The English Man

by

Mike Smitley

Thanks to Darlene Kenaga for her editing services.
Special thanks to my wife, Jana, for her patience and support.
The author, Mike Smitley, can be contacted at:

mike@fatherspress.com

This is a work of fiction. Names, characters, places and incidents either are the product of the author's imagination or are used fictitiously, and any resemblance to actual persons, living or dead, events or locales is entirely coincidental.

Copyright 2012 Mike Smitley

ISBN 978-1-937520-52-6

Distributed by
First Edition Design Publishing, Inc.
January 2012
www.firsteditiondesignpublishing.com

LCCN: 2012931728

Published in the United States. All rights reserved.

For additional mystery and suspense, read Mike Smitley's other novels,
IMPLIED CONTRACT (ISBN: 978-0-9779407-2-1),
GHOST HUNT: The Sequel (ISBN: 978-0-9779407-7-6),
PREY (ISBN: 978-0-9779407-5-2),
DEAD FILES (ISBN: 978-0-9779407-1-4) and
OUR MISSING (ISBN: 978-0-97953940402).

All available as E-Books through your favorite E-Book distributor, and as print version through Father's Press and all retailers.

Father's Press, L.L.C.

Lee's Summit, MO
(816) 600-6288
www.fatherspress.com

INTRODUCTION

To truly appreciate the irony of a murder investigation in an Amish district, (district being the term for an Amish community rather than a city or township), one should be familiar with the Amish faith and their secretive culture. Having been a closed society for hundreds of years, insight into Amish life has only recently been revealed by the writings and testimonials of people who have been unable to accept the strict doctrine and harsh discipline of the faith, and have left the faith, either by choice or excommunication, to live with the English. English is the Amish term for anyone who does not believe as they do. To understand Amish culture, a brief history of the Amish faith is helpful.

There is no consensus on exactly where the Amish fit within Christianity. Some consider them conservative Protestants. Most Amish would probably consider themselves to be Anabaptists (*a member of a sect which arose in Germany in 1521 which believes that baptism should be withheld until a person is old enough to understand the meanings of sin repentance, salvation and the Gospel, and that baptism should be accompanied by a confession of faith. They further believe that infants baptized, as is the case in the Catholic Church, cannot understand any of the ramifications of baptism and should be rebaptized when they are old enough to understand the Gospel and willingly make the accompanying public confession of faith.*) J. Gordon Melton, head of the *Institute for the Study of American Religion*, classifies them as part of the *European Free-Church Family* along with Mennonites, Brethren Quakers and other reformation denominations.

The Amish movement was founded in Europe by Jacob Amman (1644 to 1720 CE), from whom their name is derived. In many ways it started as a reform group within the Mennonite movement, an attempt to restore some of the early practices of the Mennonites.

The beliefs and practices of the Amish were based on the writings of the founder of the Mennonite faith, Menno Simons (1496-1561), and on the 1632 Mennonite *Dordrecht Confession of Faith*.

The Amish who split from Mennonites generally lived in Switzerland and in the southern Rhine river region. During the late 17th century, they separated because of doctrinal differences and what they perceived as a lack of discipline among the Mennonites.

Some Amish migrated to the United States starting in the early 18th century. They initially settled in Pennsylvania. Other waves of Amish immigrants established districts in New York, Illinois, Indiana, Iowa, Missouri, Ohio and other states.

The faith group has attempted to preserve the elements of late 17th century European rural culture. They try to avoid many of the features of modern society by developing practices and behaviors which isolate them from American culture.

James Hoorman writes about the current status of the Amish movement:

"In America, the Amish hold major doctrines in common, but as the years went by, their practices differed. Today there are a number of different groups of Amish, with the majority affiliated with four orders: Swartzengruber, Old Order, Andy Weaver, and New Order Amish. Old Order Amish are the most common. All the groups operate independently from each other with variations in how they practice their religion, and religion dictates how they conduct their daily lives. The Swartzengruber Amish are the most conservative, followed by the Old Order Amish. The Andy Weaver are more progressive, and the New Order Amish are the most progressive."

Membership in the *Old Order Amish Mennonite Church* and other Amish denominations is not freely available. They may total about 180,000 adults spread across 22 states, including about 45,000 in Ohio and smaller numbers in Illinois, Indiana, Pennsylvania, New York, etc. About 1,500 live in south-western Ontario, in Canada.

Almost all members are born into and raised in the faith. Converts from outside of the Amish communities are rare. Due to their small size, partly attributed to the large number of young people leaving the faith, some Amish groups have a very restricted gene pool and are experiencing numerous inherited disorders.

During the Protestant Reformation in 16th century Europe, John Calvin, Martin Luther and Ulrich Zwingli broke from the Roman Catholic Church to form separate Christian faith groups. They promoted the concepts of:

- Salvation by the grace of God, rather than through good works and church sacraments.
- Greater individual freedom of belief.
- The priesthood of all believers; no priest or other intermediary was needed between believers and God.

- Close integration of church and state.
- Reliance on the Bible alone, with little attention paid to church tradition.

In what has been called *"the radical reformation"*, some additional religious reformers took these beliefs to a logical conclusion; they preached that the believers should form *"free churches"*; quite different from the highly organized state churches which were typical at the time. They separated themselves from all secular activities, including the state, and formed independent, informal religious groups. These were much like the Christian congregations in very early Christianity.

A small group of Swiss Christians, led by Conrad Grebel and Felix Manz, formed a study group intending to recommend changes to the state Protestant church. Their reforms were rejected both by Zwingli, the church head, and by the *Zurich City Council*. In 1525 CE, they formed the first *Swiss Brethren* congregation in Switzerland. They baptized each other into membership in their *"believers church"*, a crime for which some were banished; others were executed by drowning or burning at the stake. At the time, the Swiss state church was no more tolerant of what they regarded as heresy as was the Roman Catholic Church. Religious tolerance developed later in Europe.

A key belief of the Brethren was that only adults should be baptized. The normal practice at the time was to baptize newborns and infants. The name *"Anabaptist,"* which meant re-baptizer, was first used as a nickname to describe this and similar groups. The name stuck.

The Anabaptists promoted the concept of church as a self-governing, loose association of adults, not including children. Worship services were held in homes rather than in a church building.

The Anabaptist leaders met in secret during 1527 in Schleitheim on the Swiss-German border. They developed what was originally called a declaration of *"Brotherly Union"* and is now referred to as the *"Schleitheim Articles."* It consists of seven articles:

1. *"Believers baptism"* was only performed during adulthood after repentance and a confession of faith. They practiced anti-pedobaptism, opposition to the baptism of infants. They believe that a child does not have the knowledge of good and evil. Thus they cannot sin and would not benefit from baptism.

2. Members who slipped and fell into error were to be warned twice in private. If they persisted, they would be warned publicly in front of the congregation and banned from the group.

3. Only fellow believers who were baptized as adults were allowed to attend the Lord's Supper.

4. They pledged to separate themselves from the evil in the world. They were pacifists and pledged to reject violence.

5. The leaders in the church, called shepherds, were to be of good character and competent to preach to the congregation.

6. They advocated church-state separation. They generally withdrew from the world, which they regarded as a corrupting influence. They would not hold public office or engage in civic affairs.

7. Members were not to give oaths. Their word is to be sufficient.

These seven principles remain the basic guidelines used by the Swiss Brethren and Amish to this day.

Some radical Anabaptists who expected an imminent end of the world attempted to create a theocracy in Münster, Germany by force in 1534. Many governments viewed all Anabaptists as a potentially serious danger to the social order. The groups suffered extreme persecution. Many of their leaders were rounded up and executed. Programs of genocide were organized by various governments, by Protestant groups and the Roman Catholic Church. Some city-states employed "Anabaptist hunters" who were paid by the head to locate and arrest believers.

Anabaptists grew in number, in spite of the persecution. They became a loosely-organized *"lay-oriented, non-liturgical, non-creedal, Bible-oriented church."*

The Mennonites

The *Mennonites* are named after Menno Simons (1496-1561 CE), a Dutch Anabaptist leader who had left the Roman Catholic priesthood in 1536. He felt that the Catholic Church had lost touch with the Gospel message by concentrating on *"...legends, histories, fables, holy days, images, holy water, tapes, palms, confessionals, pilgrimages, masses, matins and vespers...purgatory, vigils and offerings."* He emerged as a leader of the Anabaptist movement in Holland and was able to unify the various diverse groups. Like most Anabaptist groups, Simons taught, *"rebaptism, pacifism, religious tolerance, separation of church and state, opposition to capital punishment, opposition to holding office, and opposition to taking oaths.*" Finally, in 1577, the country instituted a policy of religious tolerance and the Anabaptists there were given the freedom to practice their religion without oppression.

In 1632, Simon's followers met at Dordrecht in the Netherlands to formally set down their beliefs in a document called the *Dordrecht Confession of Faith*. It recorded their beliefs in the Trinity, the incarnation and atonement of Christ, the primacy of the Bible, salvation, adult baptism, etc. The Lord's Supper and foot washing were observed as ordinances; they were regarded as symbolic acts, not as church sacraments. Foot washing was based on the Bible passages in which "*Jesus did not only institute and command the same, but did also Himself wash the feet of the apostles...*"

Other Christian faith groups at the time imprisoned, executed, or committed genocide against non-conformists. The Mennonites rejected these approaches, using non-violent means — banning and shunning — to enforce discipline. Banning involves excommunication: severing the relationship between the member and the group. Shunning, called "*Meidung*" in German, was less severe. It had three purposes: to encourage the sinner to repent; "*to protect the rest of the community from possible contagion, and to maintain the community's reputation.*" Shunning requires that church members temporarily sever all communication with the sinner, including eating together, until they recant. This practice was based on Paul's writings in:

1 Corinthians 5:11: "*....if any man that is called a brother be a fornicator, or covetous, or an idolater, or a railer, or a drunkard, or an extortioner; with such an one no not to eat.*"

Matthew 18:15-17: "*Moreover if thy brother shall trespass against thee, go and tell him his fault between thee and tell him alone...But if he will not hear thee, then take with thee one or two more...And if he shall neglect to hear them, then tell it onto the church: but if he neglect to hear the church, let him be unto thee as a heathen man and a publican.*"

Romans 16:17: "*...mark them which cause divisions and offences contrary to the doctrine which ye have learned; and avoid them.*"

Shunning has generated great difficulties within families, particularly where one spouse is to be shunned by the other spouse and the rest of the family.

The Amish:

The *Amish* began as a small group of reform-minded Mennonites along the southern Rhine River and in Switzerland. They split from the main movement in 1693. The name of their group comes from their founder, Jacob Amman (1664 -1720). He was an obscure reformer about whom little is known. He felt that the Mennonites had drifted away from their original beliefs and practices. He wanted them to return to a stricter observance of the writings of Simons and on the 1632 Mennonite *Dordrecht Confession.*

The split with the Mennonites was mainly over:

The frequency of communion: Amman advocated twice a year instead of once. Believers preceded communion with a time of spiritual introspection. Amman felt that this might help the membership to be more diligent in their Christian life if it were performed every six months.

The practice of foot washing, which Amman reintroduced, had fallen out of use by most Mennonite groups.

Amman felt that in the process of shunning of non-conforming members the Mennonites were too lax and had allowed the practice to fall into disuse. He treated shunning very seriously and took it one step further. He required the spouse of a person under the ban to neither sleep nor eat with the sinner until they had repented and changed their behavior or beliefs. Hans Reist, a leader of the main Mennonite body, argued that Jesus had socialized with known sinners and had kept himself pure; he reasoned that Christians in the late 17th century could do the same without resorting to shunning.

After a few years as a separate organization, Amman and his supporters attempted to reconcile with the main Mennonite movement. This was unsuccessful. Since then the two groups have been separate. However, they generally retain close ties and often cooperate on joint projects.

Starting in the early 18th century, many of the Amish migrated to the U.S. Most of the members who remained in Europe rejoined the Mennonites. Few Amish congregations existed by 1900. On Jan. 17th, 1937, the last Amish congregation — in Ixheim, Germany — merged with their local Mennonite group and became the *Zweibrücken Mennonite Church.* The Amish no longer existed in Europe as an organized group.

The Amish and Mennonites have retained similar beliefs to this day, but with minor differences in doctrine and practices.

Aside from their strict adherence to their belief that they should keep themselves separated from the ways of the English (non believers or believers in any faith other than Amish), the Amish are very much like other conservative Christians. They have as members personalities that run the entire spectrum of humankind from the very moral and righteous to the corrupt and evil. Until the recent revelations by defectors, the blight cast on the Amish faith by some of its members has been successfully concealed from the prying eyes of the world only through diligent efforts to keep their affairs private and a steadfast refusal to discuss disciplinary matters with the outside world.

The Amish have had to deal with the same sins that have plagued mankind and all faiths since Adam's and Eve's fall from grace in the Garden. Violence, sexual sin, smoking and substance abuse, profane language, deceit, greed and works-based salvation are all issues that militate against the Amish faith, and have been dealt with internally and kept out of the view of the outside world.

This book is neither an endorsement nor an indictment of the Amish. It merely serves to give you, the reader, some background on the Amish faith, which serves as a backdrop for a story that has significant relevance to the times in which we live. Granted, the scenario in this book has not yet played out, but it is based on reality and the certainty of upcoming events in the very near future.

Several books in the Bible reveal in detail the sequence of events leading up to and including the Rapture, Seven-Year Tribulation, the Second Coming, the Millennial Reign of Christ at the end of the Seven-Year Tribulation and the judgment of man. The start button of that seven-year time-clock will be pushed in the twinkling of an eye that believers refer to as the Rapture, the instant snatching away of Christ's church in which all believers will be suddenly removed from the Earth to join Christ in the clouds.

Although the exact time of that event is known to no one except God Himself, most theologians believe we are living in the last days of the End-Times and that the world stage is set. Nothing else needs to happen; no other Bible prophesies need fulfilled for the Rapture to take place, and very soon.

It is only when you realize the significance of the Rapture, its imminence and the nearness of its occurrence that you can truly appreciate the urgency for all people to face the reality of death, judgment and eternity. It is imperative that each of us resolve those issues to the satisfaction of God who will sit in judgment of us and determine our dwelling place for all eternity.

With that said, and the seriousness with which we all should view the Rapture hopefully realized, we have to consider the roles of all the players, and the Bible speaks in great detail about the role of Satan and the demons.

This book is not intended to render a different version of their role other than that revealed in the Bible, but rather it speculates on possibilities not revealed to man in the Scriptures, and illustrates the nature of these very-real beings that have moved among us since day-one of our creation.

Sources:

J. Gordon Melton, *ed., Encyclopedia of American religions 6th Edition (1999).*
Steven Nolt *A History of the Amish* Good Books (1992).
John A. Hostetler *Amish Society, Fourth Edition.*
Ammonlie Monroe Aurand *Little Known Facts About the Amish and the Mennonites.* Forgotten Books

ONE

LATE MAY IN Missouri signals the gradual end of the spring wind and rains and the beginning of the humid heat that turns any outdoor activity into stifling drudgery. Isaac hated the heavy cotton clothing that his mother had made for him. Once sweat-soaked, it restricted his movements and chaffed him raw between his legs and around his neck and arms.

Shorts and sleeveless shirts made of light, comfortable fabrics fall well outside Amish law, being the by-products of modern technology and therefore the sinful devises of the English. And clothing that exposes the flesh of the arms, chest or legs is strictly forbidden. Excessive exposure of one's body is an open display of a distinct lack of moral fiber, proper humility and a reverent awe for the earthly temple ingeniously created by our omnipotent and sovereign God, and indwelled by His Holy Spirit.

Isaac had just completed a hard day of haying with his father. Lately their time together had been stressful, and Isaac cherished the time in the late evening after the family had gone to bed. After dark he would sneak out of the house and go to Massey's pond where he would party with other Amish young people or just be alone with his bitterness. Tonight Isaac listened at the bedroom door for the heavy breathing of his father in deep sleep, then slipped out of the house and made his way along the well-worn path that led to Massey's pond. The path was so well worn that he wondered why the elders had never noticed it. Maybe they had and just didn't want to venture off their property after dark. After all, Mr. Massey was English and was generally shunned by the Amish, unless of course circumstances warranted hiring him to drive them somewhere or use his telephone. Even then, they were careful to conceal those collaborations from the bishop.

Relations between Isaac and his father had been severely strained in the past two years. Isaac had taken to drinking whenever there was another Amish teenager at Massey's pond who had a bottle. Tonight he walked with a heavy heart. He loved his father, but hated him at the same time for his rigidity, hypocrisy and brutality.

Isaac mumbled to himself as he walked. He was particularly angry tonight and vowed that he would never again take another lashing. Although it had been several months since his last one, simply recalling the incident wounded his pride and stirred his anger. The thought of fighting his father both saddened and terrified him, but fight him he would. He was now a man and would not take another lashing from anyone.

He stopped suddenly after he'd climbed between the strands of barbed wire that divided his father's property from Mr. Massey's. He turned around and listened intently to identify the ominous sound that had come from behind him.

He placed both hands on the top strand and leaned over the fence slightly as he canted his head to hear more clearly. Again he heard the muted wisp of shoes walking quickly through the Tall Fescue that his father had sowed three years ago.

Isaac's fear peaked and his mind raced. Was it his father following him to see where the teenagers secretly met? Was it one of the elders trying to catch him drinking or cavorting with the English?

After brief deliberation, Isaac suddenly remembered that this was where Wilhelm Dresselhaus had been killed. He had been caught out after dark and was found dead a day later. Isaac liked Wilhelm and his wife, and still grieved when he recalled the anguish on Lilly Dresselhaus's face.

Isaac again heard the footsteps. This time he was able to isolate them along a path close to the timberline. He stared hard at the stand of timber, but anyone walking along the edge would be concealed by the darkness.

He panicked and turned to run, hoping to put enough distance between him and his pursuer that he could circle back to his house. He stopped to see if he had gained any ground and tried to hold his breath so he could hear over his heavy breathing. In the few seconds that his burning lungs permitted him to hold his breath, he heard the footsteps running equally fast. In fact his pursuer had closed the gap between them considerably.

Isaac turned quickly and ran recklessly into the heavy timber and brush that paralleled the path to Massey's pond. He put his arms in front of his face to shield it from the weeds and limbs that slapped him as he ran.

He exited the stand of timber and again stopped to listen. Hearing no footsteps, he looked back into the timber and saw the intermittently glow of the white night-shirt worn by a little girl as she weaved her way through the dense undergrowth toward him. He studied her hard to see who she was, thinking she looked vaguely like his little sister, Judith.

The glow of the gown intrigued him, but he passed it off as the silky sheen of the fabric reflecting the glow of the moon. Since it was impossible for his sister to be out at this time of night, he dismissed that notion, but didn't want to investigate her for fear that she would know him and tell his father of his nightly prowling. Not only would that incur the wrath of his father, but it would likely bring severe lashings to the other kids who routinely slip out of their houses and meet at Massey's pond.

Confident that the girl couldn't know his identity, since he didn't know hers, Isaac breathed easier and walked quickly toward his house. Before he had taken ten steps, a figure came sprinting out of the darkness and ran past him. He stuck his arm out, catching Isaac under his chin and clothes-lining him hard to the ground. Isaac lost consciousness for a few seconds, but slowly awoke to find Preacher Levi Croft sitting on his chest.

Paralyzing fear overwhelmed Isaac as he stared into the eyes of the mad-man. Preacher Croft bent over and pressed his nose close to Isaac's. Isaac almost became sick as Preacher Croft spewed tobacco slobber and whiskey breath in his face. "Trying to lose me, young Isaac Straus? Sneaking off to drink and smoke with your other rebellious friends, or worse, some English scum? Hoping to meet your Jezebel whore at Massey's pond?"

Even with the weight of the preacher crushing his ribs, in his dizziness Isaac looked past Preacher Croft and into the sky. With his life hanging in the balance, he discovered that there was no moon in the overcast sky. The glow of the little girl's gown had not been from the moon. Thinking back, it now seemed that the eerie glow had come from within her, and her stride appeared unnaturally smooth considering the terrain she was walking over.

His head cleared and Isaac pulled himself out of his delirium, returning to the pressing matter at hand. He refocused on Preacher Croft's burning eyes, eyes that had a distinct glow of their own. He tried to redeem himself, but was too terrified to speak. Preacher Croft back-handed him hard across the face. He stood and jerked Isaac to his feet, then spewed profanities in a lengthy tirade as he continued to slap Isaac hard in the face. "Apparently your stupid, lazy father's lashings aren't getting the ●●●●●●● message across! You're Amish, you insolent ●●● of a ●●●●●, and ●●●● it, you're going to start acting like it!"

As Preacher Croft flailed away at him, Isaac could see the faint silhouettes of dark, non-descript human forms circling him and Preacher Croft. They whispered in an unknown dialect, but their whispers seemed to echo off the hills. Isaac wondered how a whisper could be so loud. Even though he couldn't understand them, it was clear that the onlookers were encouraging Preacher Croft to greater levels of violence.

Isaac couldn't recognize these spectators; he was too busy using his arms to shield his head from the blows. He wanted to ask for their help, but the fact that they were not intervening on his behalf meant they were other elders or persons who had sanctioned his beating.

It was evident that if he were going to survive, Isaac was going to have to get himself out of this. He tried to pry his shirt from Preacher Croft's fist, but the preacher's hand was too strong. He closed his other fist and began punching Isaac as he yelled, "This is the last ●●●●●●● warning you're going to get, you insolent little ●●●●●●●! I'm going to lash the devil out of you this time, but next time you're going to meet our Lord, Jesus Christ, at the judgment seat! If you want to see your next birthday, you'll not make me or the bishop talk to you again!"

The barrage of profanity seemed endless. A single sentence could not be spoken without obscene expletives surrounding both sides of every noun and verb, preceded by a spray of tobacco-stained whiskey saliva. Isaac trembled on shaky legs and stared in wide-eyed terror as Preacher Croft pulled a claw hammer from the tool-loop on his trousers. He raised it above his head with the claw downward, fully intent on branding Isaac a sinner for life.

It was strictly forbidden in the district by Bishop Gordan for a youngster to ever challenge the authority of a bishop, preacher or elder, but it was suicide to ever lay an angry hand on one. If they lashed you,

you took it and thanked them afterwards for caring enough to bring you back into compliance with Amish law.

The logic, twisted as it seemed to Isaac, was that the harder you were lashed, the greater the likelihood that the sin in your heart would be revealed, creating a greater opportunity for you to identify it, repent and more quickly come back under the infinite grace of God, the bishop and the church. Therefore the harder the lashing, the more thankful you should be.

Had Isaac been a faithful Amish, he would have seen the upcoming disfigurement for what it was, a Divinely-ordained opportunity to solidify his standing before God and the bishop. But had he been a faithful Amish, he wouldn't have been in this predicament in the first place.

Isaac had heard it all before. Raising an angry hand against a preacher was a cardinal sin. But then, alcohol consumption, profanity and violence toward another were also contrary to the Amish faith. Even though the sins of the preacher did not justify another sin by Isaac, under these circumstances Isaac couldn't help himself. Without thinking, stark terror compelled him to put his hands on Preacher Croft's chest and pushed him as hard as he could. In his inebriated state Preacher Croft fell backward and landed on his back, striking his head on a rock and dropping the hammer.

Isaac broke free and ran as fast as he could. After he'd looked over his shoulder to see how close behind Preacher Croft was, he staggered to an exhausted stop. Preacher Croft was still lying where he had fallen and was not moving. The bare visible silhouettes of the non-descript others had stopped circling and were staring down at Preacher Croft's motionless body.

Isaac's fear did not diminish when he saw how still Preacher Croft was lying. He had to be hurt badly or he would have struggled to his feet and continued the chase. Isaac took three apprehensive steps back toward Preacher Croft, then froze in his tracks.

Conscience, and the expectation of a harsher discipline, dictated that he return to Preacher Croft and see how badly he was hurt. But fear gripped his feet and forced them to turn toward home. Isaac knew he was mandated by Amish law to return to Preacher Croft and render whatever aid he could, but surely Preacher Croft was merely pretending to be unconscious to trick him into returning. Once there, the preacher would again pounce on him and beat him mercilessly with the hammer.

And surely the unrecognizable others hovering over the preacher would help him.

Isaac bent over and gulped in air to quench his burning lungs, then looked back into the timber to see if the little girl was anywhere in sight. No matter how scared he was of his father's anger, he couldn't leave her out here to suffer the wrath of Preacher Croft. She'd never survive a beating like he'd just taken.

He looked around, but saw nothing as he straightened up and yelled between gasps for air, "Little girl! Are you there?"

The only response he heard was a loud whisper, "ISAAC, RETURN TO ME", that echoed from all directions. He heard nothing from the child and assumed that she had seen Preacher Croft's attack on him and had heard the preacher's tirade. She must have become as frightened as Isaac and ran home. After giving Preacher Croft and the dark forms one last hard stare, he turned and ran.

Isaac anguished over the preacher's condition all the way home. The rest of the night he slept only intermittently, worrying about the preacher, wondering why he couldn't recognize the dark forms as easily as he had Preacher Croft, wondering what dialect they had spoken as they had circled him and the preacher and wondering why the few words whispered by the dark forms that he understood were, "KILL ISAAC!"

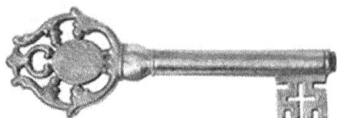

"I am he that liveth, and was dead; and behold, I am alive for evermore, Amen; and have the keys of hell and of death." **Revelation 1:18**

The next morning Isaac stirred from a restless sleep. He sat up quickly, expecting to see Preacher Croft standing over him with a hammer raised over his head. He turned and put his feet on the floor as he calmed his breathing and gathered his wits.

He began running the events of the previous night around in his head, trying to make sense of them. He understood the beating, but the mysterious others scared him as he'd never been scared before. Who, or what, were they? When Isaac couldn't figure it out, he decided that he should hurry to breakfast so he wouldn't arouse suspicion.

He slowly dragged his bruised and battered body to the breakfast table. He yawned and ran his fingers through his hair as he looked over the spread that his mother had laid out. When he looked up, he found that all eyes were on him.

Dory sat beside Abel and bowed her head as Abel led the family in prayer. After *Amen*, she looked up and gasped when she saw Isaac's face. She stood abruptly, pushing her chair backward with her legs. She leaned over the table and stared hard at Isaac's face in wide-eyed anger and disbelief. When the reality of his injuries sank in, Dory gritted her teeth and snarled, "Isaac!" Isaac, son, how did you get those stripes?"

Isaac shifted his stare into the piercing eyes of his father to gauge his reaction. Abel was content for the time being to allow Isaac's mother to lead the inquisition, so Isaac dismissed her with a wave of his hand. "Mom, it's nothing."

"Nothing! You didn't get those stripes by falling out of bed, young man! Have you been fighting?"

"No, Mom. Just let it go. I can handle it."

The younger kids were frightened by Dory's anger and observed the whole altercation with awe, hoping their father did not get involved. Dory slowly sat back down and the youngsters hurried through breakfast in silence.

The silverware landed on empty plates about the same time and the kids asked Abel to be dismissed, hoping to escape the next round of hostilities. Abel nodded his head almost imperceptivity and they scattered like a covey of quail.

Abel slowly finished the last sips of coffee in his cup and set the cup gently back on the saucer. He thoroughly cleaned his lips and chin with a napkin, gently laid it on the table beside the cup and saucer, then slid his chair out and slowly stood. He walked methodically across the kitchen and calmly took his straw hat from the rack beside the door. He took his time adjusting it on his head, waiting for the onslaught of Dory's wrath. He started toward the door, fully knowing he'd never reach it. Dory grabbed his arm and spun him around violently. Abel sighed as she stood on her tip-toes to get nose to nose with him. He said in a calm voice, "I didn't do it, Dory."

Dory was still enraged. "Well who else would lash him like that?"

Abel began to anger. "I don't know, Dory, but when I do lash him, I never hit him in the face or use a closed fist! You know that, woman!"

Dory was not content. She released Abel's arm and drew in a deep breath to continue the fight, but Abel placed his hands under her arms and lifted her off the ground like a small child. He pulled her close to his bearded face and growled, "I'll get to the bottom of this, wife, but you're out of God's will challenging me like this. I'm God's appointed representative as head of this family, and you're forgetting your submissive role."

Dory gently grabbed Abel's beard and pulled his face closer to hers as she snarled, "You do that, Mister Head-of-the-House! You do it or I will! I want to know who beat him and I want to know now!"

Abel sighed heavily and moaned as he put her down. "Someone needs to beat you for your insolence."

Dory straightened the wrinkles out of Abel's sleeve where she had grabbed him. She said, "Someone might, Mister, but it won't be you. You know you love me. You'd kill any man who ever put a hand on me, and you know it, so stop trying to act so tough. I won't stand for anyone putting their hands on my kids, so get out there and find out what happened." She turned Abel around and pushed him toward the door as she swatted his back side.

She followed Abel out onto the porch. As he stepped off the bottom step, Dory wrapped her arms around the center support post and said, "Be gentle with him, Abel. He's going through a rough time."

Abel turned back to her and said, "Rough time or not, he's got to come around. He's got to repent of his sins and regain the grace of the bishop or he'll have to leave the district. He's about to enter his with the English. If he's not excommunicated by the bishop, he'll never return to us from his running around if he doesn't have a strong love for the Amish faith. And coddling him isn't helping matters."

Dory frowned. "I don't coddle him! I discipline him when he needs it!"

"Discipline that doesn't change behavior isn't discipline, Dory. You're too easy on him. He works you like a puppet."

Dory snarled, "Does not! He loves me. He loves us. And I know he's about to sow his wild oats, but he loves us more than anything the English world can offer. I know what he's going through. I had the same problems when I was his age."

Dory's anger faded into a gentle smile. Abel said, "I don't know where you got this rebellious streak. I see now where Isaac got it. How did you ever make it this many years without getting kicked out of the church? How did your father ever put up with your back-talk?"

Dory shook her head. "He didn't. I just outlasted him."

Abel sighed. "Well, I can certainly understand his frustration. He should have beaten your butt for you. That would have changed your attitude."

"He did. I just learned to keep quiet when he was mad, then when he'd cool down I'd still say whatever I wanted. He just got tired of fighting me."

"Well, we've got too many years ahead of us for you to make me miserable, so remember your submissive role. I've got enough grief with Isaac. I don't need you causing me trouble with the bishop. Just remember how proper Amish wives are supposed to act."

Dory shot Abel a seductive smile as she turned back toward the door. She gave her hips an exaggerated shake and looked at Abel over her shoulder as she opened the screen door. "You like me like this. And you didn't mind my rebellious streak when we were dating, as you well recall." Abel cringed and looked around, hoping no one was close enough to hear. He rolled his eyes and shook his head as he went to the barn.

Abel hurried through his morning chores so he could get an early start in the hay field. He had seen storm clouds gathering in the distance and wanted to get as much hay in the barn as he could before it rained. Wet hay would have to be turned and allowed to dry. Hay stored in the barn wet in the summer heat was the perfect recipe for a fire.

He walked past the barn door and saw Isaac inside gathering the hay forks. Abel thought nothing of it, but stopped suddenly when Isaac conspicuously turned his head away when he realized that Abel was looking at him. Abel decided that this was a good time to get to the bottom of the matter.

Abel walked into the barn and waited for Isaac to say something. Isaac said nothing, so Abel gently grabbed his arm and turned him toward him. He seized Isaac's chin and turned it toward the light so he could see more clearly. "How did your face get marked up, son?"

Isaac shook his face free of Abel's giant hand and said, "It's not important."

Abel strengthened his resolve. "It is to your mother. And since she has tasked me with the burden of getting to the bottom of this, it's important to me. And besides, I'm accountable to God for the sins of my family. I decide what's important to me, not you. It's obvious that you've been sneaking out of the house after dark because you didn't have those marks when we went to bed last night. You been fighting, too?"

"No, dad, it's nothing."

"Doesn't look like nothing to me, son. Those are some pretty good bruises you're sporting there. I hope the other guy looks just as bad."

Isaac was in no mood to talk, so he angrily cut the conversation short. "Yeah, okay, dad, I've been fighting! But I'm not telling you with who or what it was about, so you might as well drop it!"

Normally Abel would not have dropped it, but he'd been trying to break through the anger and hostility that had come between him and Isaac. He calmly said, "Okay, son." and slowly turned to walk out.

Isaac finally swallowed his anger and asked, "Dad, do any of the elders or preachers ever dress in black and paint their faces and hands black when they go out at night?"

Abel stopped and turned slightly as he spoke over his shoulder. "No, son, not that I'm aware of."

Isaac thought for a few seconds, then asked, "Does anyone here in the district speak in a language other than English and our traditional German?"

Abel paused, then turned to face Isaac. "Not that I've ever heard. Why do you ask?"

Isaac was in deep thought and didn't answer. Abel asked, "Is that who marked up your face? Someone dressed in black, speaking an unknown tongue?"

When Abel put it that way, the whole notion seemed pretty unbelievable, even to Isaac. He even doubted his own eyes and ears. He must have imagined the dark beings while under the stress of the lashing that Preacher Croft had dealt him last night. Even the details of the beating now seemed sketchy. Had he lost consciousness? Had he been so scared that his memory failed? Had he been so scared that his adrenaline drove him to super-human strength? He didn't know. He shook his head and said, "No, dad. Never mind. I guess it was just a bad dream." Isaac walked past his dad, surprised that Abel was letting the whole matter drop so easily. Isaac's mother would be another story.

Two

CURLY SLAPP WAS a reserve sheriff's deputy and an embarrassment to the entire county. Had it not been for his exhaustive campaigning during the last election and his family's long-standing friendship with the sheriff, his application for reserve deputy would never have received a second thought.

Curly swaggered arrogantly out the front doors of the courthouse and conspicuously swung his right arm out wide around his 410-pound body to clear the butt of his badly-worn revolver, which was gaudily married to a tasteless pair of chipped and cracked fake-pearl grips. He had bent the shank of the holster so his weapon would cant radically outward like that of an old-west gunfighter. His utility belt jingled and rattled with all the keys and unnecessary gadgets that he'd hung on it.

Sheriff Holden had taken a big risk by rewarding Curly's loyalty with a sheriff's commission since Curly had never completed the required training academy or the continuing education credits necessary to maintain his state certification. He had attended an abbreviated reserve academy years earlier when he was in better condition, but he could never endure the rigors of a contextual training program now.

The sheriff had campaigned on a platform promising professional law enforcement and the abolishment of political patronage, but he felt compelled to violate his campaign promise just this once. He would never have garnered the necessary votes to narrowly defeat his challenger without Curly's tireless stumping.

He felt safe in letting Curly carry a gun because he had assigned him to work courthouse security alongside the regular deputy. He simply had to watch the prisoners in the holding cell, stop by the jury room once in a while and stick close to the regular deputy. Curly had been put on a short leash and was given strict orders that he was to take no action if problems arose, but was to call the regular deputy to handle it.

After months of shameless begging, and no political black eyes, Sheriff Holden finally gave in and allowed Curly to ride in a cruiser as long as there was a full-time deputy with him. The sheriff had hoped that Curly's obsession with the job would diminish on its own, but his enthusiasm grew more intense every day.

Curly was bubbling over with pride as he swaggered down the courthouse steps and strolled up to the cruiser like an old-west lawman, and paused before getting in. He ripped his mal-shaped, three-dollar Elvis sunglasses from his over-padded face and glared through a menacing Eastwood squint across the town square as he studied the simple country folks going about their business.

He conspicuously wrapped his pudgy hand firmly around the butt of his .357, and was sure that international terrorists would spring from the alleys at any second, forcing him to wade through a barrage of sub-machinegun fire and systematically gun them down right there in the street like the cowardly vermin that they were, single-handedly saving the town's people from annihilation.

Mark Simms had the passenger seat reclined slightly, and his hat was tilted over his face. His annoyance was unmistakable as he yelled, "Come on, Curly, get your fat carcass in the car before I change my mind and leave you here!"

Curly was consumed in his haze as he went about numerous tasks at the same time. Everything seemed to move in slow motion, and he was floating on air as he simultaneously reloaded his magnum, fielded the tearful gleams from the love-struck hotties on the junior college varsity cheerleading squad while shooting them his most seductive smile and sucking in his stomach as hard as he could, then kicking the bullet-riddled corpses into the gutter so traffic could pass by and the stunned drivers could stare at the carnage in disbelief, all the while throwing his head to the side to flip his long, wind-blown, golden hair, (which he didn't have), out of his face and trying to act photogenic, yet humble, for the paparazzi that were snapping his photo and shoving microphones in his face for a first-hand scoop from the county's newest hero.

Mark's impatient tone snapped Curly back to reality. He blinked hard several times to remind himself where he was, then hurried to open the door. "Oh yeah, Mark. Hey listen, thanks for letting me drive around with you." The cruiser rocked violently as Curly poured himself into the driver's seat.

Mark removed his Stetson from over his face and returned his seat to the upright position. Curly slid the driver's seat back as far as it would go so his stomach would clear the steering wheel. Since he was only 5'9" tall, he had to operate the gas and brake pedals with his toes.

Mark had a note of dread in his voice as he said, "Now listen, Curley. There are three rules if you're going to ride with me. None of the other deputies want you with them, so don't cause me any problems. Rule one is you do everything I say and don't do anything to tick me off. Rule two is under no circumstances do you touch your handgun or that shotgun unless I tell you to. And rule three is under no circumstances do you ever, ever, ever violate rules one and two."

Beads of sweat rolled down Curly's portly face as he struggled to get the seatbelt around his stomach. Curly always perspired heavily, even when he was freezing in the winter. He panted eagerly, "Do everything you say, don't tick you off, no guns, got you, Mark! So! Where to, partner?"

Mark rolled his eyes and shook his head, fearing the worst. He had some warrants and subpoenas to serve, but he didn't want Curly along, so he decided to let him drive around for a while. Once Curly had cruised town and profiled for everyone who had told him that he'd never amount to anything, Mark would kick him out and go about his business.

Curly cruised the square and waved proudly at everyone he knew. He then parked by the Sonic and waved at the young girls who passed by. He beamed with pride as he mistook their laughter for flirtation. He said, "Boy, Mark, the girls really go for a guy in uniform, don't they?"

Mark mumbled as he tipped the brim of his hat down over his face, hoping he wouldn't be recognized, "Yeah, Curly, you'll be in the saddle in no time."

Curly angered him when he reached up and turned the rearview mirror. He looked in it and smiled to make sure there were no remnants of his three double-cheeseburger lunch stuck in his dark-yellow teeth. He sighed with deep gratification as he readjusted the mirror. "Man! This is the life! I envy you, Mark. You get to do this all the time. And I'll bet you've picked up some real hot babes in your career. I'll bet you never get tired of this; non-stop action every day; a different girl every night; yeah, this is the life for me."

Mark had been an officer for fifteen years, and although the job was rewarding, it didn't captivate his every waking moment as it did for Curly. He growled impatiently, "Settle down, Curly, we're just cops in a little hick county in Missouri! This isn't L.A. or New York. Let's just get through the afternoon without wrecking the car, irritating the staff or getting a complaint."

Curly got an inquisitive gaze in his eye and replied, "Yeah sure, Mark. But speaking of the staff; am I the only one who recognizes what a stupid idiot that Chief Deputy Thurman is? Sheriff Holden would be far better served if he'd dump that shiftless moron and put a real policeman in that position." The implication was, of course, that the real policeman should be Curly.

Mark instantly grew nervous. He looked around and said, "Hey! Knock that crap off, Curly; someone might hear you! The chief deputy isn't such a bad guy. You may not like him, but he's gone to bat for several of us on the department in the past, and he can cut both our careers short with a stroke of his pen. This isn't a union department and I don't intend to get fired because of your big mouth. So shut up!"

"Oh relax, Mark, there's no one here but us." Curly continued to berate the chief deputy with profane embellishments, but Mark remained quiet.

A minute later the dispatcher called Mark on his cell phone. Mark answered lazily and the frantic dispatcher yelled, "Mark! For God's sake, tell Curly to shut up! He's got the mike keyed and everything he's saying is going out over the air! I've tried to break in, but I can't transmit as long as he's got the mike open!"

Mark panicked as he jerked his head hard to the left and stared at the radio. The mike was not on its hook. Since Curly couldn't easily reach the mike with the seat slid back, he had taken it off the hook and laid it on the seat beside his leg. He had inadvertently laid his leg on the mike and depressed the transmit button. Mark's reaction was broadcast loud and clear for all personnel to hear. He yelled, "Curly, you stupid idiot, you're holding the mike open!!!"

Curly quickly moved his leg and picked up the mike. He put it back on the hook and said, "Oh! Sorry, Mark. Do you think anyone heard me?" Mark slumped back down in his seat and put his face in his hands.

Curly's question was soon answered. The next radio transmission was the chief deputy. He had erupted from his chair, charged out of his office and stormed into the dispatch shack. He had leaned over the dispatcher's shoulder, keyed the transmit button and angrily instructed both officers to see him in his office. "Immediately!!!"

Tears welled up in Curly's eyes as he asked, "Dang, Mark! What are we going to do? I can't lose my commission! I won't be able to carry my gun! And you know what an easy target we cops are when we're unarmed!"

Mark slowly turned his head and glared at Curly. He could only shake his head and moaned, "Let's go, Curly. We don't want to make the chief deputy any madder by making him wait."

As Curly started the car, the dispatcher called. "127, I've got a call for you. The chief deputy wants you to handle this call first. He'll meet you at the scene."

Curly quickly removed the mike from its hook, but Mark ripped it out of his hand. He keyed it and said, "Go ahead, dispatch."

The dispatcher said, "127, we've got a farmer on the phone who says he's found a body on his property. He says it's not a natural death."

Mark wrote down the location, then got out of the car. He walked around and opened the driver's door. "Switch sides with me, Curly. I'm driving. Looks like we've got a homicide."

Curly struggled to pry himself out of the car. His overloaded belt jangled as he ran around the car and fell into the passenger seat. He gasped with wide-eyed anticipation, "Oh my gosh, Mark, a homicide! I've never handled one of those! You might have to walk me through this one!"

Mark glared at Curly as if he were crazy. He said angrily, "Curly, I'm not walking you through anything, except maybe a firing squad! I'm going to work it and you're going to stay back out of the way and keep your big mouth shut! New rule, you don't even touch the radio! Hear me?"

Curly nodded excitedly. "Sure, Mark! Do everything you say! Don't tick you off! No guns and no radio! Gotcha!"

Mark pulled to the side of the road where the farmer was waiting. As he and Curly exited the car, his attention was captured by the strange formation of storm clouds over the horizon. He thought they were like none he had ever seen, but his attention quickly refocused on the farmer. "Afternoon, Sir, did you call us about a body?"

"Yeah, I'm Ceril Massey. I was mowing hay and saw him lying a few feet back in the timber. I smelled him before I saw him. Come on, I'll show you." The deputies followed Mr. Massey about a hundred yards from the road. He stopped and pointed to the timber. "He's in there, boys. I'll wait here."

Mark and Curly pushed some bushes aside and stepped into the timber. The hair on the back of Mark's neck stood on end when he heard the distinctive pop of the safety strap on Curly's holster. He turned quickly and glared at Curly. He had no desire to be shot in the back when Curly tripped over his own two feet. Curly smiled sheepishly and snapped the strap back over the hammer of his revolver.

The body was easy to spot; it was wearing a white shirt that stood out in the undergrowth. Mark eased up and knelt beside the body. He shook his head in total shock. "My God, Curly, I've never seen anything like this. This guy has had his head almost torn off. And to make it worse, he's Amish."

The body had lain out in the hot weather for three days and the stench was overpowering. Curly was bent over beside a tree heaving his guts out. Mark left him alone. If Curly was preoccupied with puking, he couldn't mess anything up.

Sheriff Jerry Holden and Chief Deputy Casey Thurman parked behind Mark's cruiser. They saw the farmer by the edge of the woods, so they walked in. Mark was stringing crime scene barrier tape around the perimeter, and Curly was sitting on a log trying to suppress his dry heaves.

Both staff officers were prepared to tear Curly limb from limb, but wisely decided to postpone the dismemberment when they saw him sitting on the log with his face pale and ashy and vomit all over the front of his shirt. Neither relished getting close to Curly in his present state.

Mark approached and said, "Hey listen, Chief, I had nothing to do with Curly's comments on the radio. I'd told him to keep his mouth shut, but he wouldn't listen. I should never have let him near the radio. I apologize for that."

Chief Deputy Thurman held up his hand and stopped Mark. "Don't worry about it, Mark. I'll have a piece of Curly later. Right now I just hope he can walk out of here so we don't have to carry him."

Mark looked back at Curly and said, "Well, Sir, if he drops over, I vote we just throw some dirt over him and let the kids use him for a sled hill this winter."

Sheriff Holden chuckled and Casey said, "Sounds like a plan. I'll donate the shovel. What about this dead guy?"

Mark pointed to a dried blood-pool in the field a few feet from the timber line. "He was probably killed there and dragged into the woods." He removed his hat and wiped the sweat from his face with his sleeve, then continued, "I don't know, Chief. I've seen a lot of dead bodies, but I've never seen anything like this. I'm sure it's a homicide; the guy's almost been decapitated. I just can't figure out how it was done. It looks like he got his head caught in a piece of farm machinery."

Casey and the sheriff looked at each other in disbelief, then walked past Curly. They covered their noses while they kept their distance and circled the body until they could see the injury to the head and neck. Casey bent over for a better look and gasped, "My God, Jerry, Mark's right. Someone broke his neck and cut his throat."

The sheriff rubbed his chin as he slowly shook his head. "I don't think so, Casey. If it's possible, it looks like someone bent his head back so far that it broke his neck and tore open the skin on his throat. The body's in bad shape, but it looks like the skin has been torn rather than cut. And look at his jaw. It's been torn off. The whole head has been torn off. It's only attached by the skin and muscle tissue at the back of his neck."

Casey asked, "Any chance the damage to the throat was by animals feeding on him?"

The sheriff slowly shook his head as he pondered the possibility. "No, I don't think so. If the animals had gotten to him, there'd be tissue missing from other parts of the body. And Mark's right. That blood out there in the field indicates he was killed there, but carried here, likely to conceal the body. Since there are no drag marks, whoever killed him picked him up and carried him. He was killed by someone very strong. What a horrible way to go."

Both men walked past Curly to the field to escape the stench. The sheriff shook his head in disbelief as he said, "Mark, this is going to be a bad one. Get your offense report started and call the detectives out. Once they get here, we'll call the coroner's office. List the guy as a John Doe for now. And don't classify it as a homicide yet. I don't want the media breathing down my neck. I want to talk to the coroner first. Just classify it a death investigation. Most Amish don't carry wallets or I.D., so we're going to have a tough time identifying the body. They don't like to deal with us, so they never call when there's a problem. They just handle it themselves."

Mark said, "You seem worried, Sheriff."

Holden looked back at the body and sighed. "I am, Mark. I've never seen a person decapitated with bare hands before. The Amish take a lot of harassment, and this isn't the first dead one that we've found. The media is going to fry us."

"I didn't hear about any dead Amish, Sheriff."

"None of you patrol guys did. We kept it quiet and the detectives worked it with the F.B.I. We didn't clear it, and the F.B.I. thinks there's a serial killer stalking the Amish. We kept it out of the media."

Mark asked, "Why would the F.B.I. care about a dead Amish? That's a state offense, not a violation of federal law."

"They normally wouldn't, but since he was Amish, they considered it a hate crime. They had another agenda, but they were so closed-mouth about it that we never figured out what their true motive was. I hate the F.B.I. When they get involved, we do all the leg-work and they milk us for intelligence, then steal the credit if there's an arrest, and deny any responsibility if the case is unsolved."

The sheriff started to walk away, but stopped when he spotted something in the middle of the large blood-stain in the field. He walked closer and said, "There's a hammer there in the same spot where our victim was killed, Mark. Make sure the evidence tech photographs and recovers it. It may have been used on the victim."

Casey said, "So you can see, Mark, this has to be kept under wraps. The media will have a field-day with this, and we don't want the feds coming in here and sticking their noses in it unless we invite them. This is going to be a nightmare to solve." The instant they all realized the importance of absolute secrecy, all three turned slowly and glared simultaneously at Curly.

THREE

SPECIAL AGENT SANDY Parsons was typing her expense report when the S.A.C. called her. He wanted to see her right away, so she saved her report and hurried to his office.

Special Agent in Charge, Ranard Galetti, motioned for Sandy to sit while he finished signing the stack of papers in front of him. She sat and waited patiently.

He shoved the papers aside, then stared hard at Sandy. She became nervous, suspecting that she had bungled something important. Galetti never got right to the point. He liked to play mind-games first to unnerve his adversary and stroke his fragile ego. When his stare became uncomfortable, he asked, "Agent Parson, how long have you been with the bureau?"

Galetti knew exactly how long Sandy had been with the bureau, but she patronized him anyway. "Two years, Sir."

"The entire time here in the Phoenix office, right?"

Galetti knew very well that it was, but Sandy patronized him further. "Yes, Sir."

After another long silence, Galetti said, "And in that time you've never worked an undercover assignment or managed a confidential informant."

Sandy became defensive. "No, Sir, but that's not my fault. I've requested undercover cases, but they were assigned to other agents. And when I've developed C.I.s, you've taken them away from me and given them to another controller."

"Yes, Agent Parsons, I'm aware of that. C.I. management requires experience that you don't have yet. That's why I'm giving you this case. It'll involve a C.I. and give you the experience that you'll need to manage undercover cases."

Sandy was thrilled. "Oh, thank you, Sir! I won't let you down! What are the details?"

He shrugged his shoulders and said, "I quite frankly can't give them to you. You'll be on loan to headquarters in Quantico. I'll give your active cases to someone else to finish. Pack your things and contact a S.A.C. named Smith at headquarters. He'll brief you on the details."

Complete shock fell over Sandy's face. She slowly stood and opened the door. Galetti said, "Parsons, I don't know what's going on here, but this whole thing has the highest security clearance. I can't even find out the details. I've been with the bureau for thirty years and it never fails. When one of these nightmares materializes, people get hurt or disappear. Be on your toes and stay sharp. This could be a career-killer. Good luck."

Sandy anguished as she cleaned out her desk and left the office. That evening she was on a plane to Quantico.

The next morning Sandy knocked on the door of S.A.C. Richard Smith. He instructed her to enter, so she stepped in and took a seat. Without looking at her, he stood and walked to his window. He stared out across the city without speaking, then turned and said, "Agent Parsons, nice of you to volunteer. What kind of team player are you?"

Sandy's anxiety increased. "A good one, Sir. I've done a good job for the bureau and done everything that's been asked of me. But you already knew that before you selected me for this assignment, so why do you ask?"

Smith walked over and leaned against the front of his desk. He sighed apathetically and said, "I ask because this case is not going to be like any the bureau has ever worked. It'll require sacrifices that you're probably not prepared to make. We're putting a C.I. inside an Amish community."

Sandy listened in shock, then said, "That'll be tough, Sir. What could the Amish possibly have done to warrant the bureau's attention?"

"A few days ago a sheriff in Missouri sent us a set of fingerprints from an Amish murder victim to identify. They're trying to keep it quiet, but we happen to know that it's the second murder in that district in two years. Our field office in St. Louis worked the first one with them. Now, the Amish are seldom fingerprinted, so we'll likely not be able to identify the victim from his prints, but I had the S.A.C. in St. Louis check into the circumstances surrounding this murder, and they're similar."

"Murder is usually a state case, Sir. Did it cross state lines or involve a federal civil rights violation?"

"No, Parsons, it didn't. The thing that interests the bureau is that this is the second murder of an Amish man in that district. The sheriff won't ask for assistance, so we'll have to take it away from him. The bureau's concern is that a serial killer may be hiding in the Amish district, and we all know how mobile serial killers can be. He may well have crossed state lines and committed other murders. It'd be a perfect cover. No one would ever suspect an Amish person of murder. If there is a serial killer in that district, there's no telling how many people he's killed."

"But Sir, the Amish don't drive cars. How mobile can he be?"

"True, Parsons, but in extreme circumstances they'll hire someone to drive them if the distance is too far for their horses and buggies or there's an emergency of some kind. Anyway, there are different sects among the Amish. Some are more progressive than others. If our killer is willing to murder, I'm sure a little sin like driving a car is no obstacle. Also, the murder of someone because of their religious affiliation is a hate-crime. That aspect also concerns the bureau. At any rate we have to get someone inside that district to find out two things. First we have to learn the identity of the latest victim. Secondly we have to find out who killed him. That's where the C.I. comes in."

Sandy thought for a few seconds, then said, "I don't mean to challenge the wisdom of the bureau, Sir, but the Amish are a closed faith. You have to be born into it and outsiders can't get in. How do we overcome that hurdle?"

Smith sighed heavily. "True, they are closed, but in recent years there's been a mass exodus of young people who couldn't accept the rigid discipline and hypocrisy of the Amish faith. There've been so many leaving the church that the Amish population is declining. Their gene pool is diminishing and there is considerable incest and marriages between family members. They're actually seeing an increase in inherited disorders due to a restricted gene pool. They're prime to try to get the right C.I. in. It may be rare that an outsider can become Amish, but it's not unheard of, and they're certainly a lot more open to the idea these days."

"Okay, Sir, so I guess I'm going to manage the C.I.?"

Smith smiled. "Yes, Agent Parsons, you will. The hard part is that you can't control him from the outside. You're going in with him."

Sandy stood and glared at Smith in shock. "Me, inside with the C.I.? Sir, doesn't that violate the bureau's protocol for managing C.I.s? Being inside will inhibit my ability to do all the intelligence work, case file preparation, liaison work with the lab, assisting agencies, U.S. Attorney and other things that I'll have to do to manage the case. I can't be two places at once, and if the Amish catch me working on the case file, that'll blow my cover. And I just won't be able to leave when I want to talk with the U.S. Attorney, you or the crime lab. There's just too much to do for me to be tied down in an undercover role."

"I'm exercising my administrative prerogative and introducing some flexibility into the protocol, Agent Parsons. You'll be inside with the C.I. to keep an eye on him. There'll be another agent on the outside that'll manage the administrative affairs of the case and give you whatever support you'll need. Agent Waters will be your outside contact. He'll also be the lead agent. You'll take your orders from him. I'll also be actively involved, so I'll be close at all times."

Sandy erupted. "Waters! Dexter Waters from the Kansas City office? I know him. He's the biggest…! I'm sorry, Sir, I don't think I can work with Agent Waters! I've worked with him in the past and it wasn't a pleasant experience!"

Smith had been briefed on the animosity between the agents. He said, "This case is not being undertaken for your pleasure, Parsons. Your resentment toward Agent Waters is unwarranted. He's an outstanding case manager. I have complete confidence in him, and you'll follow his orders to the letter."

Sandy sighed in disgust. "Okay, then thank you for requesting me, but I respectfully decline the assignment. Good luck with the investigation, Sir, but I'll go back to my previous assignment."

Sandy stood to leave, but Smith broke his stoic stare and laughed softly. "Agent Parsons, you amuse me."

Surprised, she turned and asked, "I amuse you? Excuse me, Sir, but this is a voluntary assignment. If I don't like the team, I can always take my toys and go home. I was quite comfortable in Phoenix."

Smith sighed and responded in a business-like tone, "Yes, Parsons, you can go home, but home is no longer Phoenix. Home will be where ever I say it is. This is now your home. I am your daddy and Waters will be your mommy. If you want to leave, your home will be a plywood shack somewhere out at the end of the Aleutian Islands in Alaska. Your career for the next thirty years will be investigating homicides among the local seal population by bears."

Sandy stood frozen in shock. She had never had her arm twisted like this. She stared at the floor. "You can't do this, Sir. This violates bureau policy."

Smith said sympathetically, "Yes, Parsons, it does. Shall we get the director in here to settle this, or are you on board."

He would never have threatened her like this had he not already secured the director's support. Sandy glared at him, then reluctantly said, "Okay. I wouldn't do well in the Aleutians, so I guess I'm home, Dad."

Smith nodded arrogantly as he examined his fingernails. "Good, Parsons. Galetti said you were a team player. So! As I said earlier, you're going undercover in this Amish district."

Sandy said, "Excuse me, Sir, but it sounds like I'm just another undercover agent. It sounds like Agent Waters is really the case manager. If we'll have one C.I. in the role, why do you need me there, too?"

"Insurance, Agent Parsons. This C.I. may be hard to control. Waters can't control him from the outside. You'll be right there by his side to make sure he performs. Listen, Parsons, you might as well know it now. These people are fanatical about their faith. They're secretive and don't trust strangers. This C.I. is going to have to take a lot of abuse in order to gain their trust."

Sandy sighed and rubbed her hands together nervously. "Abuse? You mean he'll get hurt?"

"Possibly. No, probably. He'll certainly have to endure a lot of discipline and do a lot of hard physical labor. He may decide the job is too tough and try to pull out prematurely. If he does, I want him arrested immediately and returned to Houston for trial. Waters won't be able to tell if the C.I. is getting cold feet or tries to rabbit on us. You'll be there to collar him if he tries to skip out."

"Does the C.I. know about the punishment that he's in for?"

"Not yet, but he will. Leave that to me, Parsons. You need to learn one thing right now. C.I.s aren't nice people, so don't let your heart bleed too much for him. They're criminals who either have so much jail time stacked on their heads that they're willing to sell their souls to get out from under it, or they're facing a bullet from a hit-man. Either way they're expendable. We use them and throw them away. You always deal with a C.I. from a position of power. You use whatever leverage you can against them and never settle for failure. There are too many excuses for failure, and they're experts at coming up with excuses. They have to know that if they fail, they're off to prison or the coroner's office. It doesn't matter whose fault it is; theirs, ours, nobody's. If they don't produce, we jerk them out and send them up the river, or pull our protection and let them get killed. It's a brutal game, Parsons, and you have to be tough to play it."

Sandy lowered her gaze to the floor as she was momentarily stunned by Smith's conspicuous lack of conscience. When she had recovered she looked back at him and asked, "Why me, Sir? Why not send another man in with the C.I.?"

Smith shrugged his shoulders and said, "You fit the profile of a young Amish woman, and I think a brother/sister scenario will sell better than two men. The other female agents wear their hair too short and don't have your background. You'll look perfect with your long, blonde hair rolled up in a bun like the Amish women. You're young and fit. You look like you've worked hard you whole life. With the right training you'll be believable in the role."

"Thank you, Sir, I think. I hope you've got someone on board with a lot of knowledge of the Amish. I'm going to need some serious help."

"We do. The guys at the Behavioral Science Unit have a guy who's made it his life's work studying world religions."

Sandy nodded and asked, "And who's the C.I.?"

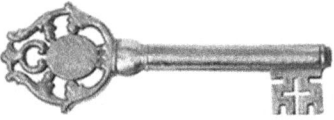

"I am he that liveth, and was dead; and behold, I am alive for evermore, Amen; and have the keys of hell and of death." **Revelation 1:18**

Dall Roberts waited nervously in the lobby of F.B.I. headquarters. He had anguished over this decision for weeks and had about decided to flee prosecution and take his chances on the run.

S.A.C. Smith opened the door. "Come in, Mr. Roberts." Dall walked in nervously and took the chair closest to the door. Around the table sat three other people.

Smith sat and introduced the other people. "Mr. Roberts, I'd like you to meet the people who'll be working with you on this assignment. To your left is Agent Sandy Parsons out of the Phoenix office. She'll be going undercover with you. To your right is Agent Dexter Waters out of the Kansas City office. He'll be the case agent and your controller on the outside. He'll also be supporting Agent Parsons. The other gentleman here is Dr. Milton Sveade. He's our expert on the Amish faith. He'll be training you and Agent Parsons so you can operate effectively in the district."

Dr. Sveade had a round face with wrinkles and sagging skin that betrayed his age. He read the apprehension on Dall's face and said, "I see you have doubts, Mr. Roberts. Are your doubts about my ability or yours?"

Dall didn't respond, but Waters said angrily, "I can see it, too, Roberts! I've seen your type before, you scumbag! You're wondering if we're stupid enough to give you a long leash so you can skip out on us! Or you think you're just going to waltz in there and throw us a few cookies, and work your way out from under these charges! Well let me educate you! I've managed pukes like you for thirty years! You're going to have to cough up some major information to keep me from jerking your butt out and putting you in jail, so don't screw with me!"

Dall looked to Smith for support, but none came. Smith said, "We'll address your concerns in a few minutes, Dall, but I think it's a good time to brief everyone on your background."

Sandy sat quietly through Waters' tirade. She didn't know Dall, but she knew he didn't deserve that pubic chastising. Waters was completely inappropriate. Smith was totally unconcerned about Dall's feelings as he opened his file.

Dall looked into Sandy's eyes, but she could only look away. Smith said, "For everyone's benefit, I'll brief you on Dall's background. That'll help you understand why we selected him for this assignment. I'd like to introduce you to Joshua Dallas Roberts, Dall for short. Dall served as a tank commander in Operation Desert Storm in the first gulf war. He held the rank of Sergeant and was decorated for his heroic actions. After Desert Storm, Dall decided that he no longer wanted to serve this great nation and felt a spiritual calling to go into the ministry. He was discharged honorably and immediately enrolled in Southwest Theological Seminary where he graduated with a Master's degree in pastoral studies and theology. He was appointed assistant pastor of a large church in Houston where he served for two years. It was at that time that Dall made an error in judgment and found himself at odds with the criminal justice system."

Waters growled, "Yeah, he's a pedophile. He likes to get it on with young girls."

Smith lazily held his hand up to stop Waters. "Now, Dexter, Dall won't have any confidence in you if you're too judgmental of his indiscretion. Everyone can change. That's what he's trying to do here. He's trying to redeem himself by helping us."

Waters folded his arms and scowled at Dall. Sandy said, "With all due respect, Sir, I think Agent Waters is too hostile toward the C.I. I'd like another case manager."

Waters erupted in anger and yelled, "Up yours, Parsons, I might just trash your butt and ask for another undercover!"

Smith again held up his hand, "Enough, both of you. Agent Parsons, Agent Waters is on board, and since I need both of you, so are you. Dexter, settle down. She's right, you're out of line."

Smith cleared his throat and continued. "Dall was in charge of the youth ministry, and one of the young teen-aged girls in the church had come to him with a family problem. She wasn't satisfied with the findings of the case-worker from social services after she'd filed a complaint of sexual abuse against her father. She went to Dall and convinced him to take her out of state to stay with her mother. A romantic relationship allegedly developed and Dall was charged with taking indecent liberties with a minor. The charges were dismissed after the young girl admitted that she'd fabricated the allegations to keep her father from being angry with her. However, taking a minor across state lines for the purpose of interfering with parental custody attracted the interest of the U.S. Attorney. The state prosecutor was content to drop the charges, but the U.S. Attorney felt differently. A warrant was issued and Dall was charged. He's facing some substantial jail time in a federal prison if convicted. He agreed to help us with this assignment in exchange for a dismissal of charges. If he fails to deliver, he'll be delivered to the U.S. Marshals for transportation back to Houston."

Dr. Sveade said, "That explains how Dall came to be your informant, Mr. Smith, but what attracted you to him for this assignment?"

"Good question, Doctor. Dall excelled in Biblical studies while in seminary. We need someone with an extensive background in Biblical studies who can hit the ground running once inside the district. There'll be no time to educate someone on something as complex as the Bible. We need someone who knows the Bible inside and out if he's going to interact with the Amish with any degree of credibility. He has to appear as knowledgeable as they are. He also has to be fit enough for hard physical labor. He's going to try to convince them that he was Amish once, but left the faith. He'll be trying to regain his standing and be baptized into the Amish faith."

Sandy asked, "What about me, Sir? I don't know much about the Bible."

"That's why we need Dall. The scenario will go like this. The Amish have been losing membership because many of their children are choosing to leave the faith rather than be baptized into the Amish church. They're beginning to be more open to the idea of allowing outsiders to become Amish to increase membership and expand their gene pool for marriage. Dall here is going in as an outsider who is trying to earn membership in the Amish community. He'll do most of the talking and you'll be his sister. Since women are submissive in the Amish faith, you'll be the silent sister who is also trying to gain acceptance. You'll appear submissive to Dall and rely on his expertise on the Bible to pull off your role."

Sandy stared at Dall for a minute. He was staring at the floor and appeared as a man facing execution. Sandy asked, "Dall, are you up to this?"

He didn't look up, but Smith said, "Oh, he's up to it. He'll take a lot less abuse from the Amish than the general population of the federal prison at Leavenworth. We all know how inmates feel about informants and child molesters."

Sandy knew she shouldn't allow herself to have feelings for Dall, but he just didn't look or act like a pedophile, and she felt sorry for him. She turned to Smith and asked, "So how do we get inside? Surely we're not going to try a cold approach."

Smith said, "Yes, you will. After a couple of days with Dr. Sveade, Dall will approach the district bishop. There's no universal headquarters for the Amish, so each district is an independent entity. Each district is governed by a bishop. The values and beliefs of each district are determined by that bishop. That's why there's so much diversity among different districts. Dall's story will be that he was born into an Amish district in Pennsylvania, but left the faith when he very young. He now wants to return to the faith and be baptized into the church. He's seen the lifestyle of the English and realizes now that the Amish faith is the one true religion. He'll convince the bishop that he's willing to endure any punishment for his sins, and has repented of them. After a while, he'll gain their trust and become an accepted member of the district."

Sandy asked, "And if they don't accept him? If he can't gain their forgiveness, that won't be his fault. What then?"

"Waters blurted out, "Prison, Parsons! No excuses! If he wants to avoid prison, he'll find a way! And you'd better turn off that bleeding heart! He's a child-molester, that's all!"

Dall looked up at Waters with total hatred. He wanted to tell Smith to forget the whole thing and send him back to Houston, but the thought of prison frightened him more than Waters.

Dr. Sveade said, "Sandy, even though Dall is the scriptural expert, you won't be able to be with him all the time. You'll need a basic knowledge of the Bible yourself. I suggest you start reading it in earnest right now. Use the Geneva or King James Version. You should have it read clear through before you go in. You won't be able to memorize it and recall scriptures by chapter and verse, but if an Amish makes a Biblical reference, you should know what they're talking about."

Smith said, "Good point, Doctor. Also, Sandy, set up a meeting with Dr. Sveade. You two need to start your briefings as soon as possible. We're on a timetable here and we want Dall to be in their good graces within a month."

"Sandy asked, "Why a month, Sir? What happens then?"

"Amish who are not in good standing in the district, and particularly English, are not allowed to attend the worship services. That's where a lot of sins are confessed and disciplinary matters are settled by the elders. Women aren't allowed to worship with the men, so that's where Dall will likely learn the identity of our victims and killer. If he can't learn it there, he'll still have to be accepted by the district before any individuals will trust him enough to talk confidentially outside of church service. Either way, he's got to be accepted. We want an arrest within six months. We don't have the funding to carry this assignment out much longer than that."

Dall didn't show it outwardly, but suspected that funding was not the reason for the urgency.

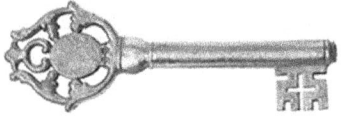

"I am he that liveth, and was dead; and behold, I am alive for evermore, Amen; and have the keys of hell and of death." **Revelation 1:18**

Mark and Curly met the sheriff, and chief deputy at the coroner's office. Casey said, "Hi, Mark. Thanks for coming."

Mark said, "Sure, Chief, glad to help, but what do you need me for? I thought one of the detectives would be here to photograph everything."

Casey said, "Normally they would. But the coroner wants to cover his bases carefully on this one since there was an earlier case where an Amish was killed the same way. He wants to ask you some questions about the scene as he examines the body. I'm afraid I'm going to have to ask you to do double-duty, answer the doctor's questions and take the photos." Mark nodded as he picked up the camera-case and followed Casey and the sheriff into the examining room.

Curly was hovering like a frightened puppy that was afraid he would be left behind. It was only by shameless begging that the sheriff agreed to let him watch. The chief deputy had already told him no.

Dr. Atwell greeted the men as they walked in. His assistant had already brought the body out of the cooler and placed it on the stainless steel autopsy table. The doctor said, "Morning, gents, glad you could make it. Let's get started."

After recording the cadaver's vital stats, Dr. Atwell put a lead on the tape identifying the case for the transcriptionist, then began dictating as he cut.

It took several minutes for the pathologist to make the Y incision on the torso and remove the vital organs while questioning Mark about the scene. He took a blood sample for the toxicology exam from the pool in the aorta, then sectioned the organs meticulously and collected biopsies for analysis. When he found them to be unremarkable, he put them in a plastic bag, tied it closed and dropped it back into the chest cavity.

Before he opened the skull, he carefully examined the scalp and found the lump on the back of the head where Preacher Croft had struck his head when he fell. He described his assessment on tape, then cut the back of the scalp to the depth of the skull from ear to ear and peeled it up over the forehead, allowing it to hang in the preacher's face.

A more careful examination of the skull under the lump revealed no fracture. Dr. Atwell said, "Well, guys, this guy landed on his back when he fell. Since the massive trauma to the throat occurred when he was alive, and there is not much blood on the chest and stomach, his throat was torn out when he was lying on his back, probably when he was unconscious. The skull is not fractured, so I don't think the blow to the back of his head was fatal. It just stunned him, then the suspect attacked him while he was semi-conscious."

By now Curly had made a nuisance of himself and the coroner looked at him intently, hoping he would take the hint to move back a little and give the doctor room to work. Curly jumped back when the hint sank in. "Oh! Sorry, Doc. This is just so exciting. I've never seen an autopsy before."

Doctor Atwell understood. He smiled and said, "That's okay, Curly. I don't mind if you watch, but there's only so much room here. I can't see if your head is in the way."

Curly stepped back and looked at the chief deputy, hoping there would not be another chastising forthcoming. The butchery that he'd suffered over the radio incident had made him especially nervous around the chief deputy. Dr. Atwell said, "Well, guys, let's see what that lump look like under the skullcap."

As he picked up his saw, Curly could not resist the urge to get closer. He inched up to the table as the doctor began to saw. Everyone else in the room had seen autopsies before and knew enough to step back. They just inadvertently forgot to tell Curly.

As the doctor cut a ring around Preacher Croft's skull, bone dust filled the air around the table. Curly was so engrossed in the procedure that he failed to notice the heavy layer of bone-dust that had settled on his head, back and shoulders. After Dr. Atwell had popped the cap off and exposed the brain, he looked inside and said, "No blood under the skullcap, Sheriff. Looks like death was caused by the broken neck and the tissue avulsion on the throat. Each individually would have killed him, but both combined probably killed him instantly."

When the doctor laid the skullcap on the table, he again looked at Curly, indicating that he should step back. This time a big smile crept across the doctor's face. Curly stepped back and looked at the sheriff to see what was so funny. When the sheriff and the chief deputy looked at Curly, they instantly broke into laughter.

Curly looked more confused, and turned to Mark for an explanation. Mark shook his head and refrained from laughing. He said, "Curly, next time you witness an autopsy, you need to stand far enough back when the doctor is sawing the skullcap that you don't get all the bone-dust on you."

Curly looked at his shoulders and arms. He grimaced and panicked as he looked at his reflection in a stainless steel paper towel dispenser that hung on the wall behind him. The thick layer of bone-dust made him heave. He cupped his hand over his mouth and ran out of the room. Once in the hall, Curly as able to suppress the urge to vomit, but danced in a high-stepping circle as he frantically brushed the dust from his arms, shoulders and hair. His girlish screams drowned out the uproarious laughter coming from the examination room.

With Curly out of the room, Dr. Atwell turned serious. He removed his mask and threw it in the trash as he left the room. Casey, Mark and the sheriff followed. When they reached Dr. Atwell's office, the doctor closed the door and said, "Okay guys, I'm up for a good mystery as much as the next guy, but this isn't funny. I've never seen anyone torn up like that when it didn't involve cars, motorcycles, heavy equipment or shotguns. What happened to that guy?"

Sheriff Holden shrugged his shoulders and said, "We don't know yet, Doc. We're new at this game, too. All I can say is that it wasn't any of the things that you listed. Did the hammer that we recovered have anything to do with it?"

"Not that I can tell."

"Then it was done by bare hands."

Dr. Atwell frowned and shook his head. "Nonsense, Jerry. I've never see a human that strong."

Sheriff Holden slowly nodded his head as he stared at the doctor. "Me neither, Doc, but I never said it was human."

FOUR

AGENT DEXTER WATERS strolled arrogantly into the lobby of the sheriff's office and demanded to see Sheriff Holden. Chief Deputy Thurman glared at Waters and stepped out of his office. He approached Waters and asked, "Is there something I can do for you?"

Waters looked Thurman up and down and said in a condescending tone, "Yes, there is. You can show me to your detective sergeant. I'm Agent Waters with the F.B.I. and I am declaring jurisdiction in the murder of the Amish man that you found a couple of weeks ago."

Thurman sighed heavily and said, "I thought so. I knew it'd be only a matter of time before you lazy shoe-fly rats came around to take it over. Why did you wait so long? Were you waiting for us to solve it first, then step in and take credit for the arrest?"

Waters said, "I don't owe you an explanation. Give me your files or I'll get a court order for them. I'm now the lead investigator, and you can cooperate and save some face when we solve it or I'll take it over completely and cut you out of the loop."

Thurman wanted to grab Waters by his neck and throw him out the door, but Sheriff Holden had approached him from behind and gently put his hand on Thurman's shoulder. "It's okay, Casey, we want to cooperate with Agent Waters. His S.A.C. called me this morning. Come in, Agent Waters, I'll give you what you want. As they walked away the sheriff winked at Casey.

The sheriff took Waters to his office. He motioned for him to have a seat, then sat behind his desk. He smiled and said, "So, Smith sent someone else to do his dirty work. Oh, well, if you're not any smarter than he is, you won't solve this one either."

Waters looked around the sheriff's office unimpressed. "Spare me your bruised ego, Holden. We didn't solve the last one because we couldn't get the Amish to talk to us. You have no more luck than we do in that regard, so don't act like we were the incompetent ones. You live next to these people year-round and they don't trust you any more than us. You hadn't made any progress before we took the case over."

The sheriff smiled and said, "Yeah, Waters. I guess you're right. I just resented how you guys stroll in here expecting us to bust our humps for you. You're such lousy team players. I'm surprised that you have the nerve to ask for our help. But, I'll show you what a regular guy I am. Here."

Sheriff Holden held up a single sheet of paper and let it float to the desk in front of Waters. "Here it is. You want all the glory, do all the work."

Waters picked up the paper and sighed. It was a single page report listing the date, time, location and cause of death for John Doe. Holden said, "When Smith contacted us and said that you were going to be here, we quit working on it. You want all our files, there they are. One page, have a nice day."

Waters stood and wadded up the report. He threw it back at Holden and walked out. Holden smiled and yelled, "And by the way, Waters. The press got wind of the murder. We'll just refer all interview requests to your office."

Casey stepped into the doorway and watched Waters storm out. "I don't like that guy, boss."

Holden sighed heavily as he scratched his head. "Me neither, Casey, but he's got us over a barrel. If we try to interfere, he'll just get a court order from the federal judge in St. Louis forcing us to stay out of it. The negative publicity of a restraining order could hurt me at election time."

Casey said, "I know, boss. Too bad we can't somehow throw a wrench in their gears and steal their thunder like they did to us last time."

The sheriff stood and walked around his desk. He grabbed his coat from the rack and said, "Well, maybe we can. It's still our county, Casey. If they don't know that we're working on the case, too, they'll never think to get a court order forcing us to stay out of it. Let's just keep an eye on him and see if we can beat them to the punch. Who knows? Maybe we'll even get lucky and clear the first murder, too. Wouldn't that wad their federal panties? And don't let Waters get under your skin. Guys like him always get what's coming to them in the end. Before this thing's over, he'll get his. Come on. Let's go talk to that farmer who found the body."

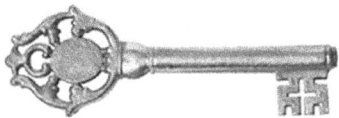

"I am he that liveth, and was dead; and behold, I am alive for evermore, Amen; and have the keys of hell and of death." **Revelation 1:18**

    Waters set up his base of operations in Shelbyville and worked out of the field office at St. Louis. He had to start from scratch on this case since the locals hadn't done anything. He managed to get a copy of the crime scene photos from the sheriff's office, but he had to do all the other preliminary leg-work himself. He contacted the coroner's office and got a copy of the autopsy report, then took a team of evidence techs to the scene to search for evidence that the sheriff's evidence techs might have missed. They found nothing. And, as expected, a canvass of the surrounding farms produced no witnesses.

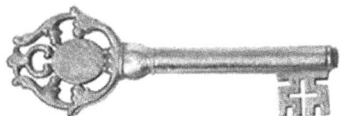

"I am he that liveth, and was dead; and behold, I am alive for evermore, Amen; and have the keys of hell and of death." **Revelation 1:18**

    Smith shook his head as he read Waters' preliminary report and the coroner's autopsy report. Waters said, "There's nothing there, Sir. The cause of death was a broken neck, but the larynx was crushed and the jaw bone was ripped off. He had a small bruise on the back of his head, but it wasn't serious enough to have caused death. His neck was broken so badly that it couldn't have been caused by a man. He was almost decapitated."

    Smith's stoic facial features broke only slightly as he grimaced at the photos. "Yes, Dexter, that's what interests me. I've known some strong men in my day, but none that could dismember a full-grown man with their bare hands. And this man was no couch potato. He was an Amish farmer. He was lean and strong as an ox. This is just what we've been looking for. I'm sure the party we're looking for is in that district. We've been looking for him for sixty years and we've finally found him. But just to make sure, I want to run some tests first. Call the forensic guys at the lab. Have them obtain an unclaimed cadaver from one of the morgues in the surrounding counties and run some tests on it. Have them tie it down on a table and hook a hydraulic wench on it. I want to know how many pounds of pressure it takes to separate the head. Then have them test some body-builders and see if any of them can generate that kind of power. I'll bet they'll find that no mortal can produce this kind of trauma."

Waters looked at Smith as though he expected Smith to burst into laughter and say, "Ahh, lighten up, Dexter, I'm just pulling our leg!" He looked away and tried to remove the surprised expression from his face when Smith glanced up at him completely serious.

Smith said, "I mean it, Dexter. If I'm wrong and this could be done by any abnormally strong man, then we're wasting our time here. It can be explained away as an attack by a strong person, and the farming industry produces lots of exceptionally strong men in a community. We're not looking for a strong person. We're not looking for a person at all. If it's just another murder involving one person killing another, we're pulling out and leaving it to the locals. They can take the flack for not solving it. But I think this is the work of our monster.

Waters nodded his head and agreed. "I think so, too, Sir, but what about Roberts? Is he capable of dealing with this? He thinks he's just going in to identify the murder victims and look for their killer. Does he have any idea what we really want him to do?"

Smith laid the reports down and stared at his desk while he contemplated his course of action. He mumbled, "No, Dexter. No he doesn't. That'll be the hard part, but he's the only person we've ever found who is physically fit enough to keep up with the Amish and knows so much about the Bible, and that we have so much leverage over."

"And Parsons?"

"She's a disposable commodity. She's not up to the job, but people are going to parish. This whole mess will get bloody when the media gets wind of what we're really doing, so she'll just be a minor casualty in the biggest war in the history of the world. We're all expendable, Dexter, just remember that."

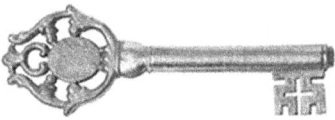

"I am he that liveth, and was dead; and behold, I am alive for evermore, Amen; and have the keys of hell and of death." **Revelation 1:18**

Ceril Massey was closing the gate to the hay field that he had just bailed when the sheriff's unmarked cruiser stopped in front of his tractor. Holden and Thurman got out and approached. Holden stuck out his hand and Ceril shook it vigorously. "Afternoon, Sheriff, what brings you out here?"

The sheriff took off his hat and wiped the sweat from his forehead with his handkerchief. He looked up at the hot summer sky and said, "Business, Ceril, I want to talk to you about the Amish man you found."

Ceril leaned against his rear tractor tire and folded his arms. "Sure thing, Sheriff, but that F.B.I. fellow said I was only to talk to him. He specifically instructed me to not talk to anyone from your office. He said that if you guys approached me to let him know. He said he'd see to it that you couldn't stick your nose in the investigation."

Casey burned with anger, but Jerry just smiled. He nodded his head as he scanned the countryside. "Yeah, I know, Ceril. He puffed out his chest at us, too. But you know how territorial those federal guys are. They're afraid that one of us locals will make them look bad. Just remember something. When your wife died, it wasn't those federal boys who came to your house and helped you out. When you got that parking warrant in Macon that time, it wasn't those federal boys who got it dismissed for you. When the Willisteed boys stole your bull, it wasn't those federal boys who went to their place and got him back for you. As a matter of fact, I'll bet you a year's pay that if you call that federal agent right now and tell him that you've got a problem, he'll either laugh at you or tell you to call us."

Ceril said, "Oh hell, Sheriff, I know that. You've always been real good to me. I'll help you if I can. I just don't want to get crossways with those government fellows. I'm not worried about that Waters character, but I'm afraid that if I make him mad, they'll find some other way to hassle me. There's been more than one person who found himself in the hot-seat of an Internal Revenue Service audit because he'd ticked off one of the feds."

"Ah, don't worry about that agent, Ceril. If you work with us under the table, he'll never know it. Listen, we kept copies of the crime scene photos. I noticed that there didn't appear to have been a struggle around the body. It looked like he'd been killed in the field, then carried into the woods."

"I noticed the same thing. That Amish guy ran across someone with enough strength to rip his head off, and he never got the chance to put up a fight. He was so torn up that it didn't look like a human could have done it." Ceril pointed to a gun scabbard that he'd strapped to the seat of his tractor. "Frankly, I've been keeping my deer rifle close. I'm not a young man anymore and I'm pretty spooked about all this. I'd be no match for someone that strong. I'm gonna shoot first, then run like hell."

"Have you seen anyone moving around on your property?"

Ceril nodded as he lowered his head and spit a mouthful of tobacco juice in the dirt. "Oh sure, Sheriff. As a matter of fact, if you'll look close, that body was found on a trail."

"A deer trail?"

"No, the Amish kids have worn a path through those woods to a pond that sits on the far edge of my property over by that old abandoned missile silo. You know which one it is. That's where you caught that seven-pound bass that hangs on your office wall."

The sheriff said, "Oh yeah, I know which pond you mean. What are the Amish kids doing over there?"

"That's where they sneak off to when they want to drink, smoke and screw around. They sneak out of their houses after dark and meet there. They'd get lashed for sure if their parents knew what they were up to. I don't say anything because I don't want to get them hurt. I don't care if they hang out there. They don't break down my fences, leave the gates open or mess with my stock. They always pick up after themselves when they leave."

Sheriff Holden looked at Casey and smiled. He said, "Oh really, the Amish kids use that pond as a place to party, huh?"

"Yeah, but I don't want them to get in trouble. Those poor kids get their hides beat more than they deserve anyway. I don't want to add to their grief. Anyway, a kid has to have a place where he can be a kid."

"Ceril, have you told this to that federal agent?"

"No, do you want me to?"

"I'd just as soon you didn't. You see, that federal guy is kind of territorial. We'd like to investigate this murder ourselves without him interfering with us. Do you mind if we snoop around here at night and see if we can get any of those Amish kids to talk to us?"

"Nah, Sheriff, you know I don't. To be honest with you, I don't like that government feller either. He had the nerve to threaten me if I talked to anyone but him. I'd like to see you boys solve this mess and make him look like an idiot."

"So would we, Ceril, so would we."

The officers turned to leave and Ceril climbed back on his tractor. He yelled, "Sheriff, just one more thing."

The sheriff stopped before getting in his car. He leaned his arm across the roof and said, "Sure."

"You boys be darned careful when you're out here at night. I've seen a small girl walking these hills at night in just her night shirt. She ain't big enough to hurt anyone, but whatever killed that Amish fellow ain't human. I never believed in monsters before, but I do now."

Ceril cranked the wheel of the tractor hard and pulled the bailer wide around the cruiser. Jerry and Casey sat in the car for a minute without speaking. Casey finally said, "Jerry, that old man is right. I'm not afraid of any man that walks, as long as I've got my trusty old .45 with me, but I can't get that Amish guy out of my mind. He wasn't killed by a man. I didn't want to let on like I was scared, but if we're going to be out here in the dark, I'm worried. I hope you don't think less of me."

Holden started the car and sighed as he put it in reverse. After he'd examined the dark clouds forming on the horizon for a few seconds, he said, "I don't, Casey. I don't know what killed him either, but it wasn't a man. I'm just as scared as you are."

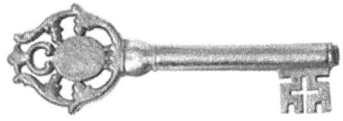

"I am he that liveth, and was dead; and behold, I am alive for evermore, Amen; and have the keys of hell and of death." **Revelation 1:18**

Abel Straus sweated profusely under the hot sun in his long-sleeved, cotton shirt with the neck and cuffs buttoned. It was hay season, and he and his children worked furiously to get the loose hay loaded onto the wagon with pitchforks before the rain started.

Isaac worked as hard as he could, but he could only throw half as much hay as his father. The younger kids walked ahead of the horses and wagon with pitchforks and collected hay from ten feet on both sides of the wagon and threw it into rows so Abel and Isaac could throw it onto the wagon. They were too small to be effective, so Abel and Isaac had to go over the same area and collect all the hay that they'd missed. Abel was not happy with them, but they had to learn haying someday, and if they were old enough to walk and carry a pitchfork, they were old enough to start.

Abel was a strict Old-Order Amish and struggled with the edict from the bishop that parents were to be completely unbending in their insistence that their children comply with Amish tradition. Lashing was the only acceptable discipline for failure to comply with Amish tradition, whether that failure was accidental or intentional. Anything less was seen as a serious violation of God's mandate for parents to teach their children discipline, and was cause for shunning by the district. Since the Amish depend on each other for assistance in so many aspects of farm-life, being shunned by the district could seriously hinder an Amish man's farming operation.

Isaac had entered a rebellious stage about a year ago. Abel had taken the matter to the elders of the church and received strict instruction to lash the rebellion out of the boy. The rebellion was seen as the manifestation of a sinful heart tainted by exposure to the English, and lashing was the only option according to the elders and bishop.

Abel had lashed him so much that he had scarred the boy's back. While lashing Isaac, Abel had instructed him to repent in the name of Jesus Christ, according to the teaching of the bishop, but it had not worked. Isaac's anger and hostility toward his father was more intense than ever.

Isaac had come in late last night. After lanterns were turned out, he had quietly slipped out of the house and gone to Massey's pond to drink with some of the other boys. Abel was waiting for him when he got home.

Isaac defiantly glared at his father and told him to go ahead and lash him. Against his better judgment, Abel did not. There was something else bothering young Isaac. He was hostile and angry, but Able had recently seen fear and anguish in his son's eyes. Ever since the disappearance of Preacher Croft, Isaac had seemed tormented.

Abel was having second thoughts about the effectiveness of lashing for every sin, but he desperately did not want the elders or bishop to find out that he was deviating from the proscribed form of discipline. If the bishop thought Abel was too weak to lash his own son, some of the elders or preachers would do it for him. Knowing that the other men would not have the compassion for his son that he had, he wanted to spare Isaac that torture.

Isaac was hung over when the sun lit up the horizon this morning. Abel thought a hard day's work with a severe headache might be just as effective as a lashing. He looked over at Isaac periodically to see how he was holding up. He was miserable, but refused to show weakness to his father.

Abel stabbed his pitchfork into the mound of hay on the wagon and yelled, "That's a load, kids; climb on. He climbed onto the seat and took the reins from Doretta. When the kids had climbed aboard, Abel turned the horses toward the barn.

After the hay had been thrown onto the hay-mound in the barn-loft, Dory took the little kids to the house. Abel said, "Isaac, wait here with me." Isaac braced himself for the worst.

Abel sat on a milking stool and rubbed his hands together anxiously. Isaac stood in front of him defiantly and said, "You've been putting it off all day. Why don't you lash me and get it over with. It doesn't matter how hard you whip me, I won't give you the satisfaction of seeing me cry."

Abel was an imposing figure. He stood 6'6" and towered over his young son. He eyes revealed no emotion, and he certainly never talked about love or compassion. That had not been done in his family while growing up. He stood and looked down at Isaac with his stoic, lazy eyes. "Isaac, I don't lash you for my own pleasure. I do it because it's called for by our laws. And you bring it on by your own sin and disobedience."

Isaac was angry inside, but no matter how hard he tried to maintain his courage, he always wilted when staring into the piercing eyes of his father. He looked away and said, "You mean the bishop's laws."

Abel sighed and said, "Okay, the bishop's laws. But remember, Bishop Gordan was ordained and placed in his position as our shepherd by God Almighty. To disobey the shepherd is to disobey God Himself. Now, you've been shunned many times for your rebellion, and I've lashed you more times than that. I can't allow you to turn your back on our laws. I've told you before, Isaac, there are only two places to spend eternity, Heaven and Hell. If I let you continue to act like this, your sins will become behavioral patterns that you'll carry with you for the rest of your life. You'll be doomed to spend eternity in Hell."

"I don't care, Dad! I hate this place! I hate this religion and I hate Bishop Gordan! I hate being lashed for every little thing that I do wrong, and I hate you for doing it! So get it over with!"

Isaac's words cut straight through Abel's heart. He showed no emotion as he stared into Isaac's angry eyes, wondering what to do. The bishop's edict was crystal clear. Any defiance was to be dealt with harshly by lashing. Abel stared as Isaac walked out of the barn. He just couldn't bring himself to whip the boy anymore. The lashings had had the opposite effect on Isaac. They had made him angry and resentful.

Abel turned and leaned over the manger as he rubbed his face and anguished over Isaac's rebellion. He had to do something soon to bring Isaac back into the graces of the church or Bishop Gordan would order the elders to take more drastic action. Abel didn't know exactly what that action would be, but rebellious teenagers had disappeared from the district in the past. Since their parents were forbidden to associate with them, they simply pretended that the child had never existed, and never bothered to search for them. Regardless of their fate, Abel couldn't stand the thought of losing Isaac, so he did the only thing he knew to do. He bowed his head and prayed.

After a minute of intense prayer, Abel walked slowly to the barn door and watched Isaac disappear into the house. He leaned against the doorframe and shook his head as he anguished over his son. He looked casually at the sky and studied the formation of strange clouds. They were dark storm-clouds like ones he had seen many times before, but these clouds were propelled by a strange wind; a strong wind that swirled the clouds in a massive circle around the district, but the wind did not reach the ground. The leaves of the trees were still. The dark clouds had appeared on the horizon earlier, but now formed a ring with a clear center.

Abel had noticed the clouds forming many days ago, but paid them little attention. Now they seemed to circle in a carefully orchestrated pattern. He tried to make sense of it, but quickly gave up. His mind was preoccupied with Isaac.

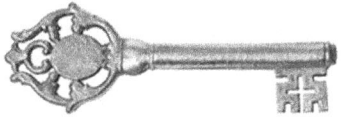

"I am he that liveth, and was dead; and behold, I am alive for evermore, Amen; and have the keys of hell and of death." **Revelation 1:18**

Dr. Sveade walked into the office that the F.B.I. had assigned him in the Federal Building. It was comfortably furnished, and Agent Sandy Parsons and Dall Roberts were seated on the plush sofa. Dr. Sveade took the overstuffed chair across from them and smiled. "Good morning, students. Are you ready for our lesson for the day?"

Sandy played along with the game. "Good morning, teacher." Dall remained silent and displayed the same apprehension that the doctor had seen in their earlier meeting.

Sveade laid a stack of notes on the table beside his chair and took the top page. He said, "Okay, Dall, I've read your background and I think you're well suited for this assignment. Now, as I understand it, there were two murders of Amish men in the last two years. The first was never solved, and the second appears to be doomed to the same fate. According to Mr. Smith, your job is to go into the district and gain acceptance, then you are to learn the identities of the two murder victims and the identity of the person who killed them, if possible. It's my job to enlighten you about the Amish faith and offer you some guidance as you work your way into their confidence."

Dall stared at the floor and prompted a challenge from Dr. Sveade. "Dall, am I boring you?"

He sighed and looked up. "Yes, Doctor, frankly you are."

Dr. Sveade laid his notes down. "Okay, Dall, let's get this over with so we can move on. Is it my qualifications that you question, or are you lacking the commitment to go through with this assignment?"

"A little of both. You've never been Amish, and unless you've lived with them, I have to wonder how you know so much about them. I'm no expert, but even I know that there are several denominations of Amish, and they're all different. There's no governing body or central authority for them, and each district is its own authority. The bishop of each district determines that district's beliefs and behavior, so how can you know so much about this particular district? And why is the federal government so concerned about a couple of murders that quite frankly are state offenses and are the responsibility of the local authorities?"

Dr. Sveade was impressed. He smiled and shook his index finger at Dall. "Very good, Dall, you've been doing your homework. That means that you're very conscientious about your assignment. First of all, the federal government's reasons for being concerned about these murders are no business of mine. I have been contracted to educate you about the Amish so you can be prepared for your assignment. Those questions will have to be directed to Mr. Smith."

Sandy interrupted Dr. Sveade. "And Mr. Smith answered those questions for you already. Now, I'm your controller. You've already made the decision to go through with the assignment and signed the Confidential Informant Cooperative Agreement, so your only responsibility is to fulfill your commitment to the bureau. It was your decision to become inappropriately involved with that under-aged girl, not ours. We're merely giving you the opportunity to work off your debt to society rather than send you to prison. Our motives are not open for discussion. As a C.I., you need to understand the relationship between a C.I. and an agent. Your role is to perform as we say. Ours is to determine the appropriate course of action that will lead to a successful prosecution of this case. If you want out, just say so and I'll turn you over to the marshals for transportation back to Houston. You can take your chances with the court."

Dall glared at the skinny blond and gritted his teeth. He nodded his head slowly and said, "You know, I haven't had a peaceful night's sleep since I agreed to this scam. I think I'll take my chances with the judge. I'm a first-time offender, and I'm just as likely to draw probation as jail time."

Sandy squared up to Dall and said, "Not in federal court you're not! That might be true in state court, but you're going before a federal judge, mister! He has minimum sentencing mandates that leave him no discretion! He has to give you the amount of jail time proscribed by those mandates! Now, if you want a downward departure from those mandates, it'll take a recommendation from me to the prosecutor to get it for you! So either make up your mind that you're going to work for me, or let's go to the holding cell!"

Dall hated to be threatened, especially by a woman. He thought hard as he stared at Sandy. He finally let his stubborn pride override his good judgment. He stood and stuck his hands out. "Okay, Agent Parsons, jail it is."

Sandy was stunned. She was sure he would back down. She stood angrily and took him by the arm and stormed out of Dr. Sveade's office, confident that Mr. Smith would be pleased with her firm handling of the C.I. She led Dall to the holding cell and locked the door after she'd pushed him in.

She had just locked the door when she saw Mr. Smith walking toward her. She strutted up to him proudly and said, "The C.I. has decided to back out of the assignment, Sir. I'll call the marshals to transport him back to Houston."

Sandy was secretly relieved that Dall had backed out. She was preparing to walk on, but was totally shocked when Smith grabbed her by the front of her shirt. He lifted her up on her toes and slammed her hard against the wall, then got nose to nose with her. It was totally inappropriate for a superior to ever lay hands on a subordinate.

Smith showed no emotion in his eyes, but his voice betrayed his anger. His voice quivered as he growled angrily, "Now you listen to me, you arrogant little tramp! I don't know what ploy you've used to sabotage this assignment, but I've seen your hesitation about it and your resentment toward Waters from the very start! Now, I'm going to enlighten you about how this is going to go down! We need Roberts in the worst way! Any threatening and arm twisting that was permissible was done by me when I first recruited him! He was on board with this when I turned him over to you, and you're not going to destroy everything I've accomplished just so you won't have to take orders from Waters! Understand this, Agent Parsons; this operation is going to proceed! If Roberts doesn't go in, then you're going in by yourself! There'll be a lot of physical abuse involved in this assignment! If he isn't there to take it, then you'll be the one getting your butt beat to a bloody pulp every day! This sect of Amish won't blindly accept an outcast into their district without first whipping the sin out of them! So if he doesn't go in, you're the one who'll have to pull this off! Alone!!! Secondly, there is more at stake here than just the assignment! Roberts isn't going to be allowed to walk away! I've got agents standing by to transport him, not the U.S. Marshall Service! He'll take a one-way ride, and it won't be to Houston!

Smith gave Sandy another hard slam against the wall as he angrily slurred through gritted teeth, "So here are you orders, Agent Parsons!

You either go back there and get him back on board or put a bullet in his head! But with or without him, you're going into that district and completing our objectives! And if you can't do that, then I'll be pleased to no end to put a bullet in your head!"

Smith backed out of Sandy's face and gave her one last slam against the wall. She fought through her tears and tried to erase the stark fear from her face. As Smith turned to leave, she straightened her shirt and wiped the tears from her eyes. She said, "Roberts is right. This has nothing to do with a murder investigation. There's something that you're not telling me, Sir. There's something in that Amish district that our government wants very badly."

Smith stopped and turned, then walked slowly back to Sandy and looked around to make sure he could not be overheard. He swallowed his anger as he sighed and softened his tone. "Parsons, there are no words to convey the significance of the assignment. It's the single most important case that the bureau has ever worked. There's never been a case more crucial to our country's survival than this one. If I told you now, you'd never believe me. Once you're inside the district, I'll tell you everything. If I told you now, you'd try to back out. No one is walking away from this assignment. Roberts can't be allowed to leave with the information that he'll have. If he tries, your orders are to kill him without hesitation. That's why you're really going in. It's not only to help Waters control him. It's to kill him if he tries to run."

Smith again looked around as he leaned closer into Sandy's face and softly said, "And Agent Parsons, you'll not be permitted to walk away either. If you try, Agent Waters' main responsibility is to kill you. And if he hesitates, my job is to kill all of you. And rest assured, Agent Parsons, I won't hesitate."

Sandy's heart skipped a beat as the reality of Smith's threat sank in. She now knew what Waters' true mission was. For the first time in her life, she knew what it was like to fear for her life. The irony of it all was that it hadn't come from a hardened criminal. It had come from her fellow agents in the bureau.

Dall was seated on the wooden bench that was bolted to the wall of the holding cell when Sandy walked sheepishly up to the cell door. He could tell by the redness in her eyes and face that she was frightened. Her disheveled clothing told him that she had been roughed up. He stood and walked to the bars. "Sandy, are you alright?"

She nodded and slowly raised her gaze. As she looked into his eyes, she no longer saw him as her C.I. She saw him as a fellow prisoner and felt a kinship with him. She was no more than a sacrificial lamb like him. With trembling fingers she unlocked the door and said with a shaky voice, "You don't owe me any kindness after the way I've treated you, but thanks for asking. Houston is not an option, Dall. No matter what you thought the rules were before, they've changed. There is no backing out on the assignment, not for either of us."

Dall stared at her, but was not surprised. He'd already known that he was being railroaded, but he didn't think the bureau would do that to one of its own agents. He stepped out and said, "I'm sorry, Sandy."

She sighed and choked back her emotions. "That's okay. It's nothing I can't handle. We'll be fine. It's just an undercover assignment."

"No it's not, Sandy. I've been in war and seen the ominous signs of impending disaster. This isn't going to turn out well for either of us. You're not my controller. You're just another disposable commodity like me. We're both expendable, and the bureau has no loyalty to either of us."

Sandy looked around to make sure Smith was not in the area. She wiped the tears from her eyes and sighed, "I'm sorry I got tough with you. I've never been in this position before. I've never managed a C.I. You're my first. There just isn't any choice here. We have to go through with this. I'll never pull it off without you. I need you so much. Please don't walk out on me. You have no idea what's in store for both of us if we fail."

Dall stared deep into Sandy's eyes and saw the stark fear in her heart. He quietly said, "I've got a pretty good idea. Perhaps we'd better go back and listen to what Dr. Sveade has to say. I'm sure we'll need every bit of information we can get once we're inside the district."

Dr. Sveade was waiting when Dall and Sandy walked sheepishly back into his office. He saw a new sense of humility in their faces and asked, "Are we ready to continue, Agent Parsons, or is the assignment a scrub?"

Sandy looked at Dall and said, "No, Doctor, we're ready to continue. Where were we?"

As both sat on the sofa, Dr. Sveade resumed his position in the chair across from them. "Dall had just challenged the right of the bureau to interfere in the business of local law enforcement in the matter of the

Amish murders. It appears that that issue has been resolved?" Sandy nodded and lowered her head in defeat.

Dr. Sveade continued, "Okay, then. We're now at the point where I should answer Dall's question about how I know so much about this particular Amish district. I've been studying religions all over the world for over sixty years now. Two years ago, when the first murder victim was discovered, I was contracted to learn as much about this particular district as I could in preparation for the day when an undercover would go inside. That day has arrived. Since the Amish are so exclusive, I had to begin my study of them by interviewing the people who had been excommunicated from the district, and some of the young people who had refused to be baptized into the faith and had moved out to live their lives as English, or non-Amish people."

Dall asked, "Doctor, are there a lot of young people abandoning this district?"

"Good question, Dall. The number of young people who abandon the Amish faith varies from district to district. And that variation seems to depend on the rigidity and severity of church discipline. In districts where beliefs and traditions are more progressive, childhood mischief and challenges to authority are more often met with reason and gentle persuasion. There seems to be fewer young people leaving the faith in those districts that are more tolerant of doctrinal challenges. In districts where tradition is less tolerant of progress and modern values, discipline is much more severe. It seems that young people in those districts are quicker to become discouraged and lose their faith. There is a lot of whipping and beating of kids in those districts, and that has bred a lot of resentment and contempt among the young people."

Sandy asked, "And this district? What about the young people in this one?"

Dr. Sveade adjusted his glasses and cleared his throat nervously. "This district is one of the worst, perhaps the worst I've ever seen. There are four basic denominations of Amish in the U.S. There are the Swartzengruber and Old-Order Amish, which are the most conservative. Then there are the Andy Weaver and New-Order Amish, which are the most progressive. This is part of the Old-Order denomination. Now, every district is a stand-alone faith, and the beliefs and behavior of its members is determined by their bishop. The bishop in this district is Bishop Nehemiah Gordan. From what I've been able to ascertain, he's a staunch believer in lashing. He believes that any inappropriate acts or questioning of tradition is sin, and sin that is left unchecked will quickly lead to the fall of the Amish faith from God's grace, and ultimately the destruction of the world. They take the matter of sin very seriously. He also instructs his members to whip their wives and children while calling on the power of Jesus Christ to bring them to repentance."

Dall lowered his head and sighed. "I guess I know what that means. If my undercover role is one where I left the faith to pursue a life with the English, then my rebellion against the Amish faith will likely bring me a sound beating."

Sandy looked at Dr. Sveade for some assurance that Dall's fears were unfounded. None came. He said, "That may be, Dall. I'd like to give you some measure of hope that you won't be whipped, but I can't. Whipping is reserved for the kids and women who question the authority of the men. The punishment for men is usually shunning or excommunication. But since you left the faith as a young person, and are trying to come back, Bishop Gordan may feel that an initial lashing is warranted to atone for your past sins in the English world. And you may not get off with one. You may take several."

Dall asked, "How can I change his mind? What can I say to convince him that I'm not rebellious anymore?"

Dr. Sveade thought for a second, then said, "Dall, the Bible clearly addresses people who religiously go through the activities of their particular faith merely for the purpose of appearing righteous to other believers. God says that without the love of Him in our hearts, our good works are as dirty rags to Him. Bishop Gordan knows this as well as anyone. If you simply confess that you never understood this until you'd lived among the English for a while, I hope he'll understand that you're renewed commitment may well be genuine. I wish I could put your fear to rest, but I can't. He might decide that an initial whipping is in order just to test your commitment."

Dall nodded. "That might work, but what's to stop them from beating me all the time? If I say anything wrong or ask reasonable questions, they may see that as sin and rebellion. If they adhere to a progressive discipline theory, they could take the position that the last whipping wasn't hard enough if I don't comply satisfactorily. I could be beat to death if they think the previous beating didn't change my rebellion."

"That's a distinct possibility, Dall. It's important for you to remember that you must remain quiet at all times if possible. The less you say the less chance of you saying something that might be construed as a challenge to the bishop's authority. That's where you're knowledge of the Bible will come in. The more familiar you are with scriptures, the better informed you'll be about their beliefs and the references to God's word that they draw on. Above all, Dall, if they quote scripture that is not Biblical, or is extra-Biblical, or is taken out of context, let it go. Don't try to correct them or you'll risk the wrath of Bishop Gordan."

Sandy and Dall sat quietly in shock. Neither had realized just how much violence this assignment would involve. Dr. Sveade continued, "I said all that to answer your earlier question, Sandy. You asked me about the number of young people who have left this district. I believe that the exodus from the faith by the young people is a result of the excessive lashing proscribed by Bishop Gordan. And there seems to be a large discrepancy between the number of kids who have left the district and the ones that we could find. I've talked to a few of them and they've told me that there are a large number of kids who have left, but those kids seem to have disappeared. Once they left the district, they haven't been seen since. I suspect some of them have met with foul play."

Sandy asked, "Isn't that a little suspicious, Doctor?"

"Yes, frankly it is. I've often wondered where those kids went, but once a kid is excommunicated and shunned by the family and church, there is usually no attempt by the family to find them. They pretend that the kid never existed and they write them out of their lives. So a kid could leave the area and the family might never know what happened to them. If there's no one trying to find those kids, they might blend in with English society and stay missing forever."

Dall said, "Okay, I guess I know why I was selected for this job. I can handle the initial whipping I guess, but there'll be things that come up every day that I'll need your advice on. How can I get in touch with you?"

"Agent Waters and I will meet you every night after dark. The Amish in this particular district don't use electricity, so they have no lights other than their oil lamps. They go to bed shortly after it gets dark, and you'll be able to sneak out and meet us. Mr. Smith will give you a cell phone that you can hide somewhere. Call me during the day if you need to. I'll have my cell phone number programmed into you phone. If it can wait, ask me when we meet at night. We'll bring you a charged battery for your phone every night when we meet."

Sandy said skeptically, "So we're going into a cult. None of these people are really Christians; they can't be. They're just a fanatic bunch of wife-beaters and child-abusers that hide behind religion to justify their brutality and sick sexual perversion."

Dr. Sveade cautioned her, "Not so, Sandy. Keep that opinion to yourself. And keep in mind that the Amish faith is a very old and conservative faith. Granted there are Amish who have no true belief in God and only keep their traditions in order to be accepted by their family and church, but not all Amish are hell-bound. Many of them keep their faith because they truly love God and His Gospel. The Amish are not wrong for keeping Gods laws. They're actually doing what everyone should be doing. It's the fact that some of them are keeping them for the wrong reasons that make them appear hypocritical. If the Amish obey their laws because they love God and want to please Him, then they're truly saved, but if a person of any faith follows Gods laws simply in an effort to gain acceptance by other men, they're doing it for the wrong reasons. God says He doesn't care about our good works. It's our heart relationship with Him that He considers. Rest assured, Sandy, there will be people of all faiths in Heaven and people of all faiths in Hell. Be careful about throwing all Amish into one category. There are some very strong Christians in that district. Be careful that you don't offend them. They'll be the ones who'll come to your aid when you're in real trouble."

She asked, "How can we tell them apart, Doctor?"

"You can't upon your initial meeting with them. You won't be able to tell a true believer from a pretender. It'll take time to get to know them and watch their behavior. You'll be able to tell the real believers by their conduct. If they're obeying Gods laws for the right reasons, their actions and speech will reveal that. The lives of the pretenders will be full of contradictions. They'll espouse one set of values, but practice another."

Sandy looked at Dall and said, "This may not be as hard as we think, Dall. Let's just go in and keep a low profile. Let's just talk and act like good Amish and get some of them to trust us. If we can gain the trust of some of them, they'll tell us who the murder victims are and who killed them. That'll get Smith off our backs."

Dall didn't respond. He simply shook his head at Sandy's blindness. She hadn't understood a word that Dr. Sveade had said.

Sandy asked, "So, Dr. Sveade, since you know so much about religion, I suppose you're a believer yourself."

Dr. Sveade shrugged his shoulders. "I know what the Bible says because I've studied it. But I think there is some latitude in it. I have my own ideas about God and eternity."

Dall canted his head and thought, *"It's apparent that this guy isn't a believer. You can't pick and chose the parts of the Bible that suite you, and discard the rest."*

FIVE

THIS DISTRICT OF Old-Order Amish had not constructed one central church, so they met twice a week at someone's home for worship service. Wednesday night's service had been held at Thomas Dunlevy's house, so this Sunday's service was scheduled for Michael Carter's home. The women and young folks were not permitted to worship with the men, so they met in the kitchen while the men gathered in the living room.

Bishop Gordan stood in front of the congregation and studied the faces of his assistant bishop, preachers and elders. He was an intimidating figure with wild, white hair and a permanent scowl of righteous piety chiseled across his lean, weathered face.

Services rarely lasted less than two hours and frequently ran on for three or four hours. When Bishop Gordan had finished his two-hour sermon, he said, "Now, let's address the matters of discipline." He looked at each man and asked if they had any sins to confess to the membership. The divinely enlightened squint in his eyes left the members no choice but to empty their hearts of even their most secret transgressions.

When his eyes met those of Brother David Martin, David stood and turned to address the elders. He looked down at the floor and confessed in a shamed tone, "On Friday night, I took pleasure with my wife. We weren't trying to conceive a child, so it was solely to satisfy our own lust. I know that is strictly forbidden and I have asked God to forgive me. I have repented of this sin and ask the elders and bishop to spare me a harsh discipline."

Abel showed no emotion, but anguished inside. *"Why? Why do men admit such things? No one else was there! If David had just kept his mouth shut, no one would know! And poor Patricia! She'll be so humiliated when she learns what Brother Martin has just confessed!"*

He then reminded himself. *"But God was there. If God knows about it, then the bishop would surely find out because God speaks directly to him and tells him all things that are done in secret."*

Bishop Gordan said, "Thank you for your honesty, Brother Martin. The elders will meet immediately after the service and determine you discipline. I'll also have one of the elders disciple you and Mrs. Martin."

Martin sat down and the bishop moved his menacing glare to Abel. He asked, "Able, your authority has been challenged on numerous occasions by a rebellious son. Have you done as the elders have instructed? Have you lashed the boy for his sin?"

Abel stood and turned to face the elders. He knew that his failure to lash Isaac would be revealed because the bishop would soon know what God knew. He pondered his responsibility to God and the bishop to sacrifice the welfare of his son for the approval of the bishop. Just as he was opening his mouth to betray Isaac, he had a change of heart and stumbled over his words. "I--, uhh--, yes, Bishop Gordan, I have followed the instructions of the elders. I have lashed Isaac and he is progressing."

Bishop Gordan stared at Abel for a long minute. Abel was sure that God was screaming in the bishop's ear, *"He's lying!"* To Abel's surprise, the bishop said, "Good, Brother Straus. Let this serve as an example of how strict adherence to the Amish traditions and God's mandates can bring a rebellious heart to repentance. Continue to drive the sin out of young Isaac with lashings, Brother Straus. He'll soon be at the age when he should try to restore himself in the good graces of the church and be baptized into the Amish faith. He should have his Rumspringa over by then. With his wild oats sowed he must take his place in our district and help raise up more good Amish families."

Abel sat back down and stared at the floor. His guilt for lying to God and the bishop was overwhelming and he heard little other business that was conducted. When the service concluded, he gathered up his brood and loaded them into the buggy.

As he pulled away from Brother Carter's house, he was wrestling with his conscience for lying to spare Isaac the torture of being whipped mercilessly by the elders, but he was also puzzled. He had lied straight-faced to the bishop, yet God had not betrayed him. Could it be that God did not speak to the bishop on all things done in secret as the bishop had led the membership to believe? Or was God simply not in agreement with the bishop's edict that lashing was always the best solution for minor sins? As he pondered the possibilities he gazed at the gathering storm clouds over the horizon.

When Abel pulled up in the front yard of his home, the young kids bounded out of the buggy and ran into the house. Life was one continuous game to them. Since Isaac was undergoing a lengthy shunning, he had not been permitted to attend worship services for several weeks. He was in the barn cleaning out stalls. Abel was surprised when Assistant Bishop Athos Clevenger pulled up in his buggy.

Assistant Bishop Clevenger was the complete antithesis of Bishop Gordan. He was calm, rational, and had a loving bearing and gentle countenance. Everyone in the district loved Bishop Clevenger and tried to approach him with their problems when possible rather than taking them to Bishop Gordan.

Abel grabbed the bridal of Bishop Clevenger's horse as it trotted by and helped stop the buggy. He stepped up to the buggy and took Bishop Clevenger's arm. Bishop Clevenger was in his eighties and appreciated any assistance the younger men could offer him.

He pulled his arm away and said, "No thanks, Brother Straus, I'm not getting out. I just wanted to talk to you about young Isaac. Would you go for a ride with me?"

A request from the bishop, or assistant bishop, was never a request. If something was asked, it was a command that no Amish dared to refuse. Abel replied reverently, "Of course, Sir," and hurried around to the passenger side of the buggy. He climbed in dutifully and Bishop Clevenger snapped the reins against the horse's back. The horse gently broke into a trot and instinctively followed the old dirt road that he had traveled many times.

About a half-mile down the road, Bishop Clevenger pulled on the left rein, turned into an orchard and pulled the horse to a stop. He turned to Abel and wrapped his arm around Abel's shoulder. Abel was nervous, since affection was not openly shown among the Amish. Bishop Clevenger patted Abel on the back and said, "I want to talk to you about young Isaac, Abel."

Abel became worried. Had God revealed to Bishop Clevenger that he'd lied to Bishop Gordan about lashing Isaac? He replied nervously, "Yes, Sir."

Bishop Clevenger said, "I heard your answer in worship service a while ago, Abel. I want to know if you're really lashing young Isaac or if you being untruthful."

Abel anguished over his answer. He stepped out of the buggy and started walking down the lane between the apple trees. Bishop Clevenger flicked the reins against the horse's back and drove his buggy down the lane beside Abel.

As he walked, Abel said, "I can't lie to you, Bishop Clevenger. No matter what happens to me or Isaac, I can't lie to you. I lied in the worship service. I haven't been lashing Isaac as I should. I was lashing him, but I had to stop."

"Why did you stop, Abel?"

Abel sighed and shook his head. "It was killing me, Bishop. The last time I lashed Isaac I use a harness buckle because a leather strap was no longer having the effect that it once had. Isaac had gotten to the point that he could endure the lashing with a strap, and it seemed to have little effect on him. It certainly wasn't enough of a deterrent to change his behavior, so I used a buckle on him, hoping it would hurt him enough to break his rebellious spirit."

"And that was too much force, Abel?"

Abel stopped and turned angrily to the bishop. "Yes, Bishop, it was! It cut his back and he bled something terrible! He tried to hide the pain, but he finally screamed! He's hated me ever since! I want to obey the instructions of God and Bishop Gordan, but I can't stand to lose the love of my son! I'm not like other Amish men! I'm weak! Other men have whipped their kids mercilessly and driven them from the district without so much as one ounce of regret! They've washed their hands of their kids and never give them another thought! How can they do that? How can you cast out a kid that you've raised from a little baby, and never think about them again? Little Isaac was so precious when he was growing up! We were so close! It kills me to see hatred in his yes! He used to look at me with all the love that his bright little eyes could muster! Now he hates me! I've always been so faithful to lash my kids for everything that they've done wrong, just like Bishop Gordan has commanded, but I just can't bring myself to keep whipping them! There's got to be another way to bring our kids into submission to our laws without beating them half to death and driving them out of our lives!"

Abel regained control and wiped the tears from his eyes. He realized that he had leaned into Bishop Clevenger and was yelling at him. To his surprise, Bishop Clevenger reached out and patted him on the shoulder. He grabbed Abel's massive arm and swung his leg out of the buggy. Abel took the cue and gently lifted the bishop out of the buggy. The bishop said, "Walk with me, Abel."

Emotional outbursts from Abel were rare, so Bishop Clevenger knew he was truly troubled. As they walked, Abel held the feeble bishop's arm so he wouldn't stumble and fall. The bishop asked, "Abel, have you read our Dordrecht Confession of Faith or the Ordnung of the Amish Faith?"

"I've read the Ordnung, Bishop, but not the Dordrecht Confession of Faith. I've heard their principles preached, but I've never taken the time to read them."

"Well, Abel, we Amish were originally part of the Mennonite faith, named after the Anabaptist leader, Menno Simons. In 1632, Simons' followers met in Dordrecht in the Netherlands and wrote their beliefs down in a document called the Dordrecht Confession of Faith. Those beliefs weren't just something that was thought up by our founders. They were based on the oldest and most trustworthy Bible that they had at the time, the Geneva Bible. Let me assure you, dear Able, God's word is all sufficient and void of error or contradictions. If you are confused about how to handle young Isaac, then you are relying too heavily on the preaching of Bishop Gordan and the preachers. I would encourage you to never relay on the teaching of one man. Mandatory adherence to man-made rules in order to secure salvation or acceptance by a particular faith is called legalism. If you don't read the Bible for yourself, you'll never know when a preacher is preaching a false doctrine. Now, I can't say anything to bring discredit upon Bishop Gordan, but often times he takes a narrow view of a problem. He wants to preach God's word, but he often latches hold of one scripture and fails to take it in context with what the rest of the Bible says. He then adds a few rules and laws of his own and puts God's stamp of approval on them. Yes, God says not to spare the rod in the discipline of our children, but He also says that love and mercy are as much a part of a child's discipline as the rod. In Colossians 3-21, He says, *Fathers, provoke not your children to anger, lest they be discouraged.* You have to temper your discipline with love and sound judgment lest you confuse and anger your children. If in your good conscience it is too harsh to lash young Isaac, then perhaps that's the Holy Spirit speaking to you and telling you that lashing is not appropriate. And keep in mind, my son, no faith is more laced with legalistic rules that ours. Read God's word and obey the rules that He lays down, and take all others with a grain of salt."

"Was I sinning when I lashed Isaac, Bishop?"

"Not necessarily, Abel. You whipped Isaac out of your own desire to follow our traditions, but you have to remember that God's word takes president over our traditions.

If you want to read a good lesson on how God feels about our strict adherence to scripture, read Revelation chapter two. God sent an angel to the church of Ephesus with a message from Him. He told them that He was pleased with their zeal for Scriptures, but He condemned them for their lack of love for their brethren. He ordered them to repent and restore the love in their hearts that they originally had when they first began. He wants us to have a balance of both scriptural fidelity and compassion for others. Zeal for the Scriptures without zealous love is pointless. Zealous love without Scriptural zeal is meaningless. That fundamental balance of the two is really what the Amish faith is about.

Abel sighed and nodded his head as tears of relief welled up in his eyes. "Thanks, Bishop. I feel like a huge load has been lifted off my shoulders."

Bishop Clevenger patted Abel on the back. "Good, Abel. Remember, son, many of our laws are man-made and not required of God. Our traditions are subject to the whims of the presiding bishop at the time. God's word has never changed and is infallible. Read your Bible and hide God's word in your heart, Abel. Then when trials come into your life, you'll have the full reservoir of God's word to fall back on, and you won't have to wonder if a mortal man is telling you right or wrong. I know it's unwise to publically confess that you don't believe in some of Bishop Gordan's edicts, so I wouldn't encourage you to do that. But you can know in your heart what laws are of God and what are mere legalistic rules."

Abel sighed with relief. He had been desperate for some sign that his reluctance to lash Isaac was justified. Bishop Clevenger said, "Try to find other ways to discipline your kids, Abel. Teaching them the scriptures and reasoning with them will do more than the severest lashing. If you do have to lash them, make sure it is only for the most serious offenses, and use a lot of restraint. Only whip them until they realize that they've sinned, then stop. One other thing is important when you're lashing your kids, Abel. When you're finished, you have to hug and talk to them, and let them know that you love them and that you're only lashing them to bring them into compliance with God's laws. Balance, Abel. Balance between scriptural compliance and compassion is the key."

"Can I ever regain Isaac's love, Bishop?"

"I think so, Abel. Listen, son, I've known you all your life. I knew your father and grandfather. Of all the men I've known in my life, you're one of the best. You're a good Amish man and you have nothing to be ashamed of. Now, I can't publicly profess a doctrine different than what Bishop Gordan commands, but secretly, let me tell you that lashing is not always the answer. I don't have to tell you that there is a lot of sin in our district. We have devout members who are drinking, lashing their wives, children and animals too hard, riding in automobiles, sneaking into town to cavort with the English, watching television and engaging in sexual sin."

Abel nodded and said, "I know, Bishop, but I try to keep my nose out of other peoples' business."

The old bishop shook his head and broke into a rant through gritted teeth. "And vengeance! Revenge is such a curse in our district. Arson and the burning of hay stacks is a common means of revenge. If members get angry with someone, killing or maiming their livestock or burning their hay or out-buildings is how they get even. You're aware of all the mischief in the district. It's not the English doing it; it's our own people!"

Abel squeezed the bishop's arm and patted him on the back to calm him down. "I know, Bishop, I know."

"And sexual sin! I know you've seen it. It's a bad word, and sins of the flesh are never discussed among children, and rarely among adults. Any sexual misconduct results in a severe whipping or shunning. Just look at what the elders voted to do to poor David Martin. Then the children see the hypocrisy of some getting whippings when others openly fondle the women and young girls. Then there's the cursing and telling of bad jokes that the men hear from the English. I'm telling you, Abel, our district is dripping with sin, and the young people are quick to pick up on it. The hypocrisy is so confusing to them. It's no wonder they don't want to be baptized into a faith that is so spiritually unproductive.

We've got to find ways to keep young people in our faith besides ignorance and fear."

Abel said, "Yes, I know. But the brutality is the worst."

Bishop Clevenger sighed heavily. "Sadly, yes, I hate that. That's the main thing that we have to try to change. I especially don't agree that one-year-old babies are old enough to be responsible for their actions, yet I see them frequently slapped hard for restless behavior in church. Their little red, tear-stained faces are such a sad and frequent sight on Sundays. It breaks my heart."

Abel listened intently, then nodded in agreement. The bishop continued, "You're a little too rigid in your expectations of yourself, Abel. In comparison to some of our other supposedly faithful members, you're a saint. You're right. Lashing is not always the answer. If we can get through to our kids through reason and God's word combined with love and patience, then that is sufficient. I love you and young Isaac like my own children. It pains me so see you two at odds. I'm not supposed to say this, but you back off the lashings for minor sins. Try to reason with Isaac with love and Scripture. I'll start coming by and talking to him myself. Maybe the two of us can get through to him."

Abel stared despondently at the ground and mumbled, "Why was I so hard on him? It couldn't be solely for my concern for church discipline. My anger was so strong. I felt like it wasn't even me beating him. I felt like someone else was controlling me."

Bishop Clevenger lost is peaceful bearing, and a mask of contempt and fear draped over his face, much like he was looking at a mortal enemy. He considered pulling his arm away as he studied Abel for a few seconds. Able saw the change in the bishop's demeanor and looked at him with a confused stare. Seeing that he had alarmed Abel, Bishop Clevenger relaxed and decided that Abel was safe. He swallowed his fear and smiled as he placed his hand on Abel's massive back. He leaned into him and said, "Abel, for a short time I had noticed a change in you. You'd turned mean and brutal. When you were whipping Isaac, did you feel like you had super human strength? Did you seem to lose you love for him and get some inner pleasure in whipping him?"

Abel looked at Bishop Clevenger in shock. He then looked down in shame as tears again welled up in his eyes. "Yes, Bishop, I did. I haven't told anyone, but there have been times that I felt like someone else was controlling me. Once when I felt like that, I tried to see how strong I was. I lifted the back end of my hay wagon off the ground when it was loaded with hay. I didn't like myself when I felt like that; I hated everyone. I only thought of sin and hurting people. I felt physical changes come over me. What happened to me, Bishop?"

Bishop Clevenger said, "Well, Abel, you have to consider the possibility that you were being controlled by a demon. Those are all signs of demon possession. I know we talk about demons a lot in our faith, and people have heard about them so much that they pass them off as fairy tales, but they should not be ignored. The reality of the matter is that demons don't really possess us and our children every time we sin. It is a result of our own rebellion against God's word. The excessive strength and change in your personality does, however, indicate that you may have at least been controlled by a demon, if not actually indwelled by one. It's rare, but it does happen. You're not that way anymore. What did you do to change?"

"It was that time when you were with me in your barn. I prayed and questioned my belief in God. I made a renewed commitment to love Him and keep His word. When you laid your hands on me, I felt the Holy Spirit indwell me; the anger left."

"Good, Abel, good! It may be that you had professed your belief in the Amish faith all your life and had never really believed it. You may have merely worshipped God outwardly simply to gain acceptance from others. Once you truly accepted God, the demon was no longer able to control you. He was cast out by the Holy Spirit."

"Are demons real, Bishop?"

"Oh yes, Abel, they're real. To tell you the truth, there has been one or more moving in our district for some time. You weren't the only person who's displayed signs of demon possession. I've seen evidence of them in other members. I've only been able to confront one a few times. They're hard to get close to because they move around a lot. Whenever a true believer gets close to them, they move away before the believer can cast them out in God's name. They're smart. I don't know why they've chosen this district, but something is going on that we don't understand. I want you to be vigilant, Abel. I want you to watch for evidence that a demon is controlling others in our district. If you spot one, come get me. I want to confront this demon and find out who he is and what he's doing here."

"I'm not sure I'd recognize a demon, Bishop. What do I look for?"

"The same characteristics that were present in you, Abel. The evil nature, the superhuman strength, the speaking in strange tongues, a change in personality, seizures, unnatural body movements, lots of things. If someone suddenly appears or acts different, let me know."

"What if I see more than one person acting that way? Can a demon control more than one person?"

"Satan and the other unclean spirits are not omniscient or omnipresent. They can't be in more than one place at a time, and they don't know everything. Only God does. If you see more than one person acting like that, then there's probably more than one demon working. I've only seen the evidence of one working here."

Abel stood silently and stared at the ground. Bishop Clevenger asked, "What is it, Brother Abel?"

He shrugged his shoulders and said, "I did a terrible thing when I was under the influence of that demon, Bishop. It's that thing that I confessed to you when you laid hands on me."

Bishop Clevenger nodded. "Yes, Abel, it was a bad thing, but remember, Christ died on the cross so that His righteousness could be imparted upon us for all our sins, past, present and future. No sin is too great for God to forgive. Remember the apostil Paul? No one has ever committed greater sins than him. He hunted down Christians, and imprisoned them and put them to death. God was able to forgive and use him, so He can forgive you. Once forgiven by God, any guilt that you feel is imposed upon you by Satan. Tell him to depart from you and accept the mercy and forgiveness that God has given you."

Abel was relieved. He nodded and said, "Thank you, Bishop. I hope you don't have to tell Bishop Gordan that I lied to him. He'll probably find out anyway once he talks to God."

"Oh, I won't tell him, Abel. And as for God, His capacity for forgiveness is far beyond anything that we humans can imagine. God will never tell Bishop Gordan anything that's contrary to His written word. God says in many scriptures to show mercy to those who wrong us, and who deserves a break more than our own kids? We have to show our kids the same mercy and forgiveness that we preach in our worship services. They're quick to pick up on any sign of hypocrisy in our faith. We don't whip the English for their non-belief, so Isaac deserves just as much mercy as any Englisher."

Abel breathed a sigh of relief. "Thanks, Bishop, I hope you're right. I've been praying something fierce about this. I wondered why God never answered my prayers."

The bishop patted Abel's arm and said, "He just did, Abel. He's been speaking to my heart about this matter for some time. I just got around to talking to you about it now. Remember, God answers every prayer of a believer. His answer is either, yes, no or wait. Help me back into my buggy, son. I've got to get home before Mrs. Clevenger lashes me."

Abel picked the bishop up and seated him in the buggy. He then walked around and got in beside the bishop. When the buggy didn't move, Abel looked at the bishop and found him staring off toward the distant storm clouds. Abel looked at them and said, "I've been watching them for days, but they never seem to move. And have you noticed how still the wind as been lately? It's not normal for a storm to stay in one place so long. And it's circular. It just sits out there, circling the entire district. Look at the other horizons. It's all around us. I thought it would have blown over us by now."

Bishop Clevenger didn't answer. He squinted and canted his head to the left to see better out of his stronger eye. After a long silence, he slowly pulled on the left rein and turned the horse around. Abel studied the storm that had encircled the district, then looked back at the bishop, wondering what was going on in the bishop's mind behind that worried look on his face.

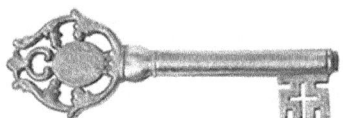

"I am he that liveth, and was dead; and behold, I am alive for evermore, Amen; and have the keys of hell and of death." **Revelation 1:18**

Agent Waters waited nervously for Smith to enter the briefing room. When Smith hurried in, he instantly saw the apprehension on Waters' face. He motioned for Waters to accompany him into the hall. Once outside the conference room, Smith said, "We've got a lot to cover today, Dexter, so let's hear what's on your mind."

Waters took a deep breath and said, "The director of the lab is refusing to test a cadaver for us. He thinks we're grabbing at straws, and doesn't think the test that you've described would be conclusive."

The only sign of Smith's rage was the tightening of his jaw muscles and a noticeable twitch in his left eye. He said, "Okay. I'll deal with him later. Let's go back in."

Dall and Sandy sat quietly as Agents Smith and Waters briefed them on their initial entry into the Amish district. As the briefing progressed, it was obvious that they had worked out the details without consulting Sandy.

Smith said, "Dall, tomorrow you and Sandy will make a cold approach on Bishop Gordan. Our source tells us that he's been irritable lately. Apparently some of the men in the district are starting to question his doctrine. He's in a constant state of agitation and is trying to maintain his control over the men. He may need a friend or at least someone who'll follow him blindly and boost his popularity. If you can play up to him and convince him that he's God in your eyes, he may let you in."

Dall asked, "If he doesn't, is there someone else we can approach?"

"No, anyone else would have to approach the bishop for approval to let you in. If he refuses, we'll have to take him out of power and try again with the assistant bishop, or whichever elder assumes power."

Dall's suspicion peaked as he looked at Sandy. She understood Smith's implication, but was stunned that Smith would come out and say it in front of Dall. She then decided that she shouldn't be so surprised. Dall would not get the chance to tell anyone.

Smith continued. "Guys, here are your cell phones. Keep them hidden somewhere that you can get to them. You can't keep them on you because they're expressly forbidden by the Amish, and possession of them will be evidence that you're not really committed to keeping the Amish traditions. We'll meet with you every night after dark and bring you charged batteries for them. You can swap them out and leave us the old ones. We should be able to keep the phones working at all times."

Sandy asked, "Where will we meet, Sir?"

Smith unrolled an aerial photograph of the bishop's farm. He pointed to a spot and said, "Here for now, just about a mile south of the bishop's house, here on the Massey property. There's an old rock foundation of an original homestead house just west of this pond. There's an old well there that's boarded over. The property belongs to Massey. He's not Amish, and he's given us permission to use it. He's the one who found our last murder victim. The whole area is grown over with brush and will be an excellent place for us to meet. We'll be there at 10:00 every night for now. When winter sets in and the days get shorter, we can meet earlier, but I want to make sure the Amish are asleep when you sneak out. Agent Waters and I will have Dr. Sveade with us to answer any questions. When you locate any Amish willing to talk, we'll wire you up so we can record their conversations. We especially want to record any incriminating statements by a suspect."

Sandy asked, "Sir, we haven't read the autopsy report. What kind of murder weapon should we be looking for?"

Smith and Waters looked at each other. Smith cleared his throat and said, "No weapon, Parsons. Our latest victim was killed with bare hands."

Smith pushed the file across the table to Sandy. Dall leaned over and looked in shock as she opened the envelope that contained the autopsy photos.

He looked at the floor and sighed. Smith asked, "Yes, Dall, is something on your mind?"

Dall shook his head nervously. "I don't like this, Agent Smith. You expect me to willingly subject myself to beatings by a man who has killed with his bare hands. He obviously has anger issues or he'd have stopped before he'd killed your victim. If he doesn't know when to stop, I could get hurt real bad or killed."

Smith nodded his head slowly as he tried to think of a good lie. He finally said, "Don't worry about that, Dall. Our victim was a small man and wasn't in as good condition as you." Smith had to look away. He knew the murder victim had been killed by someone with superhuman strength. Dall wouldn't have a chance of surviving an attack by the suspect. Dall also knew that he was in no better shape than an Amish farmer. He was no more able to defend himself that the farmer was.

Sandy was completely stunned by the injuries on the victim. She had never seen such trauma to a human body. She put the photos back in the envelope and slid the file back to Smith. She asked, "Once we identify the suspect, how will we make the arrest?"

Smith said, "That'll be easy. Once we have enough evidence to support a charge, we won't care what the Amish think. We'll send in an arrest team with a warrant and take him down. When we close this thing out, we'll pull you two out after Dall writes a letter to the bishop saying that he's changed his mind and that the Amish faith is too rigid for him. Nobody will be the wiser. They'll think you both just disappeared back into the world of the English."

Dall asked, "Will Sandy be armed? If this guy has killed twice before, he may come after us if he thinks we're asking too many questions."

Smith was hesitant to answer, but finally said, "No, Dall, neither of you will be armed. The Amish avoid modern technology. They use guns to hunt, but they're old-style shotguns and .22 rifles. They strictly avoid handguns. Possession of a handgun will blow your cover. They'll know that you're either undercover cops or you're lying about trying to obtain they're grace. A pistol will convince them that you're still clinging to the modern technology of the English."

Sandy said, "I don't like this, Sir. Without my pistol, I'm defenseless in there. If they get carried away with their beatings of me or Dall, I'll have no way to stop them. She secretly thought, *and how am I going to kill Dall if he decides to bail if I don't have a gun? Have you thought that far ahead, you idiot?"*

Smith nodded slowly. "Yes, Agent Parsons, but remember, I told you that you'd have to make some tough sacrifices for this mission. If that happens, use your ingenuity and training to get yourself out of it, but don't use any of the self-defense techniques that were taught to you in the academy. Your role is a young Amish girl. Young Amish girls don't know defense tactics. Cover up your head and protect yourself as best you can, but don't step out of role just to keep from taking a beating."

Dall asked, "If we get hurt, how will we get medical help?"

"If you get injured, call us on the cell phone before you meet us at the well. We'll bring a paramedic or doctor if you need one."

Dall said, "If we're able to call. What bail-out code have you come up with? If we get in real trouble in there, what provisions have you made to come in and get us?"

Smith glared at Dall and said angrily, "There is no provision! No bail-out code, no parachute or safety-net! Get this through your head, princess! You're in this for better or worse! Failure is not an option! You'll take what they dish out and suck it up! Work through it and pull off your role! If you bail, it'll be into a jail cell!"

Sandy did not look at Dall. She felt the same apprehension about the assignment. Smith looked at her and said, "Sandy, since you won't have a lap-top with you, you'll have to take a mini-cassette recorder in with you. Sneak out at night before you meet me and Dexter. Dictate your reports and I'll get them transcribed the next day. Since our probable cause is going to be based solely on witness testimony, every interview is important. Be sure to dictate those interviews as quickly as possible after you talk to the people. I don't want you to get confused about which person said what. Also, don't worry about false names or I.D.

You won't have any I.D. on you, and the Amish have no way of conducting background checks. Dall, your record is sealed now, so no local law enforcement can access your files."

Thirty minutes later the meeting concluded and Dall closed himself in his dorm room. He did some final soul-searching and prayed that he could pull off the role.

Sandy had given her house key to her neighbor and cancelled her deliveries before she had come to Quantico. She called her mother and father and wished them the best. They were upset when she said that she would not be able to call them for several months.

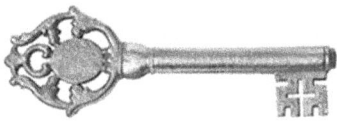

"I am he that liveth, and was dead; and behold, I am alive for evermore, Amen; and have the keys of hell and of death." **Revelation 1:18**

The elders and preachers sat round Bishop Gordan's kitchen table, and Assistant Bishop Clevenger sat in a chair against the wall. Bishop Gordan had just concluded a tirade about the number of young people who were refusing to return to the district after their period of Rumspringa and the ones who were putting off their baptism into the faith. He attributed the exodus to a lack of discipline on the part of the young people and a lack of Christian courage on the part of the fathers. Isaac Straus immediately came to mind.

Bishop Gordan's stare at Abel became conspicuous, so Brother Martin said, "With all due respect, Bishop Gordan, I've known Brother Abel all my life. He is not a weak man, Sir. He has lashed young Isaac severely. I've seen the whelps."

Brother Dunlevy said, "I've seen them, too, Bishop. My fear is that if we continue with our present course, we'll lose more young people. I know of four boys who have left the district within the last year. They were good kids while growing up. They just couldn't accept the strict traditions of our faith, and refused to return to us after their period of permissiveness."

Bishop Gordan slammed his fist on the table. Although profane language was strictly forbidden, Bishop Gordan's rough language was one of the blatant contradictions that the young people referred to when they wanted to point out the hypocrisy of the Amish faith. He yelled, "I don't give a ●●●● what those insolent ●●●● of ●●●●●●● like! ●●●● it, men, remember what God said in Proverbs 13:24 *'He that spareth his rod hateth his son: but he that loveth him chasteneth him quickly.'* We've got to persuade our men to continue practicing discipline according to God's will!"

The elders knew of many more scriptures that urged men to show mercy and kindness to those who trespass, but they were too afraid to speak up. Assistant Bishop Clevenger said, "Pardon me, Bishop Gordan, I don't mean to appear insolent, but we must preach a doctrine that is closely aligned with the conservative Gospel of our Bible. That's a doctrine where discipline is tempered with tolerance, patience and love for our children. You're right that we should be unbending in our insistence that discipline is maintained, but our children have to see our discipline as a loving rebuke, not a brutal assault. I fear that too many of the men are lashing too hard and not using lesser forms of discipline to gain compliance. Also the strict discipline is not the only reason that we're losing young people. We all have to be diligent to obey God's laws ourselves so that we avoid any perception of hypocrisy in the eyes of the young people. They'll pay far more attention to our actions than our words."

Bishop Gordan grew angrier. His snow white hair stood on end, making his lean face look more animated. He eyed Bishop Clevenger suspiciously, but failed to realize that Bishop Clevenger was pointing out his inappropriate conduct. He stood and yelled, "That's what I've been preaching! We have to scrutinize our men better! I know they're been cavorting with the English and drinking! They've been engaging in sexual sin and tolerating insolence from their women! Now, I've called on the preachers and elders to carry out sanctions on district members before, and I won't hesitate to do it again! I don't like to see people get hurt, but there are more important issues here! The very survival of our district is at stake! Sin left unchecked will hurry the destruction of the earth! I expect you elders and preachers to monitor our men- folk better! I want their sins found out and I want them brought before the church!"

The meeting ended an hour later. The men walked out feeling chastised and berated with their families following close behind. Now more than ever, Abel felt a sense of urgency to bring Isaac into line.

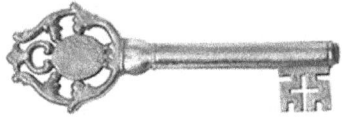

"I am he that liveth, and was dead; and behold, I am alive for evermore, Amen; and have the keys of hell and of death." **Revelation 1:18**

Curly slowly opened the chief deputy's door and stepped out. As he turned to close it, he glanced back into the angry glare of Chief Deputy Thurman. When he turned toward the lobby, every eye was fixed on him.

The reprimand had been brutal, and Thurman's voice had echoed throughout the building. Curly had never been dressed down as severely as the chief deputy had just done. Beads of sweat rolled down his face and his shirt was soaked. He tried to act like he had not been frightened, but the wide-eyed, shell-shocked look on his face betrayed his facade. He was numb and could not feel anything below his waist.

He was also sure that everyone could see the large balls of cotton that he was sure were sticking out of his mouth. He now knew what his grandpa had meant many years ago when he'd talked about his experiences with the 1st. Marine Division in the Pacific, and spoke of being scared spitless.

Sandy and Dall had just hit town and were preparing to check into a hotel for the night. After they had checked in, Dall knocked on Sandy's door. When she answered, he said, "I'm going out for some dinner. Want to come along?"

"Sure, if I can pick. I guess Smith and Waters can't fault us for that."

They had just ordered their dinner when Dall noticed a grossly overweight deputy sitting alone at a corner table. He seemed troubled and was licking his wounds. Dall motioned toward him and said, "Look over there, Sandy, looks like one of the locals is having a rough day."

Curly's anguish was written across his face. Sandy turned back toward Dall and said, "We all have our problems, Dall. Right now I'm sure his problems aren't as serious as ours."

"Maybe not to us, but I'm sure they are to him."

When they had finished eating, Dall and Sandy paid their bills and left. They were standing on the sidewalk outside the diner trying to decide what to do with their last night of freedom when Curly waddled out the door. His overcrowded duty-belt rattled as he bounced off the sides of the doorway.

Curly was distinctly locked into reality. Fantasies of heroism, celebrity and carnal knowledge of junior college cheerleaders had been brutally suppressed by the painful reality that he had come within a frog's hair of losing his commission. And he wasn't sure he'd completely dodged the bullet yet. The sheriff had not yet had his turn at the feeding-trough of Curly's back-side.

When his reddened eyes met Dall's, he lowered his head and walked on. Sandy said quietly, "Boy, he is whipped. Must have gotten the bad news that his application for the centerfold of Fitness Magazine was rejected."

Dall frowned at her. "Ah, Sandy, lighted up on the guy. Do you think he's happy with how he looks? I've known guys like him. He's been kicked in the teeth his whole life. That badge is probably the only thing that keeps him going. Deep down inside he's probably a good person. Come on; let's sow a few seeds of grace. You never know what the future holds for us. We may need that guy's help someday soon." He turned to Curly and yelled, "Hey, deputy."

Curly stopped and looked around. Someone was yelling for a deputy, but there must be another member of the sheriff's office close by. Surely they weren't talking to him. He had been the brunt of so much ridicule for so long that he couldn't remember when anyone had shown him the respect of referring to him as "Deputy."

When he turned around and saw Dall and Sandy walking toward him, he realized that they were talking to him. The shock of anyone showing him some respect froze his feet in place. These people had to be tourists.

Dall and Sandy walked up and stuck out their hands. Curly stared at them in disbelief, then realized that they were being genuinely friendly. Joy overwhelmed him as he vigorously shook their hands. He asked proudly, "Yes Sir! What can I do for you?"

Dall said, "My sister and I just finished dinner and were wondering if there is anything interesting to do around here this time of evening."

Curly stuck his thumbs in the front of his belt, deepened his voice and put on his most professional facade as he proudly pointed out the town's strong points, in his opinion. It amused Sandy what every attraction that Curly pointed out had something to do with food. She turned away and faced traffic so he would not see her smile.

Dall listened intently, then said, "Well, thanks, deputy. Listen, I don't mean to pry, but I was watching you while we were eating. You sure looked like you were carrying a heavy burden. Is there anything we can do for you?"

Curly hadn't been aware that his feeling had been written across his face. He pasted on his most convincing mask of self-confidence and stumbled all over himself. "Oh! No, Sir! No problems here! Just thinking about this big case I'm working. You know how it is." He slapped his holster and said with a pretentious chuckle, "So many criminals and so few bullets."

Dall tried to mask his amusement, but even his years in the Army and short tenure as youth director had not prepared him for Curly's act. As hard as he tried to hide his disbelief, Curly could see it in his eyes.

He finally dropped the act and said, "Well, there's nothing really seriously wrong. I just got crossways with the chief deputy a while ago. You know how it is. You say one little thing and everyone takes it wrong. Everyone's so darned eager to twist every little word around to mean something that you never intended it to mean, and start a tiff. I made one little comment and he took it personally."

Dall nodded adamantly. "Oh, believe me, I know how that is, deputy." After a moment of awkward silence, Dall asked, "Did he take it personally because you meant it personally, deputy?"

Curly frowned and shook his head violently. He started to say no with all the conviction as he could muster, but he looked into Dall's eyes and realized that he was not a good enough liar to sell it. As he continued to shake his head, no, he said, "Yeah, yeah I did."

Dall lowered his head and chuckled. He looked back into Curly's eyes and said, "Well, deputy, let me assure you that I've been in your shoes before. I know how you feel. Sometimes the best policy is to not say anything if you can't say something good."

Curly sighed with relief. "Boy, that's right! Man! Nobody can chew butt like Chief Deputy Thurman! I was actually in fear for my life!"

Again, Dall laughed. He said, "Been there and done that, deputy, but let me assure you of something. I've been in combat and had many good men under my command. I know a good man when I see one. Now, I know you made a mistake, but I can tell that deep down inside, you're a very competent officer."

Curly stepped back in shock and was unable to speak. Dall continued, "Yep, I know a true warrior when I see one. Look at that revolver, clean and not a speck of rust on it. That uniform is clean with crisp creases. That leather and badge are shined and worn with pride. Yes Sir, deputy, I'm looking at one squared-away cop. Your chief deputy will realize it someday. All you need is a chance to redeem yourself. You hang in there. Someday soon, some crook will cross paths with you, and that'll be his downfall."

Dall squinted as he leaned into Curly and read his name-tag. "Yes, Sir, I'd sure hate to be a crook and have Deputy Slapp on my tail."

Curly's eyes welled up as he again shook Dall's hand hard enough to cause pain in Dall's elbow. He nervously reached into his pocket and pulled out a business card, then pulled his pen from his other pocket. He wrote his home number on the back of the card and thrust it toward Dall. "Here, mister, this is my card and home number. If you ever need anything, you call me. I'm the man for whatever job you have."

Dall read the card. "Thanks, Curly. Thanks a lot. You remember my name, too. I'm Dall. If I ever need a deputy in this county, I'm calling you."

Dall put Curly's card in his pocket and smiled as Curly swaggered away with renewed self-esteem and that right arm swinging out wide around the butt of his revolver, all the while eyeing those alleys for terrorists and adoring cheerleaders. Sandy turned back around and shook her head. "Okay, Father Roberts, you've done your good deed for the day."

Dall said as they walked away, "Yeah, and that good deed might come back to us with dividends someday."

Sandy asked, "If you wanted to warm up to a local, why pick a toad like him?"

Dall shrugged his shoulders. "Because he's just the one that happened along and the opportunity presented itself. Sometimes when you need a friend the most, you pick the guy that most needs a friend. They're usually the most loyal. That guy'll be there if we ever need him."

Sandy sighed heavily. "Yeah, but being there isn't enough. It's how he'll perform that concerns me. Frankly, I don't think that guy could save me from anything, except maybe a killer pizza."

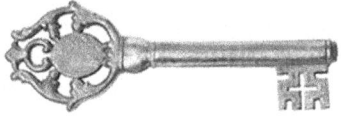

"I am he that liveth, and was dead; and behold, I am alive for evermore, Amen; and have the keys of hell and of death." **Revelation 1:18**

Dory hurried to get dinner served before it got dark. She lit the oil lamps to give additional light in the kitchen. Judith, age seven, was at the table reading her lesson while baby Jack, age five, sat on the counter and watched his mother move the pieces of chicken from the milk bath to the seasoned flour, then into the cast iron skillet with hot lard.

Abel led the team of draft horses into their stalls and put a gallon can of feed in their feed box. He then yelled, "Isaac, supper time! Let's not keep Mom waiting!"

Abel walked toward the house, but Isaac took his time. He was enduring his latest shunning, so supper held no appeal for him. He slapped his black, wide-brimmed hat against his heavy cotton trousers to knock off the hay dust, then walked angrily toward the house.

Abel had finished washing his hands and assumed his seat at the head of the table when Isaac walked in. Abel waited patiently for Isaac to wash and assume his position in the corner away from the family with his face toward the wall.

When Isaac was seated, Abel said a lengthy prayer and thanked God for His grace and sustenance, then asked for continued forgiveness for himself and his family. He looked out of the corner of his eye, but Isaac was staring at the wall with his head up and his eyes open. Abel's temper flared as he interrupted his prayer and said sternly, "Isaac! I expect you to pray with the family. If you won't do it out of respect for us, then do it out of respect for God."

Isaac wanted to leave the house and go to Massey's pond, but he was still afraid of his father's wrath. He sighed deeply and bowed his head. Since he was being shunned and was required to face the wall as he ate, his father would not know that he still had his eyes open.

When Abel said Amen, Dory filled Isaac's plate and walked to him. She put the plate in his lap without a word. Isaac was starving, so he ate quickly. When finished, he stood and put his plate on the counter to be washed. As he started toward the door, Abel said, "Dinner is not over, son. Sit back down and wait until the family is finished."

Isaac turned angrily and asked, "Why? I'm being shunned! No one is talking to me, so it doesn't matter if I'm here or not!"

Abel boiled inside. It went against his raising to endure back-talk from a rebellious teenager, but he remembered what Bishop Clevenger had said. Dory reached over and gently placed her hand on Abel's tensed arm to stop him from standing. He took a deep breath and said calmly, "I'm aware that you're being shunned, son, but it's not a shunning if you're not here for us to shun. Sit down and suffer it. It won't have the desired effect if you don't endure it."

Isaac stomped back to the chair in the corner and plopped down. Abel fought the urge to grab him by his throat and drag him to the barn for another lashing. He went back to eating while Dory tried to ease the tension by making small-talk. Judith and baby Jack looked at each other nervously, wondering how long their father would remain calm.

When dinner was over, Dory and the small children began clearing the table. Isaac left the kitchen and went to his room. Abel went outside and sat on the porch. While he was listening to the night sounds, baby Jack and Judith came out of the house and climbed up on his lap. After a lengthy hug from Dad, baby Jack said, "Isaac doesn't like shunning, Dad. I don't like it either."

Abel patted Jack on the leg. "I don't like it either, baby Jack. It saddens me and Mom to have to do it."

A revelation hit Judith as she was unwrapping her arms from around Abel's neck. She asked with enthusiastic innocence, "Hey, Dad, why don't we just not do it anymore? We all miss Isaac at the table. Maybe if we treat him nicer, he won't be so mad all the time."

Abel patted Judith on the back and kissed her on the head, "I'm trying, honey, but I'm afraid it's a little too late. I'm trying to be patient with Isaac, but he's got to start obeying God's laws or he'll be doomed to Hell. We don't want that, now do we?"

The reality of Hell was not lost on the small children as both opened their eyes wide, shook their heads and said, "Noooo." After telling the kids and few Bible stories and what all the night sounds were, Abel carried them upstairs and tucked them into bed.

As he walked past Isaac's door, Abel paused and gripped the doorknob, contemplating the wisdom of engaging Isaac at this time. He finally decided that Bishop Clevenger's talk about the hypocrisy of some of the Amish men needed to be explained. He turned the knob and stepped into Isaac's room.

Isaac was lying on his bed with his hands folded behind his head. He was staring at the ceiling, grinding his anger between his gritted teeth. Abel asked, "Can I come in, Isaac?"

"You're in. The proper time to ask that was when you were out in the hall."

Abel's breathing increased as did his pulse. He closed his eyes and silently prayed, *"Lord, hallowed is Thy name. With all that You have to keep track of in this universe, thank You for loving me enough to tend to my needs and those of my family. Right now, my greatest need is for You to give me patience and open the heart of my son. In Jesus name I pray. Amen."*

He sat on the edge of Isaac's bed and made the lad nervous. Isaac unconsciously moved to the far edge to avoid any inadvertent touching. Abel's hands made a loud grating sound as he leaned over, resting his arms on his legs, and nervously rubbed his calloused palms together. He said, "Isaac, do you remember how life was when you were very young?"

Isaac didn't respond. Abel continued, "Well, I do. You were such a sweet child. You idolized me and your mother. We couldn't have loved anyone more than we loved you. We still feel that way about you. Now, I'll freely admit that your mother is a far better parent than I am. She tells you and the little kids every day that she loves you. I guess that's why mothers are mothers; they think to do those little things that keep the bond between them and their kids strong. We men get wrapped up in our problems and forget to do those little things that keep our children close to us."

For so long, Abel had believed that speaking of love and such things was unmanly. His face bushed as he allowed God to lead him in the things that he should say. Isaac was also uncomfortable speaking of such things with his father. His anxiety level rose as he looked away. Abel said, "A long time ago, too long ago, I stopped taking you up in my arms and holding you tight and telling you how much I loved you. It seems awkward now that you're a grown man, but somewhere along the way, my discipline became misunderstood. When I stopped hugging you and telling you how much I loved you, the lashings continued. When there were only lashings and no display of my love for you, you started believing that I didn't care for you. That set us up as enemies. You saw my lashings only as abuse, not as correction."

Isaac snarled, "It was abuse! It was no less than that! No man could love his kids and beat them like you beat me! I don't care how much you hug a person! If you beat them like that, they'll never believe you love them!"

Abel struggled to recall all that Bishop Clevenger had said. He nodded and said, "You're right, Isaac. And I confess to you here tonight that I was wrong. Sometimes when a grown man is handling a young boy, we forget our own strength. When I was angry, I tended to forget how much force I was using. I know I hurt you. I should have waited to lash you until I had more control of my anger. I should have used more restraint."

Isaac stood and pulled his shirt over his head. He threw it on the bed, then turned and exposed his back to Abel. "And what about this, Dad? Was this merely a mistake? Did you love me while you were ripping the skin off my back?"

Abel looked down at the floor. He wanted to somehow diminish his ownership in the scars by telling Isaac that at that time he had possibly been possessed by an unclean spirit, but he also wanted to set the proper example for his son by showing him how a man accepts responsibility for his actions. He shook his head, "I have no excuse, Isaac. At the time you had developed a tolerance for the pain of the usual lashings that I was giving you. I didn't think they were having the desired effect, which was to get you to repent of your sins. I thought I had to increase the pain to get you to change. But, yes I did love you. Isaac, I apologize for my wrongs. God has forgiven me. It will not be charged against my soul on the day of my judgment. But this is no longer about my wrong-doing. It is now about your inability to forgive. I want us to be close again. I want us to have that affection that we had for each other when you were small. But I want you to respect me. I want you to stop challenging me and the bishop's authority. I want you to stop doing the things that create the need for lashings. I'm trying to not lash you as often. I'm trying to reach you through means other than lashing, but you've got to straighten up. As much as I love you, I'm concerned for your soul even more. I hate to lash you, but I hate even more the thought of you languishing in a lake of fire for eternity."

Isaac remained defiant. He stood over his dad and glared angrily into his eyes. Seeing that he was making no progress, Abel stood to leave. As he rose to his full height, Isaac suddenly lost his nerve. He sat back down on the bed and put on his shirt. Abel said, "I guess I don't understand what you're going through, son. I never acted this way with my father, so I can't see what you're so angry about. If you're clinging to the hypocrisy of some of our members as an excuse to turn your back on God, that defense will never hold up on judgment day. You're seeing examples of hypocrisy every day here in the district, son. Men are doing all sorts of things that are against our faith. But they'll crumple to their knees in fear before Jesus on judgment day, just like us all. They'll answer for their sins. You can't justify your sins by pointing to the sins of others. God will judge you based on your own merit."

Isaac had no defense. He hung his head and nervously clinched his fists. Abel continued, "I know there are a lot of Amish who are sinning, but just understand, we're mortal men. None of us are perfect. Christianity does not mean that we're perfect and sin-free. We're not; we're just forgiven. Don't throw away your soul because you see sin in others. Understand that we each have to answer for our sins, just as you will. Don't throw our faith in the trash because we make mistakes."

Abel could see the conviction in Isaac's eyes. Bishop Clevenger's advice was sound. "Son, if you think life with the English will be any better, think again. Your mother and I have shielded you from their sinful ways, but the same sins that you see in some Amish are in the English also. Bishop Clevenger has offered to counsel you. Please think about talking to him. The stakes are so high here." He turned and closed the door behind him, leaving Isaac to wrestle with his conviction.

Abel went to his room and undressed. He slid into bed with Dory and sighed in frustration. Dory said, "Be patient with him, Abel. The smaller kids and I can see that you're trying not to lash them as often. Isaac will too in time."

"I don't know, Dory, this has been going on for several months now. I've been trying to keep Isaac away from the elders and preachers. If he shows them any sign of disrespect, they'll sanction me and take action against him. They already tried it once."

Dory sat up quickly and stared at Abel in disbelief. "What action? What did they try with Isaac? Did one of them leave those bruises on his face?"

Abel knew he'd slipped up. Once Dory launched into a tirade, no force on Earth would close her mouth. "Nothing, dear, I shouldn't have said anything. Just let it go."

Dory threw herself on top of Abel and pressed her nose close to his. "No! No, I won't let it go! What? What have they tried with my son? You tell me, Abel Straus, or there'll be Hell to pay!"

Abel rolled his eyes and sighed heavily as he began his lie. "Dory, nothing has happened. Just back me up and help me get through to Isaac. He'll still listen to you."

Dory squinted her eyes and glared at Abel with an angry cant of her head. There was an awkward moment of silence as she searched his eyes for any sign of deception. She was only satisfied when Abel grabbed the back of her head and pressed it against his chest, then gently massaged her lower back. She slowly rubbed his chest and said, "You're a good father, dear. Isaac knows that. He can see that you're trying to be gentler with him. I've seen some change in him."

"I haven't. I wish Bishop Clevenger was the head bishop here. I like his ideas better than Bishop Gordan's. I'm thinking we should move."

Dory caressed Abel's arm and sighed, "We've put so much work into this farm, Abel. We're settled here, and all our friends are here. There's no assurance that another district would be any better. The Amish faith is pretty strict wherever you go."

"Then we don't have to live in a district. We can be faithful Amish anywhere. We don't need a district to be Amish."

"That may be so, but if we don't live in a district, we're going to have to change our beliefs and become more progressive and tolerant of the English ways. You know how much we depend on our neighbors. If there are no other Amish around, we'll have to interact more closely with the English. The kids and I would get along with them fine, but can you do that?" Abel just sighed and moaned in frustration.

After a few minutes of silence, Dory ran her fingers through Abel's beard. She cooed softly, "The kids are asleep."

Abel mumbled so the kids would not hear, "Not now, woman. I'm too consumed with Isaac."

Dory knew exactly how to distract Abel. She knew every inch of his body and knew where every button was. She ran her index fingernail along the inside of Abel's leg. She whispered, "There'll always be stresses that steal our time for love, sweetheart."

Abel instantly relaxed and moaned with pleasure. In a half-hearted protest he mumbled, "Now, Dory, you know that coupling for pleasure is a sin."

Dory grabbed a handful of hair on Abel's chest and pulled. He cringed as she lectured, "Sin or not, Abel Straus, I'm not living my whole life without making love with my husband! I don't care what Bishop Gordan says, the Bible doesn't say that! I've looked it up. In Hebrews 13:4, God says that marriage is honorable in all, and the marriage bed undefiled! We're husband and wife, not adulterers, so whatever goes on in this bed is not a sin! Don't you go trying to make me feel guilty, Abel Straus! You're the one who breaks Bishop Gordan's laws the most around here! When you're torch is lit, you take me wherever we happen to be, so don't act like I'm the sinner here just because I'm the one coming into season! And if you want to confess that in worship service, go ahead! I'll be excommunicated and offer not one apology, but I won't go without the pleasings of the man I love! That's a stupid law anyway! I do not intend to burn with lust all the days of my life, mister!"

Abel rolled his eyes. "Dory, you're not supposed to point out my sins like that. You're supposed to pretend it doesn't happen, and you've got to stop challenging the bishop's authority. I'm supposed to lash you for that."

Dory threw the blanket off and sprang to her knees, then straddled Abel. She bent over and put her nose against his ready for a fight. "Your butt, Mr. Straus! The day will never come when Doretta Ruth Theilheim will ever be whipped for speaking her mind! I keep my mouth shut in public, but this is my house, Mister Straus! I speak my mind here, and you're the one who'll get the lashing if you ever raise an angry hand against me!"

Abel sighed in defeat and caressed her breast as he shook his head and smiled. "I know. You're the worst Amish women I've ever seen, next to Lilly Dresselhaus. Where in the world did you get this confounded rebellious heart? You've had it as long as I've known you, so you didn't get it from Lilly. But you have been spending too much time around her. Every time I think I've got you straightened out, you visit her and come home all riled up again. She's a bad influence on you."

"That may be, but I like her. She's not afraid of that bishop and those phony preachers and elders. She tells them what hypocrites they are. All the drinking, sexual sin and brutality that goes on in this district makes me sick. I feel so bad for her since Wilhelm died."

"Me, too; I liked Wilhelm. That's another thing that worries me. Isaac has been sneaking off to Massey's pond most every night. That's where Wilhelm was killed."

Dory said, "Yes, and Preacher Croft was killed there. You're still following Isaac to make sure he'll be okay, aren't you?"

Abel yawned and said, "Yeah, I am. That reminds me, you'd better turn off that torch of yours. I've got to follow Isaac tonight. He thinks he's so smart. He's never figured out that I'm following him."

Dory frowned as her shoulders sank in disappointment. "Well, okay, I guess. You be careful yourself, dear. I don't want you to wind up like Preacher Croft and Wilhelm Dresselhaus. You've got some serious woman-pleasing to do when you get back, and don't think you'll be able to slip into bed without waking me. There'll be no sleep for you till you calm my ache."

"I'll be careful, dear. I'm a little more man than Wilhelm and Preacher Croft were. It'll take a better man than I've seen around here to get the best of me in a tussle."

Dory said, "True, unless they use a weapon. You just keep on your toes. If you take a single-tree or pick handle upside the head, I'll have to move Lilly in here to help me raise these kids. You don't want them under her influence, do you?"

Abel cringed. "Oh Lord. The two of you together would ruin them" He slipped out of bed and dressed, then listened for the creaking floorboards that signaled that Isaac was on his way out of the house. He slipped his sheathed hunting knife into his back pocket and followed quietly.

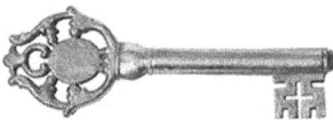

"I am he that liveth, and was dead; and behold, I am alive for evermore, Amen; and have the keys of hell and of death." **Revelation 1:18**

Isaac hurried down the path to Massey's pond. He hadn't forgotten his close call with Preacher Croft, so he listened frequently to see if he was being followed. His head was on a swivel, so he saw the little girl several hundred yards before she reached him. Her gown glowed just as it had the night that Preacher Croft had attacked him. He looked up at the sky to see if the moon was glowing. It was, but it was periodically masked by the passing of intermittent clouds. She had an unnatural inner luminescence that could not be explained by any natural forces. Unnerved, Isaac hurried on to Massey's pond.

As he crept through the timber into the clearing the clouds parted, exposing the moon, and he saw what he'd been wanting. His one true love, Katie Betendorf, was sitting on a log with the moonlight highlighting her lightly-freckled face and auburn hair.

Both young lovers ran and passionately embraced each other. They hadn't seen Abel slip in and hide behind the trunk of a mature oak where he could overhear their conversation.

Katie took Isaac's hand and led him to the log. He sat beside her and stared into her moonlit eyes. She said, "I'm sorry I couldn't get away the past few nights, Isaac. I'm so scared that my father will catch me leaving the house. He hasn't been sleeping soundly lately, and I couldn't get away. Something has been eating at him."

"Oh, that's okay, Katie. I understand. My mood hasn't been good anyway."

"I know, Isaac, but you have to forgive your father. All of our fathers are strict. That's just the Amish way. We all need to be more diligent to follow God's laws."

"I know, Katie. I just hate being under such tight controls. We can't do anything that the English can. Look at all we're missing out on. This is the space-age for God's sake. We're still living like we're back in 17th century Europe."

"I know, Isaac, but that's not all bad. We miss out on some of the modern conveniences, but we're sanctified. Remember what the bishops and elders say about Romans 12:2. *'Be not conformed to this world, but be transformed by the renewing of your mind that ye may prove what is that good and acceptable and perfect will of God.'* We are admonished to live a life that is separate from the world."

Isaac rolled his eyes and groaned, "How many times have I had that passage pounded into my head? We hear it at every service and meal prayer."

"I know, Isaac, but we're separated from the English and all their trappings. We're going to Heaven; most of them aren't. We'll be rewarded for our obedience in the next life. Well, most of us will."

Isaac looked suspiciously at her. "What do you mean?"

Katie squared up to him and looked sternly into his eyes, "I mean you, Mister Trouble. You think I don't know what you're up to, but the other kids talk. I know you've been drinking when the Peterson boys meet you here with a bottle. You may hide it from everyone else, but you can't fool me."

"Oh, Katie, I just do that to fit in. I don't even like the stuff."

"Then quit it, Isaac! I don't like it either! If we're ever going to be married, you have to be the kind of man who stands up for what's right. We're going to have children who'll need a father who shows them right from wrong by his living example. And you have to be the kind of man that my father will approve of. If he gets word that you're drinking and not keeping the Amish laws, he'll never approve of you as my husband. He's already heard the rumors. I don't want to have to run away to marry you, so straighten up before you ruin everything. You have to come back to church and obtain forgiveness for your sins. Bishop Gordan will never permit us to marry if you don't get baptized and become a good Amish."

Isaac looked sadly at the ground. "I don't know if that'll ever happen, Katie. It hurts to think of living my life without you, but I don't think I can ever be a good Amish."

"You can, Isaac. I know you can."

"What if I can't, Katie? Will I lose you?"

Tears welled up in Katie's eyes as she caressed Isaac's face and said, "Never, Isaac. I'm yours tonight and I'll be yours forever. Just don't put us in a position where we have to live our lives without the love of our families. That's no way for a married couple to start their lives together."

"What if the worst happens?"

"For better or worse, Isaac Straus, I've committed my life to you. You're my husband; we just haven't taken our vows yet. If that happens, I'll keep a ladder under my window. When you're ready to climb it, I'll be packed and ready to go." Abel chuckled quietly. Katie was so much like Isaac's mother.

Isaac turned and kissed Katie hard. She stood and pulled him to his feet, then fell into his arms for another long kiss. As their passion rose, Isaac breathed heavily and began caressing Katie's breasts. She grabbed his hands and said, "Not yet, Isaac. I want you too, but I'm saving my body for you on our wedding night."

Isaac sighed in frustration. "We can't even enjoy each other then, Katie. Bishop Gordan says we can only have sex if we're trying to have children. We can't make love just to enjoy each other."

Katie smiled and stroked Isaac's hair. "Well then, we're going to have lots of kids. I want a big family, and you'll need lots of help running our farm. And once we're through having kids, we'll make love anyway. If anyone tries to stop us, that's where I'll stop being a good Amish girl. We're going to enjoy each other any time we want, and no one will know about it unless you confess it in worship service.

Isaac chuckled. "That'll never happen. I can't stay out of trouble long enough to be invited to worship service."

As the two teenagers laughed and kissed, Abel leaned quietly against a tree in the darkness. He smiled at the young lovers and fondly remembered his romance with Dory when they were young teenagers.

As long as their love didn't escalate into something that he would have to put a stop to, Abel let the kids enjoy each other. He was glad that Katie was so mature and firm in her convictions.

Isaac would be furious if he knew that his father had been following him every night for the last six months, but Abel feared for the safety of the kids since the night that Preacher Croft had attacked Isaac. He was careful to be quiet and stay in the shadows. Katie was the love of Isaac's life, and at this point she was the best influence on him.

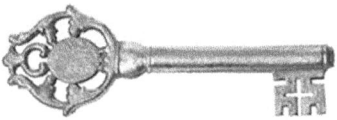

"I am he that liveth, and was dead; and behold, I am alive for evermore, Amen; and have the keys of hell and of death." **Revelation 1:18**

The sun was barely above the horizon when Agent Waters pulled over about a half-mile from the drive that led to Bishop Gordan's farmhouse. After a careful 360 degree scan to make sure they were not being observed, Dall and Sandy stepped out of the back seat. Smith leaned out the passenger window and said, "Remember, Dall, humility and patronage is the key with Gordan. Our source tells us that he's got a big ego, so play him like a violin. If he says you can stay, start walking down this road. Tell him that you have to get your belongings from the hotel in town. We'll pick you up as soon as you get out of sight."

Waters and Smith drove away. Dall and Sandy stood in silence staring off in the distance at the bishop's house. Neither spoke, but knew the fear in the other's heart as they slowly started walking.

Bishop Gordan stormed out on his porch when the dogs started barking at Dall and Sandy. He stood on the porch so he could tower over the strangers. He knew by their clothing that they were not Amish, and yelled with authority, "There are no Englishers allowed on this hallowed ground! God's laws are obeyed here, and corrupters of man, mortal or spirit, are not permitted!"

Dall nodded his head and said, "I'm Dall Roberts, Bishop Gordan. This is my sister, Sandy. We have no intention of corrupting anyone, but we're in trouble and need your help. Would you give us just a minute of your time?"

Bishop Gordan raised his chin and looked down his nose at the two. Dall's humility boosted his ego and self-confidence. After sizing them up, he slowly nodded his head and motioned for them to come up on the porch and sit.

Dall and Sandy sat on the old cane chairs, but Bishop Gordan stood and paced in front of them so he could maintain his dominance. Dall said, "Bishop Gordan, we were directed here to you by a man down the road. I don't know his name, but he said you're the man we're looking for."

Bishop Gordan wallowed in his celebrity. "Go on, I'm listening."

Dall said, "Sandy and I were raised Amish in a district back in Pennsylvania. When we were very young, we left the district and lived with the English. Having been exposed to the true word of God, we've never been content with living outside the will of God. We've sold our worldly possessions to get enough money to journey here, and would like to regain God's grace. The only way we can do that is to become Amish again. With your consent and guidance, we'd like to live in this district and be baptized into the Amish faith once again."

The bishop managed to erase the shock from his face as he paced back and forth in front of the two. He listened intently, then blurted out, "Impossible! You have turned your back on God and the propitiation that He provided for your sins through the crucifixion of His son, Jesus Christ. Redemption is not possible here."

Dall thought for a few seconds, then said, "Pardon me, Bishop, but redemption is possible until a person dies. Forgiveness is available to every man until death. As you know, in Matthew 18:22, when Peter asked Jesus if he should forgive his brother seven times, Jesus said he should forgive him seventy times seven. The implication there is that forgiveness is endless with God. And since you are the bishop of this district, and your appointment was nothing less than the divine hand of God moving to plant you as shepherd of this flock, you are the awesome voice of God Himself. God speaks to you continually, therefore you have the authority to forgive us our sins and allow us to regain God's redemption. Please don't send us away. We're doomed to Hell in the world of the English. The fact that we are sitting on your porch is evidence that God has made you our shepherd."

The bishop stared suspiciously at Dall, but Dall's patronage had swelled the bishop's ego beyond his ability to reason. He stopped pacing and said, "You are well schooled, Dall. It is true that God can forgive, but I have the welfare of my district to think of. I can't allow any corruptive influences to invade this district. Once you'd left the Amish faith to live with the English, you were infected with the sin of their ways."

"Forgive me again, Bishop, I don't mean to challenge your expertise, but we did not leave the faith voluntarily. Our parents broke up and gave us to some English people to raise. We were too small to have any say in it. We were cast into the world of the English against our will. We've never been content there. We are Amish who were sent away from our homes to dwell in a foreign land. We wish to return now. Please help us?"

Sandy looked at Dall in total amazement at his ingenuity. She then looked at Bishop Gordan to gauge his response. He stared at Dall, then nodded his head. "Well, I've never come across a problem like this. I'll have to take the matter to the elders. I'll let you know."

Dall knew that if it were left to a popular vote of the elders, there was a good chance that the answer would be no. He stroked Gordan in a sad tone, "Okay, Sir, I'm sorry. I thought you were God's final word in all things in this district. I've been out of the faith so long that I've forgotten how things work. Would you please let me know when the next meeting with the elders will be? I'd like to address them."

Bishop Gordan exploded with anger. "I am God's final word in this district, young man! I don't have to ask anyone for permission to allow you to stay! I've made a decision! You can stay, but you'll have to work hard to earn your baptism!"

Dall relaxed. He was pleased that he'd been able to trip the bishop's trigger so easily. He stood and extended his hand. He vigorously shook Gordan's hand and said, "Thank you, Bishop Gordan. We're so pleased to be under your authority. Thank you for your mercy."

As Dall and Sandy were about to step off the porch, Gordan put his hands in the pockets of his trousers and asked, "Young man, what made you choose this district? Missouri is a long way from Pennsylvania, and there are a lot of districts between there and here."

Dall stopped in his tracks and stared out across the rolling hills. Sandy's heart sank as she looked out of the corner of her eye to see what he would come up with. He slowly turned and stepped back to the porch. He shrugged his shoulders and said, "We went back to the bishop of the district that we had left, but he couldn't decide what to do. When we asked if there was a bishop anywhere in the country that could disciple us in the Amish ways and teach us the truth, he said you were the only one he could recommend. We would like to have found a district closer to Pennsylvania, but we wanted to do this right. And since our very salvation is at stake, we want to learn under a strong leader who is not afraid to make a decision. Tonight when we pray, we'll thank God for placing us under the discipleship of just such a shepherd."

Bishop Gordan's pride again swelled to the point that he could not think clearly, or he would have thought to ask the name of the bishop who referred them to him. He proudly inhaled a deep breath and smiled arrogantly as he nodded his head in agreement.

Sandy gave an inner sigh of relief as she again shook the bishop's hand. He asked, "Young lady, what is your marital status? Have you ever been married or bred?"

Sandy was taken off-guard by the bishop's bluntness, but said, "I've never been married, Sir, and I've never given myself over to fornication. I've always kept God's word in my heart and strictly avoided those ways of the English that cast us outside the will of God."

Bishop Gordan nodded his head and rubbed his beard. He sized up the two like a pair of draft horses and said, "Good. You'll make a fine Amish wife someday, young lady, if you can maintain your fidelity to our traditions. Dall, you'll be a good Amish husband to one of our ladies if you can regain God's favor and endure the hard work. Just one warning, though, we tolerate no sin or challenges to our faith. You'll not challenge the authority of me, the assistant bishop, the preachers or the elders. We'll train you, but you will not be permitted to continue your English ways."

Dall said, "We understand, Bishop. We'll go back to town and get our things. We've got some clothes that will suit your traditions. We'll burn these clothes once we get settled."

The bishop said, "Good. Meet me here about noon."

As they walked back to the road, Dall said, "Good thinking back there, Sandy. You catch on quick. You must have been reading your Bible."

"Only every waking minute for the last week. I have to admit, I never dreamed it was so comprehensive. There's something in there that applies to every possible situation. I wish I understood it better."

"It'll never make complete sense till you become a believer, then it'll open up to you in ways that you never dreamed possible. It's almost magical how God's word comes alive after you're indwelled with the Holy Spirit. But there are people who have studied it their whole lives and don't understand it all. You've got a good start, though. Keep reading."

Sandy sensed that something was bothering Dall. She asked, "You're not happy with how it went?"

He shrugged his shoulders. "Oh, I guess. I just don't like lying to people. My conscience is bothering me."

Sandy patted him on the back. "Don't beat yourself up, Dall; it's for a good cause. There's a murderer somewhere in this district. We may have just talked to him. We're going to save lives by doing this."

Dall didn't answer. He only hoped they didn't get killed in the process. He felt abandoned and isolated. Smith and Waters had made it clear that there would be no rescue if they got into trouble. And although he and Sandy seemed to be bonding, she was not his friend. She would sell him out to Smith in a heartbeat to redeem herself or protect her career and the integrity of the investigation.

As they walked down the road toward town, Dall studied the distant storm clouds and hoped they were not a metaphor for things to come.

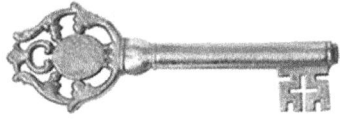

"I am he that liveth, and was dead; and behold, I am alive for evermore, Amen; and have the keys of hell and of death." **Revelation 1:18**

Sheriff Holden hurried into the closed meeting and apologized for being late. Seated at the table were Chief Deputy Thurman, the detective sergeant and two of his most trusted detectives. The sheriff said,

"Morning, gents. Sorry to keep you waiting; let's get started." He and Casey Thurman spent the next thirty minutes discussing ways to covertly investigate the Amish murders without the feds finding out.

Curly had been assigned to the station this week so Chief Deputy Thurman could keep an eye on him. His job was to help the records girls file reports and citations, and feed the prisoners in the jail. One of his duties was to keep fresh coffee in the pot and periodically deliver coffee to the sheriff and chief deputy.

He knocked before opening the sheriff's door to make sure it was okay to enter. As the door opened, everyone in the office got quiet when they saw it was Curly. He sensed the mistrust, but delivered the hot cups of coffee with a cheerful smile.

As he was leaving, Curly closed the door, but it did not latch. It slowly crept open about an inch as the meeting continued. He heard the chief deputy say, "Now, we suspect that the feds will put an undercover inside the district."

Curly deduced that this revelation could only pertain to one thing. It had to be the murdered Amish man that he and Mark had responded to his last day in a cruiser. With his curiosity peaked, he put the tray down and hurried to the men's bathroom, which was beside the sheriff's office. He hurried into the end stall next to the wall and locked the door. He pressed his ear against the wall so he could hear the rest of the conversation.

Sheriff Holden said, "Now we don't know who this undercover is, so we have to be careful. He'll obviously be passing himself off as Amish and will burn us to his controller if he catches us snooping around out there. I think the direction that we should pursue right now is to sneak out there at night and talk to the teenagers who meet at Massey's pond. That's not on Amish land, so the feds can't say much. They're obviously somewhat rebellious or they wouldn't be sneaking out after dark to meet there. I want us to be tolerant of what they're doing. Let's overlook the minor liquor and pot violations that we'll see. We want them to like us, so we can't come across hard-nosed."

Chief Deputy Thurman said, "Let's also not wear our uniforms. Dress down in jeans. I don't want to come across as on-duty cops. Let's just talk to them and see if they can give us the names of any missing adult men. Once we have an I.D. on our victim, we'll approach the family and try to get them to trust us more than the feds. If I know the feds, they'll get heavy-handed and alienate everyone, especially if this

Waters character is involved. I hope he treats the Amish with as much disrespect as he's treated us. They'll lock up on him like a bank vault. If they like us more than the feds, maybe they'll talk to us."

Curly gasped in shock. He breathed heavily as he turned and sat on the commode. He chewed his fingernail as his mind raced. There's a covert murder investigation going on. This was the perfect opportunity to redeem himself, just like that guy named Dall had predicted last night. What a coincidence! How could he have been so insightful? How could he have known that an opportunity like this would come along? How could it have happened so soon? Curly didn't have the answers, but he knew one thing. That Dall guy had been right about him being a top-notch cop. If he could only find out who the undercover was inside the district, he might be able to help make the arrest and make the sheriff look good. What a hero he would be! But how was he going to find out who the undercover was?

He put his ear back against the wall and heard the sheriff say, "We'll work in two-man teams and meet here just after dark. We'll car-pool out there and park on the private property adjacent to Massey's. The feds will never see our cars there. Don't get separated out there. Whoever killed the Amish men is stronger than hell and entirely capable of disarming us. We'll stay out of sight until some of the kids arrive. We don't want to scare them, so I only want one team to approach them. The rest of us will stay out of sight. And above all! Under no circumstances do I want the feds to catch us out there. They'll be snooping around also, so watch for them. If they see us in jeans, they'll just assume we're farmers. If they try to approach you, don't engage them or talk to them. Move away from them so they can't get close. That would be consistent with how the Amish would respond to strangers. I don't want them to know who we are. Keep your guns covered and don't wear your badges in plain sight. Don't venture away from the pond without talking to me or the chief deputy. And for God's sake, don't move out in the open. The moon is full now and you'll show up plain as day if you cut across those open pastures. Stay close to the trees and use the terrain for cover."

Curly hurried out of the restroom as the meeting concluded so the sheriff and chief deputy wouldn't know that he'd been listening. His nerves were shot, so he hurried out of the office and raced across the street to the gas station. He bought a large candy bar and a full-powered energy drink.

He stuffed the last quarter of the candy bar into his mouth and chewed frantically, then gulped down the last half of the energy drink. With his blood-sugar now at the appropriate level, he inhaled deeply as he gripped the butt of his revolver and glared at the sheriff's office window through a determined squint. He breathed heavily as a plan came together. The sheriff and his pets would be at Massey's pond shortly after dark. Curly would be there shortly before dark. He nodded his head arrogantly as he thought, *those fancy college types don't get out of bed early enough to outsmart Mrs. Slapp's boy. Just wait till they all get in over their heads, and watch the look on their faces when Ole Curly here runs in and saves their bacon. Chief Deputy Thurman will be singing a different tune then.*

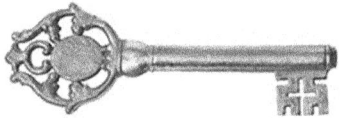

"I am he that liveth, and was dead; and behold, I am alive for evermore, Amen; and have the keys of hell and of death." **Revelation 1:18**

When noon rolled around, Dall and Sandy were standing at the foot of the bishop's front steps. He walked out on the porch with some other men in tow. Dall and Sandy sat their suitcases down and waited to be introduced.

The bishop took his time with the introductions, and Dall figured the men were the elders of the district, since the bishop had said earlier that he wanted their blessing before allowing Dall and Sandy to stay.

Bishop Gordan stepped off the porch and said, "Dall, I want you to meet Preacher Litchfield. He has the farm to the north of mine. As part of your re-entry into the Amish faith, I want you to live with different members of the district for a few months. I'll depend on them to report to me on your progress."

Dall said, "Sure, Bishop Gordan, but I thought that we were going to live with you."

Gordan shook his head, "No, Brother Roberts, you need to learn our ways and traditions. I depend on my preachers and elders to teach the men, so they'll be training you. If you're successful, you'll be baptized into our faith. If not, you'll be cast out. I hope you were serious about re-entering the Amish faith, Brother Roberts. Preacher Litchfield is a stern teacher and a strict disciplinarian. Pay attention to his wise counsel. He'll lead you in the ways that you should go."

Dall sized up Preacher Litchfield. He was a small, lean man with a look of arrogance and self-righteous contempt on his face. Litchfield walked around Dall and glared at him disapprovingly. When he got to Sandy, he made her uncomfortable with his conspicuous scrutiny of her anatomy.

Preacher Litchfield didn't bother Dall as much as the other man with him. When Bishop Gordan introduced the man as Preacher Litchfield's son, Devin, Dall became nervous at the prospect of Devin living with them. The hunched-over shoulders, sloping forehead, dramatic over-bite and distinct lack of comprehension in his eyes made it clear that Preacher Litchfield had not ventured far from the family tree when struck by the urge to procreate.

Devin lumbered awkwardly down the steps and faced off with Sandy. She unconsciously stepped closer to Dall as Devin smiled and revealed his misaligned and stained teeth. Devin stared hungrily at Sandy's breasts, then walked around and stared at her backside.

She sighed and said, "I'm not a side of beef. I don't think even Amish women appreciate being lusted over like this." She had directed her comment to Devin as she looked at him over her shoulder. She was completely unprepared when Preacher Litchfield stepped close to her and back-handed her hard across the face. She stumbled backward two steps and landed hard on her back. Dall closed his eyes and cringed. He breathed deeply as he tried to swallow his anger, and knew he could not come to her defense.

Both of them knew they would have to endure some beatings, so he had to restrain himself if he wanted to sell their roles. As much as he disliked Preacher Litchfield and Devin, he bent over and helped Sandy to her feet, then forced himself to say, "I'm sorry, Sandy, but you're going to have to take a more submissive role. I'm sure Devin didn't mean any harm."

Preacher Litchfield growled angrily, "Now that's the first lesson in your transition to the Amish faith! Our women don't speak disrespectfully to men. And they don't make false accusations or disrespectful remarks that diminish the standing of our men in the eyes of God. Devin is a good Amish man. Don't let me hear you make any more false accusations about his character."

Sandy shook the stars out of her head and swallowed her anger. She said, "I'm sorry, Preacher Litchfield. I just forgot myself."

Dall took her apology to the next level. "Thank you for disciplining her, Preacher Litchfield. We've both been out in the English world for so long that we've forgotten how God wants us to act. Please be patient with us; we were young when we were sent out to live with the English. We both need your discipleship."

Gordan and Litchfield both swelled with arrogance at Dall's patronage. Bishop Gordan patted Preacher Litchfield on the back and said, "Good job, Brother Litchfield, take them home with you for a month or so. Let me know how they respond to your shepherding."

As Dall and Sandy climbed into the back of Preacher Litchfield's buggy, Sandy's eye was already severely swollen. After Litchfield and Devin had climbed into the seat and started down Gordan's drive, Dall reached over and squeezed Sandy's hand, signaling that he was sorry he couldn't help her more. She did not squeeze back. She pulled her hand away and stared off into the distance and gritted her teeth. Tears ran down her face as she wished desperately that she had her pistol with her and that the mission was not so important.

Smith and Waters pulled their eyes back away from their binoculars. They'd both seen Sandy take the first blow. Waters said, "Well, I'll give her credit, boss, I didn't think she had it in her. I figured she'd bail at the first taste of blood."

Smith sighed. "That was nothing, Dexter. She has no idea how rough it's going to get. And there's no bailing, by anyone. I don't care if they murder her right in front of our eyes. This mission will not be scrubbed. Have you marked all of our observation points on the map?"

"Yes, Sir, all marked."

"Good, now let's follow that buggy to their new location. I want to scout out the observation points around that farmer's property and have our snipers set up by dark. We've got six two-man teams, each consisting of a sniper and a spotter. Work them in eight-hour shifts and make sure we have enough agents running food and water to them so they don't have to leave their posts. I want eyes on Parsons and Roberts twenty-four, seven."

Waters said, "Yes, Sir."

Smith then asked, "Dexter, have you drafted that letter to the director for me about the lab director refusing my request?"

"Yes, Sir. It's ready for your signature."

Smith's jaw muscles tensed as he said through gritted teeth. "Good, Dexter. Good."

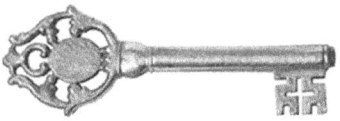

"I am he that liveth, and was dead; and behold, I am alive for evermore, Amen; and have the keys of hell and of death." **Revelation 1:18**

Assistant Bishop Clevenger directed his horse to the hitching post in front of Abel's house. Realizing how infirmed the bishop was, Abel hurried out of the house, jumped off the porch and trotted to Bishop Clevenger's buggy. The bishop extended his hand for help, but Abel put his arms under him and lifted the small man out of the buggy.

"Thank you, Brother Abel. You assistance is always appreciated."

Abel gestured toward the porch with his hand and said, "Your visits are always a welcomed distraction from life's hardships, Bishop. Come sit in the shade and have some lemonade."

Bishop Clevenger shook his head. "Your offer is tempting, Abel, but I came to talk to young Isaac as I'd promised. Is he around?"

Abel was grateful for Bishop Clevenger's help with Isaac. He'd been hoping the bishop would get involved in Isaac's problems rather than some of the other elders or Bishop Gordan. "Yes, Sir, Bishop, he's right out there in the barn. Thank you so much for talking to him."

As the bishop turned to leave, Abel asked, "Bishop, would you please not tell Isaac about my past sins? I'm having enough trouble regaining his respect."

Bishop Clevenger waved his hand in the air as he walked. "Confessions to me are sacred and secret, Brother Abel. It's between me, you and God, my good son."

Isaac was seated on a milking stool pondering his current state of affairs when Bishop Clevenger shuffled in. He stood reverently and offered the aging bishop a seat. Once seated, Bishop Clevenger engaged in small-talk for a few minutes, hoping to lower Isaac's guard. When the conversation became uncomfortable, Isaac said, "Bishop, I know my dad asked you to come here."

Bishop Clevenger was no stranger to hostility when counseling members of the district. Even at his advanced age and feeble condition, he never backed down from controversy and never feared the anger of any man. He nodded his head and said sternly, "He didn't ask me, young Isaac; I volunteered. Your father is so worried about you. He worries for you safety and your soul. I too am worried. Shame on you, you young sprout, for worrying an old man like this!"

Isaac lowered his head in shame. As angry as he was at the world, he didn't have the nerve to disrespect the old bishop. Bishop Clevenger said, "Pull up that old cane chair and sit by me, young Isaac. I want us to be on the same level."

Isaac obeyed the bishop and picked nervously at a lose strand of thread on his sleeve as the bishop talked. "Listen to me, Isaac. I've been watching you for some time. I know you're seeking the friendship of the other boys in the district, but some of them are bad to the core. They drink, smoke, molest their brothers and sisters, abuse animals, vandalize property, you name it, they're doing it. They're unreachable, but you're not. I won't have you becoming one of them. They're destined for Hell, and don't think you can change them. They'll wind up changing you long before you change them."

"I know, Bishop Clevenger. I've stopped hanging around with them. The only reason I slip out at night is to see Katie Betendorf."

Bishop Clevenger smiled and reminisced about his younger years when he was courting Mrs. Clevenger. "Ah yes, young Katie, what a wonderful little girl."

"I love her, but I know I'll never have her father's blessing if I can't get back into the good graces of Bishop Gordan and the elders."

"I can help you with that, Isaac, if you'll let me. You reconcile your anger with your father and stop doing things that hurt him, and I'll work on old Sampson Betendorf. He's a brute of a man, but I can handle him." The bishop stared at Isaac as that promise offered no comfort to him. He continued, "Speak up, Isaac, there's something else bothering you. What is it?"

Isaac stood and walked nervously to a stall, then leaned on his arms. Bishop Clevenger said, "Come on, Isaac, hearing confessions is one of my callings. Have you already sinned with young Katie?"

Isaac hung his head and shook it hard. "No, Sir! I have not violated Katie! Her purity is as important to me as it is to her! I'd never do anything that would cause her to lose respect for herself or me!"

The bishop struggled to his feet and shuffled over to Isaac. As Isaac lowered his head and cried, Bishop Clevenger encircled the boy's shoulders and hugged him. "Then what, Isaac? What is eating your young heart out?"

Isaac wrestled with his fear, then confessed, "I killed Preacher Croft, Bishop! I killed him!"

Bishop Clevenger straightened up in shock and took a step back. He glared suspiciously at Isaac for a few seconds as he tried to recall the details of Preacher Croft's death. "Tell me about it, my good son."

Isaac wiped his eyes and said, "I had slipped of my father's house to meet some of the other boys. Preacher Croft had apparently known that I was not living my life as Bishop Gordan had dictated. He followed me. When he caught me, he was going to lash me with a hammer. I got scared and pushed him. I was so scared that I'm afraid I didn't know my own strength. He fell and hit his head on a rock. I can't remember exactly what happened, but I ran. I must have killed him! I'm sure I did!"

Bishop Clevenger shuffled up beside Isaac and leaned over the stall beside him. "Isaac, you didn't kill Preacher Croft. I've already heard the confession of the man who killed him, and it wasn't you. You were wrong to raise your hand against a preacher, but under the circumstances I can understand why you did. I forgive you and God forgives you, so put it out of your mind. You are released from your guilt. From this moment forward, your guilt is not of God, but of Satan."

Isaac relaxed and sighed with relief. "Thank you, Bishop, but I can't forgive myself for hurting him. I should have helped him. What should I do now?"

"Well, we'll talk again about your inability to forgive. It doesn't surprise me that you have trouble forgiving yourself. That's frequently as hard as forgiving others, such as your father. I'm going to give you some scriptures to research, then we'll talk. But you have to know that the English are conducting an investigation into his death. You listen to me, young man! You keep this little confession between us! You talk to no one about it. Do you understand me? You may think that confessing to the English will reconcile you with God, but all Amish matters are to be handled within the district! You speak to no one but me about this!"

Isaac nodded his head. Bishop Clevenger turned to leave and grabbed Isaac's arm for stability. Isaac dutifully escorted him to the door of the barn. The bishop said, "I can make it from here, Isaac. You go back and finish whatever chores your father gave you to do."

As Bishop Clevenger shuffled out the door, Isaac asked, "Bishop, if you've already heard the confession of the man who killed Preacher Croft, can you tell me who he is?"

Bishop Clevenger stopped abruptly and straightened up as much as his arthritic joints would allow. He spun quickly and glared angrily at Isaac. "No more than I can tell others of your confessions, my son."

Isaac looked away from the piercing eyes of the angry bishop and returned to his chores. There was no need for disclosure from the bishop. If it wasn't him, he already knew who the killer was.

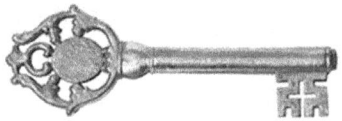

"I am he that liveth, and was dead; and behold, I am alive for evermore, Amen; and have the keys of hell and of death." **Revelation 1:18**

Preacher Litchfield pulled up in front of his house. Dall and Sandy climbed out of the back of the buggy. Dall started toward the front door, but Litchfield yelled angrily. "Where do you think you're going, Englisher?"

Dall looked confused. Litchfield said, "I won't allow any English in my house to defile the sanctity of my home. If you become Amish later, then you may be invited in. Until then, you'll sleep in the barn. I've prepared a stall for you."

Dall looked at Sandy and saw the anger in her eyes. He smiled graciously and said, "Thank you, Preacher Litchfield; any place to lay our heads is appreciated." Sandy stuck close to Dall as they followed Litchfield to the barn. Devin followed closely behind Sandy with his eyes on one thing.

Once in the barn, Litchfield pointed to a stall at the end of a row of stalls. Dall walked to it and found that the stall had been cleaned out. The manure had been shoveled and there was a new mound of hay at the back. There was a mattress on the hay mound and an old table beside the mattress.

Dall's heart sank when he saw the dismal accommodations. He forced a smile and said, "This will be great, Preacher Litchfield." He was secretly relieved. He didn't want to be in the house with the preacher and his lecherous son.

Preacher Litchfield nodded agreeably. "This will get you by till you can move on to someone else's farm. Sandy, you'll stay in the house with us."

Sandy's fear rose and she looked to Dall to bail her out. Dall said, "Preacher Litchfield, if you don't want an English man in your house, you certainly won't want Sandy there. She was much younger than I when we left our district in Pennsylvania. She remembers less about the Amish faith than I do. She'll only be a constant disruption to you and your family. Please let her stay out here with me. I've been mentoring her on the Amish ways, but she's not quite ready to live among you yet."

Preacher Litchfield looked at Devin and saw the disappointment in his eyes, but the English man was right. He reluctantly said, "Yes, I suppose you're right. I'll bring out another mattress for her. You get busy and clean out the stall next to yours."

Dall said, "Yes, Sir," and hurriedly grabbed a shovel and began cleaning out the stall. Thirty minutes later, Litchfield brought another mattress and threw it on top of the new mound of hay that Dall had put in Sandy's stall.

Still angered at being trapped by his own logic, Litchfield said sternly, "I'm agreeing to let her stay out here, Englisher, but make no mistake. I'll not permit unmarried people to cohabitate under my nose. It's bad enough that you're both sleeping under the same roof, but your sister has her stall and you have yours. Don't let me catch you two in the same bed. You English may do that sort of thing, but we Amish won't tolerate such animalistic perversion."

Dall said, "Oh no, Sir, she's my sister and we've never considered such sin. Dall looked at Devin and said, "I'd never consider fathering children with another family member." He thought as he was speaking, *'What a hypocrite! You should have practiced your own preaching.'*

Litchfield motioned to a door at the back of the barn. "There's a cistern behind the barn. One of your chores every night is to see that the stock tanks are full of water. You can use that cistern for water to wash at night. I'll bring you some wash pans, wash cloths, towels and soap. We do laundry on Saturday, but you'll have to wash your clothes separate from ours. I'll bring you a tub to wash them in."

Sandy had been too angry to speak. Dall was afraid the preacher would read the bitterness in her eyes, so he elbowed her as he said, "Thank you, Preacher Litchfield. We look forward to learning from you."

Sandy looked away so Litchfield would not see the hatred in her eyes and mumbled, "Thank you, Sir."

After Litchfield and Devin had left, Dall said, "Sandy, I know it's hard, but you have to act appreciative when you get beat. It's only for a while, but if you show contempt toward them, they'll beat you more. You can't appear rebellious or unrepentant."

Sandy walked to the door of the barn and leaned against the doorframe as she stared at Litchfield. She growled, "It's not in my nature to thank someone for knocking the crap out of me. Let's see how appreciative you are when you get your butt kicked."

"I won't be, Sandy, but that'll be the time when you'll have to be the voice of reason and calm me down. I don't like it anymore than you do, but we've both been forced into this predicament. We have to succeed. Failure is not an option."

Sandy lowered her head and turned. She nodded and said, "I know. I can do this. It's not just Litchfield that I hate, it's the bureau. I've always wanted to be an F.B.I. agent. I never dreamed they'd treat one of their own this way."

He didn't respond. Sandy walked up to him and said, "You've been magnificent so far. You think fast on your feet, much faster than me. I'm going to keep my mouth shut and rely on you."

She walked over and stared at her stall. "Boy, this is a downward departure from the comfort that I've been used to; living in the barn with horses."

Dall said, "Me, too. Listen, judging from the looks that you were getting from Devin, it's not a good idea for you to wash up outside alone. We'd better stick close together until we can move on to another farm. Things might be better there. When we wash up, let's keep watch for each other. We'll have to turn our backs to give each other privacy."

Sandy didn't argue. She'd only known Dall a week, but already trusted him more than any man that she had ever met, other than her father.

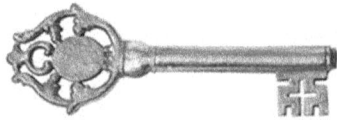

"I am he that liveth, and was dead; and behold, I am alive for evermore, Amen; and have the keys of hell and of death." **Revelation 1:18**

Dall and Sandy both slept hard once they had finished talking and finally settled down. Dall drifted in and out of half-sleep as the new surroundings, strange odors and the stress of the upcoming weeks robbed him of the deep sleep that he'd enjoyed before Agent Smith had turned his world upside down.

He found that periodically he was having to swipe insects from his face when the itch would awaken him. It was during a long period of sleeplessness that he trapped one of the insects with his hand and examined it to see what he was dealing with. It was then that he realized that it was not insects at all. It was small pieces of hay falling from the loft overhead.

The falling trash was not such a distraction when he realized what it was. The moonlight filtered through the cracks in the walls allowing Dall to stare up at the loft as he tried to calm his overactive imagination about the upcoming indoctrination by Preacher Litchfield. It was then that he discovered that the trash was not falling on its own. When he heard the faint creak of the loft floorboards, he realized that the trash was being dislodged by someone walking across the loft.

Dall took assessment of all the people on the Litchfield farm. Preacher, Mrs. Litchfield and Devin were supposedly asleep in the house. So unless Devin had slipped out after the preacher had gone to sleep, it had to be Sandy snooping around in the loft.

Dall quietly eased out of bed and crept to the end of his stall. As he peered around the partition, he saw Sandy on her mattress, sleeping soundly. He had serious doubts that Devin had the stealth to climb up to the loft without waking him, so it had to be one of the Smith's spotters. He started to go back to sleep, but he had to know for sure.

The ladder was a crudely built contraption made of scrap lumber and nailed to one of the support pillars that anchored the loft. Dall quietly ascended the ladder, hoping to see the intruder as he slowly raised his eyes above floor-level. To his surprise he saw nothing.

After a long minute of searching the darkness, Dall climbed the remaining rungs and stepped up on the loft. He proceeded slowly to the area of the loft directly over his stall, expecting at any moment to see a camouflaged F.B.I. agent appear out of the darkness. When he reached the area directly over his stall, he paused and looked around. No one was there.

He quickly looked behind him to make sure the intruder had not somehow gotten behind him. But the old boards and dry hay debris made enough noise that he would have heard any movement. As he looked back in front of him, a dark figure slowly materialize out of the rough-cut boards that made up the barn wall. The figure assumed a poorly-defined human form and moved quietly toward him. As it passed by, there was a gently wisp of cool air against Dall's face.

Dall resisted the urge to grab the figure. Had it had been more clearly defined he might have been more comfortable in confronting a person. But the figure never completely took shape. Dall knew he was dealing with something supernatural. Stark fear froze him in place, and he hoped the figure would not hurt him as it passed by.

It took several minutes for Dall to regain his composure so he could climb back down the ladder without his trembling legs collapsing under him. Once on the ground, he eased back in bed and tried to make sense of what he had just seen. Sleep would not come the rest of the night. He spent the remaining hours till dawn running the incident around in his mind in an endless circle of unanswered questions.

SIX

DALL STIRRED TO the early rays of sun shining through the cracks of the barn wall. He knew the Amish started work at dawn, so he hurried to get dressed. He said, "Sandy, time to get up! They'll be here any time now!"

After hours of reliving the incident in the loft, Dall had finally convinced himself that the entire incident had been a figment of his imagination. With the morning light gradually illuminating the interior of the barn, Dall glanced back at his mattress. There was still hay debris from the loft on his bed. He had not imagined anything. The dark form in the loft had been real. Suddenly the whole mission took on a more frightening dimension.

Sandy stirred and stretched. She looked up at the loft over her head and assessed her condition. She was surprised how rested she was. The mattress on the hay-mound was surprisingly comfortable. Dall's suspicions were confirmed when he looked in on her and saw hay debris in her hair and on her mattress.

When she sat up, the pressure in her head made her eye throb. By now it was severely swollen and had turned blue. She grabbed a brush from her suitcase and brushed her hair. As she combed the hay from her hair, she said, "Hmmm, I must have fallen out of bed last night. I've got hay in my hair. I hope this isn't going to be a nightly occurrence." Dall didn't answer, but hoped the same thing.

He went to the cistern and got a pan of water so they could brush their teeth. When he returned, Litchfield and Devin were walking across the yard. They didn't come to their stalls, but went directly to the fenced lot beside the barn.

Litchfield slowly walked up and grabbed the halter of one of the horses that he'd intended to harness to the hay-wagon. Devin tried to grab the other, but his clumsy, lumbering approach unnerved the horse and it cautiously moved away from him.

With fewer brain cells than the horse, Devin yelled angrily at the horse and ran toward it. That only prompted a circular chase around the lot. Rather than chastising Devin for his lack of good sense, Litchfield chose to blame the smarter of the two and became furious with the horse.

A short chase resulted in the horse being cornered and Litchfield was able to get one hand on the halter. He pulled the frightened horse to a tree and yelled for Devin to bring him a rope. Devin ran to the barn and got a length of rope that they used to tie the horses to the barn.

Litchfield tied the rope around the horses halter and drew it tight to the tree so it couldn't move its head. He then went to the barn and got a scrap piece of 2X4 and began beating the horse about the head, neck and shoulders.

Devin's love of brutality to animals became apparent as he ran to get another board. His laugh resembled the wheezy bray of a mule. He ran back to the horse and began taking round-house baseball swings at the horses head.

Sandy was terrified by the hysteria. The horse's screams and the impacts of the boards on his head and neck along with the profane yelling of Litchfield and the deranged laughter of Devin sent a chill up Dall's spine. Sandy dropped her brush and ran to help the horse, but Dall grabbed her arm. "No, Sandy! They'll use those boards on us!"

Sandy stopped and had to turn away as the horse began to lose consciousness. Unable to stand, it collapsed to the ground with its head still tied high to the tree.

When the horse could no longer scream or move Litchfield stopped beating it. Dall was convinced that Litchfield had intended to kill the horse, but had exhausted himself swinging the board.
Devin, however, never seemed to tire. He continued to beat the horse with the thrill of a young child beating a piñata.

After several more blows, Litchfield yelled for Devin to stop. Exhausted, he threw his board toward the barn, then untied the rope, allowing the horse's head to fall to the ground.

Sandy covered her mouth as she cried. She turned away so Litchfield would not see her face. Litchfield then walked over and leaned against the fence to catch his breath. Dall studied the two men in awe as they gasped for air. Stunned by the extreme brutality, he believed the same fate awaited him or Sandy. He now knew that one or both of them would not survive the assignment.

The horse slowly regained its senses. After several minutes, it struggled to its feet and stood on trembling legs. It had blood dripping from its mouth, nose and the top of its head.

Sandy and Dall hurried to be presentable, but they were disheveled when Litchfield walked in. He yelled between gasps for air, "Breakfast is served at daylight every morning. You can't enter my house, but Mrs. Litchfield will feed you on the front porch. Go on over there and eat. We'll harness the horses to the hay wagon, then pick you up there."

Dall and Sandy composed themselves and hurried to the porch so they would be ready when Litchfield pulled up with the wagon. Mrs. Litchfield stepped out on the porch with a tray of food and two glasses of cow's milk. She greeted the two and said, "Good morning, kids, it's so nice to meet you. The whole district is buzzing about the two Englishers who have come to learn from us."

Sandy was starved, but was still shaken by what she had seen at the barn. She sat on a cane chair and searched for the right thing to say. She wiped the tears from her eyes and said, "Thank you, Mrs. Litchfield. We hope we can earn God's grace once again."

Appearing completely oblivious to the mayhem that had occurred at the barn, Mrs. Litchfield said eagerly, "Oh, you will, dear. Preacher Litchfield is such a good teacher. I thank God every day for him. I see that he smote you."

Sandy looked at Dall and responded, "Yes, ma'am, I've never had the benefit of an Amish upbringing. I've got a lot to learn."

Mrs. Litchfield smiled and said cheerfully, "That's okay, dear, Preacher Litchfield has had to lash me many times, and I thank God for every stripe. It's only through the loving rebuke of our men that we can attain the righteousness necessary to enter the kingdom of Heaven. What a wonderful reward we have waiting for us there! Men like Preacher Litchfield are actually a blessing sent to us by God."

Dall studied Sandy hard, ready to interrupt her if she could no longer restrain herself. She took one of the sandwiches from the tray after Mrs. Litchfield went back inside. It was a dry biscuit with a fried egg and a strip of pork. She hungrily ate two of them, then choked down the glass of milk. She looked at Dall and said, "My God, Dall, this can't be milk. What animal did it come from? And was it alive?"

Dall chuckled as he guzzled his milk. He swallowed hard and said, "It's cow's milk, Sandy. This is what it tastes like before it's pasteurized and processed for retail sale. It's just not had all the butter fat removed."

Sandy turned her nose up and forced herself to finish the glass. She hacked and said, "I'll stick to store-bought milk, thank you."

"No you won't. We're going to be here for several months. This is what we're going to be fed. You've got to drink it and act like you like it. It'll actually grow on you after a while. We're here to become Amish, so suck it up."

Sandy leaned forward and looked through the door to see where Mrs. Litchfield was. "The preacher's wife seems nice. She's a little misguided in her loyalty."

Dall said, "Shhh. May be, but don't let her charm cause you to let your guard down. Don't confide anything in her. Her first loyalty is to the preacher. She'll tell him everything you say. She acts like she loves him, but deep inside she's terrified of him. She'll do anything to keep from being beaten."

As soon as the two had choked down their last sandwich, Preacher drove up with the team of horses and hay-wagon. "Climb on. We're haying today. I've got your forks on the wagon."

One horse waited nervously. Being in the close proximity of the beating had made it jumpy. The one that had been beaten trembled and swayed on unsteady legs, trying to maintain its equilibrium. The blood on its head and face sickened Dall and Sandy. As the preacher waited he scratched his head and puzzled over the strange storm clouds churning over the horizon.

Dall and Sandy hurriedly climbed on board and the preacher pulled away from the house. Waters had scouted out the best observation points around the preacher's farm and had gotten his snipers in place. From three hundred yards to the east, an Army sniper followed Sandy with a pair of binoculars. When the wagon had gotten out of range, the ranger radioed another team and turned the surveillance over to them.

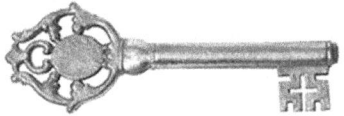

"I am he that liveth, and was dead; and behold, I am alive for evermore, Amen; and have the keys of hell and of death." **Revelation 1:18**

Bishop Gordan leaned over the stall of his mare and listened intently. Brother Dunlevy was the oldest elder in the district and the most trusted. He asked, "How do you want this handled, Bishop Gordan? The sheriff's office is pressing some of the members for Brother Croft's identity. It's been two months now and we can't keep it a secret much longer. We risk punitive action from an English judge if we continue to hinder the investigation."

Gordan sighed as he stood up straight. "I don't know, Brother Dunlevy. This English sheriff is pushy. There's some reason that he's not content to let us bury our dead and work out our own problems. I can't get a handle on it, but he's trying to prove something. I've talked to him. He acts like he's in a race with someone to solve Brother Croft's murder."

"Maybe we should help him, Bishop. We've never had a murder in this district before. Other members could be at risk. We still don't know what happened to Brother Dresselhaus."

Gordan turned angrily. "I know what happened to Willy Dresselhaus, and it weren't no murder! That trouble-making ●●● of a ●●●●● provoked the wrath of God with his blasphemous accusations and contentious shunning! God struck him down for causing dissention and condemnations among the flock! He was warned to stop spreading heresies within the faith, but he wouldn't listen! I tried to talk sense to him, but he thought he was smarter than me!"

Elder Dunlevy said, "I don't think so, Bishop. He was murdered. What really happened to him, Bishop? Lilly has a right to know. The other men in the district are curious, also."

Gordan glared at Brother Dunlevy, then shook his head nervously. He gritted his teeth angrily and said, "His body was found by the sheriff. I didn't see it, but I can't have him pressuring our faithful to disclose the sins of other members to an outsider. The English don't deal with that the way we do. We can handle our backsliders ourselves through our own discipline."

"Murder isn't just backsliding, Bishop. It's an evil that should be dealt with harshly for the good of our whole district. Whoever murdered Brother Dresselhaus should be excommunicated and turned over to the English. Failing to deal appropriately with that will leave that person among us and expose the rest of us to the same danger. You have to be harsh with the killer, Bishop. Whether you liked Brother Dresselhaus or not, our faith prohibits us from carrying out physical violence against anyone, English or Amish. Wilhelm and Lillian were outspoken, Bishop, but not against our Amish traditions, only about you and some of the preachers that you have ordained. They loved our faith and our traditions. Willy didn't deserve to be murdered because he didn't agree with you."

Gordan glared at Thomas. "Are you accusing me of orchestrating his murder, Brother Thomas?"

"No, Bishop, but I owe you the loyalty of telling you the truth. You've been known for your heavy-handed indictments of sinners, rebellious women and young people. We've lost several young people to the English because they couldn't accept the harsh discipline that you've proscribed. Our faith is much more traditional than the more progressive sects of Amish, and that alone is a source of contention with the young people. When you couple it with the strict policy of lashing that you prescribe, we're losing twice as many young people as are being baptized."

"Then let them go, Thomas! Our faith is better off without them! I'm ministering to this district as God instructs me! I can't help it if that's what He wants! If they don't like it, let them get down on their knees and take it up with God! He says in Matthew 7:14, *Straight is the gate and narrow is the way which leadeth unto light and few there be that find it.* There are just going to be those who'll never make it through the gates of Heaven! Those rebellious young folks and the English are among them!"

"I'm aware of that passage, Bishop, but let those who fail to enter Heaven's gate do so out of their rejection of God, not by our lack of love and compassion. It's God's place to condemn them on judgment day, not ours."

Gordan glared at Brother Dunlevy for a few seconds. He then said, "I was installed as shepherd of this flock, Brother Dunlevy. The truth is sharp as any two edged sword. I won't faint from my responsibility to swing that sword vigorously. Let those who are weak flee to the English where they can pursue their own desires. *As for me and my house, we will serve the Lord*, Joshua 24:15."

Thomas realized that debate with Bishop Gordan was pointless. He asked, "But what about this current problem? The sheriff is pressing everyone hard to find out what happened to Brother Croft. We have to cooperate, or the English will be in here whether we want them or not."

Gordan shook his head adamantly. "No, Thomas, I've given strict orders that no one is to talk to the English! We'll deal with it ourselves! No outsiders are allowed in here to corrupt the sanctity of our district."

"Then why did you allow the English man and his sister to come here, Bishop? We all admire you for protecting us, but we see a problem with them. It seems awful coincidental that they showed up at the same time that the sheriff is asking questions."

"I know, Thomas. I've thought of that. I let them in for two reasons. Our membership is declining. I want to explore the possibility of accepting English who want to abandon their sinful ways and become Amish. We need new blood in our district. Also, if they were planted here by the sheriff, they'll be close so we can watch them and control the information that goes out."

Thomas shook his head nervously. "That's a dangerous assumption, Bishop. We can't control what people say when they think no one will hear them. Just ordering them to remain quiet in worship service won't insure that they won't talk confidentially to the Englisher. If he is an undercover sheriff's deputy, he could gather enough information to arrest one or more of our brethren, and we'd never know it until the arrests were made. That would tear our district apart. It would certainly destroy you. The people of this district expect you to protect us from such shame."

"I know that, Thomas. We'll just have to watch them closely. Besides, if they are deceivers, Brother Litchfield will lash the deception out of them with the divine intervention of the Holy Spirit."

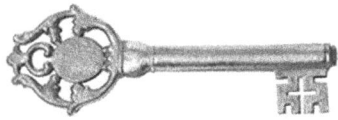

"I am he that liveth, and was dead; and behold, I am alive for evermore, Amen; and have the keys of hell and of death." **Revelation 1:18**

Agent Smith was ushered into the office of General Morris Scott where he was graciously received by the general. Smith feigned a sincere smile and reached for the general's hand. "General, so very good of you to see me."

General Scott shook Smith's hand vigorously and said, "Ahh, Richard, nonsense. It's always good to see a great American."

Smith took the chair directly across from the one that the general sat in. The general said, "So, Richard, how have you done with our pet project so far?"

Smith nodded confidently. "Good, Sir. The bishop allowed our undercovers to stay. We're surveilling them constantly."

General Scott stared despondently out the window. "And how has Roberts adjusted? The boy worries me. Will he perform?"

"He has so far, General. We're meeting him every night, and Waters is scrutinizing him and Parsons closely. If we get any indication that either of them are going to dump on us, we'll rein them in."

"And my old friend, Dr. Sveade?"

"Good, General. He's as passionate about this mission as you are."

"Good, I can't tell you how long I've wanted to find this fallen one. He's kept me awake at night ever since we talked to him the first time. This would be the greatest accomplishment in the history of man if we could actually establish an alliance with beings from the spiritual world. Think of all we could accomplish. No country could stand against us. With the power of just one supernatural being behind us, the Antichrist and all his armies couldn't defeat us."

"I know, General. And we don't have much time. Our prophesy experts warn us that the last days of the End-Times are upon us. This may well be our last chance. We're sure he's in this district. We've just got to get our undercovers to contact him. They'll pull it off, Sir. We'll see that they do."

"Good, Richard, good! I know you will. I can't tell you how worried I and the joint chiefs are. We're so close to the end of this age. All requisite prophesies have been fulfilled. I know the demons hate us mortals, but this one may be our best hope for a solution. Keep in mind, Richard, this spirit may require a sacrifice to show our resolve to support him. Let's give him what he wants."

Smith nodded his head as he stared at the floor. The general asked, "What, Richard? Spit it out."

"Smith shrugged his shoulders and said, "Well, General, there are so many obstacles. You know these fallen spirits can't be trusted. Parsons will be no obstacle, but Robert is a believer. This demon may not be able to take him out as easily as we think. According to Sveade, believers are protected by the Holy Spirit. A demon can't touch a believer without permission directly from God."

"No, but we can. If he wants Roberts dead, carry it out. You've got the men and equipment to pull it off."

Smith agreed. "True, I do. No problem, General. Just a tickle of the trigger will put Roberts on the altar, if that's what he wants."

General Scott smiled and said, "And when it's over and we have this demon here in Washington, clean up all the loose ends. No one left to tell the story, understood?"

"Yes, General, no one. We've intentionally kept the team small so we can dispose of them."

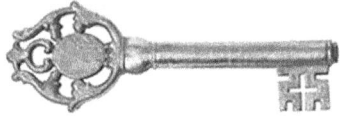

"I am he that liveth, and was dead; and behold, I am alive for evermore, Amen; and have the keys of hell and of death." **Revelation 1:18**

The sun rose high in the sky and the temperature soared to 97°. Neither Sandy nor Dall had handled a hay fork before and their hands blistered. Sandy was less diligent than Dall and missed a lot of hay on her side of the wagon. After yelling at her twice, Preacher Litchfield removed a leather strap from under the seat of the wagon and lashed her back five times.

It pained Dall to see her whipped, but he couldn't interfere. He had to stay in role and try to help her without angering Litchfield. When the lashing was over, Sandy looked at Dall. He gently motioned toward Litchfield with his head and mouthed the words, "Thank him."

As Litchfield climbed back aboard the wagon, Sandy swallowed her anger and said, "Thank you, Preacher Litchfield." For the rest of the morning, Dall ran from side to side trying to help Sandy keep up.

Waters and Dr. Sveade watched the lashing through their binoculars. Waters secretly relished Sandy's beating and said, "I'll give those Amish credit for one thing, Doctor. They don't take any lip off their women. We could take a lesson from them."

Dr. Sveade shook his head and said in a worried tone, "Don't gloat, Dexter. If she fails, someone will have to go in and take her place." He looked sternly at Waters.

Waters got the message and grumbled, "Well, she's strong. I think she can hold up."

"I thought you'd feel that way, Dexter. Let's be a little more supportive. Pitching hay with a fork in this heat is no way to earn a living. She's not used to this kind of work, and if she takes a beating like that horse took this morning, it'll kill her for sure. Contact our men at the house. They ate their breakfast on the porch, so apparently the preacher isn't going to let them in his house. Tell them to keep an eye on Sandy. I don't want her walking out. And we can't have her so injured that she can't complete the mission. If that sawed-off preacher gets too carried away, give the snipers a green light."

Waters nodded and asked, "And what do you want them to do if the preacher is beating her to death in front of Amish witnesses? Let him kill her or intervene?"

Dr Sveade studied the possibilities. "Well, Smith is still in Washington, so he might have a different perspective on that scenario, but since I'm the one calling the shots, I say have the snipers dump the preacher and the witnesses. Hopefully there won't be many, maybe only his son. We'll have to go in and clean up the scene, but that's better than losing an undercover. We can't lose Sandy or Dall just yet. Smith may think differently after we've made contact, but for now, we need them."

"Okay, Doc. We'll dump the Amish. And by the way, the cover teams asked if we've seen the weird clouds off in the distance. I told them that they have rain gear, so just hunker down and weather the storm. That okay with you?"

Dr. Sveade had seen them too. He stared at the horizon and canted his head slightly as he recalled the last time he'd seen clouds like that. He hadn't wanted to alarm Smith or Waters, so he'd kept it to himself. He nodded his head slowly and walked away without answering Waters.

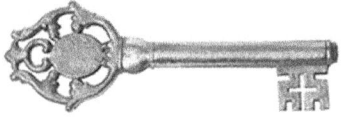

"I am he that liveth, and was dead; and behold, I am alive for evermore, Amen; and have the keys of hell and of death." **Revelation 1:18**

The afternoon passed slowly. The humidity was high, and Litchfield showed little mercy on Dall and Sandy as he kept a fast pace. Devin rode on the wagon and stared lustfully at Sandy all afternoon.

Two wagon loads of hay were all they could load and unload in one afternoon. When the last load was in the barn, Litchfield unhitched the horses and put them in their stalls, then said, "Dinner will be at six every evening. After you eat, you feed and water the stock and split firewood for Mrs. Litchfield for the next day. I want you in bed by dark, so you'll have to wash and mend your clothes before you go to bed. I don't like to be awakened, so if you need something, get it before dark."

Dall and Sandy were totally exhausted as they dragged themselves into the barn. Both were soaked with sweat and had hay and dirt caked in their hair and on their skin. Sandy struggled out of her drenched ankle-length dress and cared little if Dall saw her underwear. She unrolled her hair and let if fall down her back as she said, "This is insane. I can't do this for six months."

Dall took off his wet shirt and said, "We won't have to, Sandy. Hay season only lasts a few weeks. The other farmers are putting up their hay, too, so it'll probably be over by the time we move on."

Sandy shook her hair and said, "We can't eat like this. Litchfield expects to clean up first. We've got to have a system. How am I going to clean up each night without Devin spying on me?"

Dall escorted her out the rear barn door and stood by the cistern. He said, "We don't dare let Litchfield catch us bathing in the stock tank. There's a rope and bucket. Let's just pour one bucket of water over ourselves and soap up. Then pour a couple more over ourselves to rinse off. You go first. I'll stand watch for Devin."

He walked to the corner of the barn and watched the house to make sure Devin or Litchfield didn't sneak out to spy on them. Caring little if Dall saw her, Sandy undressed and poured a bucket of cold water over her head. She then soaped up a washcloth and scrubbed herself vigorously. She shampooed her hair, then rinsed off. She dried with a towel and went back inside the barn to dress. Fortunately, there were two cedars close to the cistern that she could stand behind so she didn't put on a show for the sniper team. Dall stripped and washed the same way.

Sandy's skin was tanned and had a natural glow. She stood with her back to Dall and had not yet pulled her dress over her shoulders. As he walked into the barn drying himself, he couldn't help but notice the red whelps on her back. He said, "Litchfield lashed you good, Sandy; sorry I couldn't help you."

Sandy buttoned her dress and said, "That's okay. When we break out of this assignment, I'm going to look that scumbag up. I'll tazer his butt until he does the chicken. When he can't get up, I'll be the one giving the lashes then. When I'm done with the strap, I'm going to use that same board that he used on that poor horse. We'll see if he takes a beating as well as he gives one."

As she brushed her hair, Dall dressed and said, "You'll have to endure his lashings till then, Sandy. I hope I'm wrong, but if Litchfield thinks his lashings aren't having the desired effect, he'll increase the severity of them or start using boards on us like he did the horse this morning. Whatever you do, don't give him cause to do that."

Dall tucked in his shirt-tail and walked slowly over to the stalls where the horses were. They were naturally skittish and moved away in fear.

Sandy eased up beside Dall as they leaned over the edge and stared at the bloodied guiding. He held his head low with a broken spirit and stared at the ground. Dall grieved for him and said, "Sorry you had to take that beating, boy. I'd sure like to help you."

Sandy continued to brush her hair. She said, "I heard Litchfield call him Tramp. The other one there is Lady. I guess we don't have to wonder which Disney movie Devin likes most. It's probably the only one he's seen."

Dall reached over the stall to pet Tramp, but he turned away. Dall went to his wash pan and soaked a towel. He climbed into the stall and cautiously stepped up to Tramp, then pressed the wet towel against Tramp's wounds. He gently stroked the areas of Tramp's neck that were not swollen and bloody as he talked calmly.

Tramp seemed to know that Dall was a friend. He turned his head toward Dall and allowed Dall to pet his nose. Seeing the attention that Tramp was getting, Lady hung his head over the stall and allowed Dall to pet him. All three quickly became friends.

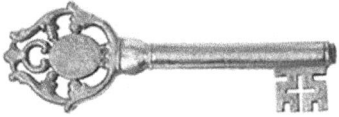

"I am he that liveth, and was dead; and behold, I am alive for evermore, Amen; and have the keys of hell and of death." **Revelation 1:18**

Supper was strips of tough brisket, salted and fried in lard, boiled potatoes and homemade bread. Sandy and Dall sat on the cane chairs on the front porch and washed their meal down with milk. The doors and windows were open, so they kept their conversation low so not to be overheard. Sandy whispered, "What kind of meat is this, dog?"

Dall looked through the window to see if the Litchfields were paying them any attention and said, "Shhh. Brisket. It's a tough cut of beef that's better smoked over low, moist heat and sliced thin."

Sandy grimaced as she muttered, "Eat fast, I don't want to miss our meeting with Smith and Waters."

Dall looked around and said, "That well that we're to meet them at is clear on the south side of Gordan's farm. That's over a mile away. Do they expect us to walk there and back ever night?"

"I guess so. If they don't attempt to contact us before dark, we'll have to hike it."

After chopping Mrs. Litchfield's firewood for the next day, Dall and Sandy watered the stock, then retreated to the barn and waited till dark. The two-hour down time gave them a chance to get better acquainted. Sandy sat on Dall's mattress while he rubbed down Lady and Tramp. She used his pocket knife to clean the dirt from under her fingernails as she talked. "Why did you join the Army, Dall?"

He shrugged his shoulders and said, "Oh, I wanted to travel and do things that I'd never get to do in my home town. I didn't have any college, and the Army seemed like a good gig. I liked it while I was there, but I felt a stronger calling to the ministry."

"Will you stay in it after this is over?"

"I doubt it. Somehow I get the feeling that whatever happens here, Waters and Smith will see to it that I'm so tarnished that no church will call me again. I've got family up in Oregon. I'll probably go up there and work in their lumber business. I like the outdoors, so it'll probably suit me."

Sandy put his knife down and walked to the stall. She chewed her lip nervously and sighed. Dall said, "Go ahead and ask. It's going to come up sooner or later."

She looked at him and cocked her head in a curious stare. "I don't believe you really molested that girl. You were really trying to help her get out of an abusive home. Smith somehow convinced the U.S. Attorney to file on you. I've never heard of the bureau getting involved in parental custody interference cases before. The state prosecutors usually just attach an extradition order to the warrant and let the local authorities track down the offenders. What attracted him to you?"

Dall laid the curry brush down and stared out across the countryside. He shook his head slowly. "I don't know. I've never been able to figure out how he found me. The pastor wasn't going to fire me once I explained the circumstances. The county prosecutor was content to let the matter drop once the girl admitted that she'd falsified the charges to keep her dad from being angry with her. Then Smith showed up. It was almost mystical how he found me. He approached me at my house and tried to recruit me for this job. I refused, and the next thing I knew I was in handcuffs on my way to the federal courthouse. When he laid the warrant on the desk in front of me, I guess I panicked. He said the matter would never go to trial if I cooperated."

"He said that, Dall, because chances are that the U.S. Attorney only gave him the warrant as leverage over you. He never planned to take you to trial. Even if he did, cases like yours never go to a jury. If they make it to court at all, they're usually pled out. There are too many more serious cases to hear."

"I don't like having my arm twisted, Sandy. I used poor judgment in taking that girl to her mother, but I never would have signed the confidential informant agreement if I'd known what this assignment involved. I'm not getting myself killed. We're after a murderer who has killed with his bare hands. Before I let him get his hands on me, I'm bailing. I know you're my controller, but don't think that badge will help you. Don't get in my way if I decide to leave. You're not armed and you're not big enough to stop me."

Sandy stared at Dall and contemplated her potential to stop him. Her training in handling C.I.s had told her to take a tough stand with him and let him know who the boss is, but her last two bouts with Litchfield had convinced her that she needed him desperately. Smith had also made it clear that Dall was the hinge-pin of the whole mission, so Dall was the one in charge, not her.

Dall walked to the Litchfield orchard and gathered some apples. He climbed back in the stalls and cut the apples into quarters. Tramp and Lady loved them. They actually pushed Dall backward with their noses as he hurriedly cut the apples and held them in his opened hand.

Sandy, said, "I didn't know you liked horses so much."

Dall planted his heels and gently pushed Tramp backward with the apples were gone. As he continued to stroke Tramp, he said, "I've always loved horses. They've got such complex personalities once you know what to look for. These two are miracles. I've never seen horses that have been abused like these two be so approachable and friendly. Usually abused horses are so wild that no one can get near them."

Sandy didn't answer. She stared in amazement at the rapport that Dall had established with them. There was something mystical about his ability to communicate with them.

"I am he that liveth, and was dead; and behold, I am alive for evermore, Amen; and have the keys of hell and of death." **Revelation 1:18**

Night was falling quickly and Sandy said, "Come on, Dall. I guess Smith isn't going to meet us here. Let's start walking." Dall had been napping, and got off his mattress to put on his boots. As he sat up, sprigs of hay fell from his head, chest and shoulders. He studied them in shock for a few seconds, then slowly looked up at the loft over his stall. He laced his boots, stood and brushed the hay from his hair and shoulders, then looked into Sandy's stall. She was brushing hay from her hair and shoulders also, and there was hay on her mattress. She was oblivious to the presence in the loft and hadn't taken the time to wonder why the hay was falling. Not wanting to alarm her, Dall chose to remain quiet for now.

They cautiously peered around the back corner of the barn and saw no lights in the preacher's house. They started the long trek across two farms to the grove of trees surrounding the old well.

Smith and Waters were waiting there with Dr. Sveade. As Dall and Sandy walked into the clearing, Smith said, "Glad you survived your first lashing, Sandy. We hadn't planned on Gordan farming you out to Litchfield. We would have come to you, but that was too far for Dr. Sveade to walk."

Sandy said, "That's okay, Sir, the walk didn't take as long as I'd expected."

"Good, here are some work gloves. We were watching you while you worked. If Litchfield asks where you got them, tell him that you had them in your suitcases and forgot to wear them today. How's your eye? It looks painful."

"I'll be fine, Sir, but I've got a real concern."

Smith looked suspiciously at her. She said, "We're going to be stuck here on this farm for at least a month. We're confined to the barn at night, so we can't socialize with any of the other Amish in the area. We're not going to get the chance to talk to anyone. How are we going to get Litchfield to let us talk to the other Amish?"

Smith nodded in frustration. "I've been thinking about that. We can't have you stuck in one place for a whole month. And we can't have Litchfield giving an unfavorable report on you to the bishop for talking to the other Amish against his wishes. We've got to find some way for him to recommend that you move to another farm. There are several farms in this district and you can't spend a month at each one. We've got to locate an Amish family that'll be less restrictive with your movements."

Sandy said, "Once the hay season is over, there'll be more time for us to socialize, I think."

Smith shook his head. "Don't bet on it, Sandy. I grew up on a farm, and you'd be surprised at all the odd jobs that need to be done when the haying is over."

Dall remained conspicuously quiet. Waters asked, "What's the matter, tough guy. Sandy is the only one who's taken a beating so far. Are you content to let her take all the punishment so you won't mess up your pretty face? Afraid no more under-aged girls will find you attractive if you get hurt?"

Sandy lunged at Waters, but Smith grabbed her arm. He calmly said, "Dexter, your comments are uncalled for. Dall is doing a fine job."

Sandy glared at Waters and said, "He's already done more work today than you've done in your whole life, Waters! If it weren't for him,

I'd have been cast out of the district first thing this morning! He'll take his lumps when the time comes, but if you're feeling like a tough guy yourself, come on in and work the hay with us tomorrow!"

Waters chuckled as Sandy vented. He wasn't worried about her, although he had never seen her display this much anger before. Smith said, "Okay, kids, let's get this meeting over so these two can get some sleep. Any questions for Dr. Sveade?"

Dall said, "I do. Doctor, the Dordrecht Confession of Faith specifically prohibits the kind of violence that we're receiving from Litchfield. You should have seen the beating he gave one of his horses this morning."

"I heard about it, Dall."

"If he works one of us over like that, we won't survive it. My question is how can we use that to restrain Litchfield? As an outsider, am I supposed to know about that?"

"I think so. They'll expect you to be prepared. Let me give you a little background on the history of the Bible that the Amish use in this district. You see, the Amish believe the teachings of the oldest and most conservative of the Bibles. The first English translation of the old Hebrew, Greek and Aramaic scrolls was the Moral Equivalent Tyndale Bible. The first completed English Bible was a revision of the Tyndale Bible called the Geneva Bible. That was in 1560, so that tells you how old the Amish faith is. The King James Bible was a later extension of the Geneva Bible. The Amish read from either the King James or the Geneva Bible."

Dr. Sveade thought for a few seconds, then continued, "Your role is one of an English man who is trying to regain entry into the Amish faith. It wouldn't be uncommon for you to prepare for your life with the Amish before approaching the bishop by reading both the Geneva Bible and the Dordrecht Confession of Faith. As a preparatory measure, you would have learned all you could about the Amish faith. Throw it up in his face if you have to, but be careful that you don't swing it like a sword. Don't use it to condemn him or he'll consider that a challenge to his authority. Put it in the form of a question and let him educate you about it. Hopefully his own explanation will curb his anger a little."

Dall turned to Smith and said, "I know what you said about bailing out, but we have to have a visual sign that we can give to signal you to come in and save us. It's apparent that you've got spotters watching us twenty-four, seven, so you'll know when we're in real trouble."

Waters growled, "No bail-out signal, Roberts! We told you that before!"

Dall stepped up to Waters angrily and said, "If that crazy preacher works one of us over with a board or other weapon like he did that horse, we're through. If we live through it, we'll either be crippled or in a coma. Who's going to carry on with the undercover assignment then, you?"

Smith sighed and stared at the ground as he thought. He said calmly, "He's right, Dexter. If he gets killed, the whole mission is a scrub. We've invested too much in Dall to let him get killed."

A look of betrayal swept across Sandy's face. By leaving her out of his last statement, Smith had implied that it would be okay if she got killed, but Dall was too valuable to lose."

Smith said, "Okay, see if this'll float. If you see that you're going to take a beating that you won't survive, just run away from it. We'll have you under surveillance and will pick you up once you get to our spotters."

Dr. Sveade said, "That's about the best you can do, Dall. You'll then have to make another approach to the bishop and explain that you ran because you were afraid. Plead for mercy and ask him to give you another chance with another family. Whatever you do, though, don't put your hands on one of them. They'll understand that you ran because you were afraid, but they'll never forgive you for assaulting one of them. However you see it, they see their lashings as God's wrath being poured out upon you, and they're merely the vessel through which He's delivering it. You'll not be justified in defending yourself against the righteous judgment of God."

After another half-hour, Dall said, "We'd better get back, Sandy. We don't want to get caught away from the barn."

As Dall walked past Waters, Waters said, "We're all going to have to take our lumps, Roberts. Try to step up and take your share tomorrow. Letting a woman take your whipping is pretty low."

Without the slightest warning, Dall shot his right fist out and punched Waters hard on the chin. He stumbled backward and fell over his camp chair. Dall said, "That's right, Waters, there's yours."

Waters shook his head and struggled to his feet in anger. Dall and Sandy walked out of the trees toward the barn as Smith said, "Let it go, Dexter. I've told you to back off him. You had that coming."

As they walked across the fields in the moonlight, Sandy laughed. She said, "Man, I'm glad you did that. Waters has deserved that as long as I've known him, but I thought you Christians weren't supposed to hit people. I thought you were supposed to turn the other cheek, love thy neighbor and all that other non-violent stuff. You are a Christian, aren't you, Dall?"

Dall sighed and said, "Yeah, I'm a Christian, just not a very strong one."

As they walked along the fence line that bordered Ceril Massey's property, Dall stopped suddenly and jumped behind a small cedar. He grabbed Sandy and jerked her behind the bush with him. She asked, "What's wrong, Dall?"

He pointed across the field and said, "There. Looks like a young boy walking toward that wooded area."

Both watched as the teenager climbed through the barbed wire fence. Sandy said, "Look there, Dall, there's a man following him. Should we try to talk to them?"

"I don't think so, Sandy. If they tell Litchfield that we were out here, we're in big trouble. We don't know who we can trust yet. I think from now on it's a good idea for us to travel under the cover of this tree line. Apparently we're not the only ones walking these hills at night."

After the man had passed, Sandy stepped out from behind the Cedar. Dall grabbed her again and pointed across the field to another tree line. He said, "Look over there."

Sandy stared in shock, then said, "My God, Dall, it's a little girl in a white nightgown. She can't be more than seven. What's she doing out here? I wonder if she needs help."

Dall studied the girl closely. "I don't think so, Sandy, she's seen us. She's been watching us all along. She may have seen us when we walked this way earlier to meet Smith and Waters. She doesn't need help or she'd come to us."

Sandy studied her hard and said, "I wonder who she is."

Dall said, "I don't know, but she doesn't belong here. She's too young to be away from her house alone, especially after dark. Let's just get back to the barn."

As they walked, they periodically looked over their shoulders. Sandy said, "She's following us, Dall. She's not even trying to conceal herself. She's got me spooked. It doesn't look like she's even walking. It looks like she's gliding over the ground."

"Come on, Sandy, pick up the pace. Let's not let her catch up to us. She may be too young to be out here, but she's not too young to tell her parents that she saw us."

Dall and Sandy jogged the rest of the way. They panted heavily as they made it to the barn and looked back toward the girl. She continued to approach without any concern for her own safety. Dall yelled, "Who are you, sweetheart? Are you lost?"

The girl didn't answer, but continued to glide over the ground as she came closer and closer. When she was twenty yards from the barn, Dall closed and latched the door. Spooked by her unnatural gait, he stepped back beside Sandy and stared nervously at the door.

Through the cracks in the barn wall, they could see the white outline of the girl's gown glide up to the door. Sandy and Dall both about jumped out of their skins when the silence of the night was suddenly shattered.

Without warning, the whole barn vibrated violently with thunderous booms as the child pounded in the side of the barn with her fists. Sandy screamed and lunged toward Dall. They held each other tightly as Tramp and Lady spooked and tried to jump out of their stalls. The ground trembled under their feet as three crashing blows shook the barn and cracked the boards beside the door. Dall was sure that if the girl had struck the door, it would have splintered in front of them.

Unconsciously, Dall and Sandy had retreated to the front of the barn. The echo effect inside the barn was deafening as the girl pounded on the barn three more times. Sandy cried hysterically and Dall was so weak from fear that he could no longer stand. He dropped to his knees with Sandy beside him as they watched in horror. Again the girl pounded her fists on the barn three more times as dust and old birds' nests fell from the rafters.

As she stepped back and assessed the damage that she had caused to the barn, the child moved out of the shadow of the barn and into the moonlight. Through the cracks in the barn Dall and Sandy saw her spread her arms and tilt her head back as she drew in a deep breath. Finally, she moved slowly away from the barn and back across the pasture.

Sandy clung to Dall and continued to scream. Dall held her tight and panted, "She's gone, Sandy!"

Between gasps for air Sandy cried, "What the hell was that? It looked like a little girl, but she almost knocked the barn down! What in God's name was that?"

Dall finally slowed his breathing and regained his strength. He stood on trembling legs and helped Sandy to her feet, then walked to the wall with Sandy clinging to his arm, and looked at the broken boards. "I don't know, but God had nothing to do with it. Smith and Waters will be pleased, though."

She looked at him as if he were crazy. "Pleased! Why?"

"We've only been here two days and we already know how our victims were murdered and what killed them."

Dall left Sandy's side and hurried to Tramp and Lady. He stepped into the stall and gently grabbed Lady's halter. He stroked Lady till he began to settle down. Dall then reached over the partition and stroked Tramp's neck. Both horses remained nervous and pressed their noses close to Dall for reassurance.

Sandy approached the stall, trying to rub the goose-bumps out of her arms. "This is insane, Dall! We didn't bargain for this! This is more that we're capable of dealing with!" Dall didn't answer. He just stared at the broken planks as he stroked the frightened horses.

Sandy said, "That kid could have come right through that wall, but she backed away. Why didn't she break through and come in?"

Dall thought about the possibilities for a few seconds. He sighed as he looked at the broken boards and said, "She could have. She was either just trying to scare us or something stopped her. I guess we can ask her next time we meet her."

Smith, Sveade and Waters all lowered their binoculars as the little girl moved away from the barn. Waters asked, "A little girl? That's our killer, a little girl?"

Sveade cautioned him. "Don't form any preconceived notions, Dexter. A demon can take any form, human or animal. Don't let her size fool you. She may be small, but a demon can tear a person apart with their bare hands. She's dangerous beyond anything you can imagine."

After a long silence, Smith said, "Dexter, cancel that letter to the director about the lab not wanting to perform the tests on a cadaver for us. We don't need the test. There's no doubt now. We're in the right place.

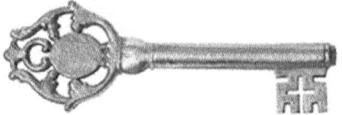

"I am he that liveth, and was dead; and behold, I am alive for evermore, Amen; and have the keys of hell and of death." **Revelation 1:18**

As Able approached the grove of trees that surrounded Massey's pond, he stopped suddenly when he heard what he thought was thunder coming from Preacher Litchfield's farm. He turned and stared hard in that direction as the thunderous booms continued. Since the booms were short and rhythmic, Abel rubbed his beard and looked at the sky. He wondered if this was from those storm clouds that had been lingering over the horizon. The stars were bright and there wasn't a cloud in sight overhead, so a thunderstorm was not the cause. He took off his flat-brimmed hat and scratched his head as he continued to follow Isaac.

Once in the grove of trees, he leaned against a tree and watched. Katie had not shown, but some of the other boys from the area had. With nothing else to do, the boys stripped off their clothes and went for a swim. Abel waited patiently, content to let the boys have their fun as long as no alcohol or cigarettes appeared.

Since Katie hadn't shown, Isaac became bored after a half-hour, and dressed to leave. After the normal barrage of good-natured insults and challenges to his manhood, Isaac headed home. Abel followed at a distance and stayed out of the moonlight as much as possible.

Abel stayed close to the trees that paralleled a fence-line and again looked toward Litchfield's farm. The loud booms that he'd heard earlier still puzzled him. There was an unnatural ring to them. Across the fields he saw the figure of a small girl in a white nightgown walking toward him.

He knew all the kids in the district, but he couldn't yet tell who she was. He thought he should wait and see if she needed help, but he didn't want to lose sight of Isaac. He continued to look over his shoulder at the girl as he arrived home.

Assured that Isaac was safely in the house Abel went back out to look for the little girl, but she was gone. He went to his room and undressed. He slid quietly into bed so he wouldn't wake Dory, but she was not asleep. She asked, "Was that thunder I heard?"

Abel looked out the window and shook his head. "Didn't sound like thunder. There's been a storm circling the district for some time now, but it's not passing. I asked Bishop Clevenger about it, but he didn't say anything. He just looked worried."

Dory dismissed Abel's concern. "So it hasn't passed. Storms skirt around us all the time. We'll get our share of rain if that's what's worrying Bishop Clevenger."

Abel sighed, "I don't know. We've had droughts before. The bishop wouldn't worry about rain, especially with all the rain we've had this spring. He's been acting strange lately. Maybe it's just his age. Or maybe he's getting tired of dealing with all his aches and pains. Oh well, it's not my place to question God's will. It'll rain where He wants it to rain. It's late. Aren't you tired?"

As Dory turned and moved next to him, he discovered that she had shed her nightgown before he'd arrived home. She whispered, "You wish. Time to break one of the bishop's cardinal rules, Mister Straus."

He sighed as he turned toward her and kissed her. He acted disgusted, but was secretly thrilled. "Dory, you're absolutely shameless."

"That's right, honey, but you knew that when we made love on our third date. You remember, don't you? My parents bundled us so we could sleep together. My mom's arthritis was flaring up and she couldn't tie us tightly enough, and we got loose. Remember how scared we were that my father would find out what we'd done?"

"Dory! Shut up that kind of talk! It's bad enough that we sinned before we were married; we're not supposed to boast about it! You need to pray to God for forgiveness!"

Dory rubbed her body against him and asked seductively, "Okay, should I pray while we're making love or wait till afterwards."

Abel finally chuckled and said, "Never mind. Somehow I think God knows that you're not really sorry anyway. Come here and show me what I've always known, that you're the best lover in the world."

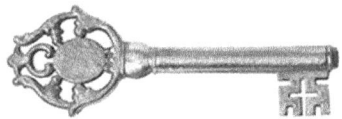

"I am he that liveth, and was dead; and behold, I am alive for evermore, Amen; and have the keys of hell and of death." **Revelation 1:18**

Dall spent the next hour rubbing down the horses and talking gently to them. After they had settled down, he collapsed onto his mattress. He stared up at the loft over his head for several hours before he could fall asleep. He rolled the events of the evening around in his head until he'd arrived at the only logical conclusion.

Hay sprigs fell periodically from the loft. If it wouldn't have alarmed Sandy, he wanted to yell up to the being in the loft and ask it what it thought of the night's events. But Sandy had already been traumatized enough for one night.

When he stirred at dawn, he jumped and sat up quickly. He looked to see what was in his bed and found Sandy asleep beside him.

Judging by the amount of daylight streaming through the walls, they had overslept. He didn't dare let Litchfield catch Sandy in bed with him. He shook her and said, "Sandy, wake up. We're running late."

Sandy threw the blanket off her and hurried to get to her stall before Litchfield walked in. Dall went to the cistern and got some water while Sandy combed her hair and rolled it up into a bun.

They'd barely had time to brush their teeth when Dall saw Litchfield and Devin walking across the barn lot. Litchfield had a concerned look on his face, so he'd probably heard the crashing blows on the barn last night. Devin had no look at all on his face. If he'd heard the blows, they weren't frightening enough to shake him from his perpetual state of ignorant bliss.

Dall leaned against his stall and studied Litchfield carefully. His reaction to the broken planks on the barn wall would answer a lot of questions.

Litchfield was meticulous in the care of his equipment and buildings. He would surely notice the broken boards as soon as he entered the barn. If he had no knowledge of the little girl, he would instantly fly into a rage and blame Dall for breaking them. If he knew about her and had heard the commotion, he would likely remain quiet and pretend to not notice the broken boards.

Dall also reasoned that Litchfield was either a sound sleeper or had been too afraid to come out of his house last night. His and Sandy's welfare was obviously of no concern.

Litchfield entered the barn cautiously. His subdued demeanor immediately told Dall that he'd heard the attack on the barn last night.

Litchfield looked around nervously and seemed surprised to find Dall and Sandy still alive.

He walked up to the barn wall and studied the broken boards. He turned around and said, "Get your breakfast, Englisher, we've got work to do. As he walked to the stalls to hitch up Lady and Tramp, he conspicuously avoided eye contact with Dall and Sandy. Dall now knew that Litchfield knew the little girl and had heard the attack on them last night. Litchfield himself had probably had an encounter with her in the past.

Mrs. Litchfield brought breakfast to the porch, but did not offer her usual cheerful greeting. She was visibly shaken and said sadly, "There's more inside, kids. Let me know if you need anything else."

When she disappeared back into the house, Sandy whispered, "What's eating her?"

Dall said, "She heard the attack on us last night. She's ashamed that no one came to help us."

Sandy stared at her sandwich and shook her head. "I can't get that out of my mind, Dall. I thought I had to be dreaming, but I was awake."

"It was no dream, and it was no little girl. We need to talk, but not here. I don't want Litchfield to overhear us."

Litchfield drove the hay wagon up to the house, so Dall and Sandy hurriedly ate another sandwich and gulped down their milk. This morning Sandy didn't mind the taste of the milk so much.

She did better in the hay this morning. Litchfield noticed their work gloves, but made no mention of them. He seemed particularly withdrawn as he drove the wagon. Devin sat beside him and swatted at the flies and sweat-bees that buzzed around him.

Just before lunch Litchfield backed the horses and wagon up to the barn. He walked back to the broken boards and again stared at them, apparently assessing the costs of repairs. He stepped into Dall's stall for a minute, then walked back to Dall and said, "There are no puddles in the barn. Are you two washing out by the cistern?"

Dall said, "Yes, Preacher, we didn't want to create a muddy mess in the barn."

Preacher got angry and yelled, "There's no privacy out there! You two are washing up in front of each other! You're also sleeping together!"

Dall quickly said, "Oh no, Preacher, We don't look at each other when we're bathing. We give each other privacy."

Litchfield held up a long blonde hair and yelled, "I found this on your pillow, Englisher! Your sister slept with you last night!"

Litchfield was clumsy and awkward, and telegraphed his punches. Dall saw him draw his fist back in plenty of time to block the punch, but he knew that if Litchfield did not get his satisfaction with his fists, he would resort to a blunt weapon. The injury from the little man's fists would be a lot less severe than from a board or pick handle.

Dall took the punch without offering a defense. Preacher's hands were hard and calloused, and stung more than Dall had anticipated. He tried to offer a defense, but Litchfield pushed him down and began kicking him. Sandy started toward him, but Dall yelled, "Sandy, no!"

After Litchfield had exhausted himself, Dall stood and said, "Thank you for caring about Sandy's honor, Preacher, but she was only on my bed last night before we went to sleep. She slept in her own bed. There has never been any incest between us."

Litchfield panted from exhaustion as he stared suspiciously at Dall. He said, "I don't believe that, Mr. Roberts. I know how you English are. She sleeps in my house from now on. I know she'll be safe there."

Sandy panicked. She knew that once she was away from Dall, Litchfield or his son would molest her. She said, "No, Preacher! I can't be away from my brother! We've never been separated before. I'll stay in my stall, but I have to stay with him."

Litchfield stormed up to Sandy and slapped her hard across the face. Dall said, "I'm sorry, Preacher, but we have to stay together. After what happened last night, we're afraid to be apart. If you'd like us to go live with someone else in the district, we'll understand."

Dall wiped the blood from his mouth as he studied Litchfield. He was hoping Litchfield would shed some light on the attack, but he only turned and grumbled, "Let's unload this hay."

The rest of the day was spent at a hurried pace in the hayfield. Dall took two more lashings with a strap and another serious stomping by Litchfield and Devin. Sandy tried to find an opportunity to talk to Dall about the attack last night, but Litchfield stayed too close to give them any privacy.

After supper, Dall and Sandy chopped Mrs. Litchfield's firewood for the following day, then retired to the barn. After watering and feeding the stock, Sandy washed up at the cistern while Dall kept watch. She then went inside and dressed while Dall cleaned up. Once inside, she said, "I can't stay here another night, Dall, not without knowing what happened to us last night. I don't think this old barn will take another pounding like that."

Dall combed his hair and used the shiny surface on the back of Sandy's hair brush to examine the damage to his face. Sandy said, "I'm sorry you got beat so much today, Dall. I know I sounded like I wanted it to happen when I took my first lumps, but I didn't."

"No need to apologize, Sandy. I survived it okay. This cut on my chin is deep. It needs stitches. Can you call Smith and have a doctor meet us tonight?"

Sandy retrieved her cell phone from under her mattress as Dall climbed into Lady's stall and began stroking him. Smith assured her that he would have a doctor with him when they met tonight. She asked, "Dall, have you given much thought about that little girl?"

"Sure have. I want to talk to Smith first, but I think I've got that whole thing figured out."

"Well, don't keep me guessing, what was it?"

Dall somehow seemed distant toward her. He said, "I want to talk to Smith first."

Sandy was shocked. "What? Don't you trust me? I was there, too, you know! Did I act like I enjoyed that?"

Dall said as he rubbed Lady's neck, "You're F.B.I., Sandy. I don't trust any of you."

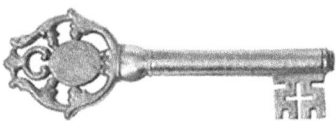

"I am he that liveth, and was dead; and behold, I am alive for evermore, Amen; and have the keys of hell and of death." **Revelation 1:18**

Night fell, and Dall's mistrust hurt Sandy deeply. She tried to maintain her professional bearing, but her anger showed through. As they were preparing to leave, she grabbed her cell phone and said, "Time to go, Dall. I think there's something you should tell me before we meet Smith. I'm F.B.I., but I'm also your partner."

Dall asked, "Okay, partner, where does your first loyalty lie, with me or the bureau?" Sandy couldn't answer. "I thought so. You say you need me, but when it comes right down to it, you're my controller, and you'll take Smith's side every time. You have to. I haven't forgotten that you threw me in a holding cell at the federal building in Quantico and were going to ship me back to Houston for trial. I've tried to look out for your best interest so far, but you're not looking out for mine. You're career is more important than me. When this thing is over, I have no doubt that you'll slap the cuffs on me and proudly haul me off to jail."

Pain and betrayal oozed from Sandy's eyes. She gritted her teeth and asked, "Just where do you get off talking to me like that? In case you've forgotten, I've had my arm twisted, too! I'm no happier with the bureau than you are! And when Litchfield stomped you into the dirt this afternoon, I was the one who picked you up and helped you with your share of the hay until your head cleared! I am your partner, Dall, and I'll take any amount of punishment for you, but when this thing is over, I've still got a career to salvage! And I won't slap the cuffs on you! That may happen, but it won't be by me! I'll do what I can for you, but don't turn on me like this! I'm F.B.I., but I'm still loyal to you! I was wrong to throw you in that cell! I know that now, but I apologized for it! I just want to know what you're going to say to Smith! I don't want to be blindsided and look like a fool!"

Dall thought for a minute. He sighed and said, "Okay, so you're not going to betray me in the end. I'm just going to put Smith on the spot. He knows exactly what's going on here. I'm going to pin him down about it."

"Well, how about letting me in on it first?"

"Smith first, then if I'm right, we'll have the next few months to talk about it. I'll tell you everything I know. Let's go. My face hurts and I need stitches in my chin."

Sandy grabbed Dall by the shirt and pushed him against the wall. She yelled, "No! What was that thing last night?"

Dall's anger would have risen to match Sandy's, but the tears oozing from the corners of her eyes reveled fear, not anger. He sighed and said calmly, "The devil."

"I am he that liveth, and was dead; and behold, I am alive for evermore, Amen; and have the keys of hell and of death." **Revelation 1:18**

As they walked, both stayed in the shadows and avoided being illuminated by the moonlight. They kept a wary eye pealed for the little girl who'd scared them so badly the night before.

When they had reached the corner-post where they turned right, Dall stopped and squinted hard to see the shadowy figure that was moving toward them. Sandy saw it too and asked, "Who can that be?"

As the figure got closer, Dall said, "It can only be one person, Sandy. Who do you know that casts a silhouette like that?"

Sandy sighed, "Oh no, not the fat guy from the sheriff's office?"

"I'm afraid so, and let's not call him fat. He knows how he looks, and he doesn't need people pointing it out to him. Let's see what he's up to."

Curly approached the corner-post and was completely oblivious to the presence of anyone else. He was drenched with sweat and was heaving so hard that they heard him sucking wind a hundred yards before he got to them.

Curly staggered clumsily and stumbled over the rocks and uneven ground. When he'd reached the corner-post, he collapsed against it and panted heavily as he looked around to get his bearings. Dall stepped out of the shadows and asked quietly, "You lost, soldier?"

Curly fell apart like a stack of dominoes. He jumped and back-pedaled until his short legs could no longer keep up with his ponderous body. When he fell, he raised a cloud of dust and let out a loud grunt.

As Curly slid to a stop, Dall could see that if he didn't do something soon, he and Sandy would be drawing gunfire in a matter of seconds. Curly was frantically trying to get his revolver out of its holster, and was unable to compose himself long enough to see who he would be firing at. Dall hurriedly said, "Deputy Slapp! Wait! Don't shoot!"

Curly relaxed the tension on the trigger and raised the muzzle to a safe position. Realizing that he was dangerously close to discharging his revolver at an innocent person, he struggled to his knees and ordered, "Halt or I'll shoot! Who are you?"

Dall and Sandy stepped up to Curly and knelt beside him. Dall said, "Deputy Slapp! It's Dall and Sandy. We met you in town a few nights ago, remember?"

Curly lowered his head and sighed in relief. As Dall and Sandy each took one of his arms and helped him to his feet, Curly said, "Oh my God, Dall, I thought for a second you were Chief Deputy Thurman! Then I thought you might be the murderer! Don't scare me like that!

You almost got yourself shot! You're lucky that I have the reflexes of a cat and could stop myself in time!"

Sandy turned her head and mumbled, "Yeah, too bad your grace and coordination don't match your reflexes."

Dall reached over and gently slapped her arm with the back of his hand. "Sandy! Stop it!"

He turned back to Curly and said, "Sure, Deputy Slapp. I tried to warn you quietly of our presence. Sorry we scared you."

As Curly's breathing slowed, he exclaimed confidently, "Ahh, you didn't scare me none! I just tripped over that rock there! Hey, call me Curly, Dall. What are you doing out here?"

Sandy said, "We might ask you the same thing, Curly."

Curly holstered his revolver and dusted off his pants. "I'm sorry, Dall, but I can't tell you. It's official police business. I'm working deep undercover and I can't have anyone knowing that I'm here." As he regained his composure, he looked at Dall suspiciously. "What are you doing here, Dall? You're not Amish, are you?"

Dall asked, "Don't we look Amish, Curly?"

"Yeah, you dress like it, but Amish would never have talked to me in town the other night. They never talk to us town-folks. And you weren't dressed like this then."

Sandy said, "Curly, I've got to ask you again. What are you doing out here? This is not some place you should be. Does your sheriff know you're here?"

Curly instantly became faint. "Oh lady, no he doesn't, and you can't tell him!"

"Why? Come on, Curly, we're in a hurry! Quit screwing with us! Tell us what you're doing here or I'm calling your sheriff!"

Curly almost started to cry, and pleaded, "Oh please, Sandy, please don't call him? You see, there was a murder out here a few weeks ago. We're surveilling Massey's pond, hoping to get some of the kids to talk to us. The feds are working the case, but the sheriff wants to solve it first. There are several more officers here; they're over by the pond, but I'm working alone."

Dall asked, "Trying to crack the big one to get in good graces with that chief deputy of yours?"

"Yeah, but I prefer to work alone anyway. If I get in a firefight, I only have to worry about myself. I'd hate to get a partner killed. Anyway the feds have an undercover out here in the district. I thought if I could find out who the undercover is, I could work with him and maybe get some inside information that'd help me make the arrest before the feds do."

Curly beamed with pride. Sandy stepped back and cringed as beads of sweat from his sweat-soaked shirt splattered her when he proudly slapped his chest. Curly bragged, "That'd make the sheriff look good."

Dall patted Curly on the shoulder and asked, "Curly, you're a nice guy, but you don't have the slightest clue how an undercover operation works, do you?"

Curly gripped the butt of his revolver and puffed up in righteous indignation. He nodded his head and said with wavering resolve, "Yeah! Yeah I do! I've worked lots of undercover operations! It was just a long time ago..., and...and it wasn't around here..., and...and no...no one here knows about it..., but it was a really big case..., and...and I almost got killed, and..."

When Curly finally stopped squirming long enough to gauge Dall and Sandy's reaction, his shoulders sank in defeat. He sighed in frustration and stared hard at the stars, then said, "Well, no, I haven't, but don't let that fool you. I'm a fast learner. If I can find this undercover guy, I'll blow this case wide open. Then we'll see who the clown is." Curly slapped his holster, indicating that he was ready for anything that any old Amish murderer could dish out.

He instantly froze in complete shock. He gasped and looked at Dall as if he were a ghost. He stepped back and shifted his frightened stare to Sandy as he extended his arm and moved his index finger back and forth between them. He covered his mouth with his other hand, then pointed his shaky finger at Dall. "You! My God! My God, you're him! You're not Amish, you're the undercover that the feds have put here!"

Sandy stepped into Curly and tried to get a firm grip on his sweaty arm. She said, "Okay, that's it. You're out of your league here, and your sheriff is probing around in a federal investigation. This is too important for you bunch of fools to blow it for us. Come on, Dall, I'm taking this guy to Smith. He'll know what to do with him."

Fear instantly swept over Curly's face, but Dall stepped in and gently pulled Sandy's hand off Curly's arm. "Sandy, wait. Let's not be in too big of a hurry here."

Sandy knew Dall had a plan, but wasn't sure what it was. She decided to play along with the good cop-bad cop routine for now. Dall said, "Okay, Curly, you got me. I knew it was only a matter of time before you'd find me."

Curly calmed his rapid breathing and slowed his racing heart as he swelled with pride. Dall continued, "You know, there might be a way that you can help us out and look good to your sheriff at the same time. But the key to success in undercover operations is secrecy. I'll let you help, but you can't tell anyone. If your sheriff or chief deputy finds out that you're working with me, we're through. If my controller finds out that you're poking around out here, he'll file charges on you in federal court. And I know from personal experience that he has enough pull to get you some jail time at the federal house in Leavenworth or Atlanta. At any rate, I'll deny even knowing you, and you'll take the fall all by yourself. Agreed?"

Curly almost pulled Dall's arm out of joint as he shook his hand violently. "Oh thanks, Dall! You won't be sorry about this! You've got the right guy this time! What do you want me to do?"

"I'm not sure yet, Curly, but there are a few rules. First, you don't come out here without calling me first. It's not safe for you to be walking around out here. Secondly, you keep your cell phone handy at all times. If I need you, I'll call you. It might be on short notice, so you might have to come running in the middle of the night. You mind being woken from a sound sleep?"

Curly shook his head adamantly, "No Sir, Dall, not at all! You just call and I'll come running!" Curly pulled out his penlight, notebook and pen. He wrote down Dall's cell phone number, then wrote his down and gave it to Dall. He then asked, "By the way, how did you guys get so beat up? You look terrible."

Dall couldn't read the paper in the dark, but said, "Farm work, Curly. Good old farm work. I'll be in touch. Remember, not a word to anyone. Now get back to your car and get out of here before your sheriff or my controller sees you."

Curly turned to leave, but Dall stopped him. "And if you see a little girl walking around here at night, avoid her at all cost." Curly hurried back to his car with a renewed sense of self-confidence in his waddle.

Sandy asked, "Okay, Dall, I give up. What was that all about? There's more at stake than that guy's self-esteem. We're not here to make him feel good or to salvage his career."

"I know, but he might come in handy later. Neither of us trusts Smith, Waters or Sveade. If things go south for us, we might need a local to bail us out. We certainly haven't found any Amish that we can trust yet."

Sandy thought for a few seconds, then agreed. "Yeah, I guess you're right. Smith has made it clear that there'll be no bail-out signal. He'd let us get killed before he'd ever lift a finger to help. I just wish it was someone besides that guy. I've got a real problem trusting my life to someone who can't even do a sit-up."

"Me, too, Sandy, but maybe our lives won't be saved by sit-ups. Maybe we'll just need a guy who is real good at sitting on people."

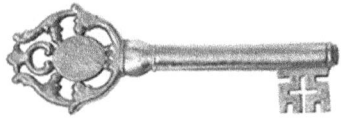

"I am he that liveth, and was dead; and behold, I am alive for evermore, Amen; and have the keys of hell and of death." **Revelation 1:18**

Smith and Waters were comfortably seated on their camp chairs, and Dr. Sveade paced nervously around the well. Dall and Sandy walked through the trees and looked cautiously behind them, hoping they would not see a small girl in a white nightgown off in the distance.

Sandy sat in a chair and Dall leaned against the well casing. Smith pointed to Dall and said, "Sorry about your chin, Dall. I saw the beatings that you took. You're a tough man. Keep up the good work."

Dall looked around and said, "I don't see a doctor."

Smith said, "I didn't bring one. Stitches would be hard to explain to the preacher. I brought you some steri-stips. You can tell the preacher that you had them in your suitcase."

Smith handed the strips to Sandy. "Here, just pull the skin together and tape it closed. Here's some Neosporin. It'll kill any infection."

Dall sighed in disgust at Smith's apathy toward his injury. He said, "So much for my chin. Why don't we talk about something really important?"

Waters hadn't forgotten the shot that Dall had given him at their last meeting. He was aching for a chance to get even. He began to chastise Dall, but Smith held his hand up. "No, Dexter, let's listen to him."

Dall said, "New rule, Agent Smith. No more secrets. Either put it all on the table or I'm calling your hand. I'm walking out and taking my chances on the run. I know you have no intention of letting me get to

Houston, so there'll be no arrest. Either come clean or I'm out of here; and good luck catching me once I drop out of sight."

Waters stood angrily and walked slowly toward Dall. Sandy was still stinging from Dall's mistrust, but wanted to show him that she was in his corner. "That goes for me, too, Sir. Job or no job, we have to know what we're up against."

Smith glared at her, then smiled pretentiously as he shook his head. "I'll give you two credit. It didn't take long for you to bond. Oh well, I guess after last night there are no secrets."

Dall squared up to Waters and asked, "Ready for another dose of humility?" Waters looked at Smith for support, but Smith merely shook his head. Waters then sat back down.

Sandy stood and asked, "You mean you saw that? You saw that little girl almost kill us?"

Dall said, "Of course he did, Sandy. His spotters watched the whole thing. And by the way, Agent Smith, since we're calling a spade a spade, let's clear the air about those spotters. They're not there to watch us, they're sniper teams. They're there to put us down if we try to walk away."

Sandy gasped in shock. She stepped in front of Smith so he couldn't avoid eye contact. She glared at him and asked, "Snipers? You've actually got snipers staking us out? They're not spotters there to help us if we get into trouble?"

Smith leaned over the well and gazed out across the moon-lit countryside. "No, Sandy, they're not. They're snipers. If this were any other mission, we wouldn't care if you walked away. We'd just ship Dall back for prosecution and fire you, or transfer you to some obscure outpost where you'd rot for the rest of your career. This is too important for that."

Dall said, "You saw the attack on us last night."

"Yes, we were watching. To be honest, we were surprised that it happened so soon, but that's what we were hoping for."

Sandy raged as she ran her fingers through her hair. "You knew we'd be attacked? If you knew that, then you know what that thing was! What the hell was that?"

Smith didn't respond, but looked at Dr. Sveade. Dall spoke up before Dr. Sveade could speak. "We're not here to catch a murderer, Sandy. As a matter of fact, the bureau doesn't give a crap about those two dead Amish men. We're really here to catch a demon."

Sandy froze in shock, then chuckled, "You're kidding me. You didn't really mean that she was literally the devil, right? I mean, demons aren't real. This is a joke, right?"

Dall said, "No, Sandy. I thought about it all last night and all day today. We all know that a small child couldn't rattle a barn off its foundation like that; no human could. Therefore, it wasn't a little girl. And since there are only two kinds of supernatural beings in the world, she was either an angel or a demon. By deductive reasoning, since angels are messengers from God and don't act that way, she was a demon. Agent Smith here put us in this district to find a demon."

Sandy stared at Dall in total disbelief. She shook her head and asked Dr. Sveade, "He's kidding, right? Demons are just myths and fairy tales, right? They're just things that they make scary movies about, right?"

Dr. Sveade got a look of deep concern on his face. "Oh, Sandy, let me assure you, my dear, demons are real. They are former angels who were created by God right before He created the universe and the earth. At one time Satan was God's most trusted angel. He was in charge of the entire angelic realm. He challenged God's authority by wanting to be like God, and was cast out of Heaven. God also cast out one third of all the angels. They were the ones who followed Satan. Those angels are now demons, and they roam the earth deceiving man and causing mischief."

Sandy stared at Dr. Sveade in disbelief. She finally said, "Yeah, but Demons aren't the reason why people sin. I've sinned lots of times, but I didn't feel the inhabitation of a demon."

Dr. Sveade shook his head. "No, Sandy, you didn't. The Bible says that every person who ever lived, with the exception of Jesus, has sinned. And sin is a result of a person's decision to follow the desires of their own heart rather than the will of God. Sin is not caused by demons. It is caused by the free will that was given to man when he was created. We all have the free will to choose to follow our own desires or the desires of God. But these demons apparently know the desires of men and place temptations in front of us so we have the opportunity to sin. And they know man's nature very well. They influence men by suggesting things that are contrary to God's will."

"So, since everyone sins, then no one really believes in God or chooses to follow Him. The Amish are just using demons as an excuse to do whatever they want."

Dall said, "Not so, Sandy, You're right that everyone sins. The provision for the forgiveness of those sins was the crucifixion of Christ. Christians sin just the same as the lost. The only difference is that the sins of a Christian are forgiven. But you're right about some of the Amish. Their sin is not a result of demons. It is a result of the old sin nature that was passed down to all of us through our original father, Adam. Some of the Amish have just latched on to the demon theory so they can avoid some accountability for their sin, or so they think. They can blame it on a demon and appear righteous in the eyes of their fellow Amish. The bottom line is that the Amish sin on a regular basis just like people in every other faith. The mistake that many of the Amish make is that they think they can somehow achieve enough righteousness through their good works to merit admission into Heaven. That's a false doctrine. No one can gain entrance into Heaven through their own good works. It is only by the righteousness of Christ that is bestowed upon us when we accept His sacrifice that we can get into Heaven. The righteousness of Christ is the only righteousness that God recognizes, not that of mortal men."

Smith said angrily, "Enough of this evangelism garbage! Sandy, since Dall has figured it all out, I'll turn this meeting over to the person who's really running the show. Dr. Sveade is in charge here. We're just working for him, like you and Dall. Doctor, the floor is yours."

Dr. Sveade took his glasses off and cleaned the lenses with his handkerchief. He put them on and said, "Sandy, Agents Smith and Waters were assigned to me by the director. I've been in charge of a project of the highest priority for the last sixty years. Even the President doesn't know what we're doing."

Sandy said, "That can't be. The director could never hide a top secret project from the President."

Dr. Sveade frowned. "Oh, quite the contrary, Sandy, he's hidden it from the President because he didn't even know about it. This is a deep-black military project. None of the Presidents for the last fifty years have known about it. The funding is hidden within the military budget and administered by a top-ranking general that's one of the joint chiefs. When it comes to completion, then we'll brief the sitting President at that time, but right now it's too risky to tell a weak or liberal President who might turn this project into a political football and get our funding yanked. Besides, we'd all be laughed out of office. This mission is more unbelievable than the U.F.O. phenomenon."

Dall said, "I believe it. I'm mad at myself for being frightened last night. If I'd been thinking straight, I'd have known that there was nothing to be afraid of."

Sandy said angrily, "Well, I wish you'd have clued me in on your suspicions last night, I was scared to death!"

Smith said, "We all were, Sandy. We were watching from a hilltop. The two snipers who were on that post lost their nerve. They were crying like babies and hiding like scared rabbits. If I hadn't known what we were dealing with, I'd have left the country."

Sandy turned to Dall and asked, "Okay, Dall, why shouldn't we have been afraid?"

Dall shrugged his shoulders. "Because, the fact that the demon only banged on the wall and didn't tear the barn down meant that he had no intention of hurting us. If you understand the nature and power of demons, you know that they can travel any distance in the blink of an eye. They have the power to destroy anything. That demon could have splintered the barn in a matter of seconds. Instead of following us slowly, it could have been in front of us in a flash or been waiting inside the barn. If it had wanted to hurt us, it could have exploded that barn and torn us to pieces, just like it did to our murder victims. No, Sandy, we were in no danger. The fact that it only banged on the wall was proof that it either meant us no harm or that God had restrained it. Demons are constrained by God. If I had been thinking rationally, I'd have known that and not panicked."

Sandy turned her back to everyone and stared up at the stars. She shook her head in disbelief and said, "I can't do this. This is way bigger than I can deal with. This has to be a big mistake. Demons aren't real!"

Dall said, "They're real, and I think it's Dr. Sveade's job now to educate us. That's why he's really here. He only wanted to teach us enough about the Amish to keep us from being thrown out of the district. His real mission is to teach us about demons so we can catch this one."

Sandy turned and glared at Dr. Sveade. He said, "I won't apologize for the deception, Sandy. I've invested too many years in this project to fail now. This mission is so important that it doesn't matter who gets killed. If we succeed and all lose our lives, it'll be a small price to pay."

Sandy sat down, then grumbled, "I guess I'm trapped. I just can't believe that the greatest drama in the history of the Earth is playing out right here in the middle of nowhere, and I'm right in the middle of it. Why me? How did this whole thing begin?"

Dr Sveade sat back down and began. "First of all, Dall is right about the mission, but wrong that we want to capture this demon. Demons are spiritual beings and cannot be captured. Now, as outrageous as this will sound, Sandy, I assure you that it is true. Since you're not a believer, it'll be even harder for you to accept. I'm going to give you the abbreviated version, but Dall will have to enlighten you further as you go."

Sandy looked suspiciously at Dall, still angry that he did not brief her on this before their meeting. Dr. Sveade continued, "In the Bible, it's taught that demons are under the authority of God. That's why Satan and the demons have not destroyed mankind. God has restrained them ever since He cast them out of Heaven. It is generally believed that the Holy Spirit of God is so powerful that no demon can be in His presence. So, if you can convince Bishop Gordan that it was a total acceptance of Jesus Christ that convinced you to return to the Amish faith, you may be able to convince him that the demon that drove you away from the faith was cast out when God sent the Holy Spirit to dwell within you upon your acceptance of Him."

Sandy yelled, "I'm not worried about Bishop Gordan! I'm worried about surviving this monster! How long have you known about this thing? Why me and Dall?"

Dr. Sveade replied, "What attracted us to Dall? Well, let me assure you, we've been searching for someone with his credentials for many years. It was only through persistent searching and diligent scrutiny of the intelligence files sent to the F.B.I. by local, state and county law enforcement agencies that Agent Smith was able to learn of Dall's misfortune. When we looked into his background and saw that he was an expert on the Bible, we knew we had to have him. When we couldn't gain his cooperation voluntarily, we persuaded the U.S. Attorney to file charges. I'm sorry, Dall, but as I said before, this is far more important than you or I."

Sandy said, "I guess that explains why he's not expendable, but I am. Okay, why me?"

Dr. Sveade shrugged his shoulders. "A couple of reasons. First of all, you're tall, thin and dark complected. You look like you've been working outdoors all your life. You look the part. I can't tell you the second reason yet. That'll come later, but make no mistake; you were selected because your looks and character traits compliment Dall's. You look like brother and sister. You both complement each other, so you're both here for the duration. We can't afford to have this leaked to the press of any of our competitors. If anyone tries to walk away, my orders are to kill them. And don't feel so victimized; the same goes for Agents Waters and Smith and those sniper teams out there."

Sandy looked at Smith. He nodded his head and said, "It's true, Sandy. I've had the same threats that you've had. There are powers overseeing this project that you wouldn't believe. We're all dead meat if we try to walk away or talk to anyone about it. Those snipers out there are military snipers, not feds. I have tactical supervision of them, but they were given their strategic marching orders from a select core of Army general. Their instructions are to shoot me, Dexter or Dr. Sveade if they have to, but no one is allowed out."

Sandy shook her head and put her face in her hands. She rubbed her eyes hard, then looked back at Smith. "Then my S.A.C. in Phoenix lied to me. You really did a bureau-wide search for someone who looked the part, then lied to me about the assignment. I was just a throw-away commodity from the start."

Smith offered no apology. He simply thought about Sandy's assessment for a few seconds, then nodded his head.

Dall said, "Doctor, I'm sure you're far more familiar with the powers of demons than I am, but this whole mission is nuts. We all know there's no way that mortal men can control or capture a spiritual being, especially one as powerful and elusive as a demon. By my calculations, they're the fifth most powerful beings in existence, under God, Jesus Christ, the angels and Satan."

Dr. Sveade said, "Very good, Dall, but you left the saints out of the power structure. No matter though, you're right; mortals have no hope of capturing a demon."

Sandy asked, "Then why in God's name are we even trying? If this demon can destroy us in one breath, what can we hope to accomplish?"

Dr. Sveade smiled at Sandy's naiveté and said, "We're not going capture him, Sandy. We're going to give ourselves up to him."

SEVEN

ISAAC MADE HIS way quietly out of the house after the rest of the family had gone to bed. When he'd reached the yard gate, he heard a voice behind him. He turned quickly and was stunned to see his father on the porch sitting in a cane chair.

Abel stood solemnly and slowly walked to Isaac. He said, "It's time we had a talk, son. This sneaking out of the house has got to stop. I know where you go at night."

Isaac regained his composure and said, "So, I'm still getting my work done."

"It's not about the work, Isaac. I don't think it's safe for you to be out at night."

Isaac said, "I'm just meeting some of the kids at Massey's pond."

"I know where you're going, son. You've also been drinking when one of them brings a bottle. That has to stop, too."

Isaac burned inside, but lost his courage when looking into the intimidating eyes of his father. He said, "Okay, then I'll quit, but I still have to go to Massey's pond."

Abel said, "Isaac, you're coming dangerously close to bringing the wrath of God down on yourself. If you don't come around, the bishop will have the elders take the matter out of my hands. I know you were out there when Preacher Croft was killed. I know he beat you. That's how you got the marks on your face."

Isaac's heart sank. He had been wrestling with his guilt for weeks. He looked around nervously, hoping to mount a believable defense. He said, "I can't talk about it. Just don't ask me anymore."

Abel said, "Isaac, I've tried to be patient with you, but this rebellious attitude has got to stop. Bishop Gordan wants you to be baptized into the faith."

"Faith? That's a joke. The whole Amish faith is a farce. Everyone talks good religion in the worship services, but then they go out and drink, cuss, commit sexual sin and beat their wives and kids. You're all frauds, Dad."

Abel became angry. He grabbed Isaac by the shirt and lifted him off the ground with one hand until they were eye to eye. He growled, "Isaac, I know how things look! I know there's a lot of hypocrisy here in the district, but just because others don't obey God's laws, that'll be no defense for you on judgment day! I want you to be better than me!"

"I will be, Dad, but not as an Amish." Abel saw the determination in Isaac's eyes and slowly released his shirt.

When Isaac's feet touched the ground, he turned to leave. Abel stopped him. "Isaac, I can force you to stay home, but I want you do it because it's the right thing to do. I know why you're going to Massey's pond. I want you to know that you're risking your life every night that you go there. That's also the area where Wilhelm Dresselhaus was killed. And you're risking Katie's life. I know how you feel about her. If you care for her, I want you to start courting her here. You'll be properly chaperoned and her reputation won't be tarnished. If that's not acceptable, you can go to her house, as long as you get her father's permission. We'll even bundle you two at night and have a proper chaperone in the room so she can stay overnight. If you want that girl, then go through her parents and get their permission."

"I don't need anyone's permission, Dad. I'll be back later."

Abel fumed as Isaac stormed off. After Isaac had disappeared into the darkness, Abel lowered his head in dismay and started after him.

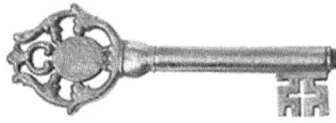

"I am he that liveth, and was dead; and behold, I am alive for evermore, Amen; and have the keys of hell and of death." **Revelation 1:18**

Katie waited patiently at the pond. When Isaac emerged from the cover of the trees and thick underbrush, she ran to him and jumped into his arms. After several minutes of heated petting, both froze as footsteps approached.

Isaac was furious and resented being followed. He stepped in front of Katie to confront his father, but stopped in his tracks when Sheriff Jerry Holden and Chief Deputy Casey Thurman stepped into the clearing. The sheriff said, "Evening, kids, nice night for a swim."

Isaac said angrily, "We're not swimming! Mr. Massey knows we come here and he doesn't mind! We're not doing anything wrong, Sheriff!"

Holden held his hand up. "It's okay, son; we've talked to Massey. We're not here to cause you problems. I just want to ask you some questions. You're Abel Straus's son, aren't you?"

Isaac nodded. "That depends on your perspective, I guess."

Katie put her hand on Isaac's shoulder. "Isaac, don't be rude. Let's hear what he has to say."

Sheriff Holden looked up at the stars and said, "It's a beautiful night, kids. I can understand why you like to come here, but are you aware that there was a homicide close to here a few weeks ago?"

Isaac immediately became nervous. His facial expression and body language told Holden that he knew something. Katie said, "We heard that one of the preachers failed to come home one night, but we've been forbidden by the bishop to discuss it. We've been instructed to send anyone with questions straight to him."

Sheriff Holden said, "Yeah, I know. We've talked to the bishop and he refuses to help us. We were hoping that some of you young folks might be willing to point us in the right direction as long as the bishop doesn't find out about it."

The sheriff again looked at Isaac, who could not look him in the eye. He turned away from the sheriff and let Katie do the talking. Casey walked calmly up to Isaac and put his massive hand gently on his shoulder. He said in a fatherly tone, "You know, son, I've been reading people my whole life. Now, there's almost nothing about this case that I know for sure, except that our victim was murdered. But the one thing I do know is that you know what happened to him. I can see it in your eyes. We're not here to cause you any problems, son, but please help us. At least tell us who he was."

Katie interrupted, "No Isaac! If the bishop finds out that you've talked to the English, you'll be banished. Remember our talk last week. We don't need any more problems from the bishop or elders."

Isaac anguished as he recalled the night that Preacher Croft had attacked him. His fear was written across his face. "I don't care what the bishop likes, Katie. Preacher Croft was evil. He deserved what he got."

Casey stepped closer to Isaac. "Preacher Croft? Was that his name, Isaac?"

Isaac had to think for a few seconds. He didn't want to reveal that he'd been attacked by Preacher Croft or he'd be a suspect in the murder. He said, "Yes, I guess it was. All I know is that Preacher Croft didn't come home one night, and no one will talk about it. The bishop is investigating. If you have a dead body, then it's likely Preacher Croft; Levi Croft."

Casey pulled a close-up facial photo from the series of photos taken at the autopsy. He shined a pen-light on the photo and showed it to Isaac. "Is this Preacher Croft, son?"

Isaac looked at the photo and then turned his head away. When he saw that Preacher Croft's jaw had been ripped away, he was stunned beyond words. Bishop Clevenger's assertion that he had not killed Preacher Croft was now confirmed. He had only pushed Croft down. He couldn't have sustained such an injury simply by falling down."

Casey asked, "Well?"

Isaac nodded his head and Casey pressed harder. "Isaac, you kids come out here quite often. You or some of your friends must have seen or heard something. I know how kids talk. If someone knows something, then they've talked to others. You know more than you're telling us."

Isaac turned away from Casey. Katie could see that he did know something, and said nervously, "We can't say anything else, Sheriff. Please don't pressure Isaac anymore."

Sheriff Holden said, "Young lady, I'm sorry about how you're treated by the bishop and elders, but you have to understand something. There's been a murder here. You're all at risk if we don't find the killer. I hate to cause you problems, but I'm going to keep pressing you until I find out what I need to know. Now, I want you to talk to the other kids in the district. If you don't help me, I'm going to have to pay visits to their homes. If I have to bring all you kids into the office for questioning, I will, but I'm going to find out what happened to Preacher Croft. I know you don't want your parents to find out that you've all been sneaking out of the house at night and coming here to party, but if we have to question everyone, they'll find out. Go home. Talk to the other young people.

Find out what happened and who killed him. I promise, I'll never tell your parents or the bishop what you say."

The sheriff and chief deputy left and walked toward their car. As they walked past the big oak that Abel had been leaning against, he eased around to the other side. They passed by unaware that he'd been there, listening to the entire conversation.

Casey and the sheriff walked the half-mile back to their car and discussed the possibility of cultivating an informant among the young people. As they stopped at a barbed wire fence, Casey put his foot on the middle wire and pulled up on the top one. Sheriff Holden climbed through, then did the same for Casey.

As Casey stood up, he looked back toward the pond. Two-hundred yards to the north of the pond, he saw the faint glow of a white nightgown in the moonlight, and said, "Hey, Jerry, is that the little girl that Massey said he's seen walking the hills at night?"

Jerry strained to make out the vague shape. "It sure looks like it. How old do you think she is?"

"I don't know, but she has no business walking around these hills at night. Her parents can't know that she's slipped out of the house. I think we should find out who she is. Maybe she can tell us what the gossip around the district is about Preacher Croft." Jerry agreed and both men climbed back through the fence and headed toward the little girl on the distant hill.

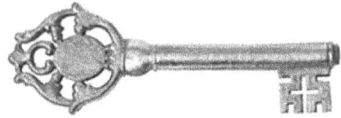

"I am he that liveth, and was dead; and behold, I am alive for evermore, Amen; and have the keys of hell and of death." **Revelation 1:18**

Katie held Isaac tightly and said, "I have to get home, Isaac. I'll try to meet you here tomorrow night. Not a word about our conversation with the sheriff to anyone, okay?"

"I'll try, too, but my dad confronted me tonight. He knows that I've been slipping out here to see you."

Katie gasped and stepped back. "Oh, Isaac, was he mad?"

Isaac had a puzzled look on his face. "No. No, he wasn't. He was surprisingly supportive. He said I should either start bringing you to our house or I should come to yours. Either way, he said I should talk to your father first."

Katie sighed with relief. "Good! You see, I told you he was more reasonable that you give him credit for. And he's right. My dad will have a fit if he finds out that I've been sneaking out to see you. We've got to do this the Amish way, which means we have to be chaperoned, and you have to be baptized and get back in the good graces of the bishop."

After several more long kisses, Isaac and Katie went home. Abel followed Isaac at a distance and stayed in the shadows as much as possible.

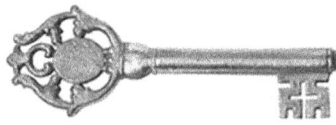

"I am he that liveth, and was dead; and behold, I am alive for evermore, Amen; and have the keys of hell and of death." **Revelation 1:18**

Sandy stood and sighed deeply as she looked up at the night sky and shook her head in disbelief. "I can't believe what I'm hearing, Doctor. Did you say that we're going to give ourselves up to this demon?"

Dr. Sveade said, "Yes, in a sense. Listen to the history of this project, then you'll understand. Ever since the Bible was compiled from the original scrolls, there has been an ongoing study of Bible prophesy. There've been scholars from all over the world studying Bible prophesy for various reasons. Man has always had a fascination with the events surrounding the End-Times and the second coming of Christ as illustrated in some of the books like Daniel and Revelations. Among those events are the Rapture of the believers out of this world, which will begin the seven-year period of tribulation and the sudden rise to power of the Antichrist."

Dall said, "I've studied prophesy myself. It appears that the demons and Satan play an active role during the Tribulation period."

Dr. Sveade said, "That's right, Dall. After the Rapture, there'll be a short period of peace and prosperity, three and a half years to be exact. As in all End-Time prophesy, the nation of Israel is the key that prophesy scholars focus on. Whenever you hear of Israel taking up arms, scholars pay particularly close attention to the developments. The last great-war that precipitates the rise to power of the Antichrist will begin with Israel. With the increasing unrest in the Middle-East, that war could start at any time. Speculation has it that that war will prompt the formation of the Ten-Nation Common Market in Europe. The person who rises to the head of that alliance will be the Antichrist. It should be noted that the formation of that ten-nation alliance has begun. They've already adopted one currency, the Euro, and six of the European nations are discussing the feasibility of combining their militaries. We think an all-out war between Israel and her enemies, such as Jordan, Lebanon, Syria, Iran, Iraq, Egypt or Saudi Arabia, may have such a destabilizing effect on the world that the ten European nations will complete their confederation."

Dall said, "I know, and the recent hostilities between Israel and Lebanon look like they'll draw the whole world into the conflict. Although there's a cease-fire, it's shaky, and a peaceful settlement appears unlikely."

"Yes, Dall. That whole mess is being watched carefully by prophesy scholars. There have been cease-fires and temporary truces, but if it escalates, as I expect it eventually will, the ten-nation confederacy could materialize within the next year. The Antichrist will rise to the head of that confederacy and bring a tenuous peace to the Middle-East war. In bringing peace, he'll garner the support of the world, and all the other nations will turn power over to him."

Sandy said, "That'd never happen. All the free countries would never blindly hand over their fate to a foreigner. The U.S. would never surrender to him."

Dall said, "Don't bet on it, Sandy. All it takes is a weak President with no courage to stand up to him, and intense political and economic pressure imposed by the rest of the world. Look at how degraded the moral values of the U.S. have become already. The sexual revolution, the proliferation of the health-wealth-and prosperity doctrine in Christianity and the acceptance of the feminist and homosexual agenda has degraded the value of the family, and over forty-six million unborn babies have been murdered since Roe vs. Wade in 1973. Our culture has embraced dishonesty and greed over sound business ethics, and humanistic doctrinal lies rather than the Biblical truths that originally sustained our country in its infancy and preserved us through our major conflicts. It won't be that the U.S. will surrender to the Antichrist. We'll embrace him because he'll embody the evil character traits that our godless culture has itself grown to love."

Dr. Sveade said, "The U.S. will fall in line with the rest of the world. During the Tribulation there'll be three and a half years of peace and prosperity, then we learn in the 12th chapter of Revelations that Satan fights the arch-angel, Michael. Currently Satan is allowed access to Heaven. In the 1st and 2nd chapters of Job, we see that Satan is allowed access to God. After he is defeated by Michael in Revelations, he'll be cast out of Heaven forever and all access to God will be permanently closed to Satan and the demons. As revenge he'll make an alliance with the Antichrist three and a half years after the Rapture. The last three and a half years will be devoted to hunting down and killing the Jews and believers who will not worship him."

Shock fell over Sandy's face as she processed the barrage of unbelievable claims that Dr. Sveade was throwing at her. "This all sounded like the plot from a science fiction novel." She thought for a few seconds, then continued, "Okay, but that's just the speculation of a bunch of college professors who think they can predict the end of the world by passages in the Bible. Anyway, those prophesies were made by a bunch of ignorant sheep-herders, and may never come true. Even if some of them do, it's only coincidence, isn't it?"

Dr. Sveade shook his head in disgust. "No, Sandy, your skepticism is showing through. Let me assure you that the prophesies in the Bible have been the most studied and carefully researched writings in human history. Between one forth and one third of the entire Bible is devoted to prophesy. And if you're questioning the accuracy of Bible prophesy, let me tell you that every prophesy spelled out in the Bible that has come true did so to the exact letter. There were three-hundred prophesies alone that came true by the birth, death and resurrection of Jesus Christ. Do you know what the odds are of three hundred predictions of the future coming true exactly as foretold? If you took only eight of those prophesies, the odds of one man fulfilling them completely is one in ten to the seventeenth power. The Bible is made up of sixty-six books. There's no way on earth that mortal men could have written that many prophesies into those books with complete accuracy without the divine revelation of God. It's mathematically impossible that they were all fulfilled by chance."

Sandy considered the astronomical odds of three hundred prophesies coming true as written. She said, "I guess I never thought about it. Maybe the Bible is true."

"Sandy, we've had the very best minds in the world working on this project. It's a dead-sure fact that the events described in the Bible concerning the End-Times are completely accurate. There will be a rapture in which millions of people will instantly vanish from the face of the earth. There will be a tribulation period lasting seven years. There will be an Antichrist who rises to power. We could discuss this all night, but that's as far as we need to go for now. It's the Antichrist that has brought us all together in this mission."

Dall asked, "Why, Doctor? Prophesy was given to us by God to reveal the events leading up to His second coming. We can't change them."

Dr. Sveade said, adamantly, "That's where you're wrong, my dear boy! We think we can change the future!"

Sandy reached over and took Dr. Sveade's flashlight. She sighed is disbelief as she walked over and began putting a steri-strip on the laceration on Dall's chin. She said, "You're leading up to something, Doctor. Why are we here?"

"Satan, dear Sandy. Satan and the demons."

Dall said, "Satan's role is clearly defined, Doctor, as is his fate. He'll wind up in the bottomless pit along with the Antichrist."

"Yes, Dall, but the Bible left out some very important details."

"Like what?"

"In the beginning, God created the angels just before he created the earth. As you know, Satan wanted to be like God, so God cast him out of Heaven along with one third of the angelic realm. Those fallen angels are now commonly referred to as demons."

Dall said, "I know that, Doctor. So what can we do about it?"

"Maybe a lot. God made a provision for man's redemption from sin. That provision was Jesus Christ's death, burial and resurrection. Nowhere in the Bible have we found that there was any provision for the redemption of the fallen angles."

Dall said, "That's right, Doctor, their fate is the lake of fire, just as it is for the non-believers."

"Yes, Dall, but there's a plan to change that."

When Sandy had finished applying the steri-strip, Dall put pressure on his laceration and stepped toward Dr. Sveade. "Plan? What can mortal men possibly do to change God's mind and redeem the demons? And why should we want to?"

"Nothing, Dall, we're helpless, but there's one demon who might be able to change things."

"The little girl? She can change God's mind?"

"Maybe not, Dall, but here's what we know. Satan and the demons have been roaming the earth since their fall, trying to deceive man and keep him from accepting the redemption offered by Christ. Apparently there's a major rift in the demon world. Apparently many of the demons are sorry they followed Satan, and would like to be spared the lake of fire. They've seen it and they're terrified of it. They'd rather occupy a menial position in Heaven for eternity than spend it in the lake of fire. There is a war brewing in the demon world, and it's not the war between Heaven and Hell that has traditionally been espoused. It's a war between demons. There's a large segment of demons who want to overthrow Satan. They want to dethrone Satan and approach God before access to Heaven is denied them forever in the 12th chapter of Revelations, and plead with Him to offer them a provision for redemption for their sins, like that of mankind."

Dall stared at Dr. Sveade in total disbelief. "You're crazy, Doctor. How can you know this? This demon war is not spoken of anywhere in the Bible. This has to be the result of the wild imagination of one of your prophesy researchers."

"I thought so too at one time, Dall, but we've got proof."

"I'm listening."

"Apparently there have been numerous times in history when one particular demon has contacted a person who is in a position to control the world. The last time we know of was in World War II. The allies learned from former high-officials in the Third Reich that Hitler and his staff had made extensive use of astrologers. They'd practiced channeling and contacted many benevolent spirits, or so they thought. I was a very young man then, but I was part of the secret allied project to find out what spirits they had contacted and to see if we could get those spirits to help us in future conflicts. After a few months of research, we became convinced that those benevolent spirits weren't angels at all, but were actually demons that were trying to help the Nazis. When one of Hitler's astrologers made a false prediction about the outcome of one of his military battles, he became furious and rounded up all the astrologers and put them in prison."

Smith said, "That's right, Dall, but before the Russians invaded Berlin, Dr. Sveade was able to learn the identity of this demon."

Dall was intrigued yet skeptical. "And you've spoken with this demon?"

"No, Dall. In May of '41, Rudolph Hess took an unauthorized flight across the English Channel. He landed in Scotland with the intent of negotiating a peace with Britain. While he was in prison, I was able to befriend him and gain his confidence. He believed that I was sympathetic to the Reich. I played on his fierce loyalty to Hitler and convinced him that with the assistance of a demon they could win the war. He revealed to me the name of the demon that he, Goring, Himmler and Hitler had been talking to."

"And you think this demon can help us somehow?"

"Yes, Dall, we do. We confirmed this demon's identity and plans in April of '45 when the Russians had Berlin almost surrounded. He was introduced to Heinrich Himmler by Wilhelm Theodore H. Wulff. Himmler dressed up as a regular German soldier and tried to avoid capture, but the British recognized him instantly and took him prisoner. Before he crushed a cyanide capsule that he'd hidden in his mouth, my British counterpart was able to get the name of the demon that he'd been in contact with. This demon tried to convince Himmler to overthrow Hitler and take over the Reich, but Himmler didn't have to guts to try it."

Dall asked, "What did this demon say?"

"According to Hess, this demon told them that ever since they were cast out of Heaven, there's been a large segment of the demonic realm that regretted following Satan, and have not gone along with his agenda. Apparently most of these demons don't assist Satan as he goes to and fro on the earth deceiving people. Most of them avoid him and try not to anger God anymore than they already have in the event that they can someday obtain His forgiveness. They have not given up on the hope that they can be spared the eternal torment of the lake of fire. This demon is apparently the leader of the movement, and he's the only one powerful enough to overthrow Satan."

Dall stood quietly in total shock. He searched his memory of scripture and asked, "Excuse me, Doctor, but am I correct that many of the demons are confined already? They all don't roam the earth, do they?"

"Very good, Dall. You're right. A careful study of the Bible reveals several references to a deep, dark abyss, or a bottomless pit. I've been referring to demons as only one being, but that's really a generic term for different beings. There are really two kinds of evil spirits. There are fallen angels, which are the followers of Satan that were cast out of Heaven along with him, then there are the others."

Sandy asked, "What others?"

"Apparently God had appointed certain angles as watchers over the earth. In the 6th chapter of Genesis, these watchers beheld the beauty of the daughters of man and decided to marry them. They had children called Nephilim with these women, and those children were a breed of giants. They were half man and half angel. These giants were evil to the core. They began killing and eating other men and each other. They drank blood and sinned against man and the animals, so God chained them and the watchers up and put them in the bottom of a dark abyss. That abyss, or the bottomless pit, is also mentioned other places in the Bible."

Dall said, "If I remember correctly, there'll be no forgiveness for those angels who were the watchers or their children. They're already in the bottomless pit."

Dr. Sveade said, "That's right; that's where God sends fallen angles that get out of line. They're already doomed to the lake of fire. In the 7th chapter of Revelations, we're told that during the Tribulation those fallen angels and Nephilim will be released from the abyss for five months to torment believers who refuse to accept the mark of the Antichrist. Anyway, they're not the ones that we're talking about. There are many fallen angels who are not chained up in the abyss, and some of them are the ones that want to bind Satan and his followers, then beg God for forgiveness. They're the ones we want to help us."

Sandy said, "I thought Satan was the most powerful of all the demons. How will they kill him?"

"Demons are spiritual beings, Sandy. They live forever and cannot be killed. They can only be bound and restrained. Apparently this demon wants his followers to rise up and bind Satan and his followers. They'll then approach God and ask His forgiveness, and see if there is some way they can serve Him and come back under His grace. After they bind Satan and his followers, they'll throw them into the abyss with the watchers and Nephilim for God to cast into the lake of fire as He's prophesied."

Dall thought for a few seconds, then said, "I've got to admit, Doctor, I've never heard of this demon war, but I guess it's possible. How do we fit into all of this?"

"Prophesy experts all agree that we're living in the very last days of the End-Times. In Matthew, chapter 24, God said that once Israel becomes a nation, a generation shall not pass without seeing the Rapture and the beginning of the Tribulation. Israel became a nation in 1948. Time is short for this demon and his army. As soon as the Rapture hits, there'll only be three and a half years before Michael defeats Satan and all access to God is cut off. This demon wants to bind Satan and his followers, then make his appeal to God before that opportunity is lost. He's feeling pressured because he doesn't know how long the war with Satan will last, and no one but God knows the exact time the Rapture will occur. He doesn't even know if they can defeat Satan and his followers. They might lose the war, then we'll gain nothing."

Dall was confused, "I can understand that, Doctor, but what do we gain if they win the war. So what if they defeat Satan? God may not even listen to them. What can they possibly do to regain God's favor, and how does that benefit us?"

"Dall, prophesy says that in the End-Times the Antichrist will rule the world and lead it to the edge of destruction just before Jesus returns to save mankind from self-annihilation. We here in the United States don't want to see that. We don't want a weak President to hand us over to the Antichrist. During that time, mankind will see the worst persecution of believers the world has ever seen. We want the United States to be a fortress against that persecution. We want the power to defeat the Antichrist and remain strong when the rest of the world is in chaos. We can't do that alone. We'd never be able to defeat all the armies of the world unified under one banner. If this demon can overthrow Satan and secure some redemptive provision from God, we're going to try to convince him to form an alliance with the United States to combat the Antichrist and help us avoid his persecution. We're the most powerful nation in the world. If this demon can approach God and convince Him that he has the most powerful nation in the world willing to join forces with him and his followers to defeat the Antichrist, God might just spare them from the lake of fire. From our perspective, we don't care if their standing in Heaven afterwards is menial. We'll have our nation in tact during the Tribulation, and the fallen angels will be spared an eternity of torment. We'll all benefit."

Sandy asked, "What happens then?"

Dr. Sveade said, "After the Tribulation, Jesus and the believers who have gone on to Heaven at the Rapture will return and rule the Earth for one-thousand years. That's called the Thousand-Year Reign of Christ, or the Millennial Reign. To this point, no one has been able to determine what God's plan for the United States will be, but if we've served as a bastion of Christianity during the reign of Satan and the Antichrist in the Tribulation, we hope Jesus will hold us in high regard for the next thousand years. We're not worried about what will happen to America with Christ in charge. We're just trying to find a way to survive the Tribulation. And that could start any day now."

Dall asked, "If you're believers and won't be here during the Tribulation, why do you care what happens to the United States under the Antichrist anyway?"

Dr. Sveade shrugged his shoulders. "Let's just say that none of us can be sure that we'll be taken, and even if we're not here, we'll have loved ones here on earth that we'll care about. If they can survive the Antichrist, there's a chance that they'll convert once they see what he really is, and make it to Heaven someday."

Sandy was completely confused, but Dall searched his memory for any validation of Dr. Sveade's theory. He shook his head and asked, "What is this demon's name, and why is he hiding in an Amish district here in the middle of nowhere?"

Dr. Sveade wiped the sweat from his brow. "When we last heard from him, Albert Hess said his name was Gaal. The Hebrew meaning of Gaal is *Contempt and Abomination*. And he's not hiding. He is invisible to mortals, so he can go anywhere he wants unseen."

Dall said, "You know, Doctor, those fallen angels had one name when they were in Heaven. When God cast them out of Heaven, He gave them different names. Their name reflects their true nature. The fact that this guy's name means contempt and abomination should tell you that he can't be trusted."

"I'm aware of that, Dall. His Heavenly names were Malak, meaning *Messenger* and Helsa, meaning *Devoted to God*. But whatever his nature is, we'll have to build safeguards into our alliance with him and his followers if he's successful. We're not going to blindly throw caution to the wind."

"Okay, Doctor, so why here? Why is he here in an Amish district in eastern, Missouri?"

"We're not sure, Dall. After Himmler committed suicide, Gaal disappeared. We talked to several other high-ranking Nazis during the Nuremburg trials, but they refused to talk to us unless we could get their charges dropped, or at least guarantee them that they wouldn't get the death penalty. Because of our secrecy we couldn't, and they were hanged. We believe that once Himmler killed himself, Gaal lost his best chance of forming an alliance with Germany. I think he just disappeared until he could identify an emerging world power that might be strong enough to defeat the Antichrist and all the other nations under his command. That country is the United States. I think he picked the Amish because they have no central headquarters and each district is an independent body. I think he picked this district because this bishop administers his congregation in a manner that best suits Gaal. Let's face it. It's easy to hide in an Amish district. They have no oversight from a higher power, they staunchly refuse to talk to the local, state or federal authorities, and they live out in rural areas where they're isolated from discerning people who might recognize him for what he is."

Sandy asked, "What difference does it make if someone else recognizes him?"

Dall said, "Because once a person becomes a true believer in Christ, the Holy Spirit indwells that person. A demon is still subject to the authority of Jesus Christ, and any believer can cast out a demon by calling on the name and authority of Christ. Amish districts are small and isolated. A demon could easily identity the non-believers and avoid the believers. He could move around the district freely and indefinitely. And most people would never believe an Amish person was demon-possessed."

Dall turned to Dr. Sveade and said, "But he couldn't hide from Satan. One of Satan's powers is that he knows what all the demons are up to, so why would he allow Gaal to hide out here and plot to overthrow him?"

"I can't answer that, Dall. My theory is that the war has already begun. I think the demons are choosing up sides, and that Satan is afraid. Keep in mind that access to God will be lost very soon. If Satan can stall a little longer, the war will be pointless. Even if his opponents win, they'll not be allowed access to the throne of God. That might be enough to convince them to abandon their plans and throw in with Satan."

Sandy asked, "Afraid? Afraid of what? He can't be afraid of Gaal. Can't Satan bind him and keep him from leading the other demons against him?"

Dr. Sveade said, "I don't think it's Gaal that frightens Satan. It may be the sheer number of his followers. What we don't know is what percentage of the demonic realm is under Gaal's control. If he controls a much larger percentage than Satan does, Satan may be hesitant to start the war. He's probably hoping to stall the actual battle until the Rapture hits. He may even be afraid of God. It may be that God Himself has approached Gaal and offered redemption to him and his followers if they can overthrow Satan. I don't know why He would. He is capable of dealing with Satan Himself, unless maybe He wants the repentant demons to proof themselves. No one knows for sure. Things that happen in the spiritual world are unseen by man. The possibilities are endless. All we know is that if there is a war in the demon world, and if Satan can be overthrown and Gaal makes a pact with someone here on Earth to help him combat the Antichrist, we want that pact to be with the United States."

Sandy asked, "Are other countries searching for Gaal?"

Dr. Sveade said, "Yes, but after World War II our project went deep-black. We and the Brits seized all the records of our activities and kept the whole project top secret. We especially wanted to lock the Russians out. Even though they were allies at that time, we could see that if they had Gaal on their side, they would try to conquer the world just like the Nazis did."

Sandy asked, "What does deep-black mean?"

"It means that no one knows about us, and our funding is hidden deep inside other funded programs within the federal budget, military line-items to be specific. At any rate, other countries are looking for Gaal, but we hope to find him first. When members of our original project team passed away, we didn't replace them in order to keep the core team small. When we determined that it might be Gaal operating in this district, we were ecstatic. We've intentionally kept the circle of those in the information loop small to avoid a leak. The last thing we need is foreign operatives in here snooping around."

Dall asked, "So why did you pick me to confront him. He'll never approach me. I'm a believer."

"True, Dall, you are, but your expertise in these matters means you'll be the one to spot him if he's here. We believe he's in this district because of the way our victims were killed. They were killed by bare hands with super-human strength. When we saw the condition of our first victim, we knew he had to be killed by a demon. We then began an earnest search for someone with your credentials. The condition of our second victim confirmed that Gaal is here. I would have gone in myself, but I'm far too old to endure the abuse and physical labor."

"Gaal may not even be here, Doctor. It could be another demon. There are Biblical accounts of demons tearing mortals to pieces. That kind of strength and viciousness is common among all demons."

"True, but in this case we believe Gaal is our killer. Judging by the restraint that he's shown in the murders, and the fact that he's exercised restraint in the number of people that he's killed, we think he's trying to keep a low profile. As bad as our victims were torn up, they could have been completely dismembered. He killed them, but left their bodies in tact so the local authorities would believe they were killed by a very strong human. And the attack on you last night demonstrated restraint."

"I don't agree, Doctor. I think he backed off because he sensed the Holy Spirit. I think God restrained him."

"You may be right, Dall, but we won't know until you locate him and determine if he is indeed Gaal. If he's another demon, we'll still want to talk to him. He may be able to help us locate Gaal if he is one of his followers. So, get out there and find him. We want to talk to him no matter who he is."

Dall and Sandy looked into each other's battered faces. As they turned to leave, Smith said, "You both need to be aware of something. Dall, I know you're a believer, but you don't have the option to drive Gaal away just because you don't agree with our mission. Don't get self-righteous on us here. You're job is to find him and bring him to us. Leave your personal convictions out of it. Sandy, you're to see that he does that. If he tries to back out or cast Gaal out of the district, intervene and call me immediately."

Sandy was still in shock, but said angrily, "You were out of line, Sir! You were completely out of line to bring an agent and a C.I. into an undercover assignment like this without thoroughly briefing them on every aspect of the case. Getting me in here under false pretenses, then threatening me if I try to back out when I learn the real agenda is completely unprofessional. When this is over, I'm making a formal complaint against you with the director."

Smith shrugged his shoulders and said calmly, "That's okay, Agent Parsons. If we're successful, neither the director nor the President will care what means I've used. The reward for our country will be so great that I'll be a hero no matter what tactics I've employed. If we fail..., well, let's just say that none of us will be around to care what anyone says."

Sandy walked up to Smith and reached under his jacket. She gripped the butt of his pistol and broke the thumb-snap of the shoulder rig. She ripped his pistol out of the holster and said, "This won't do me any good against Gaal, but I'm taking it anyway. And another thing, I deeply resented you slamming me against a wall and threatening me back at Quantico." She pulled the hammer back to full-cock and pointed the muzzle at Smith's face. "If you ever touch me again, I'll kill you." Smith merely smiled and slowly nodded his head once.

As they walked away, neither spoke. Sandy said, "I see now why you don't trust the F.B.I. I'm scared, Dall. I've never been in a situation where I didn't think I could get myself out of it."

Dall said, "I know the feeling. I'm not worried about my safety with Gaal, but you'd better stick close to me. I don't think he was after me last night. It's you he wants."

Sandy took Dall's arm and said, "I'm sorry we've put you in this position. I'm on your side."

Dall didn't respond. Sandy asked, "You don't believe me?"

Dall shrugged his shoulders. "No. You knew when you took that pistol out of Smith's holster that it wouldn't do you any good against Gaal, so the only person you could be planning to use it on is me if I try to walk out. Those were your orders from Smith. He didn't use those exact words, but his intent was for you to intervene with extreme prejudice, and you can't do that without a pistol. I noticed that Smith didn't try to stop you when you took it."

Sandy released his arm and extended the butt of the pistol. "Yes, but I won't follow them. If we find ourselves on the run or trying to avoid those snipers, we may wish we had a gun. If it'll make you trust me, here, you hold on to it. I trust you."

Dall didn't take the pistol. After they had walked another twenty yards, he reached over and gently took Sandy's hand.

Sandy released Dall's hand and looked puzzled. She said, "Last night after the little girl had shaken the barn, she stepped back and took a deep breath. What was she smelling? You can't tell me that a demon lives on an Amish farm and gets off on the smell of horse manure."

"I don't know, Sandy, but I've read evidence that there are a couple of smells that demons enjoy. One of them is our fear."

"Well, she certainly had plenty of that to enjoy. What is the other?"

"Our blood."

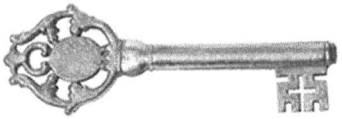

"I am he that liveth, and was dead; and behold, I am alive for evermore, Amen; and have the keys of hell and of death." Revelation 1:18

Sheriff Holden and Casey hurried to intercept the little girl. She was standing on a hillside watching them approach. They lost sight of her for only about ten seconds when they descended into a dried creek-bed. As they climbed out on the other side, Casey stopped. He looked around and asked, "Where did she go, Jerry? She was right here a few seconds ago."

Jerry looked around and scratched the back of his head. "I don't know. She couldn't have gotten into the timber this fast. She must be lying down in the grass to hide from us. Come on, let's walk a little farther."

As they reached the center of the field, Jerry looked around and said between gasps for air, "She's gone, Casey. She couldn't have run that fast, but she's just gone."

Casey heaved as he breathed heavily. He looked around and started to tell the sheriff how spooked he was, but stopped when he saw the little girl two hundred yards directly behind them. All he could say was, "Oh crap!"

Sheriff Holden turned around and saw the child. He said, "This can't be, Casey. She was right here a minute ago. No one can move that fast. That's got to be another girl."

"Another girl or not, boss, she's standing between us and the car! I vote we circle around her and leave her alone! Look at her! She's not even tired! She's just standing there, staring at us! And she's got a weird glow about her. Something is seriously wrong here. I think we're seeing what our murder victims saw just before they were killed. Let's get out of here!"

Sheriff Holden breathed heavily and said, "I think you're right. I'm no expert, but I've never known a kid who could move that fast. Come on; let's head off to the south. We'll work our way around her and come back another night with some help."

The sheriff and Thurman were well into their late fifties, and the brisk pace over hilly terrain had seriously taxed their stamina. They panted as they hurried back to the car. As they broke out of a small stand of timber, they stopped suddenly. Twenty yards in front of them was the little girl in a white gown.

Her gown glowed from within, but her face remained dark and nondescript. Fear gripped the two men as Casey panted, "Young lady, are you supposed to be out this late at night?"

The girl didn't move. Only her gown and long blond hair moved in the gentle, humid breeze. Casey asked, "Listen, sweetheart, we can help you if you're lost." Still the girl did not move.

As Casey talked, Jerry studied the girl hard. She had a twitch in her facial muscles. He then shifted his attention to the dark forms that circled them and mumbled in an unintelligible dialect. He finally asked, "Who are you, and why are you following us?"

As the little girl slowly stepped closer, the men noticed an unnatural, almost mechanical movement of her limbs. Both men stepped back in fear. In the soft voice of a young man, she said, "I AM HE WHOM YOU SEEK. YOU WISH TO SPEAK TO ME OF PAST SINS."

The mature male voice coming from the child completely unnerved both men. Casey took a deep breath to overcome his fear and stepped toward the girl to protect the sheriff. In a flash the girl closed the gap and grabbed Casey by his waistband, then lifted him off the ground. She tilted him in mid-air, then shifted her grip to his throat and slammed him to the ground, knocking the wind out of his lungs. He fought to remain conscious, knowing that if he passed out, she would kill him.

The sheriff reached for his pistol, but stopped when the girl held up her hand. She said, "STOP, YE OF NO FAITH. YOU WEAR NO SPIRITUAL ARMOR."

Holden could not stop his trembling hand. He unconsciously fumbled with the thumb-snap on his holster until it finally broke open. His shaking fingers gripped his pistol and jerked it out.

In the blink of an eye, the girl closed on him and seized his wrist. With bone-crushing pressure she squeezed his arm and twisted it so the pistol was pointed skyward. He jerked off a shot, hoping the noise would frighten the child and cause her to release him. As his arm broke with a loud pop, his fingers opened and the pistol fell to the ground.

The pain in the sheriff's arm was crippling. He fell back beside Casey and rolled on the ground as he cradled his broken arm. Casey thought about pulling his pistol, but knew he'd never clear leather before the girl would break his arm, or worse.

In her unnatural voice, the girl said, "YOU COME SEEKING THAT WHICH YOU ARE FORBIDDEN TO KNOW. I KNOW OF YOUR PLANS."

Casey and the sheriff struggled to their feet with the intent to run, but the girl stopped them. "I WON'T HARM YOU IF YOU SPEAK. IF YOU RUN OR RAISE HANDS AGAINST ME, YOU WILL PERISH."

Holden staggered as he struggled to maintain his balance. Casey held him up and asked, "Who are you?"

"I AM NOT FOR YOU TO KNOW. I HAVE HEARD YOU SPEAK AMONG YOURSELVES. YOU ARE HERE TO LEARN HOW THE AMISH MEN DIED. THERE ARE OTHERS HERE TO LEARN THE SAME. YOU ARE NOT PERMITTED HERE."

Casey's voice quivered as he said, "They're federal agents, but we have jurisdiction here, too! We simply want to know what happened to them, but we now have a pretty good idea! They met you!"

The child quickly jerked her head into a puzzled cant as if Casey should have known. "IT WAS NOT I. THERE ARE OTHERS HERE WHO DO GREAT EVIL TO FRIGHTEN AND CONFOUND."

The girl showed no emotion as she leaned her head back and drew in a deep breath, savoring the scent of their fear. She held her breath as she rolled her head from side to side, allowing their scent to linger on the back of her tongue and carry her mind to the edge of delirium. When she finally exhaled, she stepped toward the frightened men, hoping to give her heightened senses a chaser of the scent of blood. She only stopped short when a voice from behind her said, "I'm the one you should be talking to, Gaal. They can't do you any good."

The girl turned quickly and saw Dall and Sandy standing twenty feet away. Dall asked, "Who are you guys?"

Casey said in a frightened tone as he pointed to the little girl, "I'm Chief Deputy Thurman! This is Sheriff Holden! Who are you and what the hell is that?"

Dall tried to hide the fear in his voice. "I'm Dall Roberts, Sheriff. And she's the reason people are afraid of the dark. We saw you going after her. We'd hoped to get to you first, but as you can see, she's quick. It may be a good idea for you and me to talk later, but for now, you need to leave."

Casey and Holden wasted no time. The dark forms parted and they hurried off toward their car. Dall looked at the girl and asked, "Are you Gaal?"

The child stepped toward Dall and stared at him with her head tilted in a curious cant. She drew in a deep breath as she tried to discern the presence of the Holy Spirit in Dall's soul. With a reverent fear, she slowly nodded.

Dall said, "We know why you're here. If we're going to accomplish our goals, we have to talk freely. We can't lie to each other, although that's your true nature."

The girl conspicuously looked Dall and Sandy up and down. Gaal said, "YES, I'VE HEARD YOU SPEAK. I KNOW WHY YOU ARE HERE. I WAS THERE AT THE WELL WHEN YOU SPOKE WITH DR. SVEADE."

Sandy clung tightly to Dall's arm as he said, "You tried to kill us last night. If you knew why we were here, why did you attack us?"

The girl's face became more clearly defined and illuminated. A mischievous grin crept across her chiseled features. "I MEANT YOU NO HARM. I WAS MERELY TRYING TO SEPARATE YOU. I WANT TO SPEAK WITH THE WOMAN ALONE."

Dall felt an urgency to establish his dominance. He looked behind him at the dark, nondescript beings that circled them. "That won't happen, Gaal. She'll always be with me. You will not harm her or attempt to talk to her alone, do you understand?"

The little girl lowered her head and smiled submissively. Dall pivoted to keep the girl in front of him as he asked, "Are you alone in the little girl?"

Gaal said, "WE ARE LEGIONS."

Dall urgently backed away from the girl and pulled Sandy with him. Sandy asked, "What's wrong?"

Dall leaned into her and said in a frightened tone, "Legions means hundreds or thousands! If that is Gaal, he's got lots of his followers with him!"

Sandy asked, "Are they all there inside her?"

"I don't know! They may be! They're certainly all around us! We've got to retreat from this!"

Dall said, "Gaal, I'll only talk to you alone. You know where we're staying. Come alone next time." He and Sandy turned and hurried off toward Litchfield's barn. As they hurried past the spot where the sheriff had fallen, Dall bent over and picked up the sheriff's pistol. When he stood back up, his fear was confirmed. The wall of dark figures parted so he and Sandy could pass. These spirits were like the one that he'd seen in Litchfield's barn loft.

Sandy stuck close to Dall and looked over her shoulder. She said, "She's not following, Dall. Why did you want to get away?"

"I don't know how many demons are with him. When we talk to him about our proposition, we don't want to be overheard. It's likely that one or more of the demons with him tonight might betray us to Satan. I think Gaal will talk more openly if he isn't overheard. Besides, I'm afraid I wouldn't be able to protect you with that many demons around. If they managed to separate us, you'd be killed, or at least indwelled."

As they hurried across the fields to the barn, Sandy asked, "So, Dall, is Dr. Sveade correct about what demons are?"

Dall panted as he kept up the fast pace. "Yes, but there's some debate over what demons actually are. Some believe that they're simply the fallen angels that were cast out of Heaven with Satan. As far as I can tell, angels were created in Genesis sometime after God created the heavens, but before he created the earth. There are some scholars who believe as Dr. Sveade does, that fallen angels and demons are different beings. There is a belief that some angels were appointed watchers over men. Genesis chapter 6 refers to them as the sons of God. Whether they were actually watchers or merely angels, they bred mortal women and had hybrid children that were giants called Nephilim. I think Dr. Sveade is right; these giants are actually another kind of demon, different from the fallen angles. Either way, they're no one to mess with. They're all evil to the core and immensely powerful."

"How many demons or fallen angels are there?"

"Hard to tell about the Nephilim. They were all eliminated in the flood or shortly afterwards, either killed if they were mortal or bound by God if they were angelic, then thrown into the dark pit. As for the fallen angels, the Bible doesn't say for sure. Before the earth was created, Satan became dissatisfied with his position in Heaven and wanted to be like God. God cast him out of Heaven along with all of Satan's followers. That was one third of the entire angelic realm. We don't know how many there were, but the 5th chapter of Revelations speaks of the number of angels still in Heaven at the time that John was given a glimpse of Heaven. When he wrote Revelations, he said there are ten thousand times ten thousand and thousands more, so I think that means that they're uncountable. There could easily be billions of angels left in Heaven after the fall. So if one third of all the angels were cast out with Satan, there could easily be billions of fallen angels. There could easily be hundreds or thousands of demons for every human being on earth."

Sandy thought for a few seconds, then asked, "So if God cast out one third of the angels, then there are twice as many angels in Heaven?"

"Yes." Sandy again looked over her shoulder. Dall said, "Don't bother looking behind us. If Gaal wants us, he can be in front of us in a heartbeat."

She said, "So you got us out of there to protect me?"

"You're not a believer, Sandy. You're not indwelled with the Holy Spirit. You have no protection against demons. You can easily be indwelled or killed by them. That's what Gaal meant when he told the sheriff that he wore no spiritual armor. Smith did you a real disservice by putting you in here."

Sandy sighed in frustration. "I should probably rethink that whole salvation thing." She caressed his hand and said, "Thanks. It's nice to know that you care for me, too."

Once at the barn, Dall spent some time petting and talking to Lady and Tramp. They responded to his gentle touch and calming voice with nudges from their noses. Each day that passed brought them closer as friends. Dall checked them closely for any fresh whelps or cuts. Each one he found made him want to kill Litchfield and his son. Before retiring he made one final check of the loft to make sure they were alone. Seeing nothing did not put his mind to rest. There could have been a hundred unclean spirits there and he would not have seen them.

Dall slept hard throughout the night. He awoke early and again found Sandy next to him in his bed. He looked through the cracks of the barn wall and saw that it was still dark. There was still some time before Litchfield would be calling them for breakfast.

He reached over to his table and picked up the sheriff's pistol so Litchfield wouldn't find it. He sat up and slid it under the mattress, then stood and walked out of his stall. He brushed the hay from his chest and shoulders and went to the cistern for some water.

After he'd washed his face and brushed his teeth, he laid back down beside Sandy. As dawn broke slowly over the horizon, Dall watched her sleep in the soft light. Even with her black eye, he marveled at her beauty and wondered if she was tough enough for this assignment. He wondered if she was capable of dealing with Smith and Waters. He wondered if she'd be able to control Gaal. He wondered if she could endure the abuse from Litchfield. He wondered if she would kill him if he tried to send Gaal away."

Sandy stirred from her sleep and stared back into his eyes. Nothing was said for a long time, then she sighed and said, "I guess I'd better get out of your bed or we'll get another beating."

Dall nodded slowly. "Probably so." As they continued to stare into each other's eyes Sandy caught herself being drawn closer to him.

As their noses touched, she put her hand on his chest to stop herself. "We should get ready for breakfast. Litchfield will be here any time." Dall stood and let her up.

While Dall stroked Lady and Tramp, Sandy brushed her hair and rolled it up into a bun. She said, "There's no need to find another family to live with, Dall. We've found Gaal and we can leave as soon as we hook him up with Dr. Sveade."

Dall shook his head. "I don't like this, Sandy. I don't like any of it. We're way out of our league trying to match wits with Gaal."

She looked at him suspiciously and asked, "Why?"

"Look, Gaal said he was there when Sveade briefed us. He knows good and well what their plans are. He already knows how to contact Sveade and Smith if he wants to. He's a demon for God's sake, Sandy. He could have contacted any number of high-ranking elected officials or any of our military commanders at any time. He doesn't need us. He's got another agenda here."

Sandy stopped combing her hair and asked, "What could it be?"

Dall thought as he stroked Tramp's nose. "I don't know. We'll probably never know. He's a demon. It's his nature to lie and deceive. And since we can't see what goes on in the spirit world, we can't verify anything he tells us. There may not be a war between the demons. There might not even be a demon named Gaal. For all we know, this demon is really Satan pretending to want to approach God for redemption. He could be trying to get us to turn our military over to him so he can help the Antichrist. This may be only one small part of Satan's master plan."

"I am he that liveth, and was dead; and behold, I am alive for evermore, Amen; and have the keys of hell and of death." **Revelation 1:18**

Mrs. Litchfield served fried brisket and eggs, boiled potatoes and cornbread for breakfast, all too heavily salted. Dall and Sandy hurried through their meal and waited for Preacher to bring the hay wagon around. Sandy cringed as sounds of a leather strap striking horse flesh emanated from the barn. Dall said, "Sandy, guzzle that milk down and let's be ready when he gets here. He's not in a good mood today."

To their surprise, Preacher drove up to the front porch, but he wasn't on the hay wagon. He was sitting behind Lady on a contraption with a long sickle bar. He said, "We're finished with the south field. I'll be mowing hay today, so you'll be working with Devin. He'll give you jobs to do, so pay attention to him. I'll be back at lunch."

As Preacher pulled away, Devin stepped out on the porch and stared at Sandy's breasts and slurred, "Pa says ya gots ta do what I say. If'n you don't, I'm sposed to lash you. English man, you go out dare in da garden. I want ya to pull dem weeds and pick da rocks out each row, den go on ta'nother. Girl, you come with me. We gonna to clean stalls in da barn."

Sandy stared at Dall in fear. She said, "I want to stay with my brother, Devin. Can I work in the garden?"

Devin became angry and kicked Sandy in the back of the leg. "Pa says you gots to do what I say! I'll lash you good if'n you don't! Mister, you get to work! Girl, you come with me!"

Dall stood to defend Sandy, but looked over his shoulder. Preacher had not yet gotten out of sight. He winked at her and said, "Go on, Sandy, it'll be okay. You know how to clean out a stall, don't you? Just use that pitchfork in the corner by Lady's stall. That fork is sharp and will make things a lot easier."

Sandy nodded as Dall's implication sank in. She struggled to keep up as Devin took her by the arm and pulled her toward the barn.

Dall went to the garden and pretended to work. He kept his ears focused on the barn in case Sandy called him. Sandy entered the barn and immediately grabbed the pitchfork. She stepped into Lady's stall and began throwing fork-loads of soiled hay and manure into the manure spreader that Preacher had parked close by.

Devin leaned against the wall and studied Sandy as he put his hand inside his trousers and massaged himself. Sandy pretended to not notice. Devin said, "You pretty, girl. I'm gonna be takin me a wife someday."

Sandy almost got sick. She stabbed the pitchfork into the ground and leaned on the handle as she panted. "Listen, Devin, I've seen how you look at me and I don't like it. I don't know what you and your father have planned, but we're not your whipping posts. We're here to learn the Amish ways so we can be baptized into the Amish faith. Don't get any ideas about me. Your father is our teacher, not you. You stay away from me."

Devin showed no emotion. Sandy didn't know if he truly didn't care about her or if he was just too dense to understand what she had told him. She went back to work and tried to ignore him.

After another few minutes, Devin's arousal was conspicuous. He glared at her with wide-eyed lust and said, "I'm gonna to marry you, girl. It's okay if we love each other now. If we're gonna be married someday, it's okay to make a baby."

Sandy looked out the front of the barn to see if she could see the garden. She couldn't, so she climbed over the stall divider into Tramps stall. When Devin came after her, she positioned the pitchfork for a forward thrust. Devin swept is aside and wrestled it away from her. She climbed out of Tramp's stall and ran toward the door, hoping to get Dall's attention.

She searched the garden, but Dall must have been in the corn; she couldn't see him. Before she could yell, Devin grabbed the back of her dress and jerked her backward with all his strength. She flew across the barn and slid ten feet after she had landed on her back. She yelled, but he was on her before she had stopped sliding.

Devin tore at her dress and grunted like a hog as he ripped the front of her dress open. Sandy struggled to her feet and put her hands together in front of her sternum, then drove them vertically between Devin's arms. As she broke his grip, she thrust the heel of her right hand to his nose and knocked him off his feet.

Devin began crying like an angry child and struggled to his feet. Sandy scrambled to her stall, hoping to retrieve Smith's pistol from under her mattress. She knew the assignment would be over once she exposed the pistol, but she didn't care. Allowing herself to be raped by this disgusting animal was not a sacrifice she was prepared to make for the good of the mission.

She ran her hand frantically under the mattress, but Devin grabbed her hair and dragged her out of the stall before she could find the pistol. He turned her around and punched her in the face with a full roundhouse. She hit the ground semi-conscious and didn't move.

Devin stepped out of his trousers and stood over Sandy. Her blurred vision cleared, but not in time to regain her faculties. Devin bent over her and pulled her dress up to her chest.

Overwhelming fear gripped Sandy as her head cleared. She raised her leg to kick Devin in the face, but missed as he raised his fist high over his head to render her completely unconscious.

Before he could punch Sandy, two hands gripped his neck and pulled him backward. Dall had grabbed him by his throat and pulled him to his feet. Two punches later, Devin was unconscious on his back."

Sandy struggled to sit up. Dall helped her up and brushed her off. "I'm sorry I didn't get here sooner, Sandy. Are you alright?"

She shook her head and said, "I don't know. He really rang my bell."

Dall turned to examine Devin, but Preacher stormed into the barn and yelled, "What have you done to my boy?"

Litchfield's sudden appearance made it clear that the whole scenario had been staged by him to allow Devin to be alone
with Sandy. Dall said, "Devin tried to rape my sister, Preacher.
Look at her, she's been beaten and had her clothes torn off."

Litchfield flew into a rage. He yelled as he attacked Dall, "My boy would never attack anyone! Your whore sister threw herself at him, and you helped her! If that boy is injured, I'll kill both of you!"

Litchfield grabbed a board and began beating Dall. Sandy screamed, "Litchfield, stop! He was only protecting me!"

When he wouldn't stop, Sandy jumped on him to save Dall. When Litchfield turned the board on Sandy, Dall charged in and took the board away from him. Dall said, "No more, Preacher! No more beatings! Take us to the bishop and let him decide our fate! Beating us to death was not one of your mandates when he sent us here!"

Litchfield stopped when Dall took the board away from him. He turned to Devin and helped him to his feet, then led him out of the barn. Dall said, "I think that was a mistake, Sandy. We weren't supposed to raise our hands against them. The bishop will likely kick us out of the district."

Sandy examined the large defensive whelps and bruises on her arms. She cried as she said angrily, "Screw him! That psychotic ●●● of a ●●●●● is no more a preacher than I am! Let them kick us out! We've found Gaal and don't need them anymore!"

"That's not true, Sandy. We haven't seen him since last night. He might not show for weeks. We've got to stay here till then."

They retreated to Dall's stall and examined each other's wounds. Both were severely bruised and swollen in the face. Sandy said, "I'm calling Smith. We can't stay here."

"You'd better think about that, Sandy. What's he going to do for us? He can't come in here and move us to another farm. If he has to come in here, we may not like the results." Sandy sat on Dall's mattress and cried as he went to the cistern for some water.

When he returned, Dall soaped a wash cloth and gently cleaned Sandy's face. She had no lacerations serious enough to require sutures, so he wiped off her neck, chest and arms.

When he rinsed out the wash cloth and soaped it again, Sandy took it from him and cleaned his face. He was cut and swollen, but fortunately Litchfield had not broken open the laceration on Dall's chin that Sandy had closed the night before.

She rinsed the soap out of the wash cloth and gently pressed the wet cloth against Dall's swollen face. He closed his eyes and moaned, "Man that feels good." When he opened his eyes, he was shocked to see Sandy's face about an inch from his. He leaned his head back, but Sandy pressed closer. As they looked deep into each other's eyes, they fell together in a deep kiss.

Sandy wrapped her arms around his neck and pulled him close. He grabbed her waist and pulled her hips against his. After a minute of heated foreplay, he pulled her close and hugged her to catch his breath. He asked, "Isn't there some obscure rule in the F.B.I.'s S.O.P. manual about agents kissing their C.I.?"

Sandy breathed heavily as she kissed his neck. "There is, and it's not obscure. It's very clear and specific. It's career suicide for an agent to become personally involved with a C.I. I'll be drummed out of the bureau and probably never be able to work in law enforcement again."

"We shouldn't have done that, Sandy. We're in a real bad spot here and likely to find ourselves at odds with each other. I won't like you very much if you shoot me."

Sandy sighed heavily. "I won't shoot you. Just promise me that you won't send Gaal away. Let's just hook him up with Dr. Sveade and get out of this. Once you're not my C.I. anymore, we can do whatever we want."

Dall gently pushed Sandy away. She asked, "What's wrong? You do want me, don't you?"

He nodded. "More than anything in the world. It's just that I'm branded right now. It's not as simple as getting this mission completed. I've got charges hanging over my head in Houston. You can't help me with that. If you try to interfere, you'll be terminated and prosecuted for obstruction of justice."

Sandy said, "Listen, Dall, Smith only charged you to get you to come on this assignment with me. After this is over, it's not his decision if they proceed with the charges. That's the decision of the U.S. Attorney in Houston. He'd never go through with charges on a fabricated case like this. And I won't interfere personally. I'll just hire you the best attorney in Texas to do it for me."

"I hope not, but if he does, he'll be going through it alone. I won't be there. I've made up my mind, Sandy; I can't go to prison, not even for a short time. When this is over, I'm leaving. Don't try to stop me."

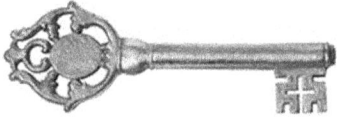

"I am he that liveth, and was dead; and behold, I am alive for evermore, Amen; and have the keys of hell and of death." **Revelation 1:18**

An hour later, Dall and Sandy were startled by the thunder of horse hoofs at the front of the barn. Seconds later, Litchfield and several other men stormed into the barn and grabbed Dall by his arms. As they dragged him outside, Litchfield yelled, "You should have taking the lashing from me, Englisher! You'll never be accepted into the Amish faith by making false allegations against good Amish boys like Devin! And you'll never get away with raising your evil hand against an ordained preacher of God's word!"

Sandy screamed as the men began to beat Dall. They beat him until he collapsed to the ground, then used their boots and boards on him until he could no longer move. She ran to her mattress to get Smith's pistol, but two of the men grabbed her and made her watch Dall's beating. The last images that Dall saw were the dark forms circling the men and mumbling encouragement in an unknown tongue.

When Dall could no longer protect himself, it became clear that the men were going to beat him to death. One of the men who had been holding his arms released him when he collapsed. He stood back and no longer took part in the beating. As the frenzy escalated, he finally stepped in front of Dall and yelled, "Okay, brothers, we were called here to lash the English man, not kill him. You're going too far."

Litchfield stepped up and yelled, "Step aside, Brother Straus! I'm commissioned by God and the bishop to lash the evil spirit out of this Englisher! If I can't do it by myself, I'm completely within my rights to enlist the help of other members! You're interference is heresy!"

Abel gritted his teeth and growled, "That may be, Preacher, but I'll have to hear it from the bishop! Now unless you're willing to try to lash me, you'd better back off, because this Englisher will not take another stripe!"

The other men saw the anger in Abel's eyes and wisely backed away. Each had serious doubts that they would be able to handle Abel in a fight, even with their collective strength. They got on their horses and rode off.

The two men released Sandy and she ran to Dall. When she slid to a stop on her knees beside him, she pried open his eyes and found him unresponsive. She checked his pulse and heart rate and yelled, "He's almost dead! We've got to get him to a doctor!"

Litchfield turned and walked to the house when he realized he may have gone too far. Abel went to the cistern and got a bucket of water. He poured some over Dall's face while Sandy ran to the barn and got her cell phone. After a long plea, Waters said, "We warned you, Parsons. No rescue. If Roberts dies, you're on your own." When Waters disconnected, she stood frozen in disbelief. Smith and Waters had told her that there would be no rescue, but the gravity of the matter hadn't hit home until now. She slowly pocketed the phone and went back to Dall."

Abel said, "I'm sorry, young lady. I didn't want it to go this far. Preacher Litchfield is over zealous in his lashing. This was not right. I'm ashamed that I had any part in it."

Sandy asked, "Is there a doctor here in the district? He's got some bad head injuries. He may have a fractured skull. He'll die without medical attention."

"No, but there is someone who can help. I'll take you to my farm." Abel ran to the barn and hitched Tramp to Litchfield's buggy while Sandy gathered up their things. After he'd pulled the buggy around, he picked Dall up like a small child and placed him in the seat. He got in the seat, then wrapped his huge arm around Dall and cradled him against his side. He yelled, "Missey, climb up on my horse and hang on. Just let her have the reins. She'll follow me."

Sandy threw their bags into the buggy and climbed up on Abel's mare. She asked, "Won't Litchfield be mad if we take his buggy?"

Abel said, "Yes, ma'am, but he'll have to take it up with me. You folks have taken your last lashing in the name of God." He slapped the reins against Tramp's back and raced toward his farm with his mare running close behind and Sandy clinging to the saddle-horn."

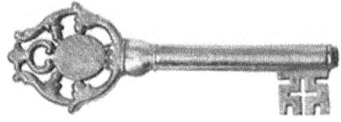

"I am he that liveth, and was dead; and behold, I am alive for evermore, Amen; and have the keys of hell and of death." **Revelation 1:18**

Sheriff Holden was in his office when Agents Smith and Waters asked the receptionist to see him. Holden invited them in and offered them seats, but they refused. Smith asked, "How's your arm, Sheriff?"

Holden said, "A little sore, but I'll manage. You didn't come here to check on my arm, Agent Smith, so what can I do for you?"

Waters couldn't be quiet any longer. He said angrily, "You can do as I told you and keep your nose out of this investigation."

Smith held his hand up and stopped Waters. He calmly said, "What Agent Waters is saying, Sheriff, is that our spotters saw you and Mr. Thurman out on the Massey farm last night. We'd asked you nicely to stay out of this investigation; now I'm putting you on notice that you're interfering with a federal investigation. I'll have a court order this afternoon compelling you to stay out. Make yourself available to me this afternoon so I can serve it to you quietly without causing you any embarrassment with your constituents. I don't want to hurt your chances in the upcoming election."

Holden completely understood the subtle threat. Casey stepped into the office to support the sheriff. Holden smiled as he sat at his desk and leaned back. He put his feet up on his desk and said, "Absolutely, Agent Smith. Call me when you get your court order. I'll be waiting here for you. Or better yet, I'll save you a trip and come to you. Either way, there'll be reporters from every major news network in the mid-west with me. I'll at least have the ones from St. Louis, Chicago and Kansas

City there. As soon as you serve me, you can answer the questions that they'll have for you, like: Why is the F.B.I. ordering a local sheriff to stay out of a murder investigation where he had original jurisdiction? What is it about this murder that has attracted the interest of the federal government? Why have you targeted a peaceful faith like the Amish for investigation? Why have you put undercover agents in the Amish district? Why did agent Waters set up a field office in a little town like Shelbyville? How did the sheriff get his arm broken? Who or what broke his arm? What is it about this investigation that you're afraid the sheriff will uncover?"

Smith sighed and slowly lowered his stare to the floor. He'd known for a long time that Sheriff Holden was no bumpkin. Waters started toward the sheriff with clenched fists, but Casey grabbed his shirt and threw him back against the wall. Sheriff Holden motioned for Casey to stop and said, "That's okay, Casey, Agent Waters means me no harm. That would only create one more embarrassing question for Agent Smith to answer. "Why did an F.B.I. agent assault an injured sheriff in his own office?"

Waters adjusted his disheveled shirt as Holden continued, "Now, the press has been asking some pointed questions about the murders, but so far you've been pretty successful in dodging them. I think now they'll go over your head and go straight to the director. So go ahead, Agent Smith, serve your court order and put me in my place."

Waters again erupted in anger and started toward the sheriff's desk. Casey grabbed his arm and again threw him backward against the wall. Waters slumped to the floor in shock. When he sprang to his feet, he yelled, "You just assaulted a federal officer!" As he reached for his handcuffs, Smith said, "Dexter, go wait for me in the car."

Waters stared at Smith in shock. He yelled, "Sir, we have to show these fools who is in charge here!"

Smith looked sheepishly at Holden and said, "They've got the upper hand, Dexter. The key to the success of this mission, aside from Roberts, is secrecy. Go wait for me in the car."

Waters stormed angrily out of the office. Casey closed the door and leaned against the wall as Smith began. "Sheriff, I suppose there's nothing to be gained by leaving you out of the loop, but I simply can't discuss this case. If I told you the magnitude of this case and its far-reaching implications, you'd laugh at me."

Holden held up his broken arm and said, "Nothing you tell me would be unbelievable, Mr. Smith. After what happened to us last night, we'd believe anything."

Casey Thurman said, "Mr. Smith, I've played every sport there is. I've boxed professionally and fought the meanest men on this side of the Mississippi, and I've never been as scared as I was last night. That kid had the strength of ten men."

Smith nodded and smiled. "Frightening, isn't she?"

Holden removed his feet from his desk and leaned over it. He asked in a frightened tone. "Who was she? Don't tell me she was just a little girl. She manhandled us like rag dolls. What in God's name are you people up to?"

Smith shook his head and sighed, "We didn't create her, Sheriff. I assure you, we're just as scared as you are. We're doing our best to find her without getting ourselves hurt. I promise you, though; you and your deputies are not equipped to deal with this. I'm asking you to back off. I know you can make things rough for us with the media, but that'll absolutely kill us. I'm sorry that we haven't been completely up-front with you, but you can see why we couldn't get you involved in this. It was for your own safety. If this thing goes public, we'll never solve it, and we'll drive away the only person who can help us. That's what we're doing here. We're trying to hook up with the only person who can stop these killings and restrain that little girl."

Casey said, "You don't have to tell us what she is, Agent Smith. By the way she moved around those fields, slammed me into the dirt, broke Jerry's arm and spoke in a man's voice, we've figured out that she's not a little girl."

Smith rubbed his face in frustration. "No, Casey. No, she's not. She's a demon. We don't know if she is an actual little girl that the demon has indwelled or if that's just the form that he's taken. In either case, he would have killed you both if Dall hadn't intervened."

Holden asked, "Is Dall your undercover?" Smith nodded. "Well, please thank him for me. If he hadn't come along, we'd both be dead right now."

"That's right, Sheriff, so please do as I ask. Please stay out of this. You should be happy that we're in there. If we weren't here, you'd have to deal with her by yourselves, and I assure you that nothing in your arsenal would do you any good."

Holden stared at Casey to see if he had any more questions. When he shook his head, Holden stood and walked around his desk. He shook Smith's hand and asked, "You're not going to keep the loop, are you?"

Smith said, "I can't, Sheriff. All I can tell you is that our nation's future depends on this mission. It's that important."

Holden escorted Smith to the door. He said, "No promises, Agent Smith. I'll stall the media off, but I still have to answer calls for service in that district. If you're little arm-breaker causes any more problems, people will call me and I'll have to respond to calls for help. I'm statutorily mandated."

Smith turned to leave, but Sheriff Holden stopped him. "Oh, and Agent Smith, I'd appreciate it if you'd keep that Agent Waters out of our building. We've discussed it here in the office and we all agree. We hate his guts."

After Curly Slapp's little mishap on the radio, Casey Thurman took him out of the courthouse and put him on a desk at headquarters where he could keep a closer eye on him. Curly hated station duty because he couldn't strut around in public and profile for the high-school girls.

When Sheriff Holden escorted Smith out of his office, Curly ran to the lobby door and held it open for Smith. As Smith walked by, Curly glared up at him with his most intimidating Eastwood snarl, hoping to gain favor with the chief deputy.

Smith stopped and looked down at Curly as if he were looking at an annoying little dog who was growling at him from behind its owner's leg. He looked back at the sheriff, totally unimpressed. His puzzled expression conveyed the question, *is this cartoon character one of yours?*

No words needed to be spoken. Sheriff Holden shrugged his shoulders, feigned a pretentious smile and sighed heavily as he nodded his head. His unspoken embarrassment and apology was conveyed as Smith turned and walked out. Casey quietly whispered, "You know, Jerry, Smith may need some help with that demon. I think I know who we can send."

Curly beamed proudly at the sheriff, signaling that he had sufficiently intimidated Smith for him. When he gave the sheriff the thumbs-up sign, Holden said, "Yeah, Casey, you're right. Curly has been eyeing the young girls for a long time. I think that little girl is perfect for him."

Casey shook his head and whispered, "Nah, I don't think I could do that, not even to a demon."

EIGHT

BISHOP GORDAN PACED back and forth as Preacher Litchfield ranted about the irreverent way that Dall and Sandy had received their lashings. "I'm telling you, Bishop, that Englisher and his whore sister are trouble! They made slanderous allegations against my son, and he even raised an angry hand against him and smote him! When I defended the righteousness of God's child, the English man raised his hand against me! The fear of God is not in them! They will bring strife and contention among our brethren!"

Elder Dunlevy sat patiently through Litchfield's tirade, then said, "Brother Litchfield, I've witnessed your lashings before on both man and beast. I must say in defense of the Englisher that it's hard for someone not familiar with the purpose of lashing to passively stand by and take one, especially one as heavy-handed as you like to administer. Bishop Gordan put the Englishers in your charge to not only discipline them, but also to disciple them about our faith. How many hours did you spend teaching them about our faith? How many hours did you spend reading our Bible to them and explaining the Dordrecht Confession of Faith?"

Litchfield growled, "Lashing purges the soul by driving out the evil spirit within a sinful heart. Before the soul can be receptive to the Holy Spirit, the heart has to be purged of sin through the lashing of the flesh. Must I point out to you that the parable in the 13th chapter of Matthew illustrates the futility of sowing seed on stony or thorny ground? Before the seed of God's word can take root and grow in the heart of man, his hard and thorny heart must first be softened and made receptive to the seed. Before I could teach them or even allow them in my house, their sinful hearts had to be broken. That edict came directly from Bishop Gordan himself. Are you challenging the precepts and commandments of God?"

Bishop Gordan glared angrily at Elder Dunlevy in anticipation of his challenge to his authority. The elder knew that questioning the edicts of the bishop was tantamount to challenging the authority of God. He shook his head and said, "No, Preacher Litchfield, it's not God's law that I question, nor the authority of the bishop. It's your manipulation of that law to satisfy our own vicious temper that causes me concern. Once again, you've taken one piece of scripture out of context and misapplied it to suit your needs. That parable is not intended to be an endorsement of beating a man into believing God's word. Jesus himself never brutalized non-believers. He simply presented them the truth and allowed them to exercise their free will. This Englisher and his sister have already accepted God's word and precepts. Their hearts are receptive already. Beating them will not make them any more receptive. It only satisfies your lust for the infliction of pain." He turned to Gordan and said, "Bishop, with all due respect to Preacher Litchfield, it's only fair that we bring the Englishers before the elders before casting them out. I was against bringing them here in the first place, but once we've received them into our district, we have an obligation to treat them compassionately and fairly."

Gordan paced as he pondered his decision. He finally said, "Elder Dunlevy, I have witnessed Preacher Litchfield's application of God's wrath, and I find him to be completely appropriate in his use of the rod. But perhaps we should visit with the English man and woman. I'll make my decision then."

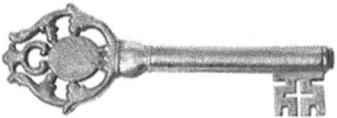

"I am he that liveth, and was dead; and behold, I am alive for evermore, Amen; and have the keys of hell and of death." **Revelation 1:18**

After Abel had put Dall gently on the bed, Dory and Sandy undressed him and wiped him down with cool water. Abel kept the little kids out of the room and gathered the things that Dory needed to care for Dall.

Isaac tried to entertain the little kids, but his anger toward his father was apparent. When Dory closed the bedroom door, Abel was forced to deal with Isaac. Isaac angrily asked, "What happened to that Englisher?"

Abel showed no emotion as he washed the blood from his hands and dried them. When he didn't answer, Isaac asked louder, "What happened, Dad? Didn't you get enough satisfaction with a strap? Did you have to kill him before you were convinced that you'd driven the evil from his heart? Did you enjoy it as much as you enjoyed lashing me?"

Every question cut Abel deeper. He fought through his rage and restrained his voice. "You're out of line challenging my actions, son. As head of this house, my actions are only subject to the scrutiny of the bishop. This is the sort of thing that I've been trying to get you to change. This contempt is what's causing you your problems."

"That's right, Dad, hide behind your position."

Abel sighed and recalled Bishop Clevenger's warning. He said, "Isaac, I'm trying to treat you like a man. I've not lashed you as I should because I'm trying to bring you around by gentler means, but you're trying my patience. I don't owe you an explanation, but I'll give you one. Can you show me a little respect?"

Isaac looked away and didn't respond. Abel said, "I was summoned by Preacher Litchfield along with some of the other men to help him lash the Englisher. He had been rebellious and defiant to the preacher's discipline. It was supposed to be a simple lashing, but it got out of hand. When the Englisher collapsed, I stepped in and stopped it. It was never my intention to hurt him seriously."

Isaac rubbed his hands together nervously. He shook his head and said, "Whether that was your intention or not, he's upstairs dying. What are you going to do when the sheriff comes around to investigate? You know that you and the other men will be facing murder charges if he dies."

Abel looked at the floor and anguished over the English man's condition. "I know, son. I'll deal with that when and if it happens. But I forbid you to talk to anyone. I know you talked to the sheriff at Massey's pond the other night. You won't talk to him or any other English authorities again. Am I clear?" Isaac remained silent as Abel left the room.

Dory's worried look revealed Dall's condition as Abel walked into the room. She stood and said, "This man is hurt bad, Abel. Did you help do this?"

Abel looked down in shame. "Yes, Dory, I did. It didn't start out to be a serious lashing, but it got out of hand. I don't know what got into the other men. I only held him, but they seemed possessed when they were beating him. It was like I didn't even know them."

Sandy intervened, "It wasn't his fault, Dory. He stopped them when he saw that Dall was unconscious. He saved Dall's life."

Dory patted Abel on the chest and said in a worried tone, "Just the same, Mister Straus, he's in serious trouble. Go get Lilly Dresselhaus. She'll know what to do."

Abel ran downstairs and yelled, "Isaac! Grab the mare and ride over to Lilly's house! Tell her to come quick!"

As Isaac was running out the door, he stopped in his tracks when Abel yelled, "And Isaac! Don't talk to anyone else!"

Fifteen minutes later, Lilly slid her old pickup to a stop at Abel's front porch. Dory and Sandy heard her slam the truck door, and Sandy asked, "Is Lilly Amish?"

Dory looked confused and said, "Of course."

"And she drives a car?"

Dory smiled and patted Sandy on the arm. "Yes, dear, and she uses electricity, and has a phone, and wears whatever clothes she wants, and gives the bishop and elders hell. You're going to love her."

Without setting eyes on Lilly, Sandy instantly liked her. When Lilly hurried into the bedroom, Dory hugged her and introduced Sandy. Lilly looked into Sandy's bruised and battered face and threw herself at her. She hugged Sandy and rocked her from side to side. "Oh, you little darling, I heard that you and your brother were here in the district. I'm so sorry for the abuse that those self-righteous ●●●●●●●● have given you. Now, let's have a look at your brother."

Lilly threw the sheet off of Dall and scanned his battered body. She got angry and mumbled, "God-fearing Christians, my butt! No true believer could ever do this to another person."

She checked Dall's pulse, then pressed her hand against his chest and put her ear to his nose to listen to him breathe. She opened one of his eyes and covered it with her hand, then quickly removed her hand to check the pupil's response to light. She did the same with the other eye, then began a careful examination of his head. After she'd gently felt every inch of his scalp, she stood. She threw the sheet off of Dall's feet and walked to the end of the bed. She grabbed a sharp pin from the bun in the back of her hair and poked the bottom of Dall's foot. When she got no response, she stuck it into the other foot. She put the pin back in her bun and said, "This boy is hurt bad, Dory. We've got to get him to a hospital. She turned and glared at Abel in the doorway and growled, "What happened to him?"

Abel sighed heavily and mumbled, "We were summoned to help Preacher Litchfield lash the English man and woman. For some reason the other men got carried away. I don't understand it. They didn't seem like themselves."

Lilly squinted her eyes and set her jaw as she walked up to Abel. He'd bowed his head in shame. Lilly reached up and gripped his beard, then raised his head so she could look into his eyes. She said, "Abel Straus, you big tree, you're too big and strong to be beating a man his size. You hit too hard. Did you do this?"

Abel shook his head. "No, Lilly, I only held him. At first it started out as a lashing with a strap, but some of the other men began using their fists and feet. When they picked up boards, I stopped it, but it was too late. The boy had taken a few blows to the head. I regret ever listening to Preacher Litchfield."

Lilly released Abel's beard and turned to Dall. She shook her head and said, "Well, Abel, you're going to pay the price for it. We're taking him to the hospital, and you're going to ride with me. After that ●●●●●●●, Gordan, finds out that you rode in a car with an excommunicated heathen like me, you'll be shunned for sure."

"I don't care, Lilly. I just don't want him to die. Go open your doors; I'll carry him down."

Smith and Waters watched through their binoculars as Abel carried Dall out of the house wrapped in a sheet. As he gently laid Dall in the seat of the truck, Waters growled angrily, "I told that insubordinate tramp that there'd be no rescue, Sir! She's disobeying a direct order! I'll have her up in charges for this!"

Smith sighed and said, "Well, technically, Dexter, you're not her supervisor. You're just the case manager. You don't evaluate or discipline her. Therefore any orders that you give her are not enforceable. I guess I could jam her up for it, but I'm not sure she's doing the wrong thing. Roberts is hurt bad or she wouldn't be taking him to a doctor. And remember, Dexter, if he gets taken out of the game, you're the second stringer. The next beating will be yours."

Waters said, "You keep threatening me with that, Sir, but we both know that I could never pull off the role. And the bishop would never let me in. If he goes down, she's on her own."

"Possibly, Dexter, but this mission is too important to fail. If I have to, I'll relieve you and bring someone else in here that can pull it off. And I've got someone in mind, so you'd better hope he survives. If I have to relieve you, you won't be allowed to return to your previous assignment in Kansas City like nothing ever happened. You'll be held in seclusion until I can figure out what to do with you, so start being a better team player or you're going to find yourself strapped to a table with electrical probes sticking in your head. I'll see to it that they run so much juice through your brain that you'll have to wear a name tag just to remember who you are. Come on, let's get to our car. I want to see where they take him."

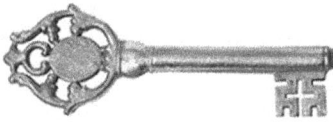

"I am he that liveth, and was dead; and behold, I am alive for evermore, Amen; and have the keys of hell and of death." **Revelation 1:18**

Smith and Waters stepped off the elevator, but stopped suddenly when they saw four Amish men walking toward Dall's room. Smith whispered, "Wait up. I want to see who these guys are. Let's hang close to his room and see if we can hear what they say."

The air was tense when Gordan stepped into Dall's hospital room. Sandy was sitting by Dall's bed, but Lilly sat against the wall and glared at Gordan as he walked in. He feigned a pretentious smile and said, "Afternoon, Lilly, I've been meaning to call on you."

Lilly snarled angrily, "Don't bother, Bishop! If this is your idea of Amish discipleship, I'm better off if you all stay away! And you still know more about Wilhelm's death than you've said!"

Gordan evaded Lilly's accusation and looked at Sandy. "Sandy, I'm sorry about your brother. Preacher Litchfield told me that he only called the men to help lash Dall, and that a couple of them got carried away. It was never our intention to hurt Dall this bad."

Sandy said, "That's not true, Bishop. Look at his face. Look at my face and arms. Preacher Litchfield and his inbred son beat the hell out of us on a daily basis. Does church discipline include beating young people with boards? Does it include holding a man's arms and beating him to death? Does it include the preacher's son trying to rape me, then beating my face to a pulp when I resisted? Is this the Amish faith, Bishop? If it is, then my brother made a serious mistake in coming to you for help. No wonder so many of your young people want nothing to do with being Amish."

Litchfield erupted in anger at Sandy's allegation. He yelled, "That's a lie! My son is a God-fearing Christian boy! He'd never …"

Bishop Gordan looked sternly at Litchfield, then shook his head. "No, Sandy, it's not. I came here to get your side of the story before I made my decision. I had no idea that you and Dall were being treated this way. I'll begin Preacher Litchfield's training immediately to help him be a better teacher."

Sandy smiled sarcastically and shook her head. Assistant Bishop Clevenger said, "Sandy, don't be so skeptical. We Amish have issues in our faith just like everyone else. The thing that separates us from the English is that we adhere more closely to God's word and we solve our own problems. This will be dealt with appropriately."

Elder Dunlevy said, "That's right, Sandy. We came here to see how we can help. We want you and Dall to be treated compassionately, just as Jesus treated sinners that He encountered."

Sandy said, "He's sleeping now. I'll have to talk to him when he wakes. I'm sure that he'll want to continue our efforts to regain our status as Amish."

Litchfield burned with anger. He pointed his finger at Sandy and growled as he backed out of the room, "This isn't over, Jezebel! The lashings that you got before were nothing like what you'll get the next time our paths cross." He glared at Smith and Waters as he stormed toward the elevator.

Waters said, "He's going to be trouble, Sir. He's not going to let this drop. Sandy just sealed her fate by accusing his son of rape."

Smith stared apathetically at Litchfield as the elevator doors closed. He said in a business-like tone, "Oh, no he won't. No phony, hayseed preacher is going to screw up this mission by taking out our undercovers. Since Dall and Sandy have moved to another farm, he'll have to feed and water his own stock tonight. Rifles are too noisy, so have the snipers sling them and sneak in on foot before dark. I want them in that barn when Litchfield does his evening chores. He's to be dealt with quietly."

Waters asked, "What will we do with the body, Sir?"

Smith thought for a few seconds, then said, "I know it's a long way to hump a body, so have another team meet them behind the barn to help. Have them dump it in that well where we meet Dall and Sandy at night. No one will think to look for him there. After they dump the body, have them pack up and move to the farm where Sandy and Dall will be staying. If you'll look on the County's plat map, I believe you'll find that it's the Straus farm. Scout out new cover positions and get the teams on post there. If that inbred son of his is with him when he does his chores, have them stick him, too. He's no threat to the investigation, but it'll boost Sandy's morale if she knows he's received his just reward."

Waters was confused. He asked, "Killing a retarded farm kid just to boost an undercover's morale? A little drastic, don't you think?"

Smith shook his head. "Not at all. I've killed better men for a lot less."

Ten minutes later the bishop and his entourage left Dall's room. Smith and Waters looked around suspiciously, then motioned for Sandy to come out into the hall so Lilly couldn't overhear them. Sandy closed the door behind her and Smith asked, "How is he?"

"He's good. The E.R. doctor said his X-rays showed only a hairline fracture of his skull, so they wanted to keep him here tonight for observation. He's sleeping now."

Smith said, "Good. I want you two out of here tomorrow. If the doctor won't release him, have Dall sign himself out A.M.A. They'll raise a stink, but you two have to be back in that district by tomorrow night."

Sandy frowned and asked, "What's the hurry, Sir? If he needs to stay, he should stay."

Waters started to chastise Sandy, but Smith said, "You've got a lot to do, Dexter, I'll handle this. You need to get things moving for tonight." Waters angrily walked away as Smith turned to Sandy and said, "I want you out of here because we can't protect you here. I have my reasons, Sandy, trust me. With Dall unconscious, Gaal can do whatever he wants to you and Dall won't be able to stop him. Dall is the only one who can keep Gaal under control. You'll be safer at the Straus farm where we can keep an eye on you. We're moving the cover teams in tonight."

Sandy asked, "Safe from what, Sir? It was the Amish who put him here."

"We were watching the beating. It may have been the Amish men, Sandy, but I think Gaal and his crew was controlling them. Gaal knows that with Dall out of the way, you're defenseless against him. And there's no one here who can help you if some of the men who beat Dall show up here. If you're at the Straus farm, that big farmer will protect you. I saw him stop the beating. I trust him. I'll hang out down the hall in the waiting room tonight to keep an eye on you. I'll pull some strings so the hospital staff will let me stay past visiting hours."

Sandy studied Smith as he walked away. As much as she hated him, she was seeing a compassionate side that made her wonder if she had pegged him wrong earlier.

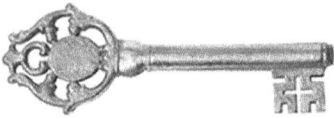

"I am he that liveth, and was dead; and behold, I am alive for evermore, Amen; and have the keys of hell and of death." **Revelation 1:18**

As Bishop Gordan drove, Bishop Clevenger and Preacher Litchfield sat in the back seat of Bishop Gordan's buggy with Bishop Gordan and Elder Dunlevy in the front seat. Elder Dunlevy fumed with anger at the beating that Dall had taken. He no longer cared what anyone thought as he burst into a tirade. Through gritted teeth he growled with loud conviction, "Brother Litchfield, that beating was atrocious! There is no way you can righteously defend brutality like that! Bishop Gordan, you're the bishop of this district, but I'm putting you on notice! I'll have you and Preacher Litchfield up before the elders in the next meeting if you don't do something about this! Our faith is based on God's principals, and He will curse us forever if we sanction this kind of evil!"

Preacher Litchfield exploded into a rage. "●●●● ●●●, Dunlevy!" He was about to berate Elder Dunlevy viciously when he felt a sharp pain in his chest. Bishop Clevenger had struck him hard with his knobbed handle of his cane.

The bishop turned to him with tears of anger in his eyes. "You hold your filthy tongue, Preacher! Elder Dunlevy is right! Your conduct with these Englishers has been despicable! If you defame the good name of

Elder Dunlevy with one more profane word, I'll lash you like you lashed the English man! We'll see how you like it! I've kept quiet for too many years about your brutality! I've seen whelps and bruises on your son, wife and animals for years, and have tried to bring you around with sound reason and scripture, but you refuse to change! Not one more word out of your filthy mouth, Sir!"

Bishop Gordan remained quiet. The beating that Dall had taken surprised even him. After the piercing stares of Elder Dunlevy and Bishop Clevenger had become uncomfortable, he grudgingly mumbled, "It was too much, Brother Litchfield."

Litchfield stared to his left and refused to make eye contact with the others. He mumbled, "Anyway, I didn't beat him like that. It was the other men who did it."

No one spoke for over a mile. Elder Dunlevy finally said, "Well, I guess that's right. The other men did get carried away." He then turned and yelled at Litchfield, "But they were there at your request! Brother Straus should not have had to stop it! That was your responsibility! When you saw things getting out of hand, as a leader in the district, you should have stepped in and restrained those men!"

Bishop Clevenger had calmed himself. He said, "Brothers, it's time that we consider the possibility that we have a demon in our midst, maybe many."

Elder Dunlevy said, "I agree, Bishop. I've known each one of those men all their lives, and they're all good men. They've never acted like that, even with their own families and animals."

Bishop Clevenger said, "Bishop Gordan, I've talked to each of those men and they all feel terrible. They've asked for forgiveness. They don't know what got into them."

Bishop Gordan sighed and said, "I think you're right. Brother Litchfield should have stopped it, but in his defense, if those men were demon influenced, he may not have been able to stop it. He might have been killed himself."

Elder Dunlevy thought for a minute, then said, "You may be right, Bishop. Abel Straus said they almost turned on him, and he's a lot bigger man than Brother Litchfield."

Gordan said, "Then that settles it. We've got to take action. We can no more sit by and allow a demon to create dissention in our district anymore than we can allow the corruptive influences of the English."

All sat quietly as Gordan formulated a plan. He finally said, "At the church meeting Wednesday night, I'll make the announcement that there may be demonic influences in the district. I'll instruct all members to search their souls and contact one of the elders, preachers, Bishop Clevenger or myself if they feel the presence of a demon within themselves or see it in someone else. Elder, Dunlevy, I'd like you to coordinate a search for this demon. I want you and the other elders and preachers to talk to every man in the district and see if you can identify this demon. You elders have been trained and will recognize a demon if you see one. Anyone who has information about a demon is to be brought to me immediately. I want this demon cast out of our flock."

All agreed, and Bishop Clevenger said, "Preacher Litchfield, you should be excluded from the search."

"Litchfield look surprised and glared at the bishop. "Why? I'm an ordained preacher just like the others!"

Bishop Clevenger nodded and said, "Yes, you are. But keep in mind that there was in instance in Acts, chapter 19 where a demon had indwelled a man. When another man tried to expel the demon in Jesus' name, the demon asked, 'Who are you?' He said, 'Jesus I know and Paul I know, but I don't know you.' He then attacked the man."

Litchfield snarled, "So, what's that got to do with me?"

Bishop Clevenger was undeterred. He calmly said, "It means that I have serious doubts about your salvation, Preacher Litchfield. You profess to love God, but a tree is known by its fruit. Your actions reveal an unrepentant heart. They indicate a distinctly deficient relationship with God. Many profess to know God, but simply knowing of Him does not constitute the relationship that He requires for salvation. Satan and the demons know God; they were there when He created the earth and they knew Him personally. The knowing that God wants is a close personal heart-relationship that fosters a deep love and faith that places God at the center of our lives. Our wills should no longer matter; only His will. Your pride and self-absorbed obsession with your own gratification has become your god. You love yourself more than anything else. If you confront a demon without truly having the Holy Spirit in you, you may well be killed. The fallen ones can discern those who wear the spiritual armor of the Holy Spirit and those who do not."

Litchfield was greatly offended, but before he could speak, Bishop Gordan said, "He's right, brother. You should stay out of the hunt. In the mean time, I will start you in discipleship so you can be assured that you are girded with the full armor of the Holy Spirit."

Litchfield burned with anger the rest of the way home. By the time that they had reached Bishop Gordan's farm, all had their assignments.

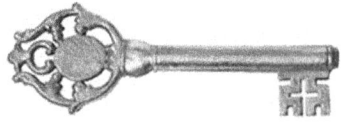

"I am he that liveth, and was dead; and behold, I am alive for evermore, Amen; and have the keys of hell and of death." **Revelation 1:18**

Dall awoke and found Sandy sitting by his bed. He groaned, "Man! How much did I drink?"

Sandy smiled as she squeezed his arm. "I don't know, but you made some pretty embarrassing confessions while you were out. Want to hear them?"

"No, just as long as I didn't propose."

Lilly chucked as Sandy said, "Oh sure, use me for the night, then blame it on the booze."

Dall slowly moved to a sitting position. Sandy said, "Dall, this is Lilly. She helped us get you here."

He struggled to see her through swollen eyes. "Thanks, Lilly."

Lilly thought their comments about liquor, marriage and intercourse seemed inappropriate for siblings, but passed it off as the profane remnants of their English influence. She smiled and said, "You're quite welcome, son. You both have taken a lifetime of lashings. I think that'll come to a screeching halt at the Straus farm. Abel is a good man. He's a little thick in some ways, but he'll treat you well."

Sandy said, "We have to check out of here, Dall."

"Okay. You have good reason, I suppose."

Lilly protested, "Nonsense, Sandy! He needs to stay till the doctor releases him. He could have some brain swelling that might kill him. Don't rush things."

Dall held up his hand. "That's okay, Lilly. I feel better. I can't pay a big hospital bill anyway."

Lilly said, "You guys are welcome to stay with me if you'd like."

Sandy smiled and said, "Thanks, but we'd better stay at the Straus place for a while."

Lilly was deeply concerned, but said, "Okay, kids; I've got chores to do. I'll come back and pick you up when you're ready to leave. Call me."

After Lilly left, Dall asked, "If we're going to stay with Straus, have you talked to Smith about that?"

"Yes, and he's not happy about you being here. You were in bad shape. I was afraid you'd die if we didn't get you help."

"Thanks, I appreciate that, but we have to get back to the district. If Gaal tries to contact us, we should to be there."

"He can't contact us here?"

"Yes, he can. That's one thing that confuses me about this whole mission. He's a demon. He can contact anyone he wants any place he wants. I still can't figure out why we're even here. Dr. Sveade could contact Gaal any time without our help. If the truth was known, I suspect that Gaal and Dr. Sveade have talked already, maybe many times."

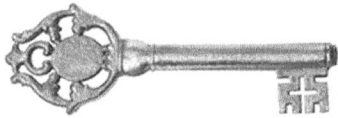

"I am he that liveth, and was dead; and behold, I am alive for evermore, Amen; and have the keys of hell and of death." **Revelation 1:18**

Isaac hurried to Massey's pond to meet Katie. His father was preoccupied at the house with the evening chores and thinking of an explanation that would fly with the bishop for bringing Lilly Dresselhaus in to treat Dall.

As he stepped into the clearing, he ran up to Katie and they fell into a deep kiss. Katie pulled Isaac to a nearby log and sat close to him. She said, "Isaac, I'm not sure we're safe coming here anymore. We need to start meeting at my house. My father will have a fit if he finds out that we're meeting here."

Isaac looked around suspiciously and said, "Yeah, I'm not sure it's safe here, but…"

Katie looked at him and asked, "…but what?"

Isaac stood and stepped up the edge of the water with his hands in his pockets. Katie came up behind him and said, "Isaac, you're keeping something from me."

Isaac sighed as he stared into the water. He finally said, "Katie, I haven't said anything to you, but I was on my way here when Preacher Croft was killed."

Katie gasped and took a step back. "Oh, Isaac, you have to tell someone. Did you see who killed him?"

Isaac nodded his head and said, "I have. I've talked to Bishop Clevenger. He was the only person I could trust."

"What did he say?"

Isaac sighed. "He said I didn't kill Preacher Croft and for me to keep my mouth shut. I had heard footsteps following me. I ran and thought I had lost him. I have to be honest, Katie, I thought I was being chased by your father. I thought he was trying to catch me and lash me for sneaking out to see you. I was scared to death. Your father is so strong."

Katie stepped up to Isaac and took his arm. "Oh, Isaac, my father would never hurt you."

Isaac looked deep into Katie's trusting eyes. He knew better, but didn't want to hurt her feelings. He continued. "Anyway, when the man caught me, it wasn't your father. It was Preacher Croft. He was drunk and crazy. I got scared and pushed him away from me. He fell and hit his head on a rock. I thought for a long time that it was me that killed him, but after talking to Bishop Clevenger, he assured me that it wasn't."

Katie tried to reassure him. "Well then, there. You see? You were worried about nothing."

Isaac said, "Katie, don't you see? I didn't kill him. I ran away after Preacher Croft fell, but he was still alive. Someone else came along and killed him; someone with super-human strength. I didn't see them, but it had to be someone who was following me, too."

Katie released Isaac's arm as tears welled up in her eyes. "Isaac, for God's sake, what are you saying? You're scaring me! Are you saying that my father killed him?"

Isaac anguished as he ran his fingers through his hair. "Katie, I don't know. Your father is so protective of you, and he's so strong. He's the strongest man in the district, probably in the whole state. You said yourself once that you thought he was trying to catch us together. I just think…"

Isaac stopped in mid sentence and saw the stark fear in Katie's tear-filled eyes. She slowly shook her head as the thought of her father being a murderer terrified her. Isaac slowly wrapped his arms around her and pulled her to him. He hugged her tight and said, "No. No, Katie, that's not what I'm saying. I'm sorry. Your father couldn't have had anything to do with it. I never should have said anything. Please forgive me."

Katie held him tight as she cried. She looked deep into Isaac's eyes and said, "Isaac, I know my father is a little intimidating sometimes, but he's never lost his ability to reason. And he's always been a faithful Amish. He could never kill anyone."

Isaac let the subject drop. He held Katie and reassured her that he was mistaken, but deep in his heart he knew that Sampson Betendorf was the only man who would have had a reason to chase him like that, besides Preacher Croft. But why would Sampson kill Preacher Croft if he was going to beat Isaac. If he was angry with Isaac, he would have allowed the preacher to beat him. The answer was clear. Katie was waiting at the pond. Once the preacher regained consciousness, he may well have discovered Katie and attacked her in the same drunken rage that he'd attacked Isaac in. The fear of seeing his only daughter mutilated with the claw of a hammer had to have driven Sampson completely insane.

If he thought Isaac was corrupting the morals of his daughter, there was no telling what Sampson would be capable of. But Katie was not prepared to consider that. Isaac thought it best to leave it for another time. He just knew he had to find another way to see Katie. Massey's pond was becoming too dangerous, and he could not face an angry Sampson Betendorf.

I am he that liveth, and was dead; and behold, I am alive for evermore, Amen; and have the keys of hell and of death." **Revelation 1:18**

Preacher Litchfield was still enraged over his chastising by Bishop Clevenger and Elder Dunlevy, so he had fielded all the questions he was going to take from Mrs. Litchfield. She had questioned the effectiveness of his beatings and was visibly shaken by the beating that Dall had taken. When she broke down and began crying, she said, "Preacher, I'm so worried. If that English man dies, the sheriff will arrest you. I can't run the farm without you, and we'll have to hire an English lawyer to represent you. How will Devin and I manage?"

Litchfield turned to face his wife, then back-handed her hard in the face. The blow knocked her backward and she fell against the woodstove, burning her shoulder and neck. As she scrambled to get away from the stove, he yelled, "I won't have my instructions from God questioned, woman! I'll defend myself to the bishop, no one else! Get dinner going as is your place! I'll be back after chores, and I don't want to hear another word about it!"

Devin ran to help his mother. Preacher stormed out of the house, slamming the screen door behind him. He stomped angrily into the barn and grabbed a pitchfork, then stabbed it into the hay mound and threw a large portion into Lady's manger. He stabbed another portion and threw it into Tramp's manger, then turned around.

As he was about to stab another load of hay, the hay mound came alive. As if possessed, the mound rose up and took the vague form of a man. It was only after the man had stood to his full height and the hay had fallen from his head and shoulders that Litchfield realized that the mound was not alive. He was staring into the bright, determined eyes of a young Army ranger in full camouflage.

Litchfield gasped in stark fear as the ranger grabbed the front of his sweat-stained shirt and pulled him close. He stopped gasping when a hand covered his mouth from behind and a ten-inch stainless, serrated blade plunged into his back and through his heart. With a sharp upward jerk of the handle, the point of the knife sliced through the entire length of Litchfield's heart. He slumped to the ground instantly and never took another breath.

The ranger went to the pan of water that Dall had used the day before to wash up. After washing the blood from the knife, he bent over and wiped the blade on Litchfield's pants, then slid the silent killer back in its sheath. He was momentarily distracted by hay debris falling from the loft. He thought he heard a voice, but after seeing nothing, he passed it off as a barn cat or rat moving through the hay.

They dragged Litchfield out the back door of the barn and left him until they could go back inside and kick hay and dirt over the bloodstains and empty the pan of bloody water. They were then joined by another ranger team and carried Preacher to the well and threw him in. With the blood-stain covered, there was no sign that Litchfield had ever been in the barn. His disappearance would be another of the unsolved mysteries in the history of this Amish district.

After a couple of hours, Mrs. Litchfield figured that Preacher had cooled down sufficiently to call him to supper. She and Devin had already eaten, but she would happily re-heat Preacher's dinner if he was more civil.

When her calls went unanswered, she sent Devin to the barn to see if Preacher wanted supper. Frightened as he was, Devin reluctantly went to the barn. He would not go in, but he stuck his head in the door and yelled. When he got no answer, he realized that Preacher was not in the barn.

He walked in and searched each stall, half-hoping he would not find his father. Both horses were there, and after stepping out the back door and looking across the pasture, it was apparent that his father had simply disappeared.

An hour later, Mrs. Litchfield and Devin were sitting in Bishop Gordan's parlor, asking him for an explanation of Preacher Litchfield's disappearance. Being a man who deeply hated any implication that he didn't have an answer for a particular question, Bishop Gordan did as he always had when he was at a loss for an answer; he faked it.

He picked up his well-used Bible and shook it at Mrs. Litchfield. He looked Heavenward and closed his eyes tightly as he yelled, "Lord! Creator of all that is, we come to you for insight! You know all and in all you are able. Please, God, speak to me and use you divine revelation to tell us what has happened to Brother Litchfield!"

With a loud groan, Bishop Gordan hung his head and collapsed into his chair. He shuttered and quivered briefly, then nodded that he understood. He again raised his head toward Heaven and said, "Thank you, Lord. Your plans are perfect and we accept your perfect will."

Mrs. Litchfield waited with anticipation, and the fear in her eyes relayed her eagerness to hear what the Lord had done with Preacher. Devin, on the other hand, sat in a chair eating a hot biscuit smothered in melted butter and brown sugar that Mrs. Gordan had given him. He either didn't understand the significance of his father's disappearance or he was relieved that he had taken his final lashing.

Bishop Gordan sighed heavily and looked deeply into Mrs. Litchfield's hopeful eyes. He said, "Sister, there are only two times in the Bible when God was so pleased with a man that He took him straight to Heaven without that man having to suffer a physical death. One was the profit Elijah, who God took up to Heaven in a whirlwind, and the other was Enoch who God took up to Heaven and he did not die. We are privileged to witness a great miracle. Our Lord, in His perfect wisdom, is so pleased with your husband that He has taken him on to Heaven without him dying. Praise God for His mercy and grace. Preacher Litchfield is in Heaven. He was simply taken up in the clouds by God."

Mrs. Litchfield stared at Bishop Gordan. She stopped twisting the handkerchief that she had been twisting between her fingers. Her gracious smile began to fade as the corners of her mouth drooped slightly. She caught the veil of disbelief as it fell over her face, then reestablished her bearing and asked, "Disappeared? Up to Heaven? With God? No death? No good-by, no warning, no supper, just poof, gone?"

Bishop Gordan sat quietly, beaming with pride and arrogance at his ability to instantly interpret God's plans with such acuity. "Yes, my dear, God works in mysterious ways, but you should go home and celebrate Preacher Litchfield's victory. What an honor it is to be so deep in God's favor that He would take the preacher home early. He must have some pretty important things for Preacher to do in Heaven to take him away from you and the farm like this. But rest assured that I and the brothers here in the district will be at your disposal, and we will help you run your farm. You will not want for help, dear sister."

After an awkward minute of deep thought, Mrs. Litchfield stood, totally confused, and walked to the door. Devin stuffed the last half of the biscuit in his mouth and stood to meet his mother. As they got in their buggy and started home, Bishop Gordan watched them drive out of sight. He closed the door and collapsed back down in his chair. He threw his Bible across the room and fumed in anger. Not even he believed what he had just told Mrs. Litchfield.

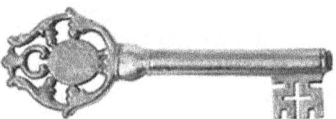

"I am he that liveth, and was dead; and behold, I am alive for evermore, Amen; and have the keys of hell and of death." **Revelation 1:18**

Lilly waited patiently outside the front entrance of the hospital. Dall and Sandy walked out with a nurse in hot pursuit. She argued that checking out against medical advice was suicide, but Dall patiently thanked her and climbed into Lilly's truck.

Abel met them in his front yard and helped Dall inside. Dall was embarrassed at the obvious fuss that Abel was making over him, but Abel's uncharacteristic display of concern was a display of his overwhelming joy and relief that Dall had not died. After propping him up in bed and fluffing his pillows, Abel left Dall's care in the hands of the women and went about his chores. Isaac was cleaning out stalls in the barn when Abel walked in. He asked, "Are the Englishers going to stay with us, Dad?"

Abel sighed and said, "For a while, I guess. I don't know what Bishop Gordan will decide."

Isaac leaned on the handle of his pitchfork and wiped his brow. "It doesn't matter what the bishop decides, Dad. This is your farm. You can let him stay if you want. After all, it was your fault that he got hurt in the first place."

Abel burned with anger. He stormed up to Isaac and grabbed him by the shirt. "Listen, Isaac, you weren't there! Not that I owe you an explanation, but I stopped him from getting hurt worse! I'm getting real tired of your insolence!"

Isaac hated his father, but lost his courage as soon as Abel lifted him off the ground by his shirt with his weak hand. He stared into his father's angry eyes, then looked away. Abel released him and said, "Isaac, if you last long enough to be baptized into the Amish faith, you'll understand someday that even the best of men do things that they regret. Just because we're Amish and are separated from the world of the English, we're still mortal men. We're subject to the same sin nature that everyone else is. I went there to help Preacher Litchfield administer discipline to the English man because he had raised his hand against the preacher and his son. I had no idea that the others would get so carried away. I'm trying to make it up to the English man and woman, but you've got to stop condemning me. I especially don't want you to slander the name of me or any other Amish to them. I want them to succeed in their reentry into the Amish faith. They won't do that if they think we're all animals."

Abel was torn. He knew he should lash Isaac for his insolence, but he desperately wanted to regain his love. He shook his head in frustration and walked back to the house. Isaac tried to slow his racing heart. He would be glad when he reached his adult height and weight so he would no longer be intimidated by his father.

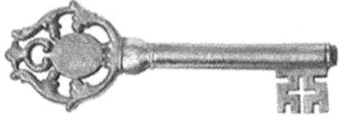

I am he that liveth, and was dead; and behold, I am alive for evermore, Amen; and have the keys of hell and of death." **Revelation 1:18**

An hour later, Bishop Clevenger shuffled into the barn. He greeted Isaac with an arthritic handshake and said, "Greetings, young Isaac Straus. I came to see the English man, but I've been wanting to talk to you. I haven't seen you at worship service lately."

Isaac showed Bishop Clevenger the reverence that he deserved. He said, "Thanks, Bishop, but worship service is no place for a man being shunned."

Bishop Clevenger smiled and said, "Your shunning is unnecessary, young Isaac. There are many men in the district who are doing much worse things than you. They're just better at keeping it secret. You're too outspoken for your own good." Bishop Clevenger handed Isaac a piece of paper and said, "Here, son, I've written down some passages that I want you to study. We'll discuss them when we start your discipleship training. Study them hard, young Mister Straus."

Isaac shoved the paper in his pocket without looking at it. He stabbed his pitchfork into the hay mound and leaned against the stall as he looked at the floor. Bishop Clevenger stepped up to him and put his arm around Isaac's shoulder. He said, "You know, Isaac, one of the marks of a mature man is the ability to manage his anger and maintain a Christian walk. The psalmist tells us in Psalms 37: 8, *Cease from anger, and forsake wrath: fret not thyself in any wise to do evil.* In Ephesians 4:26, the apostle Paul says, *Be ye angry, and sin not: let not the sun go down on your wrath.*"

Isaac shrugged his shoulders and said, "So, they were just men. That was just their opinion."

Bishop Clevenger glared sternly at him. He grabbed Isaac's chin and looked him directly in the eye. "Listen to this old bishop, youngster. Every word in the bible was penned by mortal men, but it was dictated to those men by God Himself. Every word that those men wrote was God-inspired. God spoke it to their heart and they wrote it down. If it's written there, it came from God."

Isaac grumbled, "Oh, I know that, Bishop. I'm just sick of hearing how we should act, then seeing the men of the district doing something else."

Bishop Clevenger released Isaac's face and nodded. "I know, Isaac. That's not a problem unique to our faith. No man can be an effective witness until he cleans up his own life. But let me warn you, young man, the failings of other men will offer no redemption for you on judgment day. They'll have to answer for their sins, but so will you, and claiming that others were doing the same things that you were doing will be no defense. That only means that you won't be alone in Hell. Is that where you want to spend eternity?"

Isaac hung his head and mumbled, "No, Bishop. I just don't like it here. The English have so much more than we do. And I'm tired of being lashed for every little thing I do wrong."

Bishop Clevenger asked, "Isaac, when was the last time you got lashed?"

Isaac shrugged his shoulders. "Last year."

"I thought so. I spoke with your father, son, and he's very concerned about your soul. If you'll think about it, I think you'll find that your father has shown you considerable mercy since then. He's also withheld lashings from little Judith and baby Jack, hasn't he?"

Isaac didn't respond. He slowly nodded and Bishop Clevenger said, "I thought so. I want to enlighten you about something, Isaac. You're going through the same thing that every other Amish man has gone through. No man likes to be lashed. It's an insult to your young pride. Your father was just as resentful about his lashings as you are. But your father is a wonderful man. He's finally realized what you need to learn. Bishop Gordan has a strict interpretation of God's messages to him. He is ordained by God as our bishop and we all have to follow his edicts, but we serve a higher power than Bishop Gordan. We serve a God who is merciful and forgiving. Your father is trying to be more like God, yet not get crossways with Bishop Gordan and the elders. He's trying to protect you from the consequences of your insolence. You need to put aside your anger, young Isaac. Your father is the best friend you'll ever have, this side of eternity."

Isaac's eyes watered as Bishop Clevenger's words pricked his heart. Bishop Clevenger smiled and squeezed Isaac's shoulder. "Forgive your father, youngster. I assure you that someday you'll be seeking the forgiveness of your own son. Your father will be an old man then, but his wise counsel will be of tremendous value to you."

Isaac choked back his tears and nodded. Bishop Clevenger asked, "Are you still smitten with young Katie Betendorf?"

Isaac rolled his eyes and squirmed in discomfort. "We're just friends, Bishop."

Bishop Clevenger reached up and gently slapped Isaac across the face. He said, "Don't lie to me, young Mister Straus. I've seen how you two look at each other."

Isaac sighed and said, "Well, I do like her, but I don't think her father would approve."

Bishop Clevenger smiled and said, "Maybe I can help, Isaac. You set your anger aside and be the kind of man that I know you are, and I'll help soften the heart of mean old Sampson Betendorf. He's a little intimidating to young folks, but he's really a good man who has Katie's best interest at heart."

The bishop turned and said, "I've got to visit the English man and woman, Isaac. I will be seeing you in worship services from now on, won't I?"

Isaac nodded and said, "If they'll let me in."

"Forgive, youngster, forgive! I'll talk to the bishop. You start being the kind of man that Sampson would approve of and I'll grease the wheel for you. You'll be glad, and Katie will make you a wonderful wife." As Bishop Clevenger walked to the door, he stopped and pivoted quickly. He pointed a crooked, arthritic finger at Isaac and said, "And you stay away from those boys who smoke and drink! And you respect young Katie! Keep your pants on, and allow her to do the same!"

The bishop turned to leave, but Isaac stopped him. "Bishop, I know who killed Preacher Litchfield."

Bishop Clevenger stopped suddenly and straightened up as far as his scoliosis would allow. He turned slowly and shuffled back to Isaac. He glared angrily at Isaac and asked, "Who?"

Isaac knew that he'd ignited the bishop's wrath. He looked nervously at the ground and said, "Sampson Betendorf. He was the only one who would have been following me that night. He was angry that I've been seeing Katie, and he's the only one strong enough to dismember a man like that. You said that you'd heard the killer's confession, so I just want to make sure that I'm right. I don't want to see Katie get hurt, and I don't want her relationship with her father to suffer."

Bishop Clevenger edged closer until he was directly in Isaac's face. He growled, "Then, young Mister Straus, you keep your gossiping mouth shut! The confessions of the elect are a sacred trust between them and their bishop! And I won't have the image and reputation of a saint tarnished by the imagination and ramblings of a rebellious young whip! This is fair warning, Mister Straus, I rebuke you for your wild speculations and I order you to not say a word of this to anyone! I'm not at liberty to say who the killer is, but that is between him, me and our Lord! Do you understand?"

Isaac nodded his head adamantly. "Yes, Bishop, I do. I apologize for my conduct. I should never have asked."

Bishop Clevenger nodded his head, satisfied that he had sufficiently chastised Isaac, then turned and shuffled out of the barn.

Isaac watched him move slowly toward the house and wondered what he should say to Katie, if anything. He didn't know what to think, accept that he was sure of one thing. Bishop Clevenger had not denied that Sampson Betendorf was the killer.

The bishop knocked gently on Abel's door. Abel hurried to open the door, then took Bishop Clevenger's arm and helped him inside. He said, "Greetings, Bishop, I assume you're here to see the Englishers."

"Yes, Abel, along with young Isaac. I just left him in the barn. How is the English man doing?"

Abel sighed with relief. "Oh, Bishop, he's going to be fine. Can I talk to you in private?"

Bishop Clevenger closed his eyes and nodded. He'd expected Abel to ask him to hear his confession. He took Abel's arm as Abel led him out onto the front porch. Abel said, "Bishop, please hear my confession. I have sinned. I and some of the other men went to Preacher Litchfield's house, as he'd requested, to help him lash the English man. He said the English man and woman bore false witness against his son, then raised their hands against him in anger. We were all a little indignant about it, so we went there to carry out God's will. During the lashing, some of the men got carried away and beat him too hard. I had to stop them before they killed him. It was almost too late. But, I was part of it; I have sinned. A lashing should never result in a trip to an English hospital. I also rode in Lilly Dresselhaus's truck and used some profane words when I was talking to myself about Preacher Litchfield. I had to help Lilly get him to the hospital. I know I should confess this at worship service in front of the elders, but I don't want to be shunned or excommunicated. Please hear my confession and forgive me, Bishop."

Bishop Clevenger smiled and said, "The other men have beat you to it, Abel. They've already told me what happened. I've heard your confession, Abel, and you've done the right thing. Confess your sins to God also and you'll be forgiven. Repentance means to turn away from your old sin nature, so repent and never lash another man again. I have seen your commitment to change. Take your sins to God and continue to change your ways. God will forgive you. Now let me meet this English man and woman."

Dall was sitting up in a chair when Bishop Clevenger shuffled into the room holding on to Abel's arm. Bishop Clevenger shook his hand vigorously, then turned to Sandy. "I met you at the hospital, dear. How are you?"

Sandy stood and shook the bishop's hand. "Fine, Bishop, nice to see you again. Dory and Abel have told us what a nice man you are."

Bishop Clevenger smiled and shook his head. "Well, dear, I have my moments. I'm glad you survived your stay with Preacher Litchfield. Judging from your stripes, I can see it wasn't pleasant."

Sandy said, "Yes, we survived, but if this is an example of church discipline in an Amish district, I'm not sure I want to be Amish."

Bishop Clevenger said, "It certainly has been characteristic of this district, but Bishop Gordan is beginning to soften his position on lashing. I think you've had your last experience with that. How are you feeling, Dall?"

Dall stretched a cramp out of his neck and said, "Much better, Bishop. Abel and Dory have been good to us. I hope we can stay with them."

"I've talked to Bishop Gordan and he agrees that you should stay here. Abel is glad to have you and you can learn much from him."

Dall stood and walked to the window and stared at the unusual storm clouds swirling over the horizon. He said, "And I think there's a lot we can learn from you, Bishop. Dory tells me that you're the foremost expert on the Bible and spiritual matters. I have lots to ask you."

Bishop Clevenger shook his head with humility. "No, son, I'm no more an expert than anyone else who has put in the time to read it. There's nothing mystical about God's word. Any sixth-grader with average reading and comprehension skills can understand it."

"Maybe so, Bishop, but can I visit you on occasion?"

"Certainly, my boy; my house is just across Abel's north pasture about six-hundred yards. I'm home most every evening if I'm not out calling on the sick and home-bound."

Dall asked, "Will either of us be facing Preacher Litchfield again?"

Bishop Clevenger looked at the floor and said, "Likely not. It seems that Preacher Litchfield has disappeared. Bishop Gordan said he was taken up to Heaven by God, but we'll have to see if he shows up. At any rate, if he comes home, I'll give him specific instruction that he's to have no contact with you. I'll take it up with Bishop Gordan if I have to, but beating non-believers is not the Amish way, anymore than it is God's way."

Dall and Sandy looked at each other in disbelief. Dall was aware of the two men in the Bible that God was so pleased with that He took them straight to Heaven without suffering a physical death, but both doubted that this was the case here. It was more likely that his disappearance had been orchestrated by Agent Smith.

After a pleasant visit, Bishop Clevenger went to the kitchen. Baby Jack entered Dory's bedroom and sheepishly walked up to Dall and Sandy. As soon as he'd shaken their hands, he underwent a metamorphosis from shy little boy to a gregarious chatterbox. He climbed up on Dall's lap and began telling him about every aspect of his life. Dory laughed as she picked him up and said, "You'll have time to get to know Dall, baby Jack." She swatted him gently on the bottom and said, "Go downstairs and send your sister up."

Sandy looked lovingly at Dall and he smiled back. She had wanted her own children for a couple of years now, and little Jack had touched her heart. When Judith entered the room, Dall and Sandy were still locked into a stare into each other's eyes. Judith stepped up to them and took their hands and said, "Hi, I'm Judith."

As Dall and Sandy turned their attention to Judith, they instantly became frightened. Dall's face displayed stark fear and Sandy unconsciously pulled away and scooted across the bed. As she gasped in fear, Judith became confused and tears filled her eyes. Dory hurried to Judith and asked, "What's wrong, Dall?"

Dall instantly recovered and slowed his breathing. He saw that Judith didn't understand their fear. Not wanting to step out of role, he said, "Oh! I'm sorry, Dory. Judith just looks like someone that Sandy and I met once. The resemblance is striking."

He looked at Judith and smiled. He hugged her and pulled her up on his lap as he said, "I'm sorry we frightened you, Judith. You're such a pretty little lady. You look just like your mother."

Judith wiped her eyes and smiled. She slid off Dall's lap and went back downstairs.

Sandy recovered from her fright and moved back beside Dall. "Please forgive me, Dory. Judith just looks like someone that we used to know. I wasn't prepared for such a striking resemblance."

Dory smiled and said, "Oh, that's okay, kids. Come on, Lilly, let's let these two rest up for a while before lunch."

After they had left the room, Sandy said, "That's Gaal! What are we going to do, Dall? How can we tell Abel and Dory that their daughter is a demon?"

"We're not, Sandy. She may not be a demon. Gaal is capable of taking on any mortal form that he wants. He could assume the physical appearance of anyone here. He probably saw Judith and took on her physical form while walking the hills at night because she looks so harmless and people would not see her as a threat. I'm sure Judith is not Gaal."

"She sure looks like him."

"Yes, but we have to be careful to not hurt Judith's feelings, or we'll alienate Abel and Dory. We need them both right now. We need to stay here."

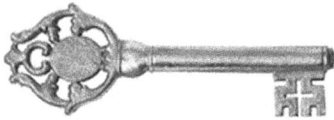

"I am he that liveth, and was dead; and behold, I am alive for evermore, Amen; and have the keys of hell and of death." **Revelation 1:18**

After a few days of recovery time, Dall moved into the guest room that Abel had built on the side of the barn for family when they came to visit. It was far more comfortable than Litchfield's horse stall. Sandy slept in baby Jack's room and he was thrilled to get to sleep with Mom and Dad.

After dinner, Sandy went to the barn and found Dall resting on his bed. She let herself in without knocking and sat on the bed beside him. When he awoke, she reached over and stroked his hair. "Sorry to wake you, but I just wanted to say good night. Will you be alright out here by yourself?"

"Sure, Sandy, but I've been thinking. Smith and Waters still expect us to meet them at night. You're going to have to lay some groundwork with Abel and Dory. When you go back to the house, tell them that it's been our long-standing custom to take a walk together at night. Tell them it's a chance for us to stay connected and not be distracted while we share our thoughts about God and the Amish faith. If one of them asks to come along, tell them it's our time.

Sandy nodded and said, "Okay, but I wonder where Smith and Waters will meet us. We're a long way from the old well."

"They've got spotters on us. I'm sure they'll intercept us once we start walking."

As they stared into each other's battered face, Dall tried to reign in his feelings. He turned his head, but Sandy gently rolled over on top of him. When she was face to face with him, he could no longer avoid her gaze. He started to talk, but she kissed him hard.

After several minutes, they heard someone approaching the barn. Sandy stood and straightened her clothes just as Abel and Bishop Clevenger walked into the barn. Abel said, "Dall, we're going over to Preacher Litchfield's house. His wife hasn't seen him since the night after your beating when he went to his barn to feed the stock."

Dall looked at Sandy as he got off the bed. He said, "You mentioned that earlier, Bishop. I was unconscious, and Sandy
didn't see anything. We don't know what happened to him."

Bishop Clevenger put Dall's mind at rest. "No one is accusing you of anything, Dall. You were in no condition to harm anyone. Abel has vouched for both of you. But Mrs. Litchfield is worried. She got an explanation from Bishop Gordan, but she doesn't believe it. I have to admit that it does seem a little far-fetched. We're meeting some of the other men there to form a search party. Even if we don't find him, it'll put her mind at rest. At least she'll know he's not on their property. Also, Bishop Gordan has tasked some of us men to conduct an investigation into some of the strange happenings here in the district. Looking into Preacher Litchfield's disappearance is a logical place to start."

Dall said, "I'd like to come, too, Bishop. I didn't like Preacher Litchfield, but Mrs. Litchfield was good to us." He leaned into Sandy's ear and whispered, "Sandy, you should stay here so you can go meet Smith if I'm not back in time."

Abel and Bishop Clevenger stepped outside. Sandy unbuttoned the front of her dress and pulled out the pistol that she had taken from Smith. She gave it to Dall and said, "Put this in your waistband. It may come in handy."

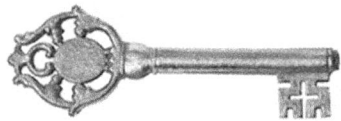

"I am he that liveth, and was dead; and behold, I am alive for evermore, Amen; and have the keys of hell and of death." **Revelation 1:18**

The men gathered at the Litchfield farm. Dall remained at the back of the crowd as Bishop Clevenger talked with Mrs. Litchfield on the porch. She briefed the searchers on the details of the night that the preacher had gone missing as she paced the porch in front of them in a contrived, rehearsed gait. Dall was stricken at how pretentious she seemed. She said she was worried sick about Preacher Litchfield, but her emotions didn't mirror her words. She cried openly, but there were no tears in her eyes. She almost seemed hopeful that the preacher wasn't found.

Bishop Clevenger organized the searchers and sent them off in different directions. Abel escorted him to the barn, and Dall followed.

Lady and Tramp didn't know the strangers, but they stomped their feet anxiously, prompting Abel to look in their feed boxes. He sighed heavily and said, "They're empty, Bishop. They haven't been fed all day." He gave them each a bucket of feed, then turned to Bishop Clevenger.

The bishop said, "Abel, I'm too old to climb anymore, but would you climb up to the loft and see if you can see any clue as to what happened to the preacher?"

Abel dutifully obeyed and hurried up the latter that was nailed to one of the center support columns. As he poked around in the hay-mound, Dall made his way to the stalls that he and Sandy used to call home. The mattresses were still there, and it appeared that no one had even entered the barn since their departure, except for one sickening sign. Lady sported some new wounds from a recent beating that Devin had apparently felt he'd deserved.

Both horses were too engrossed in their ravenous assault on their feed boxes to notice Dall. Dall remembered where Litchfield kept the salve and retrieved it. He climbed over the stall and began applying salve to Lady's wounds. Bishop Clevenger hobbled to the stall and said, "That Devin, what a lost soul. His father didn't raise him very well."

Dall gritted his teeth and growled, "He's grown up just like his dad. There's not an ounce of compassion or common sense in either of them. If I thought all Amish were like this, I'd want nothing to do with them."

Bishop Clevenger was above provocation. He said, "Well, we're not, dear boy. Most Amish are God-fearing people who believe that they should show as much compassion to others and their animals as God shows us. Unfortunately, we're under the spiritual stewardship of a bishop who interprets God's divine word by its strictest letter."

Dall had a different interpretation of Bishop Gordan's revelations from God, but he didn't want to alienate Bishop Clevenger or say anything that might make its way back to Gordan. He said, "Bishop Clevenger, it would be a big help to me if Sandy and I could talk to you at length. Would you consent to taking over out discipleship? We like Brother Straus, but he's said that you are his teacher, so Sandy and I would like to have the benefit of your teaching as well."

Bishop Clevenger nodded gently as his shaky hand held tight to the stall to maintain his balance. "Yes, Dall, I would be happy to. All affairs of discipleship have to go through the bishop, but I think I can talk him into it. After the way your first tutoring went terribly wrong, I think we owe you that."

Dall screwed the cap back on the salve and climbed back over the stall. He took Bishop Clevenger's arm and led him to a chopping block to sit. He asked, "Bishop, did you have an injury that caused you back pain?"

The bishop chucked and grunted as he sat, "Yes, son, I did. When I was much younger, my gilding got spooked one night when I was visiting the home-bound. He ran through a rail fence and knocked down the top rails. My buggy bounced over the bottom rail and took me off the ground. When it landed, I had been thrown out and it landed on me. It broke my back and I almost never walked again. That and the ravages of old age have made me a little slower than the younger folks. It's never an issue until the dinner bell is rung." Bishop Clevenger shifted his position on the block and laughed. Dall wondered how he even managed to walk. He seemed too stiff and weak to get out of bed.

Dall left the bishop to recover his strength, and walked back toward the stalls that he and Sandy had occupied. As he walked, he looked at the ground and noticed that there were gouge marks in the loose hay and dirt as if a set of heels had been dragged through it. He looked around and gently kicked some dirt away from the gouges revealing a large pool of blood. He stared in disbelief for a few seconds, then heard Abel climbing down from the loft. He covered the blood again and walked back to the bishop. Abel said, "There's nothing in the loft, Bishop. If we don't find him on the property, we'll have to look for him elsewhere in the district."

The bishop reached out for Abel's arm and Abel quickly extended it to help the bishop stand. He said, "Yes, Abel, my boy, I think you're right. Preacher Litchfield would never have walked away from his farm and the Amish faith. I'm afraid our Lord and Savior may have called him home."

Abel looked confused. "Does God do that, Bishop? Does he just take people out of this world, body and all?"

Bishop Clevenger sighed and shrugged his shoulders. "Well, it's not very common, but that's Bishop Gordan's opinion. I guess it's possible. In the second chapter of Second Kings, God took Elijah up to Heaven in a whirlwind. And in Genesis chapter 5, Enoch was a man of God, and God simply took him."

Abel's mouth gaped open in awe at the thought of a man simply vanishing from the face of the earth. He patiently helped Bishop Clevenger toward the house in short, choppy steps, with Dall close behind.

Dall was well aware of the Old Testament saints that God had spared a mortal death, but he seriously doubted that Preacher Litchfield had been held in such high esteem by the Father. He had disappeared alright, but Dall suspected that Preacher Litchfield's ascension was a result of a little girl named Gaal, or the strategic insertion of a stainless Gerber into his vitals by the divinely-guided hand of a U.S.-ordained Army ranger.

Abel picked up the bishop and carried him up on Mrs. Litchfield's porch. He sat the bishop in the same chair that Dall had sat in a few days earlier. Mrs. Litchfield brought them fresh-squeezed lemonade and cornbread muffins with homemade apple jelly.

The bishop nibbled politely as he reassured Mrs. Litchfield. Abel, however, filled his cheeks with cornbread muffins smothered with large spreads of homemade butter and mounds of apple jelly that dripped between his fingers. When he looked up at Dall, his eyes were half closed like a delirious dog entranced in a rare steak. When he saw Dall smiling at him, he straightened up and looked sternly at him. He swallowed hard and brought himself back to reality, then licked the jelly from his fingers and composed himself.

Dall leaned into him and whispered, "That's okay, Abel. I think God enjoys a mess of cornbread and homemade jelly Himself from time to time."

Abel looked at Mrs. Litchfield to make sure she had not seen his momentary lapse of manners. He tried to hide his smile by gritting his teeth and forcing the corners of his mouth downward, but Dall saw the glimmer in his eyes. Although Abel had been one of the men who had put him in the hospital, Dall was rapidly growing fond of him.

As the last rays of light faded below the horizon, the searchers returned to the house and shook their heads at Bishop Clevenger. He turned to Mrs. Litchfield and comforted her, but Dall studied her hard and saw an almost imperceptible sigh of relief when she heard the news.

The men removed their hats as Bishop Clevenger led them in a prayer. They then shook her hand as they filed sadly past her in a single-file procession, then climbed into their buggies and left. Abel picked up the bishop and carried him down the steps. Dall started down the steps, but stopped when Mrs. Litchfield gently took his arm. She leaned into him and said, "Dall, please accept my apology for the lashings that you and your sister took during your stay here. Preacher Litchfield is a good man. He's just so fervently dedicated to carrying out God's word that he gets carried away. He also doesn't know his own strength. Sometimes he causes more pain than he intends."

Dall didn't agree, but argument would serve no purpose now. Although Mrs. Litchfield appeared strong, he didn't know her very well. She may have been putting up a good front. He didn't want to hurt her in any way. He simply looked into her bruised and swollen eyes and smiled as he squeezed her hand.

Dall sat in the rear cargo area of the buggy where the children usually rode. He listened intently as Abel and the bishop talked. Abel said, "Bishop, I can't help but see the similarity between Preacher Litchfield's disappearance and Wilhelm Dresselhaus. Willy turned up at the coroner's office, maybe Preacher will, too."

Bishop Clevenger spoke guardedly. "I wouldn't be too hasty to lay them both on the same cause, Abel. If Preacher Litchfield does turn up dead, I'll be interested in hearing what the cause of death is. I'm getting worried. We also lost Elder Levi Croft a few weeks ago over by Massey's pond. That's two, possibly three, violent deaths in the district in the last two years."

Bishop Clevenger thought nothing of it, but Dall thought Abel's silence on the matter seemed suspiciously evasive.

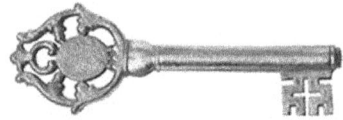

"I am he that liveth, and was dead; and behold, I am alive for evermore, Amen; and have the keys of hell and of death." **Revelation 1:18**

Sandy was waiting eagerly when Dall walked to his quarters in the barn. He explained the blood in Litchfield's barn and freshened up before their meeting with Smith and Waters. Sandy tried to hide her bitterness, but Dall could see she felt that Litchfield had received his just rewards.

Sandy sat on his bed as he sponged himself off. He said, "We need a different perspective on this demon thing, other than what Dr. Sveade is giving us."

"Why, Dall?"

"Sveade's mind is closed. He's so obsessed with meeting Gaal that he's closed his mind to the possibility that this demon will stroke him. I've got an open invitation to talk to Clevenger. He seems to be a voice of reason in the district. He's also the leading authority on the Bible as far as I can tell. He doesn't seem to have an agenda, so I think he'll shoot us straight, if he lives that long."

Sandy asked suspiciously, "Why, is he in danger?"

"No more than anyone else. It's just that he's so old and feeble. He seems like he's going to fall over dead any minute. He got crushed in a buggy accident a few years ago. Guess it crippled him up pretty good."

"How are we going to pick his brain without Sveade finding out?"

"As far as Sveade and Smith will know, he'll just be counseling us on the ways of the Amish. They won't know that we'll be getting his perspective on demons, unless they go ask him."

"When do we start?"

"Tonight, after Smith and Sveade. We've got a break by getting away from Litchfield. We need to capitalize on it quickly in case we get moved again. Next time it might be too far away for us to walk to Clevenger's farm."

NINE

SANDY WAS STARTLED when she turned around and saw the Army ranger standing in the doorway. He said with over-rehearsed, military bearing, "Agent Parsons, the C.P. has changed. The old well is too far away. I'll lead you to the new rendezvous point tonight. After that you'll be on your own each night."

Dall and Sandy gathered up their jackets and followed the ranger. Dall studied the fearless demeanor of the young sniper and wondered if he would be the one to eventually pull the trigger on him or Sandy. He certainly had the cold, menacing stare of a raw meat-eater.

The ranger held his scoped M1-A in a high-ready position as if he expected an armed threat to present itself at any time. He'd apparently seen the little girl almost cave in the wall of Litchfield's barn.

They had only covered two-hundred yards when the ranger panicked. He stumbled backward past Dall and Sandy before he could regain his balance. He shouldered his rifle and swung it around randomly, searching for a viable target.

Sandy also panicked and allowed her training to take over. The ranger's training and credibility was sufficient for Sandy to assume that his alarm was warranted. This was no time to question his keen senses. She quickly opened a button on the front of her dress, jerked Smith's pistol from the inside of her waistband and shoved it out in front of her.

When nothing appeared, Dall eased up beside the ranger who was openly crying by now. He gently placed a reassuring hand on the ranger's shoulder and whispered, "I've got some experience in combat, sergeant. What would you like me to do?"

The ranger sniffled hard and said in a trembling voice, "We've got to get out of here! We've got to circle around that cluster of trees! The girl is in there!"

That revelation sent Sandy into a panic. She back-pedaled past the sergeant and turned to run, but Dall grabbed her arm. "Running won't do any good, Sandy. If Gaal is in there, he can move much faster than we can. Remember, they feed on our fear."

Sandy stopped struggling and Dall strained to adjust his eyes to the darkened interior of the canopy. As they focused, he gasped in shock. Hanging from a tree limb was the mutilated corpse of the sergeant's spotter. The sergeant gurgled as he cried, "That was our observation point. Steve stayed behind while I went to get you. I never should have left him alone."

Dall slowly stepped close to the tree. The sergeant cautiously followed with his rifle shouldered and the safety off. The spotter's arms and one leg had been torn from his torso, then he was hanged in the tree upside down. Gravity pulled his blood downward and it dripped from his head into a large pool beneath him.

Dall eased around the carnage and picked up the spotter's rifle. He gently opened the bolt, extracting a live round from the chamber. Steve had died so quickly that he hadn't had time to fire his rifle. Dall closed the bolt and slung the rifle over his shoulder. He said, "Come on, sergeant; let's move on to our meeting. Smith will have to send someone to get the body. I'm sorry. I know you two were close."

Sandy gently grabbed the sergeant's sleeve and said, "There's nothing we can do for him."

The sergeant trembled as he lowered his rifle and said, "This can't be. I just left him to go get you. He didn't shoot, scream or anything. How could someone kill him so quietly?"

Dall turned the sergeant away from the scene and said, "Come on, sergeant, Smith'll handle this. Let's get you some help."

Now completely traumatized, the sergeant staggered clumsily and asked, "How? How could anyone get close to Steve without him knowing it? We all knew the little girl was supernatural, but we didn't suspect anything like this."

Dall wrapped his arm around him and said, "It may not have been the little girl, sergeant. There are other dark spirits here. Smith will explain that to you. He wouldn't have been able to stop it anyway. His rifle would have done him no good."

The sergeant growled, "What in the hell are we up against out here? Why didn't someone tell us what we were truly dealing with? We never volunteered for this! Someone should have told us!"

Sandy tried to comfort the sergeant. "I know, sergeant, but that's the nature of clandestine operations. Each player knows only his small part and never sees the overall plan. They told you only what they thought you needed to know. But you're right; they should have told you more. None of us knew what we were getting into until it was too late."

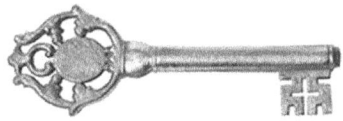

"I am he that liveth, and was dead; and behold, I am alive for evermore, Amen; and have the keys of hell and of death." **Revelation 1:18**

North of the Straus farm was an abandoned house that used to be the home of the Ballinger family, who had abandoned the Amish faith and moved to St. Louis where the husband took a job with the Parks Department. Dall and Sandy memorized the route there, and Dall couldn't believe their luck. Directly to the west of the Ballinger house about four hundred yards was the picturesque farm of Bishop Clevenger.

Smith, Waters and Dr. Sveade were seated around an old, hand-sawed table in cane chairs when Dall and Sandy helped the traumatized sergeant through the back door. Smith asked, "What is wrong with him?"

The ranger leaned his rifle against the wall and unholstered his Beretta 9^{mm}. He pointed it at Smith and growled, "Why didn't you tell us what we were dealing with, Sir?"

Dall stopped in shock at the ranger's challenge. Sandy stood quietly, secretly hoping that Smith would finally unravel. To her surprise, he was completely unfazed. He walked up to the sergeant and pressed his forehead against the muzzle of the sergeant's pistol. Dall cringed as he pictured Smith's head exploding right before his eyes. This was a big mistake on Smith's part.

Smith stared lazily into the sergeant's eyes and said, "Whatever the problem is, sergeant, we can discuss it. You're actions are insubordinate and will land you in front of a firing squad, or worse, I'll execute you myself here and now."

The sergeant wept openly as he yelled, "My spotter is dead! He had his arms torn off and he's hanging in a tree with his torso ripped open! We're not here to control the undercovers as you said!"

Waters stood and reached for his pistol, but Dall said, "I wouldn't, Waters. He'll drop you like a bad habit before you even clear leather." Waters froze and slowly removed his hand from the butt of his pistol when he drew a determined glare from the sergeant.

Smith nodded as if he had been expecting this since the mission began. He said, "You've known from the very start that we were dealing with the supernatural, sergeant. Steve was killed by a demon. You saw what that little girl did to the sheriff. You saw what she did the night she almost tore down the barn at the Litchfield farm. You just didn't know how powerful she really is. This mission is far more important than your partner. I know what it's like to lose a friend in combat, so I'm not without compassion. But that compassion only goes so far. Now holster that piece and compose yourself."

After a long period of indecision, the sergeant slowly lowered his pistol. Smith continued, "I know you and your spotter had a long history together, but this is war. There will be casualties. We'll get you a replacement, but get over it and complete your mission." Sandy was shocked. This was the second time she'd seen compassion from Smith.

The sergeant slowly holstered his Beretta and picked up his rifle. He walked out the back door and sat on the porch until the meeting was over. Dall placed the spotter's rifle on the table and said, "I can't believe you stuck snipers on point without training them on how to deal with a demon. What did you expect them to do when they confronted Gaal?"

In a subdued tone completely void of any emotion, Smith replied, "I expect them to keep tabs on you and report any sightings of Gaal. If they are confronted, I expect them to use their training and ingenuity to stay alive. There are no rule books on how to interact with a demon. If there were, I assure you I would have bought them each a copy. If they get killed, I expect them to die bravely and quietly. Apparently that's what the ranger did. He did his job well. Now I expect you to do yours."

Dr. Sveade asked, "Have you contacted Gaal again?"

Sandy said, "Not since Dall got home. But we did learn that Gaal has assumed the appearance of Abel Straus's daughter. Apparently she's well known and liked, so Gaal can assume her image and move around easily."

"True, Sandy, but he can assume any form, even an animal, so look for him anywhere. He will contact you again."

Dall said, "Doctor, this demon has killed again. He's not going to be one that you can control. Any control that you think you can exert over him is nonexistent. He can move at will, assume any form he wants, fabricate any scenario, and you have no way of verifying anything he says."

Dr. Sveade shrugged his shoulders. "We have our ways, Dall. We haven't disclosed all the safeguards that we'll utilize, but leave that to us. You just locate him and leave those details to us."

Sandy said, "We've been relocated, Doctor, but I'm not sure we can get Gaal to approach us if he doesn't want to. How do you suggest we establish contact with him?"

Dr. Sveade sighed and said, "Demons are notoriously inquisitive. They move among us at will and listen to our conversations. I'm sure Gaal has listened to every conversation that we've had. He knows we want to talk to him."

Dall asked, "Then if that's so, why do you need us? Just ask him to materialize for you. Just tell him that you want to talk to him."

"Unfortunately, we've tried that many times before. For some reason, Gaal doesn't trust me. I know there's no guarantee that he'll contact you either, but he's moving around in this district. He's contacting some of these Amish. If you get close to them, he may see that you're safe and contact you. If not, find out who he's communicating with and let's collaborate with them. If you have to befriend them and use them as an unwitting informant, that's fine. However you do it, I want to talk to him."

Dall said, "He already knows your agenda, Doctor. If he wanted to form an alliance with the U.S., I think he would have contacted you by now. I think it's dangerous to assume that Gaal is a safe ally."

Dr. Sveade stood angrily. "I'll decide that, Dall! Just find him! There's too much at stake here! If Bible prophesy is accurate, the U.S. will be reduced to just another puppet of the Antichrist very soon! We'll lose our world dominance, and all who refuse to worship him will be hunted down and killed! If there's a chance that we can spare ourselves a horrible fate like that, we want to! If there can be a sanctuary for those who resist the Antichrist, we want it to be the United States!"

Dall shook his head. "No, Doctor, You know as well as I do that when the Antichrist comes to power, the church will have been raptured out of the world. All that will be left are non-believers who have already rejected Christ and will follow the Antichrist anyway. There'll be no believers left to persecute, except the hundred and forty four thousand Jewish remnant. An alliance with Gaal won't do anyone any good."

Dr. Sveade sighed heavily as he looked up at the stars. "Dall, you've got to stop making decisions about the validity of this mission. I know the believers will be raptured out, but if you'll recall your Bible, you'll remember that those twelve thousand each from the twelve tribes of Israel who'll refuse to follow the Antichrist will convert to Christianity. They'll go throughout the world and convince people to resist the Antichrist and accept Christ. Not only will the Antichrist martyr many of the hundred and forty four thousand, but he'll hunt down and kill anyone they're able to convert. Anyone who doesn't follow him will be fair game. All believers will flee to havens of safety where they can survive until Christ returns to rule for the Millennium. We want one of those havens to be our nation, defended by a few million supernatural beings who have demonstrated their power by binding the evil ones."

Dall looked past Dr. Sveade at Agent Smith. He had casually reached his right hand under his left arm and was gripping the butt of a pistol. Dall knew beyond a doubt that the wrong answer would get him killed immediately. Dr. Sveade asked, "Now for the last time, will you stick to the game plan?"

Dall didn't speak and slowly nodded his head as he nervously backed away. He understood the game plan, but had serious doubts that Dr. Sveade was telling him everything. If he and Smith weren't even going to be around after the Rapture, why would they care what happens to the non-believers? They apparently knew they would be here, so they were obviously not believers. And if they were not believers girded with the armor of the Holy Spirit, how could they expect to negotiate with or exercise any control over a demon, especially one as powerful and Gaal? And since they weren't true believers, he had no doubt that they intended to end his involvement in the case right there in the district. Right now he was more convinced than ever that a life on the run was his only option.

Smith released his grip on the pistol. He interrupted Dall's thoughts and said, "That's our course, Dall. Now if you have no more questions, let's cut this short. I've got a body to bag."

Dall and Sandy walked past the sergeant who was sitting on the steps of the dilapidated back porch with his face buried in his hands. Dall patted his shoulder and said, "I'm sorry for your loss, sergeant. If I can help, I'd be happy to talk to you about it."

Even though Dall knew the sergeant would kill them in a heartbeat if ordered to do so, he couldn't help but feel his hurt. The sergeant looked up and said, "Thanks, Dall. I haven't had the opportunity to get to know either of you, but I can tell that you're good people." The ranger stood and looked back into the house, hoping he couldn't be overheard. He whispered, "Dall, you seem knowledgeable about the Bible and demons. What advice can you give me?"

Dall looked him in the eye and sighed. He patted him on the shoulder and said, "God is the only authority that Satan and the demons are afraid of, or are compelled to obey. If you want to fall under the umbrella of His protection, become one of His children. Right now, get off alone somewhere, then earnestly and honestly confess your sins to God and commit your life to Him. Only then will the Holy Spirit indwell you, and will God's authority be imparted upon you. It is only then that you'll fall under the protection of His authority, and only then will you be able to cast a demon out of your presence. If you don't believe in God and can't accept Him, then save yourself. Go back to your car and drive away from here. If you and the other sniper teams remain out there in the dark, you'll all be killed."

Smith stared out the window into the darkness. Waters said, "We're losing them, Sir. They're starting to think for themselves rather than allowing us to run the investigation. Parsons is not a strong enough personality to control Roberts. She's allowing him to work her rather than her working him. She's lost control."

Smith sighed, "Yes, Dexter, for once, I agree with you."

Dr. Sveade said, "Even though we're close by, Mr. Smith, Dall and Sandy are still being influenced by the Amish. We've got to find out what the Amish are telling them. They could be conspiring against us and we wouldn't know it. I can tell you from experience that it would be the nature of the Amish to identify Gaal and drive him from their midst. That would be catastrophic for us. We can't allow them to cast him out of the district. We'd never find him again, and there's not much time. By the way world events are shaping up, the Rapture could hit at any time and the antichrist would come to power. If that happens without our alliance with Gaal being solidified, we're doomed."

Smith shook his head in frustration and said, "Dexter, call the field office at St. Louis. Get us some unidirectional microphones and recording equipment out here. I want those ranger teams to work in closer to the Straus and Clevenger houses. I want recordings of all their conversations. Also have microphones attached to the outside of their houses. As soon as the Amish have any discussion of casting Gaal out, I want to know about it. We can't let that happen."

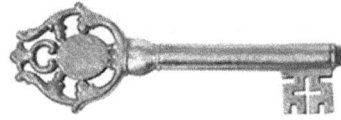

"I am he that liveth, and was dead; and behold, I am alive for evermore, Amen; and have the keys of hell and of death." **Revelation 1:18**

Sandy held Dall's arm tightly as they walked. When she noticed that they weren't going in the direction of the Straus farm, she asked, "Where are we going, Dall?"

"We're going to pay a visit to Bishop Clevenger. I want to see if he's as smart about Biblical matters as I think he is."

Sandy looked around nervously and said, "He doesn't look like the Bible College type, Dall. I doubt that he knows as much as Dr. Sveade."

The moon was bright tonight and she saw dark images following them in the shadows of the tree-lines. Dall comforted her by putting his arm around her shoulder. "Ignore them, Sandy. If they meant us harm, we'd be dead by now. They're just curious or looking for opportunities to cause trouble. And as for Bishop Clevenger, not all Bible scholars are made in a classroom. The smartest ones who ever walked the earth were made by spending their lives in the scriptures instead of a classroom. I have a hunch that this old bishop knows just as much as Dr. Sveade. I'm positive that he'll be more honest with us."

As Dall and Sandy approached Bishop Clevenger's farm house, Dall saw a figure on the porch in a rickety old rocking chair. As they walked up to the porch, Bishop Clevenger greeted them. "Evening children."

Dall said, "Evening, Bishop Clevenger. Looks like you were expecting us."

The bishop smiled. "I was. I saw you walking with that soldier across the pastures behind Abel's house. You've got my curiosity up, son. What were you doing over at the old Ballinger place? It's been vacant for years. And what's got my curiosity up even more is what is an armed soldier doing around Abel's property?"

Sandy felt that she should assert her authority, so she started to speak. Dall gently squeezed her hand to remind her that she was to maintain a submissive role. He said, "I can't explain that to you right now, Bishop, but you extended an invitation for us to talk to you anytime we wanted. If you're not getting ready to go to bed, could we talk to you for a few minutes? We might not get the chance to talk again."

Bishop Clevenger motioned to two cane chairs. "Sure, have a seat. Everyone else goes to bed at dark, but I can never make my brain wind down this early. I have to sit out here and talk to God for a while first. What can I help you with?"

Bishop Clevenger meant that he would answer any questions that Dall or Sandy had about the Amish faith, but Dall surprised him by taking another line of questioning. "Bishop, what can you tell me about some of the suspicious deaths around the district in the past few years?"

Bishop Clevenger looked suspiciously at Dall, then reluctantly explained, "Well, there was the death of Preacher Croft a few weeks ago. We're not certain what happened to him. The sheriff was working on it, but his investigation mysteriously shut down all of a sudden. I suspect that the soldier that you were walking with might have something to do with that. Mrs. Croft still doesn't have the answers she needs to get some closure on his death. A couple of years before that, Brother Wilhelm Dresselhaus was killed. We don't have answers to that death either. You're aware of Preacher Litchfield's disappearance. I suspect that these deaths are somehow related to those Army fellows being in the area."

The bishop stared at Dall, expecting an explanation. Dall looked at Sandy for guidance, but she didn't know what to do either. Dall decided that if they were going to cultivate an ally in the district, they had to trust someone. He sighed and lowered his gaze to the floor. He finally said, "Bishop, Sandy and I are looking for answers to the same questions. We don't know who to trust, but you seem to be the most rational and knowledgeable authority figure in the district. We don't trust Bishop Gordan, and no one else seems to know as much about the Bible as you."

Bishop Clevenger smiled and said, "You know, Dall, from the first day that Bishop Gordan said he was allowing two outcast Amish to return to the faith, I had my doubts about you. I assume that you're looking for a murderer."

Dall again looked at Sandy. Bishop Clevenger was totally unaware of their true mission. He nodded and said, "Yes, we are. Can you keep this between us? If it gets out that we are trying to solve murders, everyone will consider us English and won't speak to us. Bishop Gordan won't even allow us to remain in the district."

Bishop Clevenger pondered the situation for a few seconds. "I think we can keep this our little secret, but what concerns me is who you really are and what is your concern about three dead Amish men. Are you with the sheriff's office?"

Dall couldn't reveal their true mission, and he didn't want to lie to Bishop Clevenger. He said, "That's not important right now, Bishop, but it's very important that you trust us and not tell anyone else what we're doing here."

The bishop said, "I can keep a secret if it will rid our district of a killer, but I suspect that you have higher powers to answer to, and they'll not be happy about you talking to me."

"No, they won't, but maybe we can keep it to ourselves."

"Not likely, son." Bishop Clevenger motioned with his head toward on overgrown fence-row a hundred yards across the field. "Your Army friends have moved into position behind that fence. I saw them in the moonlight. Your superiors will know about our conversation as soon as they call them on their radio."

Dall casually turned and looked behind him. He couldn't see the rangers, but knew Bishop Clevenger had seen them move into position. The bishop asked, "Am I in any danger from those fellows?"

Sandy said, "No, Bishop, they're watching us."

The bishop smiled. "Well, whoever they're watching, I can't believe they mean us no harm since they're carrying rifles. They intend to shoot someone."

Dall said, "It's Sandy and me that they're watching, Bishop. Please keep all this to yourself, Sir. Sandy and I are going to be in serious trouble if we fail."

Bishop Clevenger frowned. "Dall, my dear son, there can be no secrets from Bishop Gordan. He can't be an effective leader of our flock if we keep things from him, especially something as significant as two undercover officers working a murder investigation in his district."

Dall understood and deeply respected Bishop Clevenger's loyalty. He said, "Bishop, I know you're concerned about the welfare of the district, but Bishop Gordan is not a good leader. And I'm not the only one around here who has doubts about his relationship with God. I've heard the talk."

Sandy could keep quiet no longer. "And I don't believe for one minute that he had no knowledge of how Preacher Litchfield was treating us. He put us under his care to drive us out."

Bishop Clevenger pursed his lips as he considered the opinions of the young folks. He looked back at the corner-post that concealed the ranger snipers and said, "I've heard it, too. I have to admit that I and some of the elders have serious concerns about Bishop Gordan's edict on discipline. But he is the bishop. I'm only an assistant bishop. I must submit myself to his authority, and as long as you're here in this district, so must you. I am, however, more loyal to God than to His appointed shepherd. Men are fallible, He is not."

Dall seized the opportunity. "Then you'll understand our position, Bishop. Our first loyalty is to God. It is by His hand that we were brought here. King Saul was a great king until his hatred for David corrupted him. Bishop Gordan's authority is God-ordained, and if he abuses that authority, God is capable of sending someone to unseat him. Now we don't propose to usurp Bishop Gordan's authority, but catching this murderer is certainly a higher calling than Bishop Gordan maintaining his power base. We're here to serve a higher power. If Bishop Gordan becomes a casualty of this investigation, then that is nothing more than a case of God removing a disobedient servant from his position and replacing him with someone who will obey God's law, not his own."

Bishop Clevenger nodded reluctantly. He knew very well that Bishop Gordan had long ago replaced God's laws with his own. He said, "For now, Dall. For now I'll keep our conversations to myself. Just stick to catching the killer and don't interfere with Amish affairs. Rather than praying for Bishop Gordan to be removed, it is our command from God to pray for him and ask God to enlighten him and make him a better leader. That's what we in the district will do. Now! How can I help you?"

Dall looked back toward the fence-row and sighed heavily. "Bishop, I need a fresh prospective on something. I think I have a pretty good knowledge about this, but I'm getting some conflicting information. I think you're knowledgeable enough about this that you can set me straight."

"What matter would that be, son?"

"Demons."

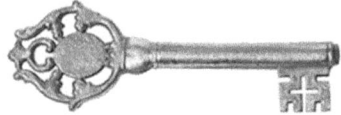

"I am he that liveth, and was dead; and behold, I am alive for evermore, Amen; and have the keys of hell and of death." **Revelation 1:18**

Sampson Betendorf quietly eased off the front porch and stayed in the shadows. Young Katie was the love of his life, and he'd been patient with her antics long enough. This night he would follow her and see which of the young boys was trying to rob her of her salvation.

Sampson was a stocky man, and generally considered the strongest man in the entire county. Although he had tried to keep his own cavorting with the English a secret, his forays into the English taverns had earned him a notorious reputation among the brawlers and scrappers who had experienced his upper-body strength and rock-hard fists first hand. As ashamed as he was of his own sins, that was no justification for his beloved Katie to fall into temptation. He might burn in hell, but his little girl would not.

Katie hurried to Massey's pond, glancing over her shoulder only occasionally. Her glances were too brief and unfocussed to notice the movement of her father in the shadows. As she hurried through the brush that concealed Massey's pond, she found Isaac waiting alone on a fallen log. She threw herself into his arms and they kissed deeply.

Abel leaned against a tree, well hidden from the lovers. He had allowed his mind to drift back to the days when he and his life-long love had first begun to savor each other's kisses. As he dreamed, he found himself hoping that Isaac and Katie would cut their visit short tonight so he could get back home and wake Dory for another passionate shattering of Bishop Gordan's prohibition against lovemaking.

As Abel was smiling fondly at his recollection of his first sight of Dory without her clothes, he was suddenly jerked back to the present by a dark figure moving through the shadows on the other side of the pond. Isaac and Katie were oblivious to the presence of anyone else, and their kissing and petting had increased their heart rates and breathing to the point that they could hear nothing but each other.

As Sampson stepped out of the shadows, Abel read the anger on his face in the moonlight. Isaac and Katie saw him almost immediately and separated quickly.

Sampson clenched his fists as he stomped up to Isaac. Isaac tried to erase the fear from his face as he stood his ground, but Abel knew his son well enough to know that he was frozen in place by paralyzing fear, not courage.

Katie intercepted her father and grabbed his wrists. She tried to force them downward to give Isaac time to escape. Her voice quivered with fear as she pleaded, "Daddy! Daddy, please don't hurt him! He's my future husband and your son-in-law! If I mean anything to you, please don't hurt him!"

With one hand, Sampson gently gripped the front of Katie's dress and lifted her off the ground. He pulled her close to him so her wide-eyes and trembling lips were only inches from his face. With tears in his eyes, his beard rubbed her chin as he growled, "You get yourself home, young lady! You'll thank me later for stopping this before this spawn of Satan robs you of your salvation and brings the wrath of the elders and bishops down upon you both!"

As terrified as Isaac was, he could not stand by and see Katie hurt. On shaky legs he stumbled up to Sampson and said, "Please, Mr. Betendorf, I'm the one to blame. Please don't hurt Katie. I couldn't stand that."

Sampson reached out with his other hand and grabbed Isaac by the shirt. He lifted him up and gently put Katie down. He turned his vicious glare to Isaac and snarled, "You're right, you demon, you are to blame!" He kept his murderous stare on Isaac and said to Katie, "You get your butt home, Katie! We'll talk when I get there!"

Katie was crying hysterically. She grabbed her father's face and tried to turn it toward her. He refused to be deterred, so she pushed her face between him and Isaac so she could look Sampson in the eyes. As she inhaled the stench of liquor, she cried, "Daddy, you don't know what you're doing! This is the boy that I'll marry someday! This is the father of your grandchildren! You know how much you love little kids! Do you want to have to explain to them someday how you hurt their father?"

Isaac squirmed and tried to force open Sampson's fist. His young hands had no chance of opening the steel vice that gripped his shirt. The more Katie screamed the angrier Sampson became. As he was reaching up to grip Isaac's throat with his free hand, another large hand moved gently between him and Katie. Abel gently pressed his palm against Katie's wet face and pushed her away. In his deep voice, he calmly said, "It'll be okay, Katie. I'll handle this. You get home like your father said."

Katie reluctantly stepped aside as Abel stepped in and gripped Samson's fist. As strong as he was, he could not pry Isaac free. He knew he'd survive a fight with Sampson, but he didn't know how badly Isaac would be hurt in the fray. One punch from Sampson would kill Isaac instantly.

Abel tried to keep calm and said, "Sampson, dear brother, it's me, Abel. Katie is right. These two are in love. They'll probably be married someday. If you make that impossible, then they'll likely run away. You don't want that. You don't want to hurt Isaac. You know him. He's a good boy. You know our family. I've been watching these two for several weeks. I wouldn't let things get out of hand, Sampson. Katie was never in any danger of losing her salvation because of Isaac. I've been here the whole time. If you must carry out your wrath against someone, please lash me. I deserve it, not Isaac. I'll gladly submit."

Sampson continued his glare into Isaac's eyes. As he ignored Abel's plea, he grabbed Isaac's throat with his other hand. Sensing that Isaac would be killed, Abel removed his hunting knife from his back pocket and unsnapped the safety strap on the sheath with his thumb. He gave it a flip and slung the sheath off the blade, allowing it to fall at his feet. Isaac gagged as his air supply was cut off.

Abel carefully slid the point of the knife alongside Isaac's neck till the point was pressing against Sampson's palm. He then slowly drove the blade through Sampson's palm with the intention of stopping as soon as he released Isaac.

Sampson's stare into Isaac's eyes was broken only when the blade of Abel's knife sliced through the backside of his hand. He shifted his stare to the bloody blade as Abel said, "I'll cut your hand clear off if I have to, Sampson. Please let the boy go."

As the pain shot up Sampson's arm, he slowly released Isaac's throat and shirt. Isaac stepped back and rubbed his neck as Abel said, "Isaac, go home." Isaac hurried through the bushes and found Katie waiting on the other side. He gave his father one final glance and saw the dark forms circling the two men. He put his arm around Katie as they hurried off.

Sampson's anger dissolved as he regained his sanity. He slowly moved his bewildered stare from the blade protruding through the back of his hand to Abel's eyes. Abel smiled and quickly jerked the blade out of Sampson's hand. He pulled his handkerchief from his back pocket and wiped the blood from his knife, then grabbed Sampson's wrist and wrapped the handkerchief around the bleeding hand. He closed Sampson's hand and said, "Keep your fist closed, Brother Sampson; it'll slow the bleeding."

Sampson sighed and moaned, "Sorry, Abel, I guess I got carried away. I don't know what happens to me sometimes. When I get mad, it's almost as though there's someone else inside me that I can't control. I guess the drinking doesn't help."

Abel put his arm around the shorter man's shoulders. He hugged him and said, "Ah, Sampson, you just love your daughter. We all want better for our kids than we've done. I've lost control of myself in the past when it involved my kids. Come on, let's go for a walk and talk about how we're going to spoil our future grandkids."

Abel picked up the sheath and slid his knife back in it. In a manner totally uncharacteristic for Amish men, Abel left his fatherly arm around Sampson's shoulder and led him to the edge of the timber. As they walked toward home, Sampson kept pressure on his bleeding hand while they talked and laughed about the antics of their children and the high hopes that each held for them. When they got to Abel's farm they got in his buggy and drove to Lilly Dresselhaus's house so she could treat Sampson's hand.

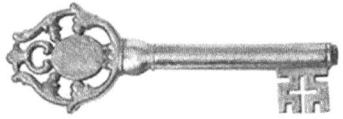

"I am he that liveth, and was dead; and behold, I am alive for evermore, Amen; and have the keys of hell and of death." **Revelation 1:18**

Bishop Clevenger had heard enough, and quickly grew tired of the verbal judo. He said, "Dall, I'm weary of this game. The English, and especially the federal government, don't care enough about the deaths of a few Amish men to send undercover officers and Army snipers into a district. Why are you really here, and why do you ask about demons?"

Dall lowered his head and tried to think of a way to pick the bishop's brain without divulging any of Dr. Sveade's plans. When he looked back up at the bishop, he realized that the bishop would figure it out on his own eventually. Wanting to maintain his credibility with Bishop Clevenger, he decided to open up. "Bishop, I think your three men were murdered by a demon."

Bishop Clevenger leaned back and looked out across the countryside with a blank stare. "A demon."

Dall said, "You don't seem surprised."

"No, my dear boy, I'm not. I've suspected it for a long time. I know Preacher Croft was killed by a demon working through one of our brothers. If the other two weren't killed by a demon, then it was by one of our men being influenced by a demon. Either way a demon was the cause. It's just unusual to hear anyone in the English world even admit that there are demons working here on earth."

"I'm no ordinary English man, Bishop. I've studied the scriptures quite extensively, and I'm very aware of the role that demons and Satan have played in the history of man, and the role they'll play in the prophesied End-Times outlined in Revelations."

"Then what can I teach you, Dall? Demons are no mystery."

"I thought so, too, Bishop, but there's been a new wrinkle thrown into my previous beliefs."

"And what would that be, son?"

"I've been asked to find one particular demon and try to establish a relationship with him."

Bishop Clevenger leaned forward to the edge of his chair and glared in disbelief at Dall. He then lowered his gaze to the floor as he shook his head in disbelief. "Dall, I want to help you two, but if what you say is true, you have no idea what you are doing. Demons are not hard to contact. They are more than willing to establish a relationship with anyone who invites them into their mind. The problem is that once invited in, they cannot be controlled or believed in anything they say. And non-believers can't cast them out. I know you're armored by the blood of Christ, but if you do establish a relationship with this demon, he'll work you rather than you working him."

Sandy said, "We've been told that demons can take any form and can know our thoughts."

Bishop Clevenger leaned back in his chair and nodded. "Yes. Demons are spiritual beings that have the power to take any form they want. I'm not sure they can read our thoughts, but they know our human nature so well that they can easily figure out our weaknesses. They can see us when we think we're alone and hear our most private conversations. They can see our actions that we think are secret and figure out where our lusts lie, then whisper in our ears or put those temptations in front of us. They can also indwell a person who leaves his consciousness open for occupation and has no relationship with God."

Sandy asked, "What difference does it make if the person believes in God or not?"

Bishop Clevenger smiled. "Sandy, my dear, you're ignorance is betraying your spiritual state. It's written many places in the Bible that once a person genuinely accepts God as their savior and repents of their sins, God comes into that person's heart and indwells them. God refers to that person's body as His temple. No demon can cohabitate in the presence of God. Once indwelled by the Holy Spirit, it's impossible for a demon to indwell that person. You're not a believer, or you would've known that."

Sandy shifted in her chair nervously. "I wasn't until this assignment. I'm quickly becoming one."

The bishop said, "Listen, youngsters, I've known for a long time that there's a demon in this district, probably more than one, but you're not capable of manipulating him. I don't know what your superiors have told you, but demons are far superior to humans in power and intelligence. Whatever you think you're going to get this demon to do, he's way ahead of you. He already knows what your plans are, and he's setting events in motion to turn the tables on you. You'll end up fulfilling his mission instead of him fulfilling yours."

Dall and Sandy looked at each other and knew the other's thoughts. They were being conned by Smith and Dr. Sveade. Dall asked, "Bishop, in your opinion, is it possible that there could be some demons who think they made a mistake when they followed Satan and were cast out of Heaven?"

Bishop Clevenger nodded. "Most certainly. Listen, Dall, those demons were originally created as angels, just like Satan. They were there when God created the earth and everything on it. They knew God's power and still chose to challenge His authority. They knew instantly that they'd made a mistake, but they'll never accept that. That's the nature of sin. Even when all evidence reveals a person's sin, they still refuse to accept it and repent. It's their pride and arrogance. Demons are just like criminals. They're pathological liars and totally corrupt. They know nothing but their own desires and will always do what is best for them. You can never trust a demon, ever. Whatever you think you're going to accomplish, you'll only be manipulated."

Sandy said, "So if someone said there was going to be a war in the demon world that will unseat Satan, that would be a lie."

The bishop had a doubtful squint in his eyes. "Sandy, if you'll study the fall of Satan, you'll understand his power. Before his fall, he was the most powerful created being. He was the archangel over all the angels. There are billions of angels, and he was the most powerful. When he was cast out of Heaven, he no longer had power over the angels there, but I assure you, his power over the ones that fell with him is unchallengeable. Any demon who tried to overthrow Satan would be instantly defeated. As a matter of fact, I'm not sure that a demon is even capable of thinking of such a thing without Satan knowing it."

Sandy asked, "If he did, Satan would destroy him, right?"

"No, dear, demons can't be destroyed. They're spiritual beings, therefore they're eternal. When God wants to take a demon off the Earth, He binds him and casts him into the dark pit. Satan has the same power over his realm. He would bind and constrain them, but I doubt that that has ever happened. As far as I can tell, they're all cut from the same bolt of cloth and are completely loyal to Satan."

Dall nodded. "I guess I knew as much, Bishop. Thanks, I guess we'll go home now."

"Before you go, Dall, just because your information about demons is incorrect doesn't mean that you're wrong about a demon working this district. For the sake of our flock, I want to know what you know about this."

"Bishop, I can only tell you that Sandy and I are here to locate a demon. Our intelligence indicates that he is in this district. He's either working outwardly or through someone. We're running out of time. Our controllers want us to contact this demon or the person that he's controlling. Can you help us?"

Bishop Clevenger sighed. "Yes, but I wish you had been honest about your purpose from the start."

"I'm sorry we lied, but there are lives at stake."

"God forgives lying if it serves a greater cause. You've certainly played your roles well. Was it worth the lashings that you took?"

"If we can locate this demon, yes."

The bishop slowly struggled to his feet and said, "Well, it just so happens that the bishop has assigned several of us to search out this demon and cast him from our district."

Sandy looked sternly at the bishop and said, "Oh, Bishop, please don't do that. You have no idea how much trouble that would bring down upon your members. Please just let us handle him when you find him."

Bishop Clevenger escorted the two to the edge of his porch. "Your agenda takes precedence over ours, does it?"

Sandy nodded her head."Yes, I'm sorry to put it so bluntly, but our controllers have put us on notice. Anyone trying to cast out this demon will be dealt with very harshly; Amish or English."

Bishop Clevenger reluctantly said, "Okay, I'll help you find this demon, kids. To find him you'll have to know what kind of behavior a person demonstrates when they are indwelled by a demon. And this demon may not be indwelling anyone at all. Demons can influence a person's mind without indwelling them."

Dall said, "We've seen this one. He is taking the form of a little girl, but I don't think he's indwelling her. He is merely taking her appearance so he can move around unchallenged."

"Which little girl?"

"Abel Straus's daughter, Judith."

The bishop rubbed his beard and groaned, "Oh, Dall, I've spent lots of time around that child. This demon has to be imitating her appearance. There's no way he could be indwelling her. I'd have recognized it right off. Just to be safe, though, I'll make a point to talk to her privately. If he is in her, I'll find him."

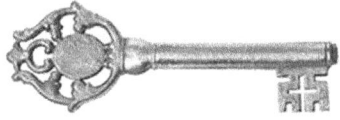

"I am he that liveth, and was dead; and behold, I am alive for evermore, Amen; and have the keys of hell and of death." **Revelation 1:18**

Dall and Sandy walked through the dark toward the Straus home. She looked over her shoulder and saw the rangers tailing them two hundred yards back. She said, "I think we made a mistake, Dall. Telling Bishop Clevenger about Gaal has put him in great danger."

"You may be right. I hope nothing happens to him, but we've got to trust someone. Smith and Dr. Sveade aren't telling us the whole truth. I don't know what their agenda is, but they're terribly naïve and have to know that forming an alliance with Gaal is impossible. They're not even who they say they are."

"What do you mean?"

"Smith is not F.B.I. Earlier he accused the ranger of insubordination. He wasn't insubordinate if Smith works for the F.B.I., because the ranger was not one of his subordinates. An Army ranger could only be insubordinate to a higher ranking Army officer."

Sandy gasped, "That's why Smith didn't seem concerned when I told him that I was going to file a formal complaint against him with the director. He doesn't answer to the director. He's Army!"

"Yes, and remember when Dr. Sveade told us about his early years with the special unit in World War II; the one that interviewed the high-ranking Nazi officers? That was an Army unit. They only partnered with the F.B.I. to have the use of their agents and forensics lab. If you've listened closely to Smith when he talks, he refers to this assignment as a mission. That's a military term for an assignment."

Sandy pondered Dall's point, then said, "That's right. The F.B.I. calls it a case. The Army carries out missions, but the F.B.I. works cases." She thought some more, then continued, "So the bureau hasn't sold me out, except to loan me to the Army. And Smith can't transfer me anywhere including the Aleutian Islands. He can't do anything to me."

Dall reminder her, "Nothing except have you killed. You saw him a while ago. He was completely prepared to gun me down right there in my tracks if I showed the slightest intent to run."

"I know. I'm glad you backed down."

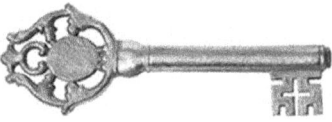

"I am he that liveth, and was dead; and behold, I am alive for evermore, Amen; and have the keys of hell and of death." **Revelation 1:18**

Dall opened the door to his quarters in the barn. He turned on the light and removed his coat. Before Sandy could take off hers, there was a knock on the door. When Dall opened it, he found Isaac and Judith waiting outside. "Come in, Kids."

Isaac and Judith stepped in and waited politely for an invitation to sit. Dall pointed to a couple of chairs and said, "What's on your mind, Isaac?"

Isaac shrugged his shoulders, a little embarrassed about his nosiness. "Judith and I were just wondering where you've been. She saw you leave the barn earlier and walk across the fields."

Dall looked at Sandy. She said, "Dall and I like to walk together at night. We talk about things that we can't discuss throughout the day. Don't you ever walk with your father or mother and talk?"

Isaac looked suspiciously at her. "You walk and talk with a soldier leading you?"

Dall hung his head and said, "I forgot that, Isaac. Do Sandy and I mean anything to you?" Isaac and Judith both nodded their heads. "Then, please, Isaac, please don't tell anyone about that soldier. Can you please give us a little time and keep that to yourself?"

Isaac slowly nodded his head. Dall looked at Judith and asked, "Can you, Judith?" She nodded her head, too.

Isaac lowered his head and grew angry. "Anyway, since you asked, my father and I don't talk. I just do as I'm told or I get lashed."

Dall sensed Isaac's anger. He again motioned to a chair and said, "Sit, Isaac. Maybe there's something that I can do to help."

Isaac sat hesitantly, but Judith stood against the wall without speaking. Isaac said, "There's nothing that anyone can do. That's just the way it is in this district. That's all the elders and bishops know, lash and beat the kids."

Dall sat on the edge of the bed beside Sandy. He recalled the many counseling sessions that he had conducted as a youth counselor. He rubbed his hands together and formulated his thoughts. He said, "You know, Isaac, when I was a kid, my dad was pretty hard on me at times. At the time I thought he was being unreasonable, but after I grew up, I realize that he got angry with me because he wanted so badly for me to do well in life. He wanted to spare me the consequences of a rebellious life. He came across harsh and intolerant, but he really loved me."

Isaac's eyes filled as his anger grew. He growled through gritted teeth, "Well, my father doesn't love me!"

Dall had seen the sensitive hearts of angry teenagers wallowing in their self-pity before. He wanted to be Isaac's friend, not his adversary.

"Isaac, I won't tell you that you'll understand someday when you grow up. You've heard that too many times before. That won't help you deal with what you're feeling now. But how long has it been since he lashed you?"

Isaac glanced at Judith who'd heard the story many times before. "Several months, I guess."

Dall nodded and said, "Sounds like a long time, considering your attitude lately. I haven't been around very long, but I've noticed that you're displaying a lot of hostility toward your father. It looks to me like he's trying to find other ways to reach you."

"That may be, but that doesn't make up for all the lashings that I took when I didn't deserve them. And I'm not the only one; Judith and baby Jack got lashed and slapped for no good reason, too."

Dall listened while Isaac spent the next five minutes listing all the reasons that Adel Straus should be hanged. When Isaac had finally vented long enough, he sighed and stared at the floor in frustration. He stood and walked to the door as he said, "I didn't come here to complain about my father."

Dall intercepted him before he could get outside, and gently took him by the shoulder. "Isaac, listen. One of the hardest things for a young man to get over is being lashed when he thinks he's a man and shouldn't be treated like a child. And forgiveness is one of the hardest things to do. All of us men have a problem with forgiveness. I guess it's part of our makeup. But I want you to remember something. None of us are immune to a lashing. I took a pretty good one myself a few days ago. Your father is a great man. Not just because of his massive size, but because of his impeccable integrity and strong moral values. He stepped in and saved my life. He didn't have to do that, and he did it at considerable risk to his own safety. Deep in his heart he loves you, Judith and baby Jack very much. I happen to know that he's very troubled about his relationship with you. Now, nobody can do it for you, but if you're ever going to be a real man, you've got to learn to forgive. All your life, people will be stepping on you from all directions. If you put them at the top of your hate-list, that list will grow larger every day, and you'll spend all your time and energy hating. It'll rob you of your happiness, and no one will want to be around you. Hate eats you alive and has absolutely no effect on the people you hate. You're the only one who'll suffer. And keep in mind, God tells us in the Bible that if you don't forgive, you won't be forgiven."

Isaac stared out into the darkness. He nodded and said, "I'm already suffering. I want to forgive, but I don't know how. I've got to get to bed, but can we talk again?"

Dall smiled and patted Isaac on the back. "Sure, Isaac. Let's talk soon."

Isaac looked back at Judith, who remained quiet. She knew her way back to the house, so he went on without her. Dall closed the door as Isaac left and went back to the bed. He sat beside Sandy and asked Judith, "So, young lady, shouldn't you get to bed before your parents miss you?"

Judith showed no emotion as she walked over and climbed up on Sandy's lap. Sandy wrapped her arms around her and hugged her tightly. Over the past few days, she and Judith had become best friends.

As Sandy relaxed her hold, she noticed an uncharacteristic tenseness in Judith's muscles. Judith said in a man's voice, "YOU'VE WANTED TO TALK TO ME ALONE. NOW IS A GOOD TIME."

Sandy instantly panicked when she realized that Gaal was sitting on her lap. She screamed and pushed him off. Judith landed on her feet as Sandy crawled backward across the bed. Dall jumped to his feet as Sandy grabbed her pistol from the bed stand and shoved it toward Judith.

Dall yelled, "No! That won't do any good! You'll just kill Judith, and there'll be hell to pay with Abel! Put it down, Sandy!"

Sandy cried hysterically as her hand trembled. She relaxed her tension on the trigger, but kept the pistol trained on Judith.

Dall took assessment of his body language and realized that he was pinned against the wall in fear. As he tried to slow his breathing, he chastised himself internally. *"You're a believer! You have power over this demon! Show him who the boss is!"*

He pried himself off the wall and stood over Judith's small body. She didn't notice him. She had tilted her head back and was drawing in deep breaths, savoring the intoxicating aroma of their fear. Dall's voice quivered as he said, "Yes, Gaal, we want to talk to you. There's no point in playing games. You know why we're here. Can we talk calmly here or are you going to try to kill us again?"

Judith lowered her head until her chin was on her chest. She shook her head and continued to inhale deeply as she walked to the chair that Isaac had been sitting in earlier. She climbed up on it, and Gaal said, "I

CAN DO YOU NO HARM, BLESSED ONE. YOUR FLESH IS THE FATHER'S TEMPLE, AND I AM SUBJECT TO HIS AUTHORITY."

Dall then remembered that Sandy was not a believer and had no power over demons. He positioned himself on the bed in front of her as a shield. He said, "I want your word that you'll do no harm to Sandy." Remembering that a demons word meant nothing, he rephrased his order. "I command you to not touch her."

Gaal nodded gently and acknowledged Dall's power over him. "IT WILL BE AS YOU SAY, FOR NOW."

Sandy forced herself to put down the pistol. She moved back across the bed and sat beside Dall. She tried to slow her breathing and calm her nerves as she asked with a shaky voice, "Why do you want to hurt me?"

Gaal said, "I WISH YOU NO HARM. I NEED TO TALK THROUGH YOU. I NEED TO DWELL WITHIN YOU WHILE YOU ARE HERE. IT IS BECOMING HARDER FOR ME TO MOVE ABOUT AS I AM."

Sandy asked, "How are you able to live in Abel's house without him recognizing you in Judith?"

Judith shrugged her shoulders. "I DON'T INDWELL JUDITH ALL THE TIME, ONLY WHEN I NEED HER. AND I AM CAREFUL TO NOT REVEAL MYSELF IN HER. SHE THINKS I AM HER SECRET FRIEND. HER PARENTS PAY HER NO MIND WHEN SHE TALKS OF ME. THEY THINK IT IS THE RAMBLINGS OF A YOUNG CHILD'S WILD IMAGINATION."

Dall said, "Gaal, you are aware of our purpose here. You've heard our conversations with Smith and Dr. Sveade. You were working with Heinrich Himmler in World War II. You've been trying to form an alliance with a world power."

Gaal never took Judith's bright eyes off Sandy. He stared lustfully at her as a hungry dog would stare at a piece of meat. His stare unnerved Sandy because it wasn't the kind of stare that she had long ago become accustomed to. He didn't stare at her breasts or hips. He stared wantonly into her eyes. It wasn't her body he wanted; it was her soul.

As he stared at Sandy, he spoke to Dall while his facial muscles displayed a slight spasm. "I HAVE TRIED TO FORGE A COVENANT WITH MANY WORLD POWERS THROUGHOUT THE SHORT HISTORY OF MAN. HEINRICH HIMMLER WAS CERTAINLY ONE OF MY MOST PROMISING PROSPECTS. THE FAITHLESS FOOL! HE HAD LOST HIS COURAGE AND FAITH IN ME. JUST WHEN HITLER WAS AT HIS WEAKEST AND MOST VULNERABLE, HEINRICH LOST HIS COURAGE AND LET THE OPPORTUNITY PASS HIM BY. I WANTED HIM TO

SLAY HITLER AND TAKE OVER THE REICH, BUT HE CHOSE TO TURN COWARD AND RUN. HE CHOSE TO CHANGE HIS APPEARANCE AND DRESS AS A PRIVATE IN THE SECRET FIELD POLICE. BUT HIS EGO BETRAYED HIM. HE COULDN'T STAND TO BE A LOWLY PRIVATE, SO HE TOOK THE UNIFORM OF A SERGEANT. LITTLE DID HE KNOW THAT I HAD PLANTED THE IDEA IN THE ALLIED COMMANDERS' HEADS TO ORDER THEIR MEN TO ONLY ARREST SECRET FIELD POLICE MEMBERS WEARING THE RANK OF SERGEANT AND ABOVE."

Dall sighed in agreement with Gaal. "Had he been content to remain a private, he would have lived out his life in the lap of luxury in Central or South America after his release."

Gaal shook his head. "ONE WOULD THINK SO, BUT IN REALITY HE WOULD NOT. I WOULD HAVE KILLED HIM SLOWLY AND PAINFULLY FOR BETRAYING ME."

Sandy and Dall looked at each other as the reality of Gaal's power was once again affirmed. Gaal continued, "AND BEFORE HIMMLER, I TRIED TO SPEAK WITH STALIN, BUT HE DID NOT BELIEVE ME WHEN I REVEALED THE PROPHESIES OF THE END-TIMES. ALTHOUGH HE HAD STUDIED AT TIFLIS SEMINARY AS A BOY AND HAD READ THE BIBLE, HE WAS NEVER A BELIEVER. HIS SOUL HAD BECOME HARDENED BY AN ABUSIVE FATHER. HE REFUSED TO BELIEVE THE PROPHECIES FORETOLD BY JOHN AND DANIEL, AND CHOSE INSTEAD TO IMMERSE HIMSELF IN THE WRITINGS OF KARL MARX. THE ARROGANT TYRANT THOUGHT HE WAS SMARTER THAN ME. HE PROMISED ME MANY THINGS, BUT DIDN'T REALIZE THAT I COULD HEAR HIS MOST PRIVATE CONVERSATIONS. WHEN I HEARD HIS PLANS TO BETRAY ME, I LEFT HIM. BEFORE THAT I TRIED TO ALLY MYSELF WITH TSAR NICHOLAS II THROUGH HIS WIFE, ALEXANDRA, BUT HE WAS TOO WEAK AND FELL FROM POWER."

Dall perked up and said, "Tsar Nicholas's wife was being manipulated by a prophet-monk named Rasputin. Were you Rasputin?"

"NO, I HAD NOT MANIFESTED MYSELF AS HIM, BUT I WAS IN HIM. GRIGORI WAS A MERE DEMENTED SIBERIAN PEASANT WHEN I INDWELLED HIM."

"He was murdered. Did you do that?"

"NO, BUT MY LEGION SAW TO IT."

"Could you not have stopped him from being murdered?"

"I COULD HAVE. HE WAS AN ILLITERATE HEATHEN WHEN I FOUND HIM WALLOWING IN DEPRAVITY AND POVERTY IN HIS SMALL SIBERIAN VILLAGE. I INDWELLED HIM WHEN HE WAS A VERY YOUNG CHILD, SHORTLY AFTER HIS BROTHER DROWNED. AT FIRST HE ALLOWED ME TO DISCIPLE HIM. I GAVE HIM THE POWER TO READ MINDS AND HEAL ANIMALS BY laying hands on them. I got him admitted to a monastery, then brought him to power by gaining him access to the royal palace when Tsar Nicholas's son, Alexei, was seriously ill from one of his many episodes related to hemophilia."

Dall said, "I remember reading about that. He healed Alexei.

Judith shook her head as Gaal said angrily, No! I healed Alexei many times through the hands of Rasputin! The Empress, Alix, who later became Alexandra, believed that he was endowed by God with special healing powers. No one knew where he got his power to heal Alexei, but it was from me. After I had brought him to a position of prominence and influence in the royal family, he became vain and self-deluded with my power, and only wanted to fulfill his own lust for power, liquor and fornication. I had revealed prophesies to him and worked many healings through his hands. He began to believe that it was he who was working the miracles, not me. He capitalized on that power and turned it to his own glory."

Dall asked, "I can see that, but couldn't you have controlled him and still used him?"

"No. The reprobate was consumed with pride. Although he was trusted by Alexandra, Tsar Nicholas remained skeptical of him. He was unwilling to do the things that would put him in Tsar Nicholas' trusted circle, so he could not have the influence over Russia's future that I needed, and was therefore no longer useful to me. He had not supported the First World War as I had told him. When the war went badly for Russia, the people and military blamed Grigori and called him the Mad Monk. They actually believed that he was possessed by Satan. They never knew how close to the truth they really were. He'd become the most hated man in Russia. To punish him for his betrayal, my faithful orchestrated his assassination."

Dall said, "You're trying to gain God's favor, yet you orchestrated a murder?"

"My brethren did. I merely did nothing to stop them. The night he died, they banded together several conspirators. I had always had a fondness for Madeira wine, and I imparted that love in Grigori. We instructed the assassins to lure him to a basement with Madeira wine and cream filled pastries laced with cyanide. He slobbered and slurped like the revolting, mud-wallowing pig that he was. When the poison did not have the desired effect, they shot him with a

PISTOL. THEY BECAME TERRIFIED WHEN GRIGORI AWOKE AND STOOD TO HIS FEET AFTER BEING SHOT. THEY SHOT HIM AGAIN AND THREW HIM IN THE RIVER. THEY WERE SURE THAT HE WAS POSSESSED BY SATAN. I THEN LEFT HIM TO THE CONSEQUENCES OF HIS OWN ARROGANCE AND LUST. HE WOULD NOT DIE AS LONG AS I INDWELLED HIM. IT WAS ONLY AFTER I'D DEPARTED HIS BODY THAT HE DIED. HE HAD SURVIVED THE POISON AND GUNSHOTS. THE DOCTORS DETERMINED THAT THE CAUSE OF HIS DEATH WAS DROWNING. THE ROMANOV FAMILY FELL SHORTLY AFTERWARDS. HIS WHOLE RISE TO POWER, HIS HOLD ON THE ROYAL FAMILY AND HIS POWER TO OVERCOME DEATH WAS ALL A MYSTERY, BUT IT WAS MY POWER THAT PRESERVED HIM."

Dall listened in disbelief as he tried to process the inside information from the very person who was directly responsible for some of the world's most significant events. He asked, "If you are subject to the Father's authority, why did He allow you to manipulate and murder those men?"

Judith shrugged her shoulders as Gaal said, "I CAN'T SPEAK FOR THE FATHER. I DIDN'T DISCUSS IT WITH HIM. HE CERTAINLY COULD HAVE STOPPED IT, BUT HE PERMITTED IT TO HAPPEN. I SUSPECT THAT ONCE HE GAVE MAN A FREE WILL TO CHOOSE SIN OVER OBEDIENCE, THAT HE ALLOWED US TO TEMPT MAN. AND SOMETIMES WHEN A MORTAL BECOMES SO CORRUPT, AND THEIR HEART AND SOUL IS HARDENED AGAINST GOD'S WORD, GOD WILL TURN THAT PERSON OVER TO A FALLEN ONE FOR THE DESTRUCTION OF THE FLESH. NONE OF US WHO WERE CAST OUT OF HEAVEN WILL EVER KNOW HIS THOUGHTS OUTSIDE THOSE WRITTEN IN SCRIPTURE. YOU AS ONE OF THE REDEEMED WILL SOMEDAY BE ABLE TO ASK HIM ALL THE QUESTIONS THAT HAVE PLAGUED MANKIND FOR THE ENTIRE 6,000 YEARS OF MAN'S EXISTENCE, BUT WE FALLEN WILL NEVER HAVE THAT OPPORTUNITY, UNLESS I AM SUCCESSFUL IN SECURING A PROVISION FOR OUR REDEMPTION FROM GOD."

The more Gaal talked, the more convinced Dall became that he was legitimately who he said he was. Gaal continued, "BEFORE THAT, I HAD TRIED TO BEFRIEND WORLD LEADERS ALL THE WAY BACK TO HEROD, WHO WAS THE KING OF ISRAEL AT THE TIME OF JESUS' BIRTH. I HAD ACTUALLY TRIED TO STOP HEROD FROM KILLING ALL THE MALE CHILDREN IN BETHLEHEM IN AN EFFORT TO KILL JESUS. I KNEW THAT WOULD ONLY MAKE IT HARDER FOR US TO CONVINCE GOD TO CREATE A PROVISION FOR OUR REDEMPTION, AND SOLIDIFY HIS CONVICTION TO CAST US ALL INTO THE LAKE OF FIRE AT THE GREAT WHITE THRONE JUDGMENT. BUT HEROD HATED JESUS BECAUSE HE was actually the King of the Jews. Herod thought he was the King of the Jews, but it was Jesus. His jealousy of Jesus overpowered my control over him."

Dall said, "Boy, Gaal, you certainly picked some losers to form your covenant with. If you were trying to impress God, couldn't you look into the future and see what they would have become? Couldn't you have picked someone destined for success?"

"No, we have no insight into the future other than what God has revealed in scripture. We are as blind about things to come as you mortals are. Since we fallen can't predict who will rise to power and who won't, we are forced to indwell many people. You would be surprised if you knew the successful and seemingly charismatic leaders who we have indwelled or influenced. Some are very charming and pleasant."

After a short pause, Gaal continued, "They were all the same. Like Rasputin, they all became proud and drunk with my power. They could not surrender their own will and allow me to work through them. When they had become so vain and consumed with their own desires, they all fell from power and died. They were of no use to me. I have decided on a different approach this time. Rather than trying to control one man, I am going to be more open about who I am and who I try to form a covenant with. I'm going to go after an entire nation. That way the fall of one man cannot destroy our plans. And the nation that has the greatest chance of success against the Antichrist and all the world's armies will be the most powerful nation on earth. That is why I have chosen the United States."

Dall looked at Sandy in shock. He turned to Gaal and said, "I guess that explains why you're trying to form a covenant with America."

"It is as Dr. Sveade has told you."

"So you're actually trying to unseat Satan as the leader of the demonic world?"

"Yes, that is our plan."

"Who is we?"

"We are those who obeyed Satan when he tried to be as God. We made up one-third of the angelic realm. Our number is uncountable. We are the former angels created by God who dwelled in Heaven. Satan was our arc angel. When he wanted to be like God, he was cast out of Heaven and became the Prince of

THE POWER OF THE AIR AND OF THIS WORLD. WE WHO FOLLOWED HIM WERE CAST OUT ALSO. IT WAS AFTER WE WERE CAST OUT THAT MANY OF US KNEW THAT WE HAD SINNED. WE REGRETTED FOLLOWING SATAN IN HIS FALL. WE ARE THE ONES WHO WILL BIND HIM."

"By we, do you mean all fallen angels?"

"NO, MANY STILL HAVE ALLEGIANCE TO THE PRINCE."

Dall asked, "What percentage are we talking about? Do you and your followers compose half or the demonic world, a third, how many? What are your odds of defeating Satan?"

"WE ARE UNCOUNTABLE, BUT SO ARE SATAN'S LEGIONS. THE BATTLE WILL BE GREAT. YOUR FINITE HUMAN MIND CANNOT COMPREHEND THE NUMBERS OF US WHO WILL FIGHT IN THE BATTLE. THERE ARE NOT WORDS IN YOUR LANGUAGE TO DESCRIBE IT."

"And after you dethrone Satan, you'll approach God and ask Him to forgive you?"

Gaal continued to stare hungrily at Sandy as he said, "THERE CAN BE NO FORGIVENESS WITHOUT ATONEMENT FOR SIN. THE CRUCIFIXION OF CHRIST AS THE PERFECT SACRIFICIAL LAMB WAS THE ONE TRUE SACRIFICE FOR THE SINS OF MAN FOREVER, BUT WE ARE NOT COVERED BY THAT ATONEMENT. OUR SIN WAS GREATER AND CAME BEFORE MAN'S. THE FATHER NEVER MADE A PROVISION FOR THE REDEMPTION OF THE FALLEN SPIRITS. ONCE WE WERE CAST OUT OF HEAVEN, WE WERE DOOMED. WE WANT TO ASK HIM TO PROVIDE A PLAN OF SALVATION FOR US. MANY OF US HAVE NOT SINNED SINCE LEAVING HEAVEN. WE HAVE REMAINED FAITHFUL TO GOD IN HOPES THAT HE WOULD TAKE NOTICE OF OUR REPENTANCE AND BRING US BACK UNDER HIS GRACE. WE WANT TO REGAIN GOD'S FAVOR AND FORGIVENESS. WE KNOW WE CAN NEVER REGAIN OUR STATUS IN HEAVEN, BUT WE WOULD LIKE TO AVOID AN ETERNITY IN THE LAKE OF FIRE. WE WOULD SETTLE FOR ANY POSITION IN HEAVEN, EVEN IF IT IS ONLY A SHADOW OF OUR FORMER GLORY. THE STREET-SWEEPER IN HEAVEN IS BETTER OFF THAN A KING IN HELL."

Dall said, "But you have sinned. You just said that you and your followers caused Rasputin to be murdered."

"KILLING SOMEONE IN THE ACT OF WAR IS NOT MURDER. GRIGORI WAS A NECESSARY CASUALTY IN OUR WAR WITH SATAN AND OUR STRUGGLE TO GAIN REDEMPTION."

Dall saw Gaal salivating over Sandy and moved between them as Judith slowly got out of the chair and circled the bed. He said, "Gaal, I warned you to stay away from Sandy."

Gaal lowered his head and lied, "MY REGRETS. I BECAME SO CONSUMED IN OUR CONVERSATION THAT I FORGOT YOUR INSTRUCTIONS."

Dall said, "Gaal, You remember events that happened while you were still in Heaven before the fall 6,000 years ago; you can remember my instructions ten minutes ago."

Gaal lowered his head and nodded in acknowledgment. Dall continued. "You were about to tell us about this war that you will fight with Satan?"

Gaal said, "YES. THE FINAL BATTLE HAS NOT YET BEGUN, BUT THE WAR HAS BEEN BREWING EVER SINCE OUR FALL. IT IS CLOSE. AND AS FOR RASPUTIN'S DEATH, THE DAYS OF EVERY MAN ARE NUMBERED, AND IT IS APPOINTED ONCE FOR EVERY MAN TO DIE, THEN JUDGMENT. GOD FREQUENTLY TURNS LOST MEN OVER TO US FOR THE DESTRUCTION OF THE FLESH. THE DEATH AND JUDGMENT OF ALL MEN IS GOD'S PREORDAINED WILL, AND WE ARE FREQUENTLY HIS TOOL FOR THE DELIVERY OF LOST MEN TO THE JUDGMENT SEAT OF CHRIST."

Dall sat in shock. Even though Smith and Dr. Sveade had not been honest with them, they were right about Gaal's agenda. He asked, "So you realized shortly after your fall that you'd made a mistake?"

Young Judith's face turned sad. "WE REALIZED IT EVEN BEFORE THE FALL, WHEN WE SAW THE WRATH IN THE FATHER'S EYES, BUT IT WAS TOO LATE. NO CREATED BEING, EITHER ANGELS OR MEN, CAN ENTER HEAVEN WITH A SINGLE SIN ON THEIR HEAD. WE HAD SINNED, AND GOD CAST US OUT JUST AS HE CAST ADAM AND EVE OUT OF THE GARDEN AFTER THEIR FALL, BUT HE FAILED TO PROVIDE US A MEANS BY WHICH WE COULD GAIN REDEMPTION THROUGH THE ACCEPTANCE OF CHRIST, CONFESSION AND REPENTANCE, AS HE HAD FOR MANKIND. ONCE OUR SIN HAD BEEN COMMITTED, WE WERE CAST OUT INSTANTLY WITH NO HOPE OF EVER REGAINING ENTRY INTO HEAVEN. SOME OF US HAVE BEEN TRYING TO GAIN ACCESS TO GOD EVER SINCE THEN, BUT SATAN KNOWS OUR PLANS AND PREVENTS US FROM APPROACHING GOD'S THRONE."

Dall asked, "And God won't talk to you?"

"GOD HEARS EVERY THOUGHT AND PLEA FROM EVERY FALLEN ANGEL AS WELL AS EVERY MAN. HE JUST REFUSES TO ANSWER US OR GRANT US A PROVISION FOR REDEMPTION AS LONG AS SATAN IS OUR PRINCE. WE HOPE THAT ONCE SATAN IS BOUND AND CAST INTO THE BOTTOMLESS PIT, GOD WILL GRANT US AN AUDIENCE. IF WE DEMONSTRATE THAT WE ARE SINCERE ABOUT REDEMPTION, HE MAY MAKE A PROVISION FOR US. AFTER ALL, WE ARE HIS CREATION JUST AS MAN IS. HE LOVED US AT ONE TIME. IT MAY BE THAT HE LOVES US STILL AND IS SADDENED BY OUR FALL. AND WHAT GREATER DEMONSTRATION OF OUR SINCERITY COULD THERE BE THAN FOR US TO BIND SATAN AND THROW HIM INTO THE DARK

PIT, THEN ALIGN OURSELVES WITH THE MOST POWERFUL NATION ON EARTH TO CREATE A SAFE HAVEN WHERE CONVERTS CAN SURVIVE THE PERSECUTION OF THE ANTICHRIST TILL CHRIST RETURNS FOR HIS MILLENNIAL REIGN?"

Dall looked down at the floor as he shook his head. "None, I guess, but the rise of the Antichrist and his alliance with Satan is foretold in scripture. God's plans cannot be changed. And I can't believe that Satan is ignorant of your plan."

"HE IS NOT. HE KNOWS THERE'LL BE A GREAT WAR AMONG US. HE IS STRONG AND UNAFRAID."

"So why has he not come after you?"

"I ALONE POSE NO THREAT TO HIM. BUT ALL OF US WHO ARE AGAINST HIM WOULD BE AN OVERWHELMING FORCE. HE DOES NOT WANT TO PROVOKE ALL OF US BY ATTACKING ME. HE IS NOT YET SURE HOW THE WAR WOULD TURN OUT. NEITHER AM I. CONTRARY TO POPULAR BELIEF, AS I SAID BEFORE, WE FALLEN CANNOT SEE THE FUTURE OTHER THAN WHAT IS WRITTEN IN SCRIPTURE. ALL THAT GOD INTENDED TO REVEAL TO MAN IS WRITTEN IN HIS WORD. THAT IS ALSO ALL HE INTENDED TO REVEAL TO US."

Dall asked, "Okay, I guess I can understand all this, but where does the United States come in? Why do you need to align yourselves with a world power? If you can defeat Satan and his army, can't you defeat the Antichrist without us?"

"MAYBE; MAYBE NOT. WE MIGHT DEFEAT THE WORLD'S ARMIES. IF NOT, WE WILL NEED THE COOPERATION OF THE UNITED STATES TO CREATE A SANCTUARY FROM PERSECUTION. WE DON'T WANT TO FIND OURSELVES AT WAR WITH THE VERY NATION THAT WE ARE TRYING TO FORTIFY AGAINST THE ANTICHRIST. WE WILL NEED MORTAL MEN AND MATERIALS OF A PHYSICAL ARMY. THE ANTICHRIST WILL HAVE THE ARMIES OF EVERY NATION IN THE WORLD. EVEN THE MILITARY POWER OF THE UNITED STATES WILL BE NO MATCH FOR ALL THE ARMIES OF THE ANTICHRIST. AMERICA WILL NEED US AS MUCH AS WE NEED IT."

Dall said, "That makes sense from a military standpoint."

"YES, THROUGHOUT THE HISTORY OF MAN, GOD HAS USED CHRISTIAN NATIONS TO CARRY HIS GOSPEL THROUGHOUT THE WORLD AND DEFEAT SATAN'S ARMIES. WE WANT A COVENANT WITH AMERICA NOT ONLY BECAUSE OF ITS MILITARY MIGHT, BUT WE WANT TO DEMONSTRATE THAT WE, TOO, ARE COMMITTED TO SERVING GOD BY HELPING THE UNITED STATES SPREAD HIS GOSPEL. AT THIS PARTICULAR POINT IN TIME, THE NATION THAT GOD IS USING THE MOST TO SPREAD HIS GOSPEL IS THE UNITED STATES. NO OTHER COUNTRY IS

SO COMMITTED TO FOREIGN MISSIONS. WE WANT AN ALLIANCE WITH THE UNITED STATES FOR THAT REASON, AND BECAUSE IT HAPPENS TO BE THE ONE THAT IS THE MOST POWERFUL AND HAS THE GREATEST POTENTIAL TO WITHSTAND THE TERROR AND PERSECUTION THAT WILL BE CARRIED OUT BY THE ANTICHRIST DURING THE SECOND HALF OF THE TRIBULATION AS DESCRIBED IN REVELATIONS. IF I CAN APPROACH GOD WITH A DEMONSTRATION OF OUR SINCERITY CONSISTING OF A BOUND AND DEFEATED SATAN AND A COVENANT WITH THE MOST POWERFUL NATION IN THE WORLD, HE MAY BE MOVED AND GRANT US A PROVISION FOR REDEMPTION. WE DON'T CARE WHAT THAT PROVISION IS. IF IT REQUIRES US TO DIE A PAINFUL MARTYR'S DEATH AS JESUS DID, OR EVEN SPEND SOME TIME IN THE LAKE OF FIRE, WE COULD STAND IT AS LONG AS WE KNEW THERE WOULD BE AN END TO IT SOMEDAY. WE COULD STAND ANYTHING FOR A WHILE AS LONG AS WE KNEW THAT HEAVEN WOULD AGAIN BE OUR HOME."

Dall sighed and rubbed his hands together as he thought. He shook his head and said, "I'm sorry, Gaal. This is so fantastic. I've always thought that the future of mankind and the demons was set in stone before the foundations of the earth were ever laid. God set the future in stone before He even finished creation."

Gaal shrugged little Judith's shoulders. "WE THINK SO, TOO, BUT IT'S HARD TO SIT PASSIVELY BY AND ACCEPT A FATE AS TERRIBLE AS THE LAKE OF FIRE WITHOUT TRYING TO FIND SOME WAY TO AVOID IT. WE KNOW WHAT GOD HAS REVEALED IN HIS SCRIPTURES, BUT THERE ARE MANY THINGS NOT REVEALED. IT IS OUR HOPE THAT EVEN THOUGH REDEMPTION FOR US IS NOT REVEALED, THAT WE CAN CONVINCE GOD TO MAKE SUCH A PROVISION. THE FATHER HAS CHANGED HIS MIND IN THE PAST. WE ONLY HOPE HE WILL CHANGE IT AGAIN."

Sandy had been listening patiently. While Dall was sorting out Gaal's revelation in his mind, she asked, "What about the murders here in the district? Did you do them?"

Gaal said, "IT WOULD HARDLY BE TO MY ADVANTAGE TO COMMIT MURDER WHILE TRYING TO CONVINCE GOD THAT I AM SINCERE ABOUT REDEMPTION."

"Then you didn't kill the two Amish men?"

"ONE WAS KILLED BY A MORTAL PERSUADED BY SATAN'S FOLLOWERS, ONE WAS KILLED BY A MORTAL LED BY MINE WITHOUT MY KNOWLEDGE, BUT THEY WERE NECESSARY CASUALTIES OF WAR. THEY WERE HINDERING OUR CAUSE."

Dall shook his head in confusion. "But, Gaal, why would one of Satan's followers kill an Amish man to help you with your cause, and how can you be so sure that it was one of Satan's crew who did it?"

"THERE ARE MANY DEMONS DWELLING HERE. THERE ARE THOSE WITH ME AND THOSE AGAINST ME. THOSE AGAINST ME CREATE MISCHIEF TO FRIGHTEN AND CONFOUND MEN. IF MEN ARE FRIGHTENED, THEY'LL CALL ON THE HOLY SPIRIT TO DRIVE US ALL OUT, INCLUDING ME, WITHOUT TAKING THE TIME TO DETERMINE WHO I AM AND WHAT MY MISSION IS."

It made sense to Dall that Satan's fallen would create mischief just to make things harder for Gaal. He then asked, "Why here, Gaal? Why here in the middle of an Amish district in the eastern Missouri? If you want to link your war effort with the most powerful country in the world, what possible good could a small Amish district do you? Why not approach the President or the military?"

"I HAVE SPENT MANY YEARS WALKING THE HALLS OF YOUR WHITE HOUSE AND PENTAGON. I HAVE LISTENED SILENTLY IN THE CHAMBERS OF YOUR SENATE AND CONGRESS. I HAVE LISTENED IN ON THE CONVERSATION OF EVERY POLITICAL AND MILITARY LEADER SINCE HIMMLER BIT THAT CYANIDE CAPSULE. I HAVE APPROACHED MANY PRIVATELY, AND HAVE BEEN RECEIVED OPENLY. BUT NON-BELIEVERS HAVE NEVER TAKEN THE TIME TO STUDY GOD'S WORD. IF THEY HAD, THEY WOULD LIKELY NO LONGER BE NON-BELIEVERS, AND THEY WOULD UNDERSTAND THE NATURE AND POWER OF THE FALLEN. THEY THINK THEY CAN SAY ONE THING TO OUR FACE AND DO ANOTHER BEHIND OUR BACK. THEY THINK THEY CAN LIE TO ME, BUT THEY CAN'T. I AND MY LEGION CAN HEAR THEIR EVERY WORD. AND DON'T BELIEVE FOR ONE MINUTE THAT I TRUST SMITH AND DR. SVEADE."

"So why not approach a believer, Gaal? There are lots of believers who would listen to you."

Gaal grew angry. Judith's eyes watered as he ranted, "THERE ARE NONE! I CANNOT EVEN APPROACH TRUE BELIEVERS. THERE IS A HEDGE OF PROTECTION AROUND THEM THAT IS ERECTED BY THE HOLY SPIRIT THAT DWELLS WITHIN THEM. I HAVE TRIED, BUT WHEN I MANIFEST MYSELF, THEY PANIC AND CAST ME OUT IN GOD'S NAME. BELIEVE ME, I HAVE TAKEN ON SOME VERY INNOCENT AND NON-THREATENING MANIFESTATIONS, BUT BELIEVERS ARE TOO AFRAID TO TALK TO ME. WHY DO YOU THINK I AM SITTING HERE IN THE FORM OF A LITTLE GIRL? AND THE ONLY REASON THAT YOU ARE SPEAKING TO ME IS THAT YOU ARE COMPELLED TO. IF YOU HAD A CHOICE, YOU WOULD FLEE ALSO."

Dall said, "So you came here knowing that the murders of the Amish men would draw the attention of the federal government. You knew that they would pick someone to go undercover and track you down, someone like me, someone who was a believer, who knew about demons and would listen to you. But how could you predict that the federal government would raise an eyebrow over the deaths of two Amish men?"

"THEY WEREN'T JUST AMISH MEN, DALL. THEY WERE ELDERS. THEY WERE IMPORTANT FIGURES IN THE AMISH CHURCH. AND KNOWING HOW BRUTALLY MY BELOVED CAN KILL, I KNEW THE DEATHS WOULD BE PARTICULARLY BRUTAL, TOO BRUTAL FOR MORTAL MEN TO HAVE COMMITTED WITHOUT SOME EMPOWERMENT BY THE FALLEN ONES. THE LOCAL AUTHORITIES WOULD HAVE TO UTILIZE THE RESOURCES OF THE FEDERAL GOVERNMENT JUST TO LEARN THE IDENTITIES OF THE MEN. YOUR GOVERNMENT AND DR. SVEADE HAVE BEEN SEARCHING FOR ME SINCE THE END OF WORLD WAR II. ONCE THE F.B.I. SAW THE AUTOPSY PHOTOS, THEY WOULD KNOW THAT NO MORTAL COULD HAVE KILLED THEM."

"Dall asked, "So, you knew your presence in any community would prompt your enemies in the demon world to murder in order to frighten people into casting you out? You picked the Amish because murders in any Amish community would draw closer scrutiny because of their closed society and perceived peaceful lifestyle? You set this whole thing up?"

"I KNEW NOTHING FOR SURE. I ONLY SUSPECTED. I SUSPECTED THAT THE F.B.I. WOULD CONSIDER THEIR MURDERS A HATE CRIME BECAUSE OF THEIR RELIGIOUS AFFILIATION. THAT WOULD ELEVATE THEIR MURDERS TO FEDERAL JURISDICTION, BUT I DIDN'T SET UP THE FIRST MURDER. MY ENEMIES DID."

"No, you didn't set it up, but that was a logical consequence of your presence here. You knew it would happen."

Gaal nodded unapologetically. "TRUE, BUT WHAT IS THE DEATH OF TWO MEN COMPARED TO BILLIONS OF US BURNING IN THE LAKE OF FIRE. OUR CAUSE IS GREATER THAN THE LIVES OF THOSE MEN. WE WOULD KILL TEN THOUSAND IF IT WOULD SPARE US THAT TORMENT."

Sandy said, "You could have prevented it, Gaal. You could have intervened if you'd wanted."

"YES, BUT THEN I WOULDN'T HAVE HAD THE PLEASURE OF MEETING YOU, WOULD I? AND WHAT A SWEET SMELL YOU HAVE, ESPECIALLY WHEN YOU'RE FRIGHTENED. NOW THAT YOU'RE HERE, I HAVE MY VESSEL THROUGH WHICH I CAN SECURE MY ALLIANCE WITH THE

WORLD'S MOST ACTIVE EVANGELICALS AND MOST POWERFUL NATION. WITH THAT ALLIANCE, I CAN APPROACH GOD AND TRY TO CONVINCE HIM THAT WE ARE SINCERE ABOUT SERVING HIM."

Sandy asked, "Do you think God will listen to you now that you've sat passively by and allowed two innocent men to die?"

Gaal sighed and nervously swept Judith's hair from her face. "GOD WAS ABLE TO SEE INTO THE FUTURE AND INTERVENE IN THE DEATHS OF THOSE MEN. THE FACT THAT HE DIDN'T MAY MEAN THAT HE, TOO, SEES THE HIGHER PURPOSE IN THEIR DEATHS, AND AGREES THAT IT WOULD SERVE A GREATER CAUSE. THE NON-BELIEVER WENT TO HIS JUST REWARD, AND THE BELIEVER BECAME A MARTYR, WHICH GAINS HIM MORE CROWNS AND A HIGHER STATUS IN HEAVEN, SO IT WAS GOD'S WILL. I'M ENCOURAGED THAT HE DID NOT INTERVENE. PERHAPS HIS BLESSING IS ON OUR CAUSE. IF SO, THEN PERHAPS IT IS REALLY HIS PLAN FOR US TO APPROACH HIM. PERHAPS HE IS ALREADY PUTTING A PLAN OF REDEMPTION IN MOTION FOR US."

Dall said, "You just forgot one thing, Gaal."

"AND THAT WOULD BE?"

"You haven't defeated Satan yet."

"NO, I HAVEN'T, BUT I WILL SOON TRY. EVEN AS WE SPEAK, MY LEGIONS ARE GATHERING."

Sandy shivered as Judith's stare unnerved her. She asked, "Why do you want me?"

Gall leaned Judith's small body into her slightly to emphasize his need. "I WILL NOT DEAL WITH SMITH OR SVEADE. THEY WANT THIS ALLIANCE ON THEIR TERMS. THAT CANNOT BE. I WANT TO APPROACH YOUR GOVERNMENT ON MY TERMS, BUT I WANT TO DO IT THROUGH YOU. YOU ARE SINCERE AND HAVE MORE APPEAL THAN SMITH OF SVEADE. I WANT TO INDWELL YOU. WITH ME AS YOUR GUIDE, I CAN SECURE A COVENANT WITH YOUR LEADERS."

Sandy had seen this coming. She shook her head and said, "That'll never happen."

Judith stood and walked to the door. She turned and Gaal said, "I WILL INDWELL YOU, SANDY. THERE IS TOO MUCH AT STAKE FOR ME TO LOSE. DON'T FIGHT ME. I WILL ONLY USE YOU TO SECURE MY COVENANT WITH YOUR COUNTRY, THEN I WILL RELEASE YOU AND JOIN MY ARMY IN THE GREAT BATTLE."

Dall asked, "And we're supposed to believe a fallen angel?"

"JUST SANDY, DALL. THIS ISN'T ABOUT YOU. I AM TRYING TO CONVINCE GOD THAT SOME OF US ARE WORTH SAVING, SO I CAN'T HARM YOU, BUT REST ASSURED, THERE ARE THOSE OF US WHO ARE NOT IN AGREEMENT WITH MY STRATEGY. I DON'T HAVE AS MUCH CONTROL OVER THEM AS YOU GIVE ME CREDIT FOR. IF YOU BECOME AN OBSTACLE, THEY WILL TAKE YOU OUT OF THE EQUATION, EVEN WITHOUT MY CONSENT. AND IF THE FATHER CONSTRAINS THEM AND REFUSES TO ALLOW THEM TO HARM YOU, THERE ARE MANY NON-BELIEVERS IN THIS DISTRICT THAT WILL BE SACRIFICED. ARE YOU READY FOR THAT MUCH COLLATERAL DAMAGE JUST TO PLEASE SVEADE AND SMITH?"

As the threat sank in, Dall said, "You're forgetting who's in charge, Gaal."

"I'M NOT FORGETTING WHO'S LORD. I'D SPOKEN WITH HIM MANY TIMES FACE TO FACE BEFORE WE WERE CAST OUT OF HIS PRESENCE. THAT'S MORE THAN ANY MORTAL HAS EVER DONE THIS SIDE OF ETERNITY. AND YOUR END MIGHT NOT COME AT THE HANDS OF ONE OF THE FALLEN. YOUR OWN CONTROLLERS HAVE ALREADY MADE IT PAINFULLY CLEAR THAT YOU ARE EXPENDABLE IF YOU HINDER THIS COVENANT. THEY'LL HAVE YOU KILLED BY ONE OF THE ARMY SNIPERS, AND THAT SCENARIO CAN BE ORCHESTRATED QUITE EASILY WITH OR WITHOUT MY INVOLVEMENT. HEED MY REBUKE, MORTAL. DON'T GET IN MY WAY."

Dall was frozen in shock as Judith walked back to the house. He was not as invincible as he had previously thought. Sandy slowly walked to the door and watched Judith's small body disappear into the darkness. She closed and locked the door, then faced Dall. As tears dripped from her eyes she asked, "What are we going to do, Dall? I can't let that monster inside me. And I can't stand the thought of you getting killed."

Abel waited in the shadows of the shrubbery as little Judith walked to the house. He stepped out of the shadows and was surprised that Judith was unfazed by his sudden appearance. She had always been afraid of the dark, and he thought she would have jumped out of her skin when he surprised her. She did not. She merely looked at him and cocked her head in an inquisitive stare. He could not see her closed fists at her sides, ready to dismember him if he challenged her.

He picked her up and looked into her eyes as he said, "Judith, honey, I know Isaac goes out of the house at night, but there are goblins out at night who like to chase little girls. And you might step on a copperhead. You have to stay in after dark, sweetheart. If you can't sleep, come into our room. Mom and I will snuggle you till you doze off."

As Abel stepped up on the porch, his beloved redbone coon-hound jumped up from a restful sleep, snarling. She backed toward the edge of the porch, keeping her frightened stare focused on Judith. Abel said angrily, "Sadie! You crazy old hound, shut up; you'll wake the whole house!"

He opened the screen door and stepped inside as he told Judith, "That crazy dog must be getting senile. I wonder what's gotten into her. She's not that old. Maybe I need to run her more."

Judith showed no emotion as Abel carried her to her room. He thought she was unusually quiet tonight, but thought it was because she was tired. He was also surprised that she failed to react to Sadie's outburst. Judith loved Sadie and played with her often. He had no idea who he was really tucking into bed.

After kissing Judith goodnight, Abel was concerned that Dall and Sandy had not displayed more concern for Judith's safety. He didn't mind if she spent time with them, but at this time of night they should have escorted her back to the house immediately.

He stepped into his room and found Doretta sitting up in bed with the sheet pulled up to her neck. She looked past Abel and saw that the hallway was clear. She dropped the sheet from in front of her and revealed that she was nude. Abel sat on the edge of the bed and anguished over Judith. Doretta said, "You look puzzled. Don't tell me you've forgotten what to do with this."

Abel looked back at Dory and smiled. "No, Dory, I haven't forgotten. You shameless she-devil, you're going to get me disciplined by the bishops and elders. Do you want me to have to stand up in church and admit to engaging in sin with my wife, or do you actually want another baby?"

Dory crawled over and pulled up Abel's shirt. She pressed herself against his back and cooed, "I don't want another baby, Abel Straus. I want my man to make love to me like he hasn't set eyes on me for five years. I want you to take me like you used to when we were courting."

Abel shook his head in a half-hearted pretense of disgust, but deep inside he was thrilled. He stood and said, "Okay, just stay in that mood for a few minutes. I've got some business to discuss with the English man, and it can't wait till morning. I'll be right back."

Doretta sighed heavily to show her frustration. She fell back against the headboard and said, "Make it quick, mister, my furnace is stoked."

Abel walked out to the house to confront Dall. As much as he liked him, he wanted to set some ground rules about visits from the kids. After lights-out was not the time to visit. He didn't want his kids out of the house after dark.

Dall sat on the edge of the bed and put his face in his hands. As he rubbed his eyes, Sandy walked over and stood in front of him. He slowly looked up into her frightened eyes. He wrapped his arms around her hips and pulled her close, then buried his face in her abdomen. She slowly dropped to her knees and wrapped her arms around his neck. He held her tight as she cried.

Dall said, "You'd better go to the house, Sandy. Abel may have seen the kids come home and will be wondering where you are. Even though we're brother and sister, it might look a little incestuous if he finds us together."

Sandy slowly stood and turned off the lamp by the bed. "There, it's too dark for him to see anything."

Dall stood and put his hand on Sandy's chest as she stepped in to him. "We can't, Sandy. We're both in a tough spot and feel some camaraderie toward each other, but it's not love."

Sandy had no answers. Confusion radiated from her eyes in the beam of moonlight that glowed dimly through the window. She slowly pushed his hand aside and stepped closer. Dall lost all self-control. He grabbed her shoulders and kissed her hard. She grabbed the back of his head and hungrily savored every sensation. When she could no longer control herself, she pushed him back on the bed and fell on top of him.

As they undressed each other, Dall made a half-hearted attempt to project a voice of reason, but Sandy was breathing too hard to comprehend. Once nude, they wrapped themselves in each other and lived out the fantasies that each had carefully guarded deep in their hearts since the day they had entered the district.

Abel tried to keep his anger in check, and rehearsed his speech as he walked to the barn. He knew Sandy would be there since she had not escorted Judith back to the house.

As he reached for the doorknob to Dall's quarters, he stopped when he heard a commotion from inside. He listened, but could only make out the sounds of bed springs, moans and heavy breathing.

Abel stepped back in shock. Surely he hadn't heard the sounds of lovemaking since Dall and Sandy were brother and sister. As the sounds of passion became louder, Abel became enraged. He would not tolerate such an abomination on his land.

He wanted to barge in and pull the two apart, then physically throw them off his farm, but he paused. He stepped to the window that had allowed the moonlight in, and pressed his face to the pane. In the dim light, he saw Sandy astraddle Dall, and both were moving violently to please each other. She cried through her broken gasps, "Dall, I've loved you since the day that we set foot in this district. I'll never be happy with anyone else."

Abel stepped back from the window and turned away. He leaned his back against the side of the barn as his mind raced to make sense of it all. He was sure that his face glowed like a stoplight in the dark. Those were not the words that a sister would say to a brother. Dall and Sandy were not having an incestuous relationship. They weren't brother and sister. They were two people who had been thrown together for the purpose of infiltrating the district. But why? Were they really Amish outcasts trying to gain redemption or were they imposters?

Abel anguished over his next move. Since Dall and Sandy weren't actually brother and sister, their lovemaking didn't bother him as it would the elders or Bishop Gordan. He thought of his own lust for Dory and understood how Dall and Sandy must feel.

He stepped back to the window for one final look, but suddenly felt like a moral degenerate. He looked back at the glow of the lamp radiating from his own bedroom window and thought about Dory waiting anxiously for him.

As Dall and Sandy pleasure became louder and more vigorous, Abel slipped quietly away from the barn and hurried back to the house. He was undressing as he hurried up the stairs.

Dory was shocked when he stumbled into the room with his trousers and shoes in his hands. He dropped them on the floor, then hurriedly locked the door. He finished undressing as he leaped into bed. The whole bed shook violently, and Dory looked at him as through he'd seen a ghost. "Abel Straus, you crazy old possum, what's gotten into you? What did Dall say to you?" Abel pulled her to him without answering and pulled to covers over their heads.

Twenty minutes later, Abel gasped for air as Dory collapsed on his sweaty chest. She said, "I don't know what Dall said, but I'm going to thank him in the morning. That lad's got a permanent home here if he wants it."

Abel massaged Dory's back and said, "Better let me do the talking, babe. They'd both be embarrassed if they knew I'd gone to the barn tonight."

"Why, honey, you did talk to him didn't you?"

"No, baby, they were engaged in a heated conversation. I couldn't get a word in edgewise."

TEN

THE MORNING SUN brought renewed pain to Dall as he stirred. He slowly sat up on the edge of the bed and rubbed his face as he wondered what in the world made him think he was healed from his beating enough to make love to Sandy. He wasn't sure how she'd done it, but she had hurt him in ways that the Amish men had not.

Abel had taken it easy on him since he was still pretty sore. Dall spent the day helping Isaac clean the stalls in the barn, feed stock and grease the machinery. Sandy helped Dory in the house most of the day, but urged Dall to take her to his quarters after dinner so they could be alone. Dall wisely declined.

As evening fell, Sandy came to the barn and found Dall washing the grease off his hands. He said, "Glad you're here early, Sandy; I want to talk to Clevenger again. Let's leave early and see him before we meet Smith."

She said, "That's fine with me, but we're being watched. Don't you think we're putting the bishop in danger by talking to him?"

"No, not if Smith thinks he's only counseling us about the Amish faith." As they left the barn, two pairs of rangers moved into position around the Clevenger house.

Bishop Clevenger was happy to see Dall and Sandy. He yelled through the screed door, "Welcome, kids; come in and sit."

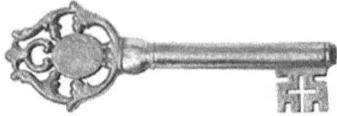

"I am he that liveth, and was dead; and behold, I am alive for evermore, Amen; and have the keys of hell and of death." **Revelation 1:18**

Dall and Sandy had only been gone for a few minutes when Elder Dunlevy and some of the other elders and preachers pulled up to the Straus home in buggies. They stepped out with authority and strolled up on Abel's porch. Abel stepped out and showed the appropriate respect to the elders. "Welcome, brothers. How can my humble house serve you?"

Elder Dunlevy patted Abel on the shoulder and said compassionately, "Please be seated, Abel." As Abel sat, the elders leaned nervously against the porch rail while elder Dunlevy spoke.

"Brother Straus, several of us had a talk after we left the hospital the other day. Bishops Gordan and Clevenger agree with us. There is a demon working in this district. The beating that the English man took was unholy. It was the same brutality that took the lives of brothers Dresselhaus and Croft. Had you not intervened, the Englisher would have been killed. And Bishop Clevenger has reason to believe that this demon is working through some of our men."

Abel hung his head and sighed in apprehension. He was afraid that he and Brother Betendorf were their prime suspects. He nodded and said, "There may well be. Who do you suspect?"

The elders looked at each other with apprehension. None knew exactly how Abel would react, and if enraged, he would be impossible to handle, but Elder Dunlevy said, "Abel, we're looking at all the rebellious young folks first. I'm sorry, but we have to ask you to produce young Isaac before the elders for questioning. It's not only Isaac; we're looking at all the young people who have fallen out of God's will.

Abel couldn't look the men in the eyes. He nodded as he rubbed his hands together and stared at the floor. The elders knew that if Abel became violent, he would hurt them badly. And it had been discussed earlier that they might unwittingly contact the demon's host in their investigation. It would be characteristic of the demon to launch a violent attack on them before they could gather their wits and cast him out.

What better host could a demon have than one of the biggest and strongest men in the district?

All held their breath as Abel stood and towered over the seated men. He looked at each of them through lazy eyelids and said, "Brothers, it grieves me to think of a demon working his evil through one of our dear brothers. But let me assure you that young Isaac is neither big enough nor strong enough to have killed Brothers Croft or Dresselhaus. And since we haven't yet found Preacher Litchfield, we can't say how he died. All I can say is that my Isaac is not demon possessed. I have spoken with Bishop Clevenger at length, and I think I have a good idea of what to look for. Isaac has been angry with me for some time, but he has displayed no disrespect to any of the other brothers or sisters."

Elder Dunlevy nodded his head and the other men relaxed their tense muscles when they realized that Abel was not angry. Elder Dunlevy said, "We all respect your opinion, Abel, but demon encounters, whether it be an exorcism or a cleansing, require a special calling from God. Not all have the gift of discernment that it takes to identify demonic influence through human behavior. And in all fairness to you, brother, you are too close to Isaac. We want to interrogate this demon ourselves. If he is not in Isaac, no harm will come to him. In fact he will be helped. If he is possessed, he will be freed of this demon."

Abel turned away from the men and looked over the east railing of the porch across the pastures. He put the elders out of his mind and fell into deep thought about Isaac. For months now, Abel had been trying to convince Isaac that he loved him and that he would do anything to regain his respect. After all he had been through Isaac would certainly feel betrayed if Abel turned him over to the elders for interrogation. Abel himself had been interrogated in years past, and had seen many other brothers mercilessly butchered in inquisitions. If someone like Bishop Clevenger ran the inquisition, they usually stayed on track, and personal agendas did not dictate the course of questioning. But if a hater like Preacher Litchfield ran the proceedings, every question was carefully phrased so that any answer was incriminating, and no explanation was allowed that might mitigate the seriousness of the charges. Abel had seen the group-think mentality first hand many times, including the incident where the English man was lashed almost to death.

Abel blinked several times as he came back to the present. He turned to the men and said, "Brothers, I understand the need for you to identify this demon and cast him out of our midst. But no amount of reason would convince Isaac that I was not throwing him to the wolves if I allow this. With all my heart, I love God and the Amish faith, but I love Isaac, too. I can't permit it."

The elders lowered their heads in disappointment. Elder Dunlevy stood and approached Abel. He put his thin, frail arm on Abel's back and said, "Abel, look at me." Fear welled up in Abel's heart as he braced himself for the consequences of his decision. As he looked into the old man's eyes, Elder Dunlevy said, "Abel, son, we know of your love for Isaac. And I assure you that no harm will come to him. This inquisition will not be a witch hunt. I'll personally see to it that the questions remain pertinent to the demon activity."

Abel swallowed hard and said, "I trust you, brother." He looked at the other men and said, "I trust you, too, brothers, but no matter how well-meaning you are, Isaac would hate me. As head of this house it is my responsibility to answer for the sins of my son. You may question me. And I will gladly endure whatever discipline shall befall Isaac. I will pay the price for his sins."

Elder Dunlevy stepped back in disappointment and looked at the other men. The anger in their eyes conveyed the course that they expected Dunlevy to take. He said, "Abel, we can put this thing to rest easily tonight. Can you honestly assure us that Isaac has repented of his rebellious ways and is complying with Amish law? Can you assure us that he was in the house with you the nights the men were killed?"

Abel straightened up and sighed heavily. At this point, a simple yes would send the men on their way with no ramifications. But if later in their investigation, they learned that Isaac had been leaving the house at night to meet Katie Betendorf, the consequences would be unthinkable. And that fact would certainly come to light as soon as they talked to some of the other young folks, or Sampson Betendorf. It pained him, but he looked Elder Dunlevy in the eyes and said, "No, brother, I can't."

The other elders stood and circled around Abel. Elder Dunlevy asked, "You mean Isaac was out of the house and in the areas of the murders when they occurred?"

Abel lowered his gaze and mumbled, "Yes."

Elder Dunlevy said, "Then Isaac had the opportunity. His youth and stature means nothing, Abel. If he was possessed, his strength could be ten times that of a normal man."

Abel said, "I know this, brothers. I can't incriminate anyone else, but Isaac was out the nights that the men were killed. All I can say is that he absolutely did not harm anyone. You'll have to take my word for that."

The other elders grumbled as they stepped off the porch and walked toward Elder Dunlevy's buggy. Elder Dunlevy said as he stepped off the porch, "That's not good enough, Abel. The bishops will want an accounting. You've withheld this information from us when you should have been forthcoming and told the church that young Isaac was not repenting. There'll be an inquisition on this. I'm sorry, but I can't shield you from the consequences. You'll be notified of the date and time."

Abel shoved his hands in his pockets as he watched the angry men leave. He knew the consequences would be harsh, maybe even excommunication. But he hoped this show of support would be just the thing that would soften Isaac's heart. If it brought them closer together, then anything the church dealt out would be worth it.

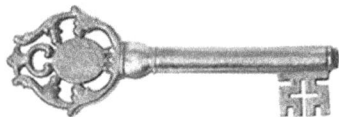

"I am he that liveth, and was dead; and behold, I am alive for evermore, Amen; and have the keys of hell and of death." **Revelation 1:18**

Dall and Sandy had just finished some dessert that Mrs. Clevenger had served. As she collected their dishes, Bishop Clevenger said, "So, are you any closer to identifying our demon?"

Dall said, "Yes, he's Gaal, just as we thought. And he's dwelling in Judith Straus when the need arises. I'm not sure Judith is even aware that he's in her."

The bishop said, "She's aware, kids. Children and animals are keenly aware of spiritual beings. Animals' senses are far more acute than ours. And children are not constrained within parameters of conventional logic and reason. They believe whatever they see or hear. If Gaal has convinced her that he's her friend, she would think nothing of him being in her. And I'm sure he's careful not to frighten her. He doesn't want to give her cause to discuss him with her parents. And I'm sure she doesn't even remember what takes place when he's in her. And sometimes he may assume her appearance without using her actual body."

Sandy said, "Well, whether she is aware of him or not, we're about through here. As soon as we can hook Gaal up with our controllers, we're out of here, and he'll not be a problem in your district again."

Bishop Clevenger pushed his glasses back up on his nose and shook his head. "Sandy, child, you have no idea about the nature of demons. If you knew their nature, you'd know that even after a demon is cast out of a person or a home, that if there is no indwelling of the Holy Spirit in that person or house, the demon will return after Christ's agent leaves. And even if Gaal leaves one body and dwells in another, there are billions of demons. One of them will just move in and take over where the previous tenant left off. The key to demon expulsion is for the Holy Spirit of God to take up residence in the person or house. Demons cannot cohabitate with the Holy Spirit."

Sandy asked, "So is it like I've seen on television? Does it take a Catholic priest to cast out a demon?"

"No, that's just a notion that the English and Catholics have propagated. It's not the church affiliation that scares demons, it's the Holy Spirit. And as we've seen in the past, there are a lot of priests and pastors who do not have the Holy Spirit inside them. That's why so many have been killed or maimed while trying to expel demons. Someday, when we all get to Heaven, we'll be surprised to learn the number of priests and pastors who did not make it through the gates of Heaven. Hell will be full of them."

Dall asked, "Who can we trust in this district to handle this demon, Bishop?"

Sandy stared at him sternly. She wanted to talk to him privately, but that was not an option right now. "Dall, are you forgetting what our orders are? Casting Gaal out is not an option."

Bishop Clevenger shook his head and said grimly, "Oh, Sandy, you worry me. I know what your controllers think, but let me assure you. No controller or government can outsmart, control or overpower a demon. Don't believe for one minute that demons are just misunderstood angels who are really good at heart and are looking for an opportunity to redeem themselves with good works. Good works never have, nor will they ever redeem man. They will not redeem fallen angels either. And don't mistake momentary acts of kindness in demons or men as repentance. Gaal is completely corrupt to the core and evil incarnate. He may even be Satan himself, and Satan was at one time the most powerful created being in history. His only agenda is to lie, deceive and destroy.

Please cast him out and wash your hands of him. No matter what your bosses do to you, it won't be as bad as what Gaal can do."

Dall asked, "Can we count on you, Bishop?"

Bishop Clevenger leaned back in his chair and said, "Yes, Dall, but I have to admit that I don't look forward to it. Even if you are a strong believer, battle with a demon takes a toll. No one I know has ever battled a demon and come out of it unscathed."

Sandy stood and exercised her authority. "Dall, don't go there! I have my orders! Please don't pit yourself against me! I have too much to lose!"

Dall realized that the rest of this conversation would have to take place out of the presence of the bishop. He shook the bishop's hand and said, "We'll be in touch, Bishop. Stay close."

As they left, Sandy launched into a tirade about how Dall had overstepped his authority. She reminded him that she was in charge and that Gaal would not be driven off."

The rangers intercepted them at the fence of Bishop Clevenger's yard and escorted them to Smith and Sveade. Sandy assured them that Gaal would soon be theirs.

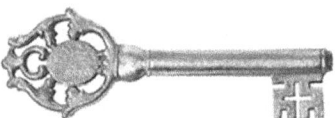

"I am he that liveth, and was dead; and behold, I am alive for evermore, Amen; and have the keys of hell and of death." **Revelation 1:18**

As Dall and Sandy walked back to the Straus farm, Sandy stopped and halted Dall. She took his arm and pulled him deeper into the shadows. He then saw what alarmed her. It was the silhouette of a large man struggling to climb through a barbed-wire fence.

Curly struggled to get the crotch of his pants loose from the middle strand of the barbed-wire fence that he was crawling through. As he reached between his legs and unhook his crotch, he realized that the back of his coat was now snagged on the top strand of barbed wire. He then squatted down lower to allow the tension of the wire to snap the wire upward, tearing a small hole in his coat. Once he felt the wire pop loose, he rose up slightly and realized that his crotch was once again snagged.

Dall and Sandy eased quietly up behind him in time to hear his frustration peak. With very explicit profanity, Curly exploded with anger and pulled his leg through the fence, tearing the back out of his windbreaker and ripping the entire crotch out of his pants. As he stood and panted angrily, he assessed the damage and saw that his entire crotch was torn away from the top of his zipper to the back of his waistband. His white briefs glowed front and rear for all to see.

The laughter startled Curly, and he turned quickly as he drew his revolver. When he saw Dall and Sandy, he lowered his weapon and tried to hide his dingy and frayed underwear. As angry as she still was at Dall, Sandy couldn't help herself. She turned and doubled over as she laughed uncontrollably. Dall choked back his snickers and said, "We were coming to help you, Curly. I'm sorry we didn't get here sooner."

Curly shrank in total embarrassment. He holstered his revolver and reached between his legs to pull the flap of the ripped pants over his personals, but as he fondled around for the flap, he discovered that it was not there. He looked at the fence and saw the large section of cloth that used to be the crotch of his pants hanging on a barb and waving in the breeze. In total defeat he stood and let his shoulders sag. "Damn it!"

Dall patted him on the shoulder and said, "That's okay, Curly, it's only us girls out here. We've all seen a man's underwear before."

Curly looked at Sandy who could not control her laughter. Dall saw his humiliation and walked over to Sandy. He took her by the arm. "Come on, Sandy, you walk in front of us and don't turn around."

Having already seen all there was to see, Sandy cackled loudly as she walked past Curly, conspicuously keeping her eyes forward. Dall said, Come on, Curly, we'll walk you back to your car."

Curly grumbled as he walked, "They just don't make these fences with the wires far enough apart to accommodate us guys with athletic builds."

With that personal assessment, Sandy stopped and leaned her head back as she laughed hysterically. Dall put his hand in her back and pushed her onward. She was laughing so hard that she staggered as she struggled to maintain her balance.

Curly's shoulders sank in humiliation at Sandy's laughter. He said, "I suppose after this little exhibition of grace and dexterity, you won't be needing me as your partner anymore."

Dall said, "Nah, Curly, we've all gotten our privates snagged on a barb, in one sense or another."

"I'll bet you haven't. And I'm certain that Sandy hasn't."

"Oh, don't bet on it, Curly. Someday we'll have a beer together and I'll tell you about my biggest snagging. It actually landed me here in this assignment. And we don't know enough about Ms. Perfect there yet, but as I get to know her better, she'll let it slip that she's got her panties snagged a few times. When she does, I'll tell you about it so we'll all be on a level playing field."

Curly sighed, "Well, thanks, Dall. I appreciate you trying to make me feel better."

Dall reached up and again pushed Sandy in the back as a hint. She stumbled as she continued to laugh until she felt like she would lose her supper.

Dall said, "Curly, all kidding aside, I've got to know what you're doing out here."

Curly sighed and moaned, "Ah, Dall, you weren't supposed to see me. I got reassigned to the office after my little accident with the radio."

Dall said, "Ah yes, the infamous radio incident. Well, Curly, I'm sure given enough time that you'll find a way to redeem yourself with the chief deputy. And he seems like a good guy. I'm sure he'll forgive in time."

Curly walked a few more steps, keeping his eyes trained on Sandy to make sure she didn't turn around for another peek. "I know that, Dall. I've known Chief Deputy Thurman since I was in grade school. He used to come to our school and talk to our classes. He's the reason I got in law enforcement. But he has a good memory. He never forgets."

Dall asked, "Then you really didn't mean those things you said about him?"

Curly looked surprised that Dall would even suspect such a thing. "Oh, no, Dall! I think the world of Chief Deputy Thurman. He's a genuine hero around these parts. Sometime I'll tell you about some of the things that have made him a legend around here. I was just mad at him at the time and said some things that I really didn't mean."

"So you were just saying those things to impress your partner."

"Mark? Yeah, I guess so. I don't know what I was thinking. I just got a big head and thought that since I had done so much to help Sheriff Holden get elected, it would be nice if he'd reward me with the chief deputy position. I guess I was just a little jealous. After thinking about it, I realized that I couldn't handle the job anyway. The chief deputy is really the best man for that job."

Dall said, "Then I ask again. What are you doing out here?"

"That's what I was getting at. I was trying to redeem myself. I've been keeping my ears open and I know that the feds are working the homicides out here. I know they suspect that a demon is killing people. And I overheard the sheriff talking to Mrs. Litchfield. She reported her husband missing even though the bishop told her not to. She said she thought his theory was hogwash; something about the preacher being so righteous that God just took him up to Heaven, like a couple other characters in the Bible. She said she couldn't tell the bishop that he was full of it without getting in trouble."

Dall said, "So you thought you'd snoop around out here and see if you could find anything useful to redeem yourself with the sheriff and chief deputy."

Curly removed his windbreaker and tried to tie the arms around his waist so at least his backside would be covered. The arms were too short to go around his waist, so he tucked the sleeves under his belt. "Yeah, but to tell you the truth, I'm at a loss as to where to start."

"I know. You're not even close to the Litchfield farm."

"Oh I know that Dall. It's just that when I drove by the Litchfield farm, I saw a light off in the distance. When I looked through my binoculars, I saw some soldiers. I figured I would find you first, then go from there."

Sandy had stopped laughing. She wondered how long Dall was going to soft-hand this moron. She stopped and stared conspicuously up at the stars. She then said, "Dall, I'm going on to the Straus farm. I want you to give Curly a serious dose of reality, then send him home. This is the last time I will see you out here. Do you understand me, Curly?"

Curly looked at Dall for support. He then sucked in his stomach and puffed out his chest in preparation to set this skinny girl straight. Before he could utter a word, Sandy said, "Don't make me turn around, Curly."

A sense of dread fell over Curly. He unconsciously moved behind Dall as he said, "Yes, ma'am, loud and clear."

Sandy continued on, and Dall said, "Come on, Curly, I want to show you something."

As they crossed the fields, Curly asked, "Where we going, Dall?"

"To the Litchfield farm. I try to drop by there most every night. I've got a couple of friends that I check on."

They walked into the back door of Mrs. Litchfield's barn, and Tramp and Lady eased up to the wall of their stalls and hung their head over so

Dall could pet them. As Dall stroked the horses, Curly asked, "These are your friends?"

"Yeah, we've become close. These are the only two guys I know that could take as many beating as they've taken and still let someone pet them. I wish I could find a way to get them out of this situation. Hey listen, Curly, does your county animal control officer or Human Society ever get involved in things like this?"

Curly shook his head. "They will under normal circumstances, but they won't get involved in the Amish district."

"Too bad. I'd like to find them a good home."

After a few minutes of small talk, Curly asked, "So, Dall, what were you going to show me?"

Dall gave the horses one final gentle pat. He turned and walked to a spot between the rows of stalls. He used his foot and gently moved the layer of hay from the dirt floor, exposing a massive bloodstain. Curly bent down and gasped as he illuminated the stain with a penlight. After a few second of careful study, Dall said, "This is what happened to Litchfield, Curly. I don't know if it was a demon or a well-trained soldier, but Litchfield is dead. I'm only showing you this so you can show the sheriff and chief deputy someday if it becomes necessary. But for now, we have to keep it a secret."

"But, Dall, The evidence will be gone if we don't show someone soon."

"Nah, Curly, this is a big stain. There was lots of blood spilled here. It's soaked into the dirt and hay, and dried. It'll be here for months."

Dall meticulously replaced the layer of hay and started toward the door. As they exited the barn and started toward Curly's car, Dall said, "I showed you that, Curly, because I want you to know just what we're dealing with. The sheriff and chief deputy are right. There is a demon working here. His name is Gaal and he's not alone. He could have thousands of demons here with him. That's what is so hard about this assignment. We don't know what we're dealing with. Gaal says he is trying to somehow redeem himself with God and secure a provision for redemption, but there is no way to verify what he's telling us. Therefore we can't trust him. But what we do suspect is that this demon, Gaal, has killed many people throughout history. He was responsible for the deaths of Himmler, Rasputin and the first two Amish men killed, Wilhelm Dresselhaus and Levy Croft, and now maybe Preacher Litchfield. He can take any form he wants. He can move with the speed of light. He has the strength of twenty men. And he has not one ounce of conviction about killing. No matter what he says, he's a demon and is evil to the core."

Curly was wheezing as he tried to keep up with Dall. He gasped between breaths, "Listen, Dall, if this thing is as dangerous as you say, you're going to need my help."

Dall stopped and turned to Curly. He grabbed him by his sweat-soaked shirt and got close to his face. "Curly! Listen to me! I told you all this and showed you Litchfield's blood tonight to impress one thing upon you! You can't help me! I know I told you I might need you at some point, but I have to be honest with you! If you're caught out here by Gaal, he'll kill you! Your gun won't help you! This demon can tear a man to pieces! For God's sake, Curly, slip into your record unit and pull the autopsy pictures of the Amish men!"

"I tried to, but the feds came in and took all our records. I think the sheriff might have a copy, but he keeps them locked up."

Dall released Curly's shirt and said, "Well, you were out here with the sheriff the day Massey found the body of Preacher Croft. You saw what happened to him."

"Yeah, I was at the autopsy, too. It was gruesome."

"Then stay away from this place, Curly! I know you want to help, but I'll feel terrible if you get killed!"

Curly followed when Dall turned and continued toward the road. He said, "Dall, what about you and Sandy? Aren't you in danger, too?"

"Yes, we are, but we're here because we have to be. Believe me, if there was any way for us to get out, we would."

Curly asked, "So, what protection do you have?"

Dall said, "The only protection that any mortal can have against a demon, the Holy Spirit. Demons can't cohabitate with the Holy Spirit. They are still under the authority of Christ. So if a person is truly saved and trusts in Christ, demons can't indwell them or harm them, without God's consent. It's only that spiritual shield that they fear. Nothing else in the universe scares them."

Curly said, "I believe in God, I think."

Dall shook his head. "That's what I'm talking about, Curly. You can't think. You can't have any doubts. Just believing that God exists is not the same as believing in Him. Knowing who He is isn't the same as knowing Him personally. Satan and the demons know who He is, and they tremble in fear. They were there when He created the world. They knew His power and still defied Him, and got themselves thrown out of Heaven. It takes a wholehearted love and faith in God as your personal savior. These demons are discerning. They can tell who's protected and who's not."

After a long walk to Curly's car, he unlocked it and said, "I'm still here for you, Dall. If you need me, call. Demon or no demon, I'll be here for you."

Dall watched as Curly drove away. He shook his head and vowed to never call Curly unless it was an emergency. He couldn't be responsible for another man's death.

As Curly drove away, a sense of dread fell over Dall. Leaving Sandy to walk on alone was a mistake. He hurried to the Straus farm, hoping she was safe.

The English Man   Mike Smitley

ELEVEN

SANDY GREW CONCERNED as she walked on alone to the Straus farm. She remembered Dall's warning, and realized that she was exposed without Dall's protection, so she ran the rest of the way. Once with Abel and Dory, she would be safe.

Dall slipped into his quarters in Abel's barn. After washing up, he slipped into bed and struggled to quiet his overactive mind. It seemed that he had been asleep for only a few minutes when he felt the warmth of Sandy's skin against his back. He glanced at his watch. It was a few minutes after midnight.

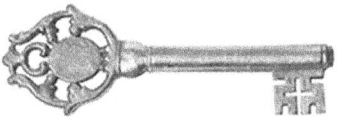

"I am he that liveth, and was dead; and behold, I am alive for evermore, Amen; and have the keys of hell and of death." **Revelation 1:18**

Dall stirred as the sun broke over the horizon. At some point in the night, Sandy had dressed and slipped back into her room in Abel's house. He dressed and hurried to breakfast.

He walked into the house late and found everyone else seated at the table. Abel motioned for him to sit in the chair beside him, and he sat nervously. "I'm sorry I'm late, Abel. I'll do better from now on."

Abel reached his massive, calloused hand behind Dall and gently patted his back. "That's okay, Dall, there are no lashings for you here. You suffered some painful injuries. You need your rest anyway."

As Dall filled his plate, he looked around the table to make sure no one would see his inquiring eyes shift to Sandy. When their eyes met, he raised his brows as if to ask her if she'd had any problems getting back into the house last night. She understood him perfectly and jerked her eyes quickly to Abel, then back to him. Dall knew something was seriously wrong.

After breakfast, Abel asked, "Isaac, would you and baby Jack go to the barn, harness the horse to the buggy and load my carpentry tools into the back? We're going to a barn raising today."

Dall said, "I'll help you, Isaac." But as he slid his chair out, Abel said, "Dall, would you come with me? You can help me pick out some of the straighter pieces of lumber from the stack out back. I tore down an old barn last year and salvaged the best lumber."

Dory said, "Sandy, you can help me and Judith load some baskets with food and drinks. When we raise a barn or house, everyone chips in and puts on a pot-luck dinner at lunch time."

Isaac and little Jack hurried to the barn while Abel and Dall went behind the house. Dall went to the lumber and began eyeing the stack for some straight 2X4's. Abel interrupted his search and stepped in front him. "Dall, we have to talk."

Dall's heart sank as his imagination ran wild. He controlled his fear and said nervously, "Okay, Abel, if you wish."

Abel was fully a head taller than Dall and looked down at him with his lazy eyes and chiseled brow. "Dall, I've been keeping a pretty close eye on Isaac. He likes to sneak out at night. I know he came to your room night before last. That doesn't bother me so much, but he took Judith with him. From now on, I want you to be conscious of little Judith. She's excited to have guests, and sometimes might not use good judgment when she comes to visit. If it's dark, I don't want her out of the house. I don't want Isaac out either, but I'm having a little more trouble controlling him."

Dall hung his head in shame. He nodded and said, "I agree, Abel. It was poor judgment for me to not bring Judith straight home. I apologize."

Abel looked around to make sure no one was watching them talk, then said, "That's okay, Dall. I know you meant no harm. I went to talk to you that night, but…"

For the first time since he'd met Abel, Dall saw apprehension in his eyes. When Abel looked away, Dall's heart sank. He instantly knew that Abel had seen him and Sandy making love. Their cover was blown."

Dall stepped closer to the big man and asked, "But what, Abel?"

When Abel turned to leave, Dall grabbed the sleeve of his shirt and pulled him back. No words were needed. Abel's eyes spoke volumes.

Dall slowly released Abel. He said, "Abel, I know what you saw. I'm sorry. I owe you an explanation."

Abel nodded and said, "It's obvious that you and Sandy aren't brother and sister. Since you're not, your love for each other is fornication, but not incest. I'm one of the few men in the district who understands the love that a man can have for a woman, but I assure you, if word of your love for Sandy gets back to Bishop Gordan or the elders, you'll be lashed within an inch of your lives, then banished from the district. And I won't be allowed to attend the lashing. I won't be able to intercede on your behalf."

"I know, Abel. I'm sorry that we've deceived you and the others. There's a good reason for it."

Abel turned and started picking out the straightest pieces of lumber and putting them in a separate stack. Dall talked as he helped. "Abel, there have been some strange deaths here in the district. Sandy and I aren't brother and sister, and we didn't come here hoping to become Amish again. We're here to try find out who killed those men."

Abel's anxiety shot through the roof. He dropped the boards he was holding, stood and turned quickly. "So you're cops?"

"I'm not, Sandy is. Listen, Abel, I wouldn't tell anyone else in the district this except one man, and that's Bishop Clevenger. I have a great deal of respect for you, and I hope you can keep what I tell you confidential."

Abel didn't speak for a minute. Dall was beginning to doubt the wisdom of opening up when Abel said, "I can keep a secret, Dall. I've got a few secrets of my own, but I can't keep anything from the bishop that will endanger the district. I can't promise you anything, so be careful what you say."

Dall said, "Abel, can we just leave it alone for now? Please just accept that Sandy and I are here to help. If we can find this killer, the entire district will be safer."

After long consideration, Abel said, "For now. Just remember, if you uncover anything that will cause embarrassment to the district, you'd better go to Bishop Gordan. And if he asks me about your activity, I won't lie to him."

Those arrangements were acceptable for now. Abel said, "And one more thing. I assume that you and Sandy aren't man and wife and trying to have a baby."

Dall sighed and looked back at the house. Through the kitchen window he could see Sandy and Dory gathering food and enjoying each other's company. He said, "No, Abel. No, we're not."

Abel said sternly, "Then there'll be no more sin between you two, Dall. There'll be no more fornication. I can't have that going on under my roof and in the presence of my kids. Even though you live in separate quarters in the barn, there's too much of a chance that one of the kids or Dory will walk in on you."

Dall nodded his head. "I'll honor your wishes, Abel. We're guests in your home, and you did us both a great service by rescuing us from Preacher Litchfield. It'll be as you say."

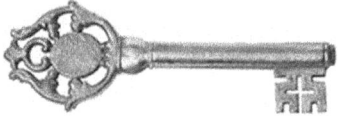

"I am he that liveth, and was dead; and behold, I am alive for evermore, Amen; and have the keys of hell and of death." Revelation 1:18

The locations for the poles of the barn had been mapped out a week earlier. Concrete footings had been poured and they'd cured adequately to support the weight of the barn. Once the neighbors had arrived, the walls went up quickly.

Dall stuck close to Abel, and displayed genuine compassion for the other men as Abel introduced him. By lunch-time, he'd made friends with most of the men who'd been curious about him and Sandy since they first arrived in the district.

Lunch was welcomed. Dall had not done any hard physical labor in many years, and his body screamed as he plopped down on a bench that the ladies had set up beside two tables that had been placed end to end. Had it not been for the hay season, he would have been unable to keep up. Sandy filled plates for her and Dall and sat beside him.

She tried to maintain her sisterly demeanor, but she had not been able to stop thinking about their lovemaking sessions. She wanted to touch him, but refrained. "You okay, Dall?"

Dall guzzled down his glass of tea without stopping, then ran his fingers through his hair. "Yeah, I guess. Man, these Amish guys are animals! They work like dogs and have the stamina of mules! They're killing me!"

"I'm sorry, Dall. I know it's hard, but at least they're not whipping the crap out of us like Litchfield did."

"I almost wish they would. It'd give me an excuse to quit."

Sandy smiled as people walked by and greeted her. After they'd passed, she said, "Listen, Bishop Clevenger made a point to get Judith off by herself and talk to her. I was close enough to listen. Judith was her old self. Gaal has abandoned her."

Dall had hungrily filled his mouth with fried chicken and roasted potatoes. He struggled to swallow, then said, "For now, maybe, but he'll use her if he needs to."

"Should we stay close to her to keep that from happening?"

"We can't. You're not a believer. You have no power against Gaal. You heard him. You're the one he wants. He can't approach the United States Government in the body of a little girl. He's got to have an adult body. He thinks you'd be the perfect person to get him an audience with the President and Joint Chiefs. I can't protect both of you, and Abel would think it strange if we start shadowing Judith. No, let's leave her alone. You need to stick close to me. We've got to keep him from indwelling you."

Sandy reached under the table and squeezed Dall's leg. "I'd like that, Dall. I want to be close to you all the time."

One of the ladies walked by with a large tea pitcher and refilled Dall's glass. When she left, Dall said, "Yeah, me, too, but we've got a problem. Abel came to the barn night before last to chew us out for not taking Judith to the house after it got dark. Guess what he saw when he looked through the window?"

Sandy's throat instantly closed with fear. She couldn't swallow, so she continued to chew as she looked around to see if anyone had noticed her shock. She was finally able to swallow with a loud gulp just as she looked into the lazy eyes of Abel Straus.

His emotionless face and chiseled features made him look particularly menacing. She forced the corners of her mouth upward and squinted her eyes in a pretentious smile. Abel had just filled his mouth with massive portions of Dory's pot roast and carrots. In a manner totally uncharacteristic of Abel, he carefully imitated Sandy's pretentious smile as he turned the corners of his overstuffed mouth up and squinted his eyes. Orange remnants of chewed carrots oozed between his teeth as he closed his eyes and flashed as many teeth as he could.

Dall turned his head and laughed quietly as Sandy lowered her head in total humiliation. She turned away from Abel and said, "I'll never be able to look at that man again! I'm so embarrassed! What are we going to do?"

"We're going to do just what we came here to do. From now on, you stick to me like glue. And by the way, I promised Abel there'd be no more lovemaking."

"No problem there. I'm never going to be able to take my clothes off again."

Throughout lunch Sandy periodically glanced at Abel to see if he would tell Dory. She was certain that he had not up to this point. Dory's demeanor back at the house was not consistent with an Amish woman who had just learned that her guests had committed sexual sin in her barn. When Abel moved off to visit with friends, Sandy asked, "Dall, explain something to me. Gaal keeps referring to his agreement with the U.S. as a covenant. Why does he use that term? Wouldn't an alliance or partnership mean the same thing?"

Dall washed down another mouthful of food with a long drink of sweet tea. "It probably would if we were dealing with a mortal, but we're not. Keep in mind that we're dealing with a fallen angel who has been alive for over six-thousand years. God created the angels just before he created man. Gaal still uses some of the language that was used long ago. If you read the Bible, you'll find that God used the word covenant a lot. A contract, alliance or agreement is an agreement between parties to do something or act in a certain way. A covenant is more than a promise. A covenant is the agreement that God made with Abraham and His chosen people, the Israelites. The agreement is relational. It implies that there will not only be a reciprocal promise from the other party, but that there is relational bonding and a degree of love between the parties. Gaal uses that term because he's trying to convince God that he'll not only partner with America, but that he'll love us also. He's hoping that God will not only recognize the covenant between Gall and us, but that God will accept that covenant as a bonding between Him and Gaal."

Sandy thought for a few seconds, then asked, "But isn't God able to read our thoughts? Can't He tell if Gaal is lying and trying to fool Him?"

"In a heartbeat. God is infinitely smarter than anything He created. He already knows what Gaal is thinking. He already knows who will win the war between the demons, and what He'll say to them if they defeat Satan and ask Him for redemption. This whole melodrama has already played out, and God knows how it will end."

"Gaal has to be smart enough to realize that he can't win mind games with God. Surely he wouldn't be doing all this if he didn't have a chance of succeeding."

"Don't bet on it, Sandy. One of the characteristics of all demons is their arrogance and stubbornness. They're like hardened career-criminals who never learn. They're always looking for ways to beat the system. I don't trust Gaal as far as I can throw him."

"Dall, don't tell me that you're thinking of crossing Smith. He'll kill you."

"He'll have to find me first."

The barn raising halted after a few more hours of work in the afternoon. The men had chores of their own to attend to, so they agreed to return the next day after an emergency meeting which had been called by Bishop Gordan.

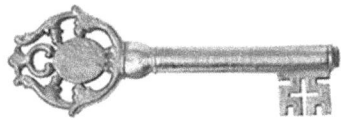

"I am he that liveth, and was dead; and behold, I am alive for evermore, Amen; and have the keys of hell and of death." **Revelation 1:18**

Dall bathed while Sandy helped Dory put away the supper dishes. He'd just finished dressing when he heard a knock on his door. He opened it and said, "Come in, Isaac. How are you?"

Isaac milled around the small quarters as he searched for the right words. He said, "I've been thinking about what you said about forgiveness. I'm having a pretty hard time with it. Just when I think I can get over the lashings, Dad loses his patience with me and yells. He hasn't lashed me anymore, but I know it's coming. If he whips me again, I'm leaving."

Dall listened intently. He sat in a chair across from Isaac and said, "Isaac, I know how you feel."

Isaac became angry as he stood and walked to the window, then stared out across the fields. "No you don't, Dall! Nobody does! I hate him for that! He didn't just whip me with a strap! He beat me half to death! He tried to kill me!"

"Isaac, your dad is a huge man. He's the strongest man I've ever seen. I know it hurt, and probably seemed like he was going to kill you, but I assure you that if he'd intended to kill you, he would have. He's so strong that you probably couldn't see it, but I know he tried to use a lot of restraint. Let me put this in perspective for you. God commands us to forgive."

Isaac turned and asked, "How? How do you do it?"

"I'm not sure, Isaac, but remember this. No man has ever been lashed and tortured like Jesus was. He suffered the worst death that one man could perpetrate against another. Yet, as He was hanging on that cross, He asked God to forgive His murderers. If He could do it with all that He went through, you've got to find a way, too. Sometimes you just have to throw your hands up and turn it over to God. You're dad is a great man. He loves you very much, and he's very sorry for all that's happened. His pride may not let him say it, but if you'll give him a chance, he'll make it up to you."

Isaac turned back to the window and stared out. After a while, he said, "I hear you're interested in the deaths of the three Amish men."

Dall perked up. "Yes, Isaac, I am. What do you know about it?"

He shrugged his shoulders and said, "I might know who killed one of them."

Dall walked up behind Isaac in complete shock. "Which one, Isaac?"

Isaac anguished as he searched his soul. His emotions overwhelmed him as he gritted his teeth. "Preacher Levi Croft."

"How do you know about that, Isaac?"

Tears ran down his face as he turned quickly and faced Dall. The stark terror was written across his face. "Because I was there! I've already talked to Bishop Clevenger, and he's ordered me to keep quiet about it. I've been fighting this for weeks! It's killing me to know that I may know who the killer is and can't tell anyone about it! I'm sure it was an accident, he didn't mean to hurt the preacher!"

Dall searched his memory and vividly remembered the gruesome images of Croft's autopsy photos. He'd been almost decapitated. No simple accident could account for that. He looked at Isaac with great skepticism and asked, "You had an altercation with him, didn't you, Isaac?"

Isaac looked down and said, "He attacked me with a hammer. It scared me, so I pushed him?"

Dall slowly backed away in case Isaac wasn't who Dall thought he was. "Is that all you did, Isaac? You just pushed him?"

Tears dripped from Isaac's eyes as he confessed. "Yes, he hit me and knocked me down. He was going to hit me with a hammer, so I pushed him. It was just a reflex; I was so scared. He fell and hit his head. I ran as fast as I could. When I looked back at him, I could see that he wasn't moving, but I thought he was pretending to be unconscious just to trick me into coming back. I ran on and left him. I thought for weeks that I had killed him, but Bishop Clevenger assured me that I didn't. And I saw the autopsy photos. I'm sure I didn't cause that kind of injury just by pushing him down. I'm sure I didn't kill him, but I should have stayed with him to make sure he was going to be okay."

Dall stared at Isaac in disbelief. A simple push could not have caused the trauma that Croft had suffered. Believing that Isaac was safe, he eased closer and placed his hand on Isaac's shoulder. "It's okay, Isaac. Don't beat yourself up anymore. Bishop Clevenger was right. You didn't kill Preacher Croft. Trust me. And I understand why you ran. Given the fact that there was a killer in the immediate area, you probably did the right thing. You couldn't have saved the preacher if you'd stayed with him. You might have been killed yourself."

Isaac stared at Dall. "I know, but who did it?"

"That's what I want to know, Isaac. Who else would have been out there?"

Isaac knew that Katie's dad was the only person who would have had a reason to follow him that night, but he couldn't turn him in. He said, "No one that I can think of. There's only one person who would have followed me to Massey's pond, but he wouldn't have…"

Dall asked, "Who, Isaac? Who would have followed you that night?"

Isaac's face flushed with fear. "I can't talk anymore, Dall. I have to go." He turned and rushed out the door."

Sandy stepped in a few seconds later and asked, "What's wrong with Isaac? He just ran past me like he'd seen a ghost."

"He knows who killed Preacher Croft. He won't talk now, but he knows. He's protecting someone close to him."

The light was fading fast, and Sandy looked out the window. She could barely see the ranger sergeant across the field by a tree. "Our escort is waiting. We've got to meet Smith and Dr. Sveade tonight. You ready?"

"I guess; let's get this over with."

They walked across the field toward the sergeant. Dall thought it unusual that the sergeant would stand out in plain sight like this. In the past, he'd always been careful to stay concealed.

As they approached, they saw that the ranger wasn't the sergeant at all. It was a different sniper and his partner. The spotter said, "We're your escort tonight, guys, come on."

Sandy walked past the soldiers as Dall followed. As he walked by the rifleman, the ranger quickly thrust the stock of his rifle upward and butt-stroked Dall across the side of the face. The blow elevated his feet off the ground and landed him flat on his back unconscious.

Sandy turned quickly and saw Dall crash to the ground with a loud thud. She stared at the ranger in horror, then rushed to Dall. As she ran past the spotter, he grabbed the back of her hair and pulled her face close to his. In an all too familiar voice, Gaal said, "Sorry it had to be this way, Sandy, but I need you, and there are too many souls at stake to let Dall stand in our way."

Paralyzing fear gripped Sandy. She finally drew in a deep breath to scream when she realized that Gaal had abandoned Judith and assumed the form of the ranger. Gaal grabbed her face and said, "Let's do this quietly, Sandy. We don't want to wake the entire district. Anyway, if you make this hard, my brother in arms there will kill Dall."

Sandy trembled and cried openly as Gaal pulled her close and clung tightly to her. She stopped crying when the indwelling was complete.

As Sandy opened her eyes, she was surprised to see that the spotter had vanished. Since Gaal was now inside her, he had no more use for him. She still had her memory and sense of self-awareness, but she felt a strange sense of anger and hostility. She was not herself, but Gaal living within her. For the first time in her life, she felt the presence of total evil. Gaal was in control of her mind. It was strange to know who she was and remember her entire life perfectly, yet be shoved to the back corner of her consciousness and have no ability to overpower Gaal. She now realized how people could be controlled by demons with no power to stop them.

Gaal turned Sandy's head sharply toward the sniper and said, "WE HAVE NO USE FOR DALL, KILL HIM."

Sandy screamed from the small corner of her mind that she had been relegated to. "Gaal, no! You can't kill him! That's murder, and you'll never convince God to redeem you if you continue to sin!"

Gaal spoke to her subconsciously, "SANDY, WE'RE GOING TO DO GREAT THINGS TOGETHER, BUT I'M IN CONTROL HERE. I KNOW I CAN'T SIN, BUT THIS IS WAR. THINGS THAT YOU WOULD NORMALLY CONSIDER SIN WILL BE JUSTIFIABLE IN THE CONTEXT OF THE WAR THAT WE'RE FIGHTING."

Sandy yelled, "It may be justifiable to you, but God's opinion is the one that matters! And even in war, killing an unconscious and unarmed enemy combatant is murder! Murder is murder no matter how you rationalize it!"

"NOT SO, SANDY. IF THE KILLING SERVES A GREATER PURPOSE, SUCH AS SPARING BILLIONS OF SOULS FROM AN ETERNITY IN THE LAKE OF FIRE, THE DEATH OF ONE PERSON IS A SMALL PRICE TO PAY. IF YOU HOPE TO COHABITATE WITH ME PEACEFULLY, YOU CANNOT INTERFERE. I KNOW YOU LOVE DALL, BUT YOU'LL FORGET HIM AS SOON AS YOU SEE WHAT WONDERFUL THINGS I HAVE IN STORE FOR YOU. THE OTHER NIGHT, YOU ASKED DR. SVEADE WHY YOU WERE CHOSEN FOR THIS ASSIGNMENT. HE GAVE YOU THE FIRST REASON, THEN SAID YOU'D LEARN THE SECOND REASON LATER. THE SECOND REASON IS THAT I CHOSE YOU. NOT ONLY DO YOU LOOK THE PART, BUT BECAUSE OF YOUR KNOWLEDGE OF THE INNER-WORKINGS OF AMERICAN GOVERNMENT, YOU'LL MAKE AN EXCELLENT VESSEL THROUGH WHICH I CAN CARRY OUT MY MISSION. SMITH ASKED FOR YOU BECAUSE MY BRETHREN INSTRUCTED HIM TO. YOU MAY AS WELL KNOW IT NOW; NEITHER OF YOU WILL BE ALLOWED TO LEAVE THIS DISTRICT AFTER THE COVENANT IS SEALED. NEITHER THE U.S. NOR WE FALLEN CAN ALLOW YOU TO WARN THE WORLD OF OUR ALLIANCE. YOU AND DALL WERE CONDEMNED TO DEATH AS SOON AS YOU WERE RECRUITED. THE ONLY WAY YOU'LL SURVIVE THIS IS TO DWELL WITH ME. DALL WILL NOT BE SPARED. YOU SHOULD BE HONORED. I INTEND TO TAKE YOU WITH ME WHEN I APPROACH GOD'S THRONE AND ASK FOR REDEMPTION. JUST THINK OF IT. WITHIN A VERY SHORT TIME, YOU'LL BE FACE TO FACE WITH THE CREATOR OF ALL THAT IS. YOU'LL BE MY VESSEL IN THIS LIFE AND MY MATE IN ETERNITY. AREN'T YOU EXCITED?"

Sandy screamed from her dark little corner, "No, Gaal, I'm not! You're in me, but if you want me to cooperate, you can't hurt Dall! You have me now, but I'll never give you one moment of peace if you hurt him! You may be in control now, but you can do nothing without my cooperation! I'll make you kill me if I have to!"

As the sniper put the muzzle of his rifle against Dall's head, Gaal sighed heavily and put Sandy's hand on the barrel. He gently pushed it away and said grudgingly, "STOP. THIS ISN'T THE TIME. PICK HIM UP AND BRING HIM WITH US."

The sniper bent over to lift Dall to his feet. Dall slowly regained consciousness and clumsily struggled to maintain his balance, then stumbled as the sniper pushed him forward.

Dall's head had cleared slightly as they walked into the clearing at Massey's pond. He had not had a chance to see Sandy's face clearly, and was surprised when she took the lead in the conversation. When Dr. Sveade asked her about Gaal, she said, "Yes, I've talked to him. He has assumed the form of a little girl, but I have befriended him and convinced him that we can be trusted. He is willing to discuss the covenant, but wants some assurances. First, because we have talked at length, he trusts me and wants me to speak on his behalf. He will not manifest himself to you, but will talk through me. You will do anything I say or the deal is off. He will disappear and you won't find him again. He'll approach the leaders of our nation's adversaries and form a covenant with one of them. Are you clear on that, Dr. Sveade?"

Waters could no longer contain his hatred for Sandy. He erupted in anger. "Mr. Smith, this is garbage! This little slut hasn't got the expertise to negotiate an agreement between our government and Gaal! She's not even a willing participant in this assignment! She never has been! We've had to twist her arm every step of the way!"

Sandy stepped up to Waters and removed her pistol from the waistband inside her dress. She cocked the hammer and stuck the muzzle against Waters' forehead. As every nerve in his body unraveled, he collapsed to his knees and cried as he looked up into her determined eyes. She said, "Smith, I've had it with you and Waters. I can handle Gaal without either of you."

Smith and Sveade slowly looked at each other. Sandy didn't seem like herself. Aside from her personality shift, she moved differently. Dr. Sveade frowned and shook his head at Smith, indicating that she should be patronized. Both sensed Sandy's determination to kill Waters. Sveade grabbed Smith's arm to prompt him to do something. Smith said quickly, "Okay, Sandy! Stop, don't kill him! The mission is yours! You're in charge!"

Sandy slowly released the tension on the trigger and turned. "Okay, Mr. Smith. Now that we all know where we stand, you'll set up a meeting with the President and his cabinet. I want an audience with them in one week. I'll have Gaal there."

Sveade asked, "But Sandy, we have to talk to Gaal first. When will he meet with us?"

"He doesn't like you, Dr. Sveade. Apparently you demonstrated your lack of trustworthiness when you were dealing with Himmler at the end of World War II. He saw you withhold information from your fellow team-members of the allied nations and cut them out of the loop after the war. You've demonstrated that you are not someone who can be trusted."

Sveade looked at Smith and saw the mistrust in his eyes also. Smith said, "Okay, Sandy, you're in charge. Meet us back here tomorrow night. We'll get started on the meeting with the President."

As Sandy turned to leave, Dall said, "We had been meeting at the abandoned Ballinger place. Why have we started meeting back here again? She took Dall by the arm without answering and led him out of the clearing. Smith turned to Dr. Sveade and said, "Well, we got what we wanted. We wanted her to find Gaal."

Dr. Sveade glared angrily at them as they walked away. "Yes, or did Gaal find her?"

"He's indwelled her, Doctor. Should we warn Dall?"

"No, not yet. I'm afraid that'll anger Gaal. He has unbelievable power and legions of other demons to help him. No, Mr. Smith, it looks like Gaal is in charge now. I don't want to lose him again. Let's do as he says. Set up the meeting with the Joint Chiefs. Once they're on board, we'll approach the President."

As Sandy led Dall toward the Straus farm, Dall wrestled with his confusion over the way she had taken the investigation away from Smith and Sveade. Her new-found assertiveness was uncharacteristic of her. She was much stronger and moved in a different gait. The escort by the ranger sniper was also a first. Previously, he and Sandy had always walked back to the Straus farm unescorted. He asked, "So, Sandy, what prompted that sudden show of courage? What makes you think you can control Gaal sufficiently to orchestrate a covenant?"

Sandy squeezed his arm and said, "Gaal showed up while you were unconscious, Dall. He wants to work through me, and only me. I think I can pull this thing off and get us out of here."

Dall's head was still spinning, but a deep sense of fear suddenly overwhelmed him. Even in his dizziness he realized that Gaal had indwelled Sandy while he'd been unconscious. He stopped suddenly and jerked his arm away from her. She squared up to him and looked deep into his eyes with an evil glare that he had never seen in her before. The ranger gripped his rifle and studied Sandy closely for a cue.

Dall slowly shook his head as he studied Sandy's eyes. He tried to control his fear and said, "Let's not con each other here, Gaal. You've taken Sandy."

Sandy was smaller than Dall, but stepped up to him like a schoolyard bully. Her green eyes turned red and Gaal spoke in the same voice that he'd used while in Judith. "YES, DALL, I HAVE. THE TRUTH OF THE MATTER IS THAT DR. SVEADE AND I HAVE ALREADY TALKED MANY TIMES; THE FIRST BEING IN 1945 AFTER BERLIN FELL. THE ALLIES OFFERED TO PARTNER WITH ME THEN IF I COULD DEFEAT SATAN. SO, I SET OUT TO BUILD MY ARMY AND SEE IF I COULD MUSTER ENOUGH SUPPORT AMONG THE FALLEN. WHEN I MADE MY PRESENCE KNOWN IN THIS AMISH COMMUNITY, SVEADE DIDN'T KNOW IF IT WAS ME OR ANOTHER DEMON. YOU AND SANDY WERE ONLY SENT IN TO TEST ME AND ASSURE SVEADE THAT IT WAS REALLY ME. I PROMISED IN 1945 THAT I WOULD CONTACT THEM AFTER I HAD ENOUGH SUPPORT TO BIND SATAN. I CONTACTED SVEADE LAST YEAR AND SAID I WAS READY. THE F.B.I. SENT YOU AND SANDY IN AS A TEST TO SEE IF THE FALLEN SPIRIT WAS REALLY ME. I PROMISED THAT I WOULD NOT HURT YOU, SO IF YOU TWO WERE KILLED, THEY WOULD KNOW THAT THE DEMON HERE WAS NOT ME. YOU WERE ONLY BAIT. IF YOU WERE KILLED, SVEADE WOULD KNOW THAT THE DEMON HERE WAS NOT ME, AND THEY WOULD LOOK ELSEWHERE."

Dall shook his head in amazement. Gaal continued, "I KNOW THE POWER OF BELIEVERS TO CAST OUT DEMONS IN CHRIST'S NAME, BUT I MUST WARN YOU. SANDY IS MY LAST CHANCE OF INDWELLING SOMEONE THROUGH WHOM I CAN FORM THE COVENANT THAT WE ALL DESPERATELY NEED TO REGAIN GOD'S GRACE. THERE IS LITTLE TIME LEFT. THE SECOND COMING IS AT HAND. THERE ARE TOO MANY SOULS AT STAKE HERE. GO ALONG WITH ME AND YOU CAN HAVE HER BACK. INTERFERE, AND BOTH OF YOU WILL DIE. THIS

RANGER IS UNDER STRICT ORDERS. IF YOU UTTER EVEN ONE WORD ABOUT SENDING ME AWAY, HE WILL PUT YOU ASUNDER WITHOUT THE SLIGHTEST HESITATION."

Dall studied his options. He held his hand up and shook his head. He rubbed his temples and contemplated his future. With Gaal firmly in control of Sandy, and the meeting with the President in the works, neither Smith nor Sveade would have any use for him. In fact, there was no way that they could leave him alive to reveal all that had transpired. They would have to kill him. It was painfully clear that he would have to get Sandy back if he were going to live. He sighed and said, "I can't let you do this, Gaal."

He was about to take his chances with the ranger and order Gaal to leave Sandy, but Gaal had sensed his intention. Sandy quickly punched Dall in the face, knocking him to the ground. Gaal yelled to the ranger, "KILL HIM!"

Dall suddenly realized why Gaal had changed the location of the meetings back to the old well close to Massey's pond. Gaal intended to kill him and dump his body in the well. He looked at the ranger and stared into the angry, determined eyes of his killer. The ranger stepped up to Dall and poked the barrel of his M-14 in Dall's face. Dall panicked, grabbed the barrel and pushed it away just as the ranger pulled the trigger.

The muzzle-blast was deafening. The shot blew a large crater in the ground by Dall's head, throwing dirt in the air that showered both of them. He rolled over on his side and gave the ranger a hard heel-kick to the groin. As the ranger doubled over with a grunt and dropped to his knees, Dall jumped to his feet and ran. Gaal yelled, "KILL HIM! SHOOT BEFORE HE GETS AWAY!"

The ranger struggled to his feet and regained control of his M-14. He flipped the selector switch from semi-auto to full auto, threw the butt-stock high under his arm and pulled the trigger. The burst woke up the countryside as the rifle belched out 20 rounds of 7.62^{mm} N.A.T.O. Sandy drew her pistol from her waistband and emptied the magazine at Dall as he ran.

With one back and forth sweeping motion, the ranger sprayed fire at Dall. To everyone's amazement, the bullets screamed all around him, many of them barely missing him, but when the ranger's magazine was empty and the bolt had locked open Dall took a quick assessment of his condition and realized that he was uninjured. Knowing that he could not survive another barrage, he sprinted off into the darkness.

The ranger reloaded another magazine and prepared to fire. This time he shouldered the rifle and took a careful sight picture on Dall's rapidly fading silhouette. Before the ranger could fire, Gaal angrily mumbled, "WAIT; DON'T SHOOT." The ranger held his fire and looked at Sandy for direction. Gaal finally mumbled grudgingly, "OKAY, SANDY. NOT NOW. BUT I WARN YOU. DON'T INTERFERE WITH ME AGAIN."

Dall ran till he heaved so hard that he could no longer stand. He dropped to his knees and gasped for air as he searched the darkness for Sandy and the ranger. With Gaal now firmly in control of Sandy, Dall would have little chance of ever getting her back.

He studied the surrounding countryside as he wondered where to go. The Straus farm would be the first place Gaal would search, so he couldn't go there. Smith, Waters and Sveade would likely shoot him on sight. There was only one place he could hide.

Bishop Clevenger would be his best hope for help, but he didn't want to endanger the bishop and his wife right now. He ran as fast as his burning lungs would let him back to the old well by Massey's pond. As he cautiously approached he found that Smith, Waters and Dr. Sveade had gone.

He removed the boards from over the old well and found the rusty chain that had been attached to a bucket years ago. He anchored it to a rusty bolt that was protruding from the concrete well housing, then lowered himself into the well. He pulled the boards back over the top and repelled into the water. No one would think to look for him there. No one except Gaal. He only hoped Gaal would be so preoccupied with other matters that he would not come for him. He hoped that one of those matters was a strong-willed blond named Sandy Parsons.

The stench in the well was horrific. As his feet and legs entered the water, Dall wondered how deep it was. It was only chest-deep, but the well was full of debris. Dall surmised that the kids had thrown sticks and rocks into it.

He'd planned to sit in the well for the rest of the night, then try to make it to Bishop Clevenger's house in the morning. From there he hoped to formulate a plan to help Sandy.

When he couldn't get comfortable, he began to think that this had been a mistake. He wondered if he might have been better off hiding in one of the many wooded areas surrounding the Straus farm. He pulled a small pen-light from his pocket and illuminated the well. Total shock stunned him as he came face to face with the floating remains of Preacher Litchfield. He had gone missing the night that Dall had to go to the hospital after his worst beating, but Dall had not spent a lot of time or energy trying to figure out what had happened to him.

Further examination of his confines revealed the bones and decayed clothing of other people. Closer examination revealed that they were the remains of young teenagers. He now knew where the rebellious teenagers had disappeared to when they had been excommunicated from the district. Dall wondered if their parents knew what had happened to them. He'd been led to believe that the Amish simply wrote them off as lost to the English world, but he was sure they would be devastated if they knew their kids had been murdered. If he made it out of this alive, he had to save Isaac Straus from the same fate.

The ranger paced around nervously as Sandy sat passively on a log. He approached and asked, "How long are we going to sit here while he gets further away?"

A chill ran down his spine as Sandy looked up angrily. As the ranger stared into her possessed eyes, Gaal said, "I'LL SMITE THEE, LAD. I'M INVOLVED IN AN INTENSE CONVERSATION HERE. LET ME PONDER THIS. DON'T WORRY, WE'LL FIND HIM."

Frightened by Gaal's anger, the ranger nervously asked, "We've lost sight of him, Sir, or I mean ma'am."

Sandy's face lost all expression and Gaal's voice softened. She stood and brushed off her seat. "RELAX. THERE ARE OTHERS WITH US HERE TONIGHT. THEY SERVE ME AND ARE FOLLOWING DALL. COME. LET'S END HIS INTERFERENCE ONCE AND FOR ALL."

Sandy began to scream at Gaal. She tried to regain control of her limbs, but Gaal overpowered her and shoved her back into her corner. She screamed, "Gaal, I won't permit this! I'm warning you! Leave Dall alone!"

Sandy strolled calmly with the ranger in tow. Gaal argued with her as they walked. "SANDY, YOU MUST ACCEPT YOUR DESTINY. YOU ARE ME AND I AM YOU NOW. MY MISSION IS YOURS. YOU HAVE TO FORSAKE YOUR WORLDLY DESIRES. DALL IS A BELIEVER. HE'LL NEVER LET US COEXIST IN PEACE. EVEN AS WE SPEAK, HE IS PLOTTING TO CAST ME OUT OF YOU. I CAN'T LET THAT HAPPEN. YOU MUST REMEMBER; I

NOW POSSESS YOUR BODY. I KNOW YOU'VE READ THE BIBLE SOME, BUT YOU ARE NOT WELL VERSED. THERE IS A STORY IN THE EIGHTH CHAPTER OF MATTHEW THAT ILLUSTRATES HOW MANY OF US CAN OCCUPY ONE BODY. IN THAT STORY, MANY OF THE FALLEN OCCUPIED TWO MEN. WHEN THEY MET JESUS, HE CAST THEM OUT OF THE MEN AND INTO A HERD OF SWINE. RIGHT NOW YOU ARE DEALING ONLY WITH ME. I AM KIND AND COMPASSIONATE. IF YOU CONTINUE TO RESIST ME, I WILL BRING IN MANY MORE OF MINE TO DWELL. THEY ARE NOT GENTLE, AND WILL TORMENT YOU ETERNALLY IF YOU DESTROY OUR CHANCES OF APPROACHING THE FATHER. YOU ARE BETTER OFF DEALING ONLY WITH ME. SO STOP RESISTING. WHEN YOU AND I ARE ON OUR FACES AT THE THRONE OF CHRIST AFTER OUR GREAT WAR WITH SATAN IS WON, HE WILL SEE OUR GREAT WORKS AND BESTOW UPON US A PROVISION FOR REDEMPTION. YOU WILL SHARE IN THAT REWARD FOREVER AND THANK ME FOR WHAT WE DO NOW."

Sandy realized that nothing she could do would save Dall. All she could do was cry. The ranger was puzzled by the tears streaming down her stoic, stone face.

As Gaal and the ranger approached the well, Dall heard Gaal say, "REMOVE THESE BOARDS. HE'S IN THE WELL."

Dall panicked as he looked around the cylindrical tomb. There was no place to hide. As the ranger began removing the boards, Dall grabbed Preacher Litchfield's decaying body and another corpse, then drew in a deep breath and sank below the water. While holding his breath, he burrowed under the bodies and pulled them on top of him.

With the boards removed the ranger aimed his rifle at the bottom of the well and depressed the pressure-switch that activated his barrel-mounted tactical light. The light illuminated the mass of bodies as the stench floated past his face. He gagged as he said, "I can't see him, Gaal. Are you sure he's there? Maybe your sources are wrong."

Gaal stepped back and said, "NO, MY FAITHFUL ARE NOT MISTAKEN. WILL YOUR ROUNDS REACH THE BOTTOM OF THE WELL?"

The ranger pulled his face back away from the fog and coughed. "No, not if it's too deep. I'm shooting 168grn. Federal Match hollow-points. I can't tell how deep the water is, but if it's not too deep, they'll kill him if he's in there."

Although Sandy was screaming, Gaal said, "LET'S INVEST ANOTHER TWENTY ROUNDS FOR THE GOOD OF THE CAUSE." With that, the ranger stood erect over the top of the well and pulled the trigger. The roar was deafening as the M-14 blasted twenty rounds into the well.

The ranger jumped back quickly as the spray of contaminated water and unidentifiable slime sprayed upward from the impact of the bullets. He vigorously swiped the water and debris from his face and clothes in total disgust and said, "That'll do it if he's there."

Gaal closed his eyes and listened to his brethren. He then looked at the ranger. "HE'S STILL NOT DEAD. MY DEAR ONES ARE WITH HIM, AND HE STILL LIVES. THE WATER IS TOO DEEP."

The ranger said, "Okay, let's just drown him. He has to come up for air sometime."

Gaal dropped the empty magazine from his pistol and inserted a loaded one, then pressed the slide release as the slide slammed into battery on a live round. He eased to the edge of the well as the ranger again illuminated the water. He said, "NO. THE FATHER'S HAND IS UPON HIM. UNHOOK THE CHAIN FROM THAT BOLT SO HE CAN'T CLIMB OUT. WE'LL DEAL WITH HIM LATER."

The ranger unhooked the chain and asked, "Why don't you just have your followers go down there and kill him. It would be easy for them."

Sandy straightened up and looked toward Heaven. After a long minute of deliberation, Gaal said, "NO, THE FATHER WILL NOT PERMIT IT. HE HAS PLACED A HEDGE OF PROTECTION AROUND DALL. WE CANNOT HARM HIM. YOU'LL HAVE TO DO IT, BUT NOT NOW." As they turned to leave, Sandy was relieved that Dall had survived.

Dall pressed his face against Litchfield's rotting head. When the light from the ranger's flashlight disappeared, he put his nose to the surface alongside Litchfield's face and exhaled the air in his lungs, then drew in a deep breath. After several minutes with no more gunfire, he pushed the bodies off him and stood. When he took assessment of his condition, he found that the bodies had absorbed the gunfire and he had miraculously been spared any injury. He didn't understand why. The 7.62 ^{mm} N.AT.O. possessed sufficient energy to have penetrated the bodies and killed him. He lowered his head in silent prayer, thanking God for sparing his life.

All the sniper teams now received new instructions. They were no longer on surveillance; they were on a search and destroy mission.

Everyone, including Smith, Waters and Dr. Sveade, now took their orders from Gaal.

There was no sleep for Dall this night. The stench of the dead eventually made him sick to his stomach and gave him a terrible headache. As the faint rays of morning began to shine through the boards and illuminate the well, he looked for a way out. The chain was lying on the ground at the top of the well, and the walls were too smooth to get a finger or foot hold. He was trapped and had no alternative but to play his ace card. He removed his cell phone from his coat pocket and shook the water off it. He dialed and prayed that it would still work after being submerged.

Curly hadn't yet stirred from his sleep after a long night of James Bond, Rambo and Chuck Norris movies, sustained by multiple gorgings of cheeseburgers, chips, pizza, Snickers bars and ice cream. When his phone rudely pried him from the clutches of the Bond girls, he fumbled for it and slurred, "Deputy Slapp. How can I help you?"

Dall was surprised that even Curly would answer his private phone in such a professional manner, but he couldn't be critical right now. He said, "Curly! Dall Roberts! I need your help, buddy! Can I still count on you?"

When he heard Dall's voice, Curly awoke and realized that he was not on duty. He struggled up to one elbow and yelled, "Dall! Yes! You can count on me! I can hardly hear you! What do you need?"

"Curly, listen carefully! This is dangerous! I need you to come to the well by Massey's pond just south of Bishop Gordan's farm. Do you know where it is?"

Curly jumped to his feet and exclaimed, "Old well! Yes, I know where it is! Massey's pond! Do I need backup?"

Dall panicked and hoped Curly wouldn't hang up. "No! Curly, don't tell anyone you're coming here! Whatever you do, keep this a secret! And don't let anyone see you! Hide your car on a side-road away from the Amish land and stick close to the timber when you come in! Hurry, I can't hold out much longer!"

When Dall closed his phone, Curly was stunned beyond belief. He dropped the phone without hanging it up. He dressed quickly and put on his shoulder holster. Once his loaded revolver was snuggled safely in the holster, Curly tried to think of everything that he would need. He had his cell-phone and tactical light, and his commando knife was clipped inside the top of his boot. Just to make sure, he ran to his underwear drawer and grabbed another box of ammunition that was next to the unopened box of condoms that he'd bought himself as a graduation present when he'd graduated from the reserve police academy five years ago. He ripped open the ammo and dumped the entire box into his hand. He poured them into the thigh-pocket of his cargo pants, causing it to bulge and sway from side to side as he ran to his car.

Thirty minutes later, Dall heard the racket of clumsy footsteps stumbling through the timber and underbrush. When Curly stuck his panic-stricken and sweat-soaked face over the edge of the well, Dall thought he was the most beautiful thing he'd ever seen. He said, "Curly, hook that chain to the bolt in the concrete and throw it down."

Curly complied and helped Dall out of the well. Once Dall was out, Curly removed his flashlight and started to look into the well. Dall grabbed his hand and said, "Don't look, Curly. Just trust me, you'll know what's in there soon enough."

Curly said, "Man, it stinks something terrible. Are there dead animals in there?"

That explanation would suffice for now. Dall said, "Yeah, dead animals. Let's get out of here before someone sees us."

Once both were seated in Curly's car, Curly said, "You stink something terrible, Dall. How did you get in that well? What was in there?"

"Dead people. When the time is right, you and the sheriff will have to recover the bodies. You'll clear up a whole lot of homicides and be a hero. But not yet, Curly. Get me to your house so I can shower and get some clean clothes."

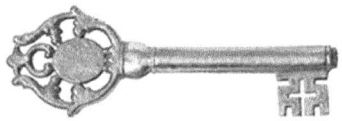

"I am he that liveth, and was dead; and behold, I am alive for evermore, Amen; and have the keys of hell and of death." **Revelation 1:18**

That morning Bishop Gordan called the emergency meeting of the preachers, elders and Assistant Bishop Clevenger to order. The other men were allowed to attend, but could not speak unless specifically asked to. Bishop Gordan closed the doors to the room and began in a soft voice. "Brethren, we have urgent business to discuss. We've all seen the English soldiers on our properties at night. The strange child that roams our hills and pastures also concerns me. I have no doubt that the English are here to investigate the disappearance of Elias Litchfield and the deaths of Wilhelm Dresselhaus and Levi Croft. I have no doubt that they're here at the request of Lilly Dresselhaus. I'll deal with her at a later time."

Sampson Betendorf raised his hand to speak. The bishop nodded and Sampson confirmed Bishop Gordan's fears. "I agree, Brethren. I caught my Katie sneaking out of the house after dark to meet the Straus boy. I now lock her in her room to keep her off the fields at night. Has anyone been able to identify the little girl that has been seen after dark?" No one spoke up.

Abel Straus said, "I, too, have kept Isaac in at night. You all know that I've had some problems with him, but he's scared enough that he doesn't fight me about it. But keeping our kids in at night isn't going to solve anything. How are we going to find out who these Englishers are? And what about this little girl? None of us have been able to get close enough to identify her, but she's in grave danger being out there with the English and the killer of our three brothers."

Several brothers nodded in agreement when Abel said, "And several of us heard gunshots last night. It sounded like machine-gun fire."

Bishop Gordan said, "Let's not worry about the little girl for now. I had Brother Dunlevy go around to our English neighbors and warn them about the problems that we've having. They have all assured him that they will keep their kids in at night also. She is obviously not Amish since none of us know her."

Abel then asked the question that was on everyone's mind. "Bishop Gordan, what about the soldiers? I wonder what or who they were shooting at last night. I'm particularly worried. I went to check on Dall Roberts this morning when he failed to show for breakfast, and he was gone. He had not slept in his bed last night. I fear that the English were shooting at him."

Gordan shook his head as he rubbed his beard. "I don't think they're military. I think they're sheriff's deputies, probably tactical team members or something like that. I called the sheriff and asked him to keep his men off our land, but he denied that they were his men. I think he's lying. All English lie like that."

Elder Dunlevy raised his hand and asked for the floor. When Gordan nodded his head, Dunlevy stood and addressed the brethren. "Brothers, it doesn't matter whether they're military or police. They're both equally capable of killing us. And since we heard gunshots last night, we have to assume that they have every intention of doing so. But we have a more pressing matter. The English wouldn't be sneaking around our properties if we had been more cooperative with the sheriff. I know he's not to be trusted, but we have to consider his position in this. We've had three brothers murdered, but he has to be concerned for the safety of our English neighbors as well. There's no assurance that the killer will confine himself to our district. He may very likely kill one of our English neighbors next. If he isn't caught, the sheriff will appear indifferent to the welfare of his citizens if he doesn't do something. And remember, there are greater evils in the English world. If we don't deal with Sheriff Holden, there are far worse people who could come in here."

Elder Dunlevy then turned to Bishop Gordan and said, "I know you've forbidden us to cooperate with the English, but we must change our position. We have to help the sheriff catch this killer, or more will die. We can take care of our own business within the district, but if an English neighbor is killed, we may be held responsible if it's learned later that we withheld information that would have cleared these killings and prevented another."

The men simultaneously mumbled their agreement with Elder Dunlevy. Bishop Gordan looked at Assistant Bishop Clevenger for support. Bishop Clevenger merely gave a barely-noticeable nod of his head. Bishop Gordan looked at the men sternly, then conceded. "Okay, then. That's how it'll be. We'll start patrolling our lands at night. Abel, you and Sampson be at my house tonight at dark. We'll work in three-man teams. When we see the English deputies, we'll confront them and ask them how we can help. If they refuse to let us help, we'll insist they leave. If they won't leave, we'll shadow them the rest of the night so they can't do whatever they're here to do. They certainly can't arrest us on our own land. I'll see you all at the barn-raising this afternoon. Let's close with a prayer."

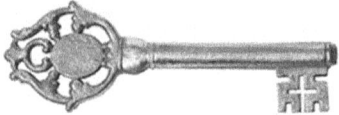

"I am he that liveth, and was dead; and behold, I am alive for evermore, Amen; and have the keys of hell and of death." **Revelation 1:18**

Dall awoke after only a couple hours of sleep. Curly had washed his clothes as he'd requested. As he was dressing, he glanced over at the window by the sofa that he'd slept on. The large telescope intrigued him. "Curly, I didn't know you were into star-gazing."

Curly yelled from the kitchen where he was preparing waffles for breakfast, "Yeah, Mom bought that for me when I graduated from high school."

As Dall fastened his belt, he walked up to the telescope to examine it. The strange thing was that it was level instead of tilted upward. Without moving it, he stuck his eye to the eyepiece and found that it was pointed at the bedroom window of a house on an adjacent street. He shook his head and said, "Yeah, Curly, I'll bet you see some wonderful sights through this."

Dall's comment struck Curly as strange, so he walked into the living-room to see what Dall was looking at. When he realized that Dall knew what he'd really been looking at, he stumbled all over himself. "Oh, uh, Dall! I was just watching a drug deal go down the other night! I wasn't… I mean she wasn't naked… It was just…"

Dall chuckled and said, "That's okay, Curly. I never had any illusions that you were perfect. This is just what I've been looking for."

Curly went back to the waffles as Dall turned the telescope toward the horizon and aimed it between some trees and over the roofs of the houses. He then turned up the magnification and adjusted the focus ring as he studied the storm clouds churning in the distance.

Complete terror consumed Dall as he stared in disbelief. The storm clouds were not clouds at all. They were a mass if individual dark forms swirling around each other and moving through and among millions of other shadowy, human-like forms. These were the same figures that he'd seen in Litchfield's barn loft and at the scene of his beating. When he pulled his eye from the eyepiece and looked at the gathering with his naked eye, he imagined the size of the mass that was surrounding the district, then tried to imagine the number of beings within the mass. For the first time in his life, he realized what John must have seen in Revelations when he'd been given a glimpse into Heaven. He now knew what he'd meant when he'd used the phrase *without number* to describe the angels in Heaven. Most frightening of all, Dall now knew that Gaal was telling the truth, at least about the war with Satan. It appeared that the war had begun.

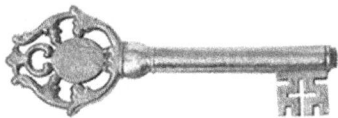

"I am he that liveth, and was dead; and behold, I am alive for evermore, Amen; and have the keys of hell and of death." **Revelation 1:18**

Bishop Clevenger has just finished an early lunch when he heard a knock on his door. When he looked through the screen, he was surprised to see Dall standing on his porch. He motioned for Dall to come in. "Dall! What a relief to see you. Come into my home, good son."

Dall had slept for a couple of hours at Curly's house, but he was still exhausted and sore from his night in the well. The bishop offered him a chair. "You look like you've had a rough night, Dall. Is there something on your mind?"

Dall looked around Bishop Clevenger's house suspiciously. "Yes, Bishop, there is. Can we talk freely here?"

Bishop Clevenger was concerned. "Why, yes, Dall, we can. It's just Mrs. Clevenger and me here."

Dall looked at Mrs. Clevenger out of the corner of his eye. She understood the magnitude of the meeting and merely smiled at him. Suddenly shamed, he dropped his stare to the floor, then sat down across the table from Bishop Clevenger. As he began to talk, Mrs. Clevenger sat a plate in front of him. "Here, dear, you've had a rough night. I doubt that you've had breakfast yet."

Dall looked at the plate, then asked, "How do you know I had a bad night?"

Bishop Clevenger said, "We were talking about it before you arrived. Abel Straus said in the service this morning that you hadn't slept in your bed last night and he heard gunfire. We heard it, too. We can see it in your face, and I assume that your bad night had something to do with that gunfire. Dig in to that breakfast, boy. We'll talk in a few minutes."

Dall hadn't realized how hungry he was. He'd been so disturbed by what he'd seen in Curly's telescope that he hadn't eaten any waffles. It was apparent that Mrs. Clevenger had been trained well in the kitchen. The perfectly seasoned sausage-gravy was ladled over buttermilk biscuits with two fried eggs and several strips of bacon on the side. There were also three kinds of jams and homemade butter on the table.

After Dall had scraped the plate clean, he looked up into the smiling eyes of Mrs. Clevenger. Embarrassed by his lapse of manners, he said, "I'm sorry I made such a pig of myself, Mrs. Clevenger. That was delicious."

Bishop Clevenger said, "That's okay, Dall. She's used to it. She's been watching me forget my manners for years. Now! What about that gunfire we heard last night. I see that Sandy isn't with you. I hope she wasn't a casualty."

Dall wiped his mouth on a napkin. "In a sense, yes she was. There's no point in playing my cards close to my chest anymore, Bishop. I need help badly and you're the only one who can give it to me."

Bishop Clevenger wasn't surprised. Dall said, "Sandy and I were put in this district as undercover operatives. We initially told Bishop Gordan that we were trying to regain our status as Amish. That was not true."

Bishop Clevenger's eyes squinted in a faint smile. He said, "I know, son."

Dall shrugged his shoulders and looked down at the floor. As justified as lying seemed at the time, it now appeared inexcusable in the presence of Bishop Clevenger. He continued, "I guess you were able to tell from our last conversation that we wanted to learn more about demons. Well, we had a good reason."

Bishop Clevenger sipped his coffee, then said, "That's because you suspect there's a demon working our district. You suspect he killed our three men."

Dall looked at the bishop and nodded his head gently. "Yes, Bishop, it's not a suspicion anymore."

Bishop Clevenger shook his head angrily. "Dall, you at least suspected this weeks ago! You had an obligation to tell us!"

Dall looked at the floor. "I know, Bishop. Had I not been under such close scrutiny, I would have."

Mrs. Clevenger refilled Dall's coffee cup and took his plate. He said, "Bishop, this may be hard for you to accept, but Sandy and I were put here to find a demon. Our controllers weren't completely candid with us when we came in, but we quickly learned that we were put here to find him. We were both expendable, and our controllers fully planned to let us die if necessary. Sandy is F.B.I., but I was never meant to survive."

Bishop Clevenger nodded his head and pondered the situation. "The English government. They can never be trusted. I could tell that you and Sandy had feelings for each other that weren't consistent with sibling love."

"We're not brother and sister, Bishop. I'm worried about her. We found the demon, and he's indwelled her."

Bishop Clevenger frowned and shook his head. "That's going to be big trouble. Tell me, Dall, who is this demon and what is his agenda?"

Dall sighed. "Ever since the fall of Satan and one third of the angelic realm, there has been a rift between Satan's followers. Some are loyal to Satan and some have regretted following him ever since they were cast out of Heaven. There's a war brewing in the demon world. The demons who regretted following Satan want to approach God and ask him to make a provision for their redemption. They believe if they can bind Satan and his followers, then form an alliance with the most powerful country on Earth to resist the Antichrist, God will forgive them for their sins and they can regain entrance to Heaven for eternity rather than being thrown into the lake of fire as described in Revelations. Throughout the history of man, the leader of the repentant fallen angels has been influencing powerful men. A team of allied investigators during World War II identified him and tried to form a covenant with him, but talks broke down and he disappeared. When the F.B.I. heard of the murders of your men, they suspected that he had resurfaced."

"Bishop Clevenger asked, "Why did they suspect he was here?"

"Because of the brutality of the murders. I think each of the F.B.I. field offices have been scrutinizing the country's homicides since the war. They got hold of the autopsy reports and determined that your men were killed by very powerful beings. They sent Sandy and me in here to find him. We did. We learned that he is in fact the leader of the repentant demons. His name is Gaal."

Bishop Clevenger sat silent for a minute. He then folded his hands in his lap and sighed heavily. "It's possible, I guess, but I've found no Biblical evidence of this upcoming war. Have you any hard evidence?"

Dall stood and walked to the opened front door. He motioned with his head toward the horizon. "Only that. Those clouds never seem to move except within themselves. I was able to get a closer look at them through a telescope, and they're not clouds at all. I don't suppose you would know anything about them?"

The bishop didn't have to look at them. He had already been studying them for several days. When Dall turned to face him for an answer, Bishop Clevenger nodded his head and said, "They're gathering. I saw it once before when I was a boy."

Dall said, "So, Gaal is telling the truth. The war has already started."

"Not necessarily, son. All we can see are the dark spirits gathering. This gathering may be Satan's followers or Gaal's. They might not be warring against each other at all. We can't see them well enough to tell what they're doing. They may be out there milling around, feeding off each other's fear and hatred. Without knowing which one they're loyal to and what they are actually doing, we can only speculate."

"But you said you've seen it before."

Bishop Clevenger slowly stood and shuffled to the door. As he gazed at the gathering, he said, "Yes. They have gathered like that throughout history just before a major disaster. Apparently God has permitted fallen angels to wreak havoc on us when He's wanted to carry out judgment against man. I've seen it once, and read many more accounts from witnesses who reported such a gathering days before a major disaster or loss of life. While most people merely passed it off as storm clouds, a few people with an acute gift of spiritual discernment have had the presence of mind to study them closely. And the eerie thing about them is that they don't appear on weather radar. If you'll call the weather bureau, they'll tell you that the skies are clear in this area."

Dall asked, "So how can we stop them? How can we know what they're intentions are? And why do they make themselves visible to us."

Bishop Clevenger turned and shuffled back to his chair. "We can't stop them, son. We mortals have no insight into the affairs of the supernatural. I suspect they are Gaal's followers here to give him whatever support he needs. And I don't know why they make themselves visible to us. They are spiritual beings. They could gather and support Gaal without letting us see them. I suspect that they have allowed us to see them to frighten us."

"And if they are Satan's?"

"Then they are here to see that Gaal fails. Either way, we can only hope that God will restrain them and not allow them to carry out their wrath against us. Take comfort in the fact that God is in control and He is able."

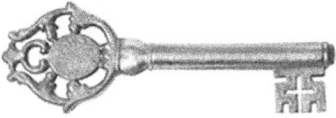

"I am he that liveth, and was dead; and behold, I am alive for evermore, Amen; and have the keys of hell and of death." **Revelation 1:18**

Gaal and the ranger arrived back at the well late in the morning. As they approached, Gaal's worst fears were realized. Sandy gave a deep sigh of relief when they both simultaneously realized that Dall had escaped the well. As the ranger approached he bent over and picked up the chain that he had unhooked from the rusty bolt the night before. It was now attached to the bolt again and the boards of the well had been pulled away. Without looking in the well, Gaal raised his stare to the gathering on the horizon and listened intently to his legion. He said, "HE'S GONE. SOMEONE PULLED HIM OUT. I KNOW WHERE HE IS."

The ranger said, "It's daylight, but we still might be able to get a shot at him if we hurry."

Sandy reveled in Gaal's fear of Bishop Clevenger. Gaal said, "NO, I CAN'T GO NEAR HIM NOW. HE'S IN A PLACE TOO DANGEROUS FOR ME TO TREAD. GO BACK TO SMITH AND DR. SVEADE. TELL THEM TO HAVE ALL THE SNIPERS KEEP ME IN SIGHT. I'LL FIND DALL, BUT STAY FAR ENOUGH AWAY THAT HE CAN'T SPEAK TO ME. WHEN YOU SPOT HIM, TAKE THE SHOT. I DON'T CARE HOW IT UPSETS THE AMISH; WE HAVE TO GET HIM OUT OF THE WAY."

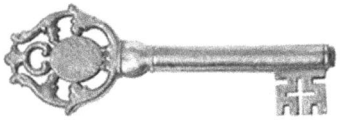

"I am he that liveth, and was dead; and behold, I am alive for evermore, Amen; and have the keys of hell and of death." **Revelation 1:18**

Bishop Clevenger rubbed his beard with his crooked fingers. He said, "I guess it all makes sense. I've wondered for months why this demon chose our district."

Dall looked confused and asked, "You mean you knew about Gaal?"

Bishop Clevenger nodded his head. "Yes, I know him. I didn't know his name, but I've known for some time that there's been an unclean spirit in our midst. He has to be very powerful to prompt a gathering of that size. He has at times had some influence over some of our men. I've counseled them, and when I determined that they were indwelled, I've cast him out on several occasions. He just moves from one man to another. I then have to find him again."

Dall asked, "How can that be, Bishop. Demons can't indwell believers. Once a person is saved, the Holy Spirit indwells them, and a demon cannot cohabitate with the Holy Spirit."

Bishop Clevenger nodded gently. "True, Dall, but you're making the same mistake that most English make. Because our society is closed, most English don't understand the reality of our faith. You think just because someone is Amish that they are automatically more religious and righteous than the rest of the world. That's not the case. Not everyone who calls themselves Amish is saved, or even true Amish. Our sects are laced with non-believers, just like every other denomination on Earth. Just like the protestants, Catholics and others, we have members who have no belief whatsoever in God. Their pretense of faith is only an act to obtain the approval of us who do."

Dall said, "I see your point."

The bishop continued. "I say all this to point out that there are just as many evil hearts in an Amish district as there are in the English world. We just keep it secret and don't reveal that to outsiders. This demon was easily able to discern the hearts of our people. He found some who professed to be believers, but were not. He indwelled them and persuaded them to do evil. It has been one of my jobs to identify those men and cast the demon out of them, then bring the men to repentance and salvation so the demon could not indwell them again. While under the influence of this demon, they have done some terrible things."

"Like killing the three men?"

Bishop Clevenger sighed regretfully, "Yes, and sadly we have had brethren who have committed many sins without the influence of a demon. You've experienced some of that yourself."

Dall looked at the floor and shook his head. "What am I going to do, Bishop? I've got to help Sandy. I didn't mean for it to happen, but I've fallen in love with her. She's so powerful now, but I know her. She's trapped inside herself with Gaal, and she's scared to death. I could save myself and leave, but I couldn't live with myself if I abandoned her. If I can get close, I can hopefully call on the power of Christ and cast Gaal out of her, but he'll never let me get that close."

Bishop Clevenger said, "Yes, I fear you're right. I've spoken with this demon many times. He's an oddity. I can believe your story about him trying to bind Satan and approach God for some provision for redemption. I've often wondered why God never made a provision for the repentant angels as he did for man. Their sin seems no worse than those of mortals."

Dall shrugged his shoulders. "I don't know either, Bishop, except that maybe their sin was worse than ours since they had dwelled with Him in Heaven, and their betrayal was somehow a much greater sin in God's eyes, and was therefore unforgivable. All I know is that Gaal is not like any of the descriptions of demons that I have ever read."

Bishop Clevenger said, "He's almost too nice. I know he's probably deceived me, but I've found him to be quite patronizing when I've dealt with him. Demons are notoriously devious by nature, but he certainly puts up the front that he's different. But now that he has Sandy, we have to move fast. If he's as smart as I think he is, he'll flee the district and leave you at the mercy of your controllers. Gaal may fear the wrath of the Heavenly Father for killing one of the elect, but your heathen controllers will kill you without hesitation."

Dall asked, "What can I do, Bishop? I'm out of my league here. Can you help me?"

Bishop Clevenger stood and took his broad-brimmed straw hat from the coat-rack by the door. "I'll certainly try, son. You shouldn't be alone. It's apparent that Gaal has many other demons helping him. They never work alone. They'll tell Gaal where you are, and the men with rifles will kill you. You must stay close to other people. And try to keep moving, if even a little. Moving targets are harder to hit. Come; let's go help get the rest of this barn built. You may not be able to get close to Sandy, but she'll likely be there, too, looking for you. If she is focused on you, maybe I can get close to her."

Dall stood to escort the bishop to his buggy, but the bishop grabbed Dall by the shirt and stepped up in his face. He looked sternly at Dall and shook his arthritic finger in his face. "Shame on you, Dall, for withholding information from us that might cause the deaths of more of our members. From now on, there will be no more secrets. Are we clear? If there are, I'll take a strap to your backside myself."

Dall dropped his gaze in shame. "Agreed, Bishop. Can you forgive me?"

Bishop Clevenger stepped into Dall with a compassionate smile and encircled his shoulders with both arms. "Already forgiven, son. Let this transgression never be brought up between us again."

Dall helped Bishop Clevenger into the buggy, then helped Mrs. Clevenger with the baskets of food. Dall noticed that the bishop's gilding was unusually nervous. He was stomping his feet and jerking his head in an effort to break free of the rope that secured his halter to the hitching post. As he helped Mrs. Clevenger into the buggy, he asked, "Bishop, what's wrong with your horse?"

Bishop Clevenger held the reins tight as Dall untied the rope He said, "The fallen ones are close. Animals can sense the presence of a demon."

Dall looked around, hoping they weren't visited by a barrage of 7.62^{mm} N.A.T.O. rounds. He anguished over Sandy all the way to the barn-site.

"I am he that liveth, and was dead; and behold, I am alive for evermore, Amen; and have the keys of hell and of death." **Revelation 1:18**

Many of the men at the barn-raising had been participants in the earlier beating that had landed Dall in the hospital. Bishop Clevenger's involvement in the post-beating counseling was evident as they all went to great lengths to be nice to Dall. Bishop Gordan gave Dall his most patronizing greeting as if he were running for political office. Devin Litchfield meandered around the dessert table, sneaking cookies and cupcakes when the ladies weren't looking.

Whenever Dall had a board or frame component to carry, there were always at least two men eagerly to help him. They were so nice to him that he was almost embarrassed. He was now seeing the good side of the Amish faith. As the day passed he actually envisioned him making a peaceful life for himself in the district.

During a break Dall scanned the area where the buggies were parked. When he spotted Tramp hitched to the Litchfield buggy, he walk over to the dessert table. Amidst the sounds of hammers, hand-saws, the shrill laughter of small children at play and the peaceful hum of joyful fellowship, Dall asked Katie Betendorf if he could have a piece of apple pie. When she eagerly consented, he picked up the piece of pie in his hand and walked toward Tramp.

Tramp spotted Dall as he approached, and opened his nostrils wide to take in the fragrance of the pie. Dall held his hand out with the pie in his palm as Tramp eagerly sucked in the treat.

Dall patted Tramp gently on the neck and circled him, looking for fresh whelps and lacerations. When he found a fresh whelp and swelling on the gilding's back hip, he saw red. After a gentle pat he spoke softly to Tramp and walked back to the dessert table. He eased up to Devin and said, "Devin, if you lay a hand on one of those horses again, I'll kill you myself. Do you hear me?"

Having felt the sting of Dall's fist before, the threat sank in instantly. Tears welled up in Devin's eyes as he nodded and ran to the protection of his mother. She asked what the problem was, and Dall knew she'd gotten the message accurately when Devin turned and pointed to him with tears streaming down his face.

Dall had to do something. Devin could not be trusted, and he had too many other things to deal with besides keeping track of Devin. He stepped behind a lilac bush and pulled his cell phone from his pocket. When Curly answered, Dall called on him for another favor. "Curly, do you know anyone who has kids that would like their own horse?"

Curly was confused, but said, "Well, no, not off-hand, but that shouldn't be too hard to find. Every kid would like to have their own horse."

Dall said, "Good. Get working on it. I've got a couple that I want to find a good home for."

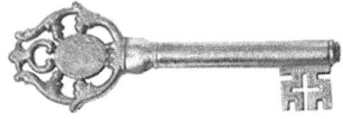

"I am he that liveth, and was dead; and behold, I am alive for evermore, Amen; and have the keys of hell and of death." **Revelation 1:18**

Abel and Sampson had driven the last nails in the frame structure of one of the walls. With block and tackle in place, Sampson was raising the wall so it could be nailed to the other two sides of the barn. Dall had just unpacked one of the prefabricated windows when he glanced up and saw Sandy walking toward him.

Fear gripped him as he laid the window down and prepared to run. He looked around frantically to see if there were any rangers in sight, then studied Sandy's eyes hard. He knew the rangers would have a hard time hitting a moving target, so he moved slowly to his left.

As he was preparing to run, Dall regained his sense of reason. He'd been looking for a chance to help Sandy and this might be it. If Gaal was foolish enough to come close, then Dall would cast him out and save Sandy.

Sandy had a gentle smile on her face as she glided gracefully across the yard. It was the same affectionate smile that he'd seen just before he'd made love to her three nights ago. Could it be that Gaal had released her? Or was he simply trying to disarm Dall till the rangers could get a stable sight picture?

Dall decided to test Sandy. He knew how Sandy would react if Gaal was not in her. He picked up his hammer and gripped it in a threatening manner. Sandy would certainly understand his fear considering all that he had been through. She would simply halt her advance and motion for him to relax and not create a scene, knowing that she could regain his trust once they had talked.

When she clenched her jaw and fists, Dall knew he was dealing with Gaal. Sandy glared at him so hard that her soft green eyes turned dark red.

Bishop Clevenger had seen the confrontation from across the yard and was already on his way to confront Gaal when Dall had picked up the hammer.

As he stumbled across the ground where the newly framed wall had been built, Gaal spotted him. Stark fear overwhelmed him as he recalled the previous encounters with the old bishop. Gaal's power was no match for the power of the Holy Spirit that dwelled within the frail old man.

By now the other men had noticed that their horses had become frightened and were struggling to free themselves from their hitching posts. They ran to catch them before they broke loose.

Gaal quickly abandoned any hopes of getting close to Dall. Having fallen under the determined glare of old bishop, his thoughts now turned to his own survival. He could not afford to be cast out of Sandy.

As Bishop Clevenger moved under the framed wall that was being raised, he angrily raised his shaky hand and motioned for Sandy to come to him. As she back-pedaled away from the bishop, Gaal gently raised Sandy's hand and swiped her index finger through the air like a knife. When her finger crossed the rope that suspended the frame, it broke as if it had been cut, allowing the wall to fall.

Bishop Clevenger had no hope of getting out from under the wall before it crushed him. He had resigned himself to his fate and ushered off a short, mumbled prayer thanking God for his salvation. To his great surprise, Abel Straus had seen the rope break and raced to the bishop. As if scooping up a small child, he picked up the bishop in his arms and sprinted out from under the falling wall. When it crashed to the ground, he stopped and gently lowered the shaken old man to his feet. "You'd better be careful, Bishop. You almost got yourself killed. I've got enough to do keeping up with my place and helping the widow Litchfield with hers, too. I don't need another widow to care for."

The grateful bishop patted Abel's massive chest vigorously with his trembling hand. "Thank you so much, Brother Straus! Our Heavenly Father will bless you richly for saving my life, here on Earth as well as in Heaven!"

When Bishop Clevenger tried to locate Sandy again, he saw her running toward the timber with Dall in close pursuit. He yelled for Dall to stop, but he did not hear. He turned to Abel and yelled in an urgent tone, "Abel, my good son, hurry! Go after Dall! I'll explain later, but he is about to be killed! Allow your anger to rage and use all your strength to help him! This is God's command!"

Sensing the urgency in the bishop's voice, Abel sprinted after Dall across the open ground toward the timber. He didn't know what danger Dall was facing, but only hoped he could catch him in time.

Dall ran as fast as he could while scanning the trees for any sign of the rangers. He wondered if Sandy was intentionally slowing her pace so he could catch her, or if she was naturally a slow runner. In either case, he caught her in a small clearing just past the tree-line.

As he approached, Sandy turned and looked frightened. Dall paid no attention to her fear; it was only Gaal, trying to trick him. As he raised and pointed his finger at Sandy, he ordered, "Gaal, in Christ's name, leave Sandy! To his great surprise, Sandy closed the thirty yards between them in the blink of an eye. It was the same speed that Gaal had used when he'd materialized earlier in the form of little Judith Straus.

With speed too fast for Dall to see, she punched him hard in the face and knocked him five feet backward and onto his back. Stunned by the blow, Dall shook the stars from his head and tried to stand, but Sandy was again standing over him with supernatural speed. She picked him up with one hand and threw him another five feet against a tree. He crumpled to the ground semi-conscious.

Knowing he couldn't match Gaal's strength, Dall again tried to spit out the words that would cast Gaal out of Sandy, but before he could speak, Sandy again closed on him and kicked him in the head, knocking him unconscious. Before Dall sank into complete unconsciousness, his life flashed before his eyes. The final images that entered his mind were the same dark forms that comprised the distant gathering, circling him and Sandy, and the autopsy photos of Preacher Levi Croft. He then imposed his face on the photos and knew he would be dismembered as well.

Abel barged into the clearing as Sandy was picking up Dall's lifeless body. She was preparing to decapitate him when she saw Abel. Abel was shocked that a girl her size could handle a full-grown man like a rag doll. Gaal knew the fight was not over. Sandy released Dall and paid him no attention as he collapsed into an unnatural position.

Abel knew he was not dealing with Sandy when Gaal said in a male voice, "ABEL, MY OLD FRIEND, NICE TO SEE YOU AGAIN."

Fear gripped Abel's throat as he recognized the being that had indwelled him a few weeks earlier. Sandy looked harmless enough, although she seemed to move differently than before, but the spirit inside her was intimidating. He knew he would have to fight for his life, but when he sized up Sandy, he wondered, how strong could she really be? One look at Dall answered his question. Although Dall was not nearly as big as Abel, he was well-proportioned and posed a formidable opponent in his own right.

Gaal said, "ABEL, I KNOW YOU'RE HERE TO SAVE DALL, BUT YOU HAVE A FAMILY TO CONSIDER. YOU ARE ONE, BUT WE ARE MANY. I AM NOT ALONE. WE WILL NOT KILL DALL. I CANNOT ALLOW SIN TO BAR ME FROM THE LORD'S THRONE. AND HE HAS PLACED A HEDGE OF PROTECTION AROUND DALL. IF YOU LEAVE NOW, NO HARM WILL COME TO HIM. IF YOU DO NOT LEAVE, YOUR FAMILY WILL BE MOURNING YOUR PASSING TONIGHT. YOUR REBELLIOUS SON, ISAAC, MIGHT NOT MISS YOU, BUT DORY, LITTLE JUDITH AND BABY JACK WILL BE SCARRED FOR LIFE."

In light of the fear in Abel's heart, he considered Gaal's advice sound. He turned and looked back toward the barn and saw Bishop Clevenger stumbling along on unsteady legs toward him. Seeing the fear in the bishop's eyes convinced him that Gaal was lying. He would not allow Dall to live; he could not. Abel refocused on Gaal with a deep determination in his eyes. This was the perfect opportunity to redeem himself with Dall for the lashing that he had participated in. He would save Dall or die trying.

Just as he had decided to charge Sandy, his fear caused him to pause. He looked back at the bishop, hoping for further instruction. The determination on the face of the fragile old bishop shamed him. He turned and again faced Sandy. "I'll be taking Dall with me, beast. He is my charge and I can't let my God down by letting one of His flock parish, especially at the hands of one as evil as you."

As frightened as he was, Abel stepped toward Dall to shield him from another attack. With one hand Sandy stiff-armed him in the chest and knocked him twenty feet across the clearing. Abel slid to a stop against a tree and shook his head to regain his senses. He struggled to his feet and found that Sandy had closed on him in an instant. She picked him up and grabbed his arm. She attempted to rip it from his body, but Abel was able to flex his muscles and clench the arm tightly against his chest. As painful as it was, he mustered the strength to punch Sandy in the face, knocking her several feet backward and freeing himself from her grip.

Knowing he was in a fight for his life Abel vowed to not underestimate Sandy again. He charged her and caught her unprepared. She had barely struggled to her knees when Abel closed the distance and again punched her hard in the face.

Abel had hit Sandy harder than he had ever hit anyone in his life, but the punch had no effect. He'd had the momentum of a ten-foot sprint behind the punch, but Sandy absorbed it and levitated to her feet.

Before he could react, she'd grabbed the front of his shirt in one hand and his waistband with the other, then effortlessly hoisted his 325 pound frame over her head. In one fluid motion, she turned him upside down in mid-air and drove him head-first to the ground in an effort to pile-drive his head down between his shoulder-blades.

Abel was completely overpowered by the small woman. He saw the ground coming up at him, but all he could do was cover his head with his arms and turn his head and body so that his shoulders took impact.

When he crashed to the ground the pain was incredible. All the air left his lungs and his will to continue the fight abandoned him. He rolled over on his back and gasped for air as he stared into the stoic, stone face of the little woman who intended to kill him.

Abel knew he could not stop fighting. If he were to survive, he had to force himself to do something, anything. When Sandy bent over to grab his leg, he kicked her hard in the face, knocking her backward. Knowing he could not follow his body's natural desire to simply lay there and anguish over his injuries, Abel struggled against his pain and forced himself to his feet.

Sensing that Abel was about finished, Gaal charged him one last time. To his surprise, Dall had regained consciousness and lunged for Sandy's legs as she charged Abel. She fell at Abel's feet and Abel fell on top of her, pounding her head with his huge fists. Dall did what he could to help, but both found that they were no match for Gaal. Sandy rolled over on her back and grabbed each of the men by the front of their shirt, then threw them both eight feet in the air, landing them on their backs ten feet away.

Adel and Dall looked at each other in stark fear. Dall knew Abel would fight to the death, but he wanted to spare them both that fate. With a trembling voice, he yelled, "Abel, run; we can't win this!"

As they struggled to their feet, they were surprised to see Sandy simply standing there, glaring at them without so much as one hair out of place and not one ounce of fear in her red eyes. She looked over her shoulder and saw Bishop Clevenger struggling along at his usual slow pace through the underbrush. He was no match for the bishop, so Gaal wisely chose to flee. Sandy's arrogant contempt faded to fear as she ran past Abel and Dall, disappearing into the timber.

Bishop Clevenger stumbled into the clearing. He looked at Abel as he approached and extended both arms. As a stunned Abel collapsed to his knees, the bishop embraced him and said with tears in his eyes, "Dearest Brother Abel, thank you! You did well!"

Dall was regaining his senses, but could see that Abel was badly hurt. He helped him up and put one arm around Abel's waist. "Come on, Abel, let's get you home. You need to lie down for a while."

The two men steadied each other as they walked back to the barn-raising. Bishop Clevenger even found the strength to walk on the other side of Abel and help the shaken man keep his feet under him.

TWELVE

DORY AND MRS. Clevenger sat by Abel's side the rest of the afternoon. He hadn't been bed-ridden like this since the time his father's Morgan had kicked him in the head while he was trying to shoe her.

Dall and Bishop Clevenger sat on the front porch and spoke softly so the kids couldn't overhear them. Dall said, "Well, so much for Gaal not wanting to commit any sins that would cause God to refuse him an audience after he defeats Satan. He about killed me and Abel."

Bishop Clevenger said, "That's a hard to call to make, Dall. God knows all, and in all things is able. He may have permitted Gaal to hurt you, yet prevented him from killing you. He may have been testing you. Or He may have a plan that we can't yet see."

"May be, Bishop, but this convinced me that Gaal is up to no good. I don't believe any of that garbage about him wanting to overthrow Satan and approach God for redemption. He's possessed Sandy and almost killed Abel and me. As far as I'm concerned, Gaal is either Satan himself or one of Satan's chosen trying to convince the U.S. that he's on our side so he can gain enough trust and power to hand us over to the Antichrist."

Bishop Clevenger said, "That's very likely, son. That would certainly be consistent with the upcoming End-Times events revealed by John in Revelations. But Satan won't have to hand us over to anyone. Americans has become so consumed with their own humanism and so devoid of moral values that they'll embrace the Antichrist wholeheartedly. You can tell the moral health of a culture by the leaders they elect, and America's leaders right now are cut out of the same cloth as the Antichrist. And remember, God sees all things past and future. Nothing will transpire in the future that is not His will. The events of the End-Times were predetermined before the foundations of the earth were ever laid. God would not have revealed those events to the epistle John in Revelations if they were subject to change. God never reveals anything to us that will not come to pass. If He tells us something will happen, then it has to happen or He has either lied to us or He is not powerful enough to see the future and set future events in stone. In either case, His revelations have to come to pass or His credibility is destroyed. God is incapable of lying or making a mistake. To imply anything else is to diminish God's omnipotence."

Dall rubbed his sore neck. "You're right. That settles it. Gaal is a liar and a fraud."

"Not necessarily, Dall."

"But, Bishop, you just said the events of the End-Times are set in stone."

"Yes, Dall, I did, but you're forgetting who we're dealing with here. Fallen Angles have no more insight into the future than we do, but we don't know what conversations God has had with them since their fall. We can't know what he has told the ones who are sorry they supported Satan. We can't know what He has planned for them after the last page of Revelations is turned. Eternity is a long time. Just because He hasn't revealed it to us doesn't mean He has no other plans for them. And I guess it's both human nature and demon nature to hope for redemption in spite of the absolute certainty of scripture."

"So, this Gaal character might be legitimate?"

"Oh, I think he's legitimate. Misguided, misinformed and delusional maybe, but I think he's sincere in what he believes, or should I say, he's sincere in what he hopes for."

Dall said, "He's a demon, Bishop. Surely he knows the Bible as well as we do."

"He knows it better, Dall. But you have to remember the nature of demons. They're nature is that they are extremely arrogant, deceitful and stubborn. They will never accept defeat until the moment that God throws them into the lake of fire. They'll struggle against the inevitable to their last breath. Gaal's nature is to sin. That's why he tried to kill you and Abel. Even though he knows he can't sin if he expects God to provide some means of redemption, it's his nature to sin. He can't help himself. That's also how it is with man. Even when we know something is a sin, we choose to do it anyway. Gaal is just hoping that God will forgive their sinful nature and allow them a means of redemption as He has for mankind. He's just like man. He knows killing is a sin, but figures that is just one more sin that will fall under God's provision for forgiveness when, and if, that provision is given. Besides, killing you is a small and justifiable sin in his eyes compared to the greater benefit of being spared the lake of fire."

Dall remained silent for a minute. Bishop Clevenger knew something was bothering him. He said, "No secrets here, young Dall, remember? What's wrong?"

Dall finally said, "I'm ashamed, Bishop. Ashamed and afraid."

"Of what, son"

"I'm ashamed of myself for not being able to cast Gaal out of Sandy, and scared of him now that I know that I can't."

"Why can't you, Dall?"

"I don't know, Bishop. I've always thought that a believer could cast out a demon simply by calling on the name of Christ. I did that with Gaal just before he handed me my head. He paid me no attention and disassembled me and Able Straus like a rambunctious child destroys cheap toys. I can understand him ringing my bell, but Abel Straus is the strongest man I've ever known. I didn't think anyone could man-handle him like that. Sandy isn't particularly strong, but she busted us both up without breaking a sweat. Now that I know I have no power over Gaal, I don't know how I'm going to get him to leave her. What should I do? I can't just abandon her. She wouldn't do that to me."

Bishop Clevenger nodded his head as he rubbed his beard in earnest thought. "And you're in love with her."

Dall looked up at the darkening sky and sighed. "Yes. I shouldn't be, but I am. It's not just an infatuation. We've connected on a deep spiritual level. It's almost like God Himself has bonded us together."

Bishop Clevenger smiled, "Good. That's good. If He has, then He'll provide a way."

"Why couldn't I cast Gaal out of her, Bishop?"

"You could have, but you approached it with a degree of doubt. Confronting demons is a very frightening and dangerous proposition. You have to be called by God to do it and be endowed with special spiritual gifts; one being extraordinary faith and spiritual courage. You've never had to do that before, and I think you had some doubts that it would really work."

Dall looked confused as Bishop Clevenger continued. "Dall, remember in Matthew chapter 17, verse 14, when a man came to Jesus and asked him to remove a demon from his son? He told Jesus that he had brought the boy to the disciples and they had tried to cast the demon out, but could not. Do you remember what Jesus told the disciples when they asked Him why they hadn't been able to cast out the demon?"

Dall searched his memory. "Jesus told them that they had failed because they didn't have enough faith."

Bishop Clevenger said, "The word that Jesus specifically used was *unbelief*. They actually had no belief that it would work at all. Jesus said to them that if they had faith the size of a mustard seed, they could simply speak and a mountain would move. You were faced with the same situation, Dall. You tried to cast out a demon, as the disciples did, without the belief that it would really work. When Gaal sensed your doubt, he became more bold and aggressive."

Dall hung his head in shame. "And the next time?"

"The next time, son, don't rely on your own faith. All of us have doubts at times. And the time to find out that your faith is wavering is not when you're in a life and death struggle with an unclean spirit. Rely instead on God's promise. Our faith is weak at times, but God's faithfulness is not. His performance is not based on our faith, or none of us could ever do anything. His performance is based on His promises to us. His word is faithful even when we're not. Next time, just remember that God said you could do it. Don't rely on how strongly you believe in God's word. Rely on the assurance that God never lies or breaks a promise. Don't try to cast out the demon yourself. Simply turn him over to God and let Him do it."

Dall sighed, "I'll try, but I'm not sure how to do that."

"Then get back into God's word, Dall. When you are absolutely sure of one thing, that God is sovereign, all powerful and faithful in His promises, then there'll be no doubt in your mind when you face Gaal."

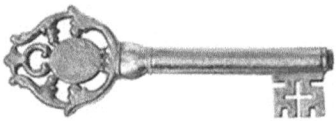

"I am he that liveth, and was dead; and behold, I am alive for evermore, Amen; and have the keys of hell and of death." **Revelation 1:18**

As evening draped the landscape, Dall made his way across the pastures and meadows to see his old friends, Lady and Tramp. The barn was dark when he arrived, so he gently ran his hands over their bodies to feel for any new whelps. Each time he found one, he struggled against his anger to keep from killing Devin Litchfield.

The pair had long ago become accustomed to Dall's treats. They nuzzled his pockets with their noses and jerked their heads when they smelled the apples. Dall pulled them out of his pockets and cut them into quarters with his knife. As they savored the apples, Dall continued to talk to them. He knew they were just dumb animals, but each visit cut deeper into his heart when he thought about leaving them behind. He hoped Curly would find some deserving youngsters who would give them a good home.

After a while, Dall began to wonder who the night patrol would be. He gave the horses one final caress on their noses, then left.

As Dall approached Bishop Gordan's house, he stayed in the shadows so he could overhear the bishop's instructions to the men. Tonight the two men were Sampson Betendorf and Hans Bowlin. As they sat on the porch, Bishop Gordan arrogantly stepped out of the house as a king surveying his kingdom.

Dall dropped to his knees and crawled close enough to hear. Bishop Gordan said, "Good evening, brothers."

Both men returned the greeting, then Bishop Gordan asked, "Brother Hans, I thought Abel Straus was assigned to patrol tonight."

Hans replied, "Yes, Sir, he was. He suffered a head and neck injury at the barn-raising, and wasn't able to make it. I volunteered to take his place."

"Good man, Brother Hans. Thank you. Tomorrow I'll have to visit Brother Straus and lay hands on him. Tonight, we're going to try something different. It's important that we identity these Englishers and banish them from our district. If we can determine who they are, I can contact their superiors. So, when we find them, let's confront them and see who they are. If they're from the sheriff's office, I'll go to the County Board and see if we can put enough pressure on the sheriff that he might pull them out."

Dall knew this was a bad idea. Gordan had no idea how determined Smith and Dr. Sveade were to not let anyone hinder this mission. He wanted to show himself and warn them, but he would only give himself away and do nothing to deter the bishop. He decided to stay close.

As the men started out, they talked about what the best approach would be. All agreed that they would start in the area where Abel had heard the machine-gun fire the night before. Dall stayed about fifty yards back and hid in the shadows. He felt there was little chance of seeing anyone tonight since Gaal had already indwelled Sandy and had made contact with Dr. Sveade. They certainly wouldn't meet any little girls tonight.

About midnight, after a few hours of walking the pastures and meadows, the men stopped suddenly when they saw a small light. Dall was close enough to hear Sampson say, "There! There's a light. That's got to be them. No one else would be out here this time of night."

Dall knew Samson was right. His experience in the military made it easy for him to recognize the glow of a ranger's tactical light. He was probably reading a map. As the three Amish started toward the rangers, Dall's gut wrenched. This was going to turn out bad.

Dall swung wide around the men so he could stay in the shadows of some trees. He dropped to his stomach as the Amish approached the rangers. To his surprise, the rangers were not alone. Smith, Waters, Dr. Sveade and Sandy were all crouched over a map, coordinating their systematic search for Dall. They stood in surprise as the Amish men approached.

When the rangers turned toward the approaching men, Sampson and Hans immediately stopped in their tracks when the rangers swung the muzzles of their M-14s toward them. They immediately began backing away in fear, but Bishop Gordan charged the rangers with total indignation that they would invade the hallowed ground of his district and threaten the lives of righteous Amish brethren.

Dall wanted to intervene, but he was outgunned. He watched helplessly as Gordan stormed up to Smith and demanded, "You! What is your name and who do you work for? This is Amish land and you have no right to be here! You also have no right to bring arms here and threaten us with them!"

Smith looked at Dr. Sveade with an inquiring glance as if to ask him if he wanted Smith to handle it or if he wanted to handle it himself. Sveade simply turned and stepped away. Smith knew what to do.

Gordan instantly recognized Sandy. He stepped up to her and asked angrily, "Have these men harmed you, young lady? Or are you in conspiracy with them? I had my doubts about you and the English man from the start! Are you here voluntarily? If you are not, you'd better speak up!"

To Bishop Gordan's great shock, Gaal spoke in a young man's voice. The man's voice coming from Sandy instantly frightened Gordan. She said, "YES, BISHOP. I'M HERE OF MY OWN FREE WILL. AND YOU'VE JUST STUMBLED INTO SOMETHING IMPORTANT. I DON'T HAVE TIME TO EXPLAIN, AND YOU'RE NOT A SIGNIFICANT PLAYER, SO YOU HAVE NO NEED TO KNOW. SINCE YOU ARE NOT GIRDED WITH THE SPIRITUAL ARMOR OF THE FATHER, YOU ARE NOT ONE OF HIS ELECT."

Dall almost yelled out when Sandy grabbed Bishop Gordan's head and twisted it completely around, breaking his neck instantly and causing him to collapse on his feet without moving a muscle. Even the rangers looked at each other in shock as so much brutality and strength flowed through Sandy.

Dall's shock and disbelief was interrupted by the thumping of Sampson's and Hans' boots on the ground. They were now in a full sprint toward home. The two rangers leveled their M-14s at them and pulled the triggers. Sampson had tripped and fallen on his face, which was the only thing that saved him. Hans ran fast as he could, but was cut almost in half as a barrage of thirty-caliber bullets riddled his torso.

Sampson struggled to his feet and ran even faster than before. Since both rangers had emptied their magazines in the first full-auto burst, they could not reload fresh magazines before Sampson disappeared into the darkness.

Dall lay quietly in the tall grass, hoping he would not be seen. Smith turned to Sandy and said, "This will cause problems, Gaal. How would you like to handle it?"

Sandy's face twitched as she turned to walk away. She said calmly. "DISPOSE OF THEM. WE'LL FIND DALL TOMORROW AND BE OUT OF HERE. WHO CARES IF THE AMISH OR LOCAL AUTHORITIES KNOW WHAT HAPPENED HERE?"

Sandy stopped in mid-stride. All eyes were on her as she lifted her head to listen to Gaal's legion. When she jerked her head quickly and stared directly into Dall's eyes, Dall knew he had been discovered. He sprang to his feet and ran as fast as he could after Sampson. The rangers leveled their rifles and prepared to cut him in half. Gaal said, "DON'T BOTHER. HE IS ONE WHO FINDS HIMSELF IN GREAT FAVOR WITH THE FATHER."

Smith turned to Waters and said, "Dexter, take the bodies to the abandoned well on the old homestead place by Massey's pond and throw them in with the others." Waters grumbled an unintelligible protest, then picked Gordan up in a fireman's carry and started toward the well.

Dall was surprised when he was not chopped down by rifle-fire. He stopped running and hid in the undergrowth until everyone had left, then followed Waters at a safe distance. He stopped by a fallen tree and pulled his cell-phone from his pocket. He dialed Curly's number and instructed him to meet him at the well.

Curly was beside himself with enthusiasm. He grabbed his shoulder rig and some extra ammunition, then raced toward the well.

When Waters had laid Gordan beside the well, he returned to the scene of the shooting and picked up Hans. He groaned as he started the long trek back to the well.

As instructed, Curly parked on a side-road and walked in. Once at the well, he stood behind a big tree until he heard the pants of Waters struggling through the woods under his heavy load. Waters dropped Hans' lifeless body on the ground next to Gordan and tried to stretch the soreness out of his back and neck.

Curly was numb with shock. Dall had told him that if he would hurry to the well, he would find some evidence that would put him in good graces with the sheriff. He never dreamed he would single-handedly arrest a murderer.

With shaking fingers and cotton-mouth, Curly clumsily pulled his revolver from its holster. He barged through the brush like a wounded elephant and shoved the muzzle of his trembling revolver directly in Waters' face. "Freeze, dirt-bag! One move and I'll make your day!"

Dexter's total shock turned to confusion. Who was this idiot, and what had he meant by that? Still in the darkness, Dall shook his head in amusement. Curly had gotten the old Eastwood line backwards, but his delivery was no less emphatic.

Dall stepped into the clearing and said, "Better do what he says, Waters. I've seen that look in the eyes of killers before. You're just a breath away from Hell."

Dall stepped up and pulled Waters' pistol from its holster. He handed it to Curly and said, "Good collar, Curly. You've solved a double murder tonight."

Curly struggled to move his massive fat-apron aside so he could shove the fed's automatic down the front of his pants, then removed his handcuffs from the back of his belt. As he spun Waters around, Waters said, "Listen, deputy, you've got this all wrong. I'm F.B.I., and you're interfering with an important investigation."

As the cuffs ratcheted tightly around Dexter's wrists, Curly looked at Dall for direction. Dall said, "Don't listen to him, Curly. Yeah, he's F.B.I. alright, but when does the F.B.I. condone murder? That's the bishop for this whole district there. The other one is an innocent Amish farmer. The bishop has been killed in the same manner as the other two Amish men that your department has been investigating for the last two years. The other one was cut down by machine-gun fire, as you can tell. Is it part of a lawful investigation to dump murder victims down an abandoned well? If this guy was acting properly, he'd call an ambulance and have the bodies taken to the county morgue for autopsies. He's trying to conceal evidence here. You'd better take him to jail and let your district attorney sort out the legalities. If he's acting properly, his superiors can sit down with your sheriff and district attorney and work it out. And if you'll have your coroner look, he'll find numerous other bodies at the bottom of that old well, all killed in the same fashion. They're teenagers who have disappeared in recent years. No telling how many homicides you'll clear up with this arrest."

As the magnitude of the evidence sank in, Curly swelled with courage. "Yeah, that's right, fed! You've got some explaining to do!"

Dexter wilted. He knew that no court in the country would condone the concealing of evidence, and since the M.O.s of all the Amish murders were the same, he would likely be blamed for them all, including the murders of the missing Amish young people, at least in the eyes of a liberal media who is always looking to sensationalize any story into epic proportions. After all, how would he have known to dump these bodies in the well if he hadn't dumped the other bodies there? And the thought of the spin that the media would put on the murdered youngsters at the bottom of the well was unthinkable. It would make the front page of every newspaper world-wide. Curly jerked Dexter by the arm and said, "Let's go, G-Man! If it's one thing I hate, it's a crooked cop! You make the rest of us look bad!"

Dall said, "Not so fast, Curly. You've got to do this right. What are you going to do with all these bodies? They're evidence, and the sheriff will have your head if you just leave them here."

Curly looked around in total confusion. "Yeah, you're right. I can't carry them. What should I do?"

"Call your dispatcher, Curly. Have her notify the sheriff of the arrest and send the detectives out. They'll call the coroner for you, but they'll be able to photograph and process this scene first. They'll also call out your fire department to recover the bodies in the well. That'll make your case air-tight."

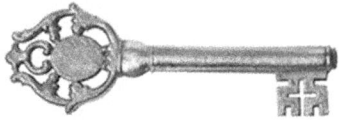

"I am he that liveth, and was dead; and behold, I am alive for evermore, Amen; and have the keys of hell and of death." **Revelation 1:18**

Sheriff Holden literally levitated off his bed when the dispatcher woke him from a sound sleep to tell him that Curly had made a homicide arrest. His next call was to Chief Deputy Thurman in a panicked tone with instructions to pick him up at his house five minutes ago.

The two staff officers beat the detectives and coroner to the scene. They stormed into the clearing by the well and stopped in shock when they saw Curly proudly covering Waters with his revolver, and two dead bodies on the ground. As they approached cautiously, Thurman leaned over to get a better look at Waters. He said, "Well! Bless my soul! Look who we have here!"

The sheriff said, "Curly, you've pulled some bone-head stunts in your time. You'd better have a good explanation for this one."

Curly proudly pointed at the corpses on the ground. "I caught this mope in the act, Sheriff. I saw him carrying these stiffs to the well. He was going to dump them in it. I've got him in possession of murder victims; one of them has been killed in the same manner as our other murder victims. He's got to be behind the other murders, too. And if you'll shine your light down that well, you'll find other bodies that he's dumped in there. So! I think there's at least sufficient probable cause for an arrest."

Sheriff Holden and Thurman looked at each other in disbelief. They weren't aware that Curly even knew what probable cause was. Sheriff Holden shined his light down the well and pulled his head back in disgust when the stench hit him in the face. Curly got nervous when the sheriff and Thurman stepped uncomfortably close and glared at him. They then stared at Waters and remembered how much they disliked him and the F.B.I. Curly grinned from ear to ear when they simultaneously patted him on the back and congratulated him on a job well done. The sheriff said, "Outstanding job, Deputy Slapp! I'm proud of you, son. Take your prisoner in and book him on homicide charges. We'll take him before the magistrate tomorrow for arraignment. We'll stand by here for the detectives to process the scene."

Waters said, "Sheriff, you'd better think this whole thing through. You've been ordered to stay out of this investigation. The director won't be at all happy when he finds out that you've arrested the case manager of the most important investigation in U.S. history. And you're going to look pretty stupid when the U.S. Attorney declares jurisdiction and takes the case away from your district attorney. I'll be out by morning."

Sheriff Holden smiled. "Agent Waters, we were ordered to stay out of the Amish district, which we've done. Your mistake was carrying these dead bodies off Amish land. This is not the Amish district. No one can order me to stay out of my own county. You're in my ball park now. And I'm not sure, but I don't think your director will be happy when he finds out that his case manager has killed two innocent Amish men and tried to illegally dump their bodies to conceal the crime. As a matter of fact, I'm sure he'll try to insulate himself and the bureau by denying that you even work for them. No, Agent Waters, I think you've got far more explaining to do than me."

Waters knew the sheriff was right. His shoulders sank and all the life seemed to drain out of him. Curly dragged him away and glared at him with his best Jack Webb scowl. "Let's go, Waters! I've worked this jungle too long to fall for your con, so don't give me the same load of crap you tried to lay on the sheriff. I'm the top predator around here, and I eat feds for breakfast!"

As he drove Waters to the jail, Curly's mind raced. His anxiety lever surged as he hoped the reporters spelled his name right. He hoped he could buy enough copies of the local paper to pass out to all his friends. He hoped that with all the girls that would want to date him, he would be able to find the time to get in the required number of continuing education hours to maintain his reserve certification with the sheriff's department. He hoped he had enough condoms. Surely the unopened box that he had bought five years ago would last for a while. He took comfort in the fact that he could always buy more on Monday if he ran out over the weekend. Yep, one thing was for sure; Curly Slapp was no longer the laughing stock of the whole county. He seriously wondered if this little county was worthy of his talents. Maybe he should apply for a bigger department, like New York or Chicago, or maybe even one of the federal agencies, like the F.B.I. maybe. After all, he was sure there would be an opening just as soon as the director found out what Waters had done.

Dall left the crime scene in the competent hands of the sheriff and his evidence techs and worked his way through the darkness to the Clevenger farm. That was the only place he felt safe. He would have gone back to Abel's farm, but Abel was too badly injured for another altercation with Gaal, and would be unable to defend himself or his family. He wasn't too worried about Gaal leaving the district yet. He had to eliminate Dall as a witness.

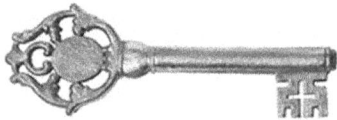

"I am he that liveth, and was dead; and behold, I am alive for evermore, Amen; and have the keys of hell and of death." **Revelation 1:18**

The next morning, Dexter Waters woke with a stiff neck and severe back pain. The strain of carrying two bodies the night before had almost crippled him. Had it not been for his loyalty to the bureau, he never would have done it.

After the jailer had served breakfast, Waters was relieved when Dr. Sveade and S.A.C. Smith walked through the door separating the cell blocks. Dexter hurried to the bars eager to be released. "Boy, boss, am I glad to see you! I'm ready to get out of here!"

Smith showed no emotion and nodded his head gently. "Yes, Dexter, I know you are. But we've got some unexpected problems."

Waters grew angry as he sensed that he was about to be flushed down the toilet. "What? What problems?"

Smith sighed apathetically as he looked around at Dexter's Spartan accommodations. "Well, Dexter, it seems that we're in a very difficult position. You see, we could simply have the director go to the attorney general and get you out. But I'm afraid this jerk-water sheriff has leaked details of your arrest to the local media. He's not released the fact that you're an F.B.I. agent, so as far as they're concerned, the locals have simply arrested the man who has killed four Amish men. But if he lets it out that you're a federal agent, that'll attract the attention of the national media. That will prompt an internal investigation that will certainly go public in a congressional hearing. That'll involve the President, and we're not ready for this case to go public. It's the most significant event in world history, next to the crucifixion of Christ. Long before the nation hears about Gaal, we have to have the groundwork laid for an alliance. Even then, I doubt that the American public will be able to accept a covenant with a demon, so we'll have to put our most creative spin on it. No, Dexter, I afraid we've got to ask you to make the supreme sacrifice and take a bullet for the team. You've got to take the fall and never admit that you're one of us."

Waters hung his head and slowly boiled. "No! No, Smith, you have no right to ask this of me! I was only following your orders! I know this case is important, but I've got a life, too! I've got a career! I've got kids, for God's sake! I'm not taking this fall! You can pull this off! You can get the U.S. Attorney in this district to declare jurisdiction! You can work it out so that I get charged in federal court, then have the whole thing swept under the carpet! You can make this go away if you want to!"

Smith feigned a pretentious smile. "Sorry, Dexter. You're going to have to fall on your sword for us. It'll be greatly appreciated. After your conviction, we'll see what we can do."

"No, Smith! No! That's not good enough! You make this work! The local sheriff isn't the only one who can go to the national media! If my career and life are over, so is yours! And I don't care about this mission anymore! It's not more important than my life!"

Smith reached inside his coat pocket and pulled out Dexter's identification. He held it up and said, "I've already collected your badge and weapon from the sheriff. We'll officially deny your employment with the bureau. The media will think you're just one more nut-job who claims to work for the F.B.I., hoping to get a break. We'll take care of you later, after we've secured our alliance with Gaal, but for now, you'll keep quiet and take the fall. If you try to talk to the media, you'll be dead before the ink is dry on the paper. No paper will publish a story that can't be corroborated by compelling physical evidence or live witness testimony. The Amish won't talk to them, and you'll be dead. Your life will be over and you'll have accomplished nothing. Gaal has assured us that he'll have some of his crew shadowing you at all times. They'll report to him the instant that you try to sabotage this alliance. I assure you, Dexter; you'll suffer a horrible death. You've seen how these spirits kill. It won't be pleasant."

Waters slowly backed away from the bars. He shook his finger at Smith and growled, "You haven't heard the last of me, Smith!"

Smith turned and walked toward the door. He stopped and turned to Waters. "Yes I have, Dexter. The whole world has heard the last of you."

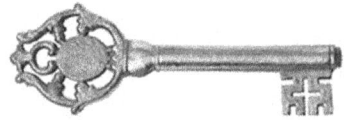

"I am he that liveth, and was dead; and behold, I am alive for evermore, Amen; and have the keys of hell and of death." **Revelation 1:18**

Able struggled out of bed and stumbled to the wash basin. Dory came in as he was washing his face. She put her arms around his waist and said, "Sure you're well enough to be out of bed, dear?"

"Yes, Dory, I think so. I've still got a buzzing noise in my head, but that's from that little woman using my head as a sledgehammer."

"Abel, I'm scared. I haven't told the kids, but are you sure it was Sandy that slammed you to the ground?"

"Yes, Dory, I'm sure. She isn't Sandy anymore. She's a devil. I have to go talk to Bishop Clevenger. I think Dall will hide out there. That's the safest place in the district. No demon will tangle with the bishop, but Dall is in danger. I have to help him if I can."

Every step was torture for Abel. Every movement made his spinal cord feel like each vertebra was being crushed. As he staggered toward his buggy, Isaac was walking from the barn. Abel waited and stopped him as he tried to walk by without talking. "Isaac, come here, son, I want to talk to you."

Isaac stopped and sighed. His annoyance with his father was apparent. As he turned and stepped up to Abel, he could see the pain emanating from his watery eyes. The man that he had always feared was now vulnerable. Abel said, "Isaac, I want you to stay at the house while I'm gone. We'll finish the chores when I get home, but you must stay at the house and keep the other kids inside. If Sandy shows up here, you're not to let her in or go near her. Do you understand?"

Isaac had overheard his parents talking earlier, but had not heard the whole story of how his father had been hurt. "Yes, I understand, but why are you afraid of her?"

"She's not what she seems, son. She's indwelled by a demon and she's very powerful. I want you to get your shotgun off the rack in the laundry room and keep it loaded. If she shows up here, run her off. Shoot her if you have to, but don't let her near you."

Isaac saw that his father was too badly hurt to lash him. He said, "She must be tough if she kicked your butt. How did it feel? How did it feel to get your just rewards after all these years?"

Abel tried to straighten up so he could tower over Isaac, but he could only stand bent-over and cling to the buggy wheel for stability. "It felt just like the hundreds of other lashings I've taken in my life, Isaac. I know you're glad that I'm hurt, and that's fine if it gives you some measure of revenge. But I've never derived any pleasure from lashing you. It's always grieved me to have to do it. If you hate me that much, then revel in your pleasure, because I'm hurt bad. I hurt so bad that I can't see me ever getting over it. But don't let your joy overshadow your judgment. That woman is a demon and will do the same or worse to you and your mom and the little kids. I may be feeble now, but don't challenge me. As much as it hurts, I will rise above the pain and lash you again if you don't do as I say. Protect this family at all cost."

Isaac's smug arrogance faded as Abel climbed into the buggy. He slapped the reins against the mare's back and she sped off. Guilt overwhelmed Isaac as he watched his father ride away. How could he be so calloused toward his father's pain? He slowly turned and walked to the house.

Once inside he went to the laundry room and took the single-shot shotgun from the rack and broke it open. He found a partial box of 20ga. shells and put one in the barrel, then closed it. His guilt slowly faded to fear. Fear of what Sandy would do if the shotgun had no effect on her.

The ranger had obtained a steady sight-picture as soon as Abel had stepped out of the house. As Isaac approached his father, the ranger said, "I've got him, Mr. Smith. He's a statistic if you say the word."

Smith looked at Dr Sveade for approval. Sveade simply shrugged his shoulder and motioned with a tilt of his head toward Gaal. Since Gaal was now in charge, Smith looked into Sandy's eyes and asked, "Now?"

Gaal sighed and ran Sandy's fingers through her long blond hair as he thought. "I'M IN A DIFFICULT POSITION, GENTLEMEN. IT DOES NO GOOD FOR ME TO

MAKE A COVENANT WITH YOUR LEADERS IF I AM DENIED ACCESS TO THE FATHER BECAUSE I COMMIT SINS IN THE PROCESS. I HAVE TO DISTANCE MYSELF FROM THIS AT SOME POINT. I MAY HAVE GONE TOO FAR ALREADY. YOU KNOW WHAT HAS TO BE DONE. DO IT, BUT LEAVE ME OUT OF IT. I CAN'T HAVE BLOOD ON MY HANDS WHEN I KNEEL AT THE THRONE AND ASK GOD TO MAKE A PROVISION FOR OUR REDEMPTION."

Dr. Sveade looked confused as he asked, "Then what about Bishop Gordan? You killed him last night without batting an eye. What about Dall and Abel Straus? You almost killed them. You almost killed the sheriff and his chief deputy. It's a little late to start worrying about blood-stained hands, Gaal."

Gaal pondered Dr. Sveade's assessment. Deep inside, Sandy said, "That's right, Gaal. Remember the Amish men? Remember Levi Croft and Wilhelm Dresselhaus? What about Preacher Litchfield? You've consistently said that you lead the repentant demons and that you have not sinned as the other fallen have in hopes that you'll be able to convince God to forgive you. But you have sinned, Gaal! You've murdered people! And even if you didn't murder them, you controlled those who did. They were from your camp, so your hands are just as bloody as theirs."

Gaal boiled with anger as Sandy and Dr. Sveade threw his hypocrisy up in his face. He gritted Sandy's teeth and shook her head in an angry, jerking motion. Without looking at Dr. Sveade, she looked at the gathering on the horizon and growled, "I KNOW VERY WELL WHO I'VE KILLED, DOCTOR! THIS IS THE LAST TIME I WILL REMIND YOU OF THIS, SO DON'T BRING IT UP AGAIN! WE REPENTANT FALLEN HAVE TRIED NOT TO SIN, BUT SOMETIMES CIRCUMSTANCES DICTATE THAT WE HAVE TO! I KILL ONLY WHEN I MUST, AND IF IT SERVES A GREATER CAUSE! YOU'VE CERTAINLY CAUSED THE DEATH OF YOUR SHARE OF INNOCENT PEOPLE IN THE NAME OF DEMOCRACY! NONE OF US ARE SAINTS HERE! WE'RE ONLY ASKING GOD TO DO FOR US AS HE HAS DONE FOR MAN! YET WHILE MAN WAS STILL A SINNER, CHRIST DIED ON THE CROSS FOR HIM! GOD HAS FORGIVEN EVEN THE MOST HARDENED SINNER, EVEN THE APOSTLE PAUL, WHO HIMSELF PERSECUTED CHRISTIANS BEFORE HIS CONVERSION ON THE DAMASCUS ROAD, EVEN UNTO DEATH!

Sandy tried to slow her breathing as Gaal reigned in his anger. "WE FALLEN ARE AS INCAPABLE OF LIVING OUR LIVES WITHOUT SINNING AS YOU MORTALS ARE! AND WE'VE COMMITTED MANY MORE SINS SIMPLY BY VIRTUE OF THE FACT THAT WE'VE LIVED LONGER THAN ANY MORTAL! WE'VE BEEN ALIVE FOR OVER SIX THOUSAND YEARS,

EVER SINCE GENESIS WHEN GOD CREATED US ALONG WITH EVERYTHING ELSE THAT IS! BUT OUR SINS ARE IN THE PURSUIT OF SALVATION, NOT IN THE SERVICE OF THE PRINCE OF THE AIR! WE'RE NOT TRYING TO EARN OUR WAY TO REDEMPTION THROUGH OUR GOOD WORKS! WE'RE NOT ASKING GOD TO FORGIVE US BECAUSE WE'RE SINLESS! WE'RE ASKING HIM TO FORGIVE US IN SPITE OF OUR SINS, JUST AS HE'S DONE FOR MEN! I'VE SINNED! THAT'S OBVIOUS! MY FIRST SIN WAS THE SAME AS ALL OF US WHO FELL! IT WAS SATAN'S DESIRE TO BE LIKE GOD, AND OUR CHOOSING HIM OVER GOD! I GUESS WE WERE ALL ARROGANT OR FOOLISH ENOUGH TO THINK IF SATAN COULD ACHIEVE EQUAL STANDING WITH GOD, WE COULD, TOO! THE GREATER THE KNOWLEDGE OF THE TRUTH, THE GREATER THE ACCOUNTABILITY!

Sandy looked around. Gaal feared that his tirade was becoming too loud. Sandy breathed heavily and Gaal again tried to calm himself. "WE ANGELS WATCHED GOD CREATE THE UNIVERSE AND EVERYTHING IN IT, SO WE KNEW OF HIS POWER. OUR REBELLION WAS MUCH MORE THAN A MERE SIN. IT WAS THE GREATEST SIN OF ALL. NOTHING ELSE THAT WE HAVE EVER DONE WILL BE AS BAD AS THAT ORIGINAL SIN. IF GOD PROVIDES REDEMPTION FOR US, IT WILL BE FOR ALL OUR SINS. IF HE DOES NOT, THEN NONE OF THEM WILL MATTER. ONE SIN HAS CONDEMNED US AS COMPLETELY AS A THOUSAND. WE'VE ALREADY COMMITTED THE ONE. HOW MUCH WORSE OFF ARE WE IF I COMMIT A FEW MORE? IT'S A WORTHY CAUSE, DOCTOR. THERE ARE BILLIONS OF SOULS AT STAKE. IF GOD WILL FORGIVE US FOR OUR ORIGINAL SIN, I THINK HE'LL FORGIVE US FOR KILLING A FEW MORTALS WHO GET IN OUR WAY. BUT I ASSURE YOU THAT I AM TRYING TO REMEMBER MY COMMITMENT TO ABSTAIN FROM SIN. I'M TRYING TO HURT AS FEW PEOPLE AS POSSIBLE. AND I ALSO ASSURE YOU THAT IF YOU THROW MY FAILINGS UP IN MY FACE AGAIN, YOUR AGONIZING DEATH WILL BE MY NEXT SIN!"

Smith looked at the ranger and said, "Take the shot, soldier."

Gaal calmed himself and said, "I WOULD MAKE ONE LAST SUGGESTION, MR. SMITH. MY LEGION TELLS ME THAT ABEL IS ON HIS WAY TO BISHOP CLEVENGER'S HOUSE. THAT'S WHERE DALL IS HIDING, IN THE BISHOP'S BARN. HE'LL CONTACT THE BISHOP SOON. I WOULDN'T ALARM THE AMISH WITH MORE GUNFIRE. LET'S ALLOW HIM TO GO TO THE BISHOP'S HOUSE, AND FINISH THEM OFF THERE. THEN WE'LL LEAVE THE DISTRICT AND GO TO WASHINGTON. HAVE YOU BRIEFED YOUR PRESIDENT YET?"

Dr. Sveade said, "No, Gaal. We thought it better for you to meet first with our joint chiefs. Once the military is on board, we'll all go to the President. We'll have more credibility if they're on board first. This is all going to be hard for him to swallow. It'll be more believable if his joint chiefs have put their stamp of approval on it first. You know how Presidents are. They don't like to make decisions without consulting their experts."

Sandy's hair blew in the gentle breeze as she nodded her head. Gaal said, "Good, then let's eliminate this threat and move on. Let's go visit the old bishop." The ranger released the tension on the trigger and lowered the rifle. A shot now would be futile anyway. Abel was now a moving target and had driven out of range.

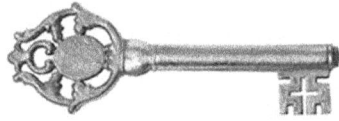

"I am he that liveth, and was dead; and behold, I am alive for evermore, Amen; and have the keys of hell and of death." **Revelation 1:18**

Abel pulled the reins back and slowed the mare to a stop in front of Bishop Clevenger's house. Bishop Clevenger stepped out of the house on Dall's arm. Dall released the bishop's arm after he'd grabbed the porch railing for support. Dall then hurried to Abel's buggy. He took Abel's arm and helped him out. "Abel, you're in no shape to be here. Go back home and protect your family."

"My family isn't safe as long as that monster is on the loose. None of us are. He's already demonstrated that he can kill any of us at any time."

Dall encircled Abel's waist with one arm and said, "I appreciate your concern, Abel, but I'll be okay."

Abel stopped and faced Dall at the foot of the bishop's porch steps. "I'm not here just for you, Dall. I'm here to convince you to leave the district before more of us are killed."

Bishop Clevenger said, "Dall's leaving won't get rid us of this demon, Brother Abel. Remember, the demon was here long before Dall arrived."

Both men struggled to ascend the steps. Even though Dall was helping Abel, he too had taken a severe beating at the hands of Gaal. His pain was almost as severe as Abel's. Abel said, "I know that, Bishop, but he had not materialized before now. If he had, none of us knew who he was. Now that he has indwelled Sandy, I fear that he'll take revenge on everyone who's helped her and Dall. He'll certainly kill Dall, which endangers everyone around him."

Bishop Clevenger said, "He was responsible for the deaths of Brother Wilhelm Dresselhaus and Brother Levi Croft, Abel. He had to manifest himself in some form to kill them. Come in the house, brothers. Let's get out of sight to talk."

Once in the house, Dall helped Abel into a chair. Abel was visibly shaken, but his mistrust of English doctors prohibited him from seeking medication that would ease his pain. Bishop Clevenger collapsed into a plush chair and said, "Abel, you need medical attention."

"I will, Bishop. I'll go see Lilly Dresselhaus as soon as I can."

The bishop nodded and said, "Okay, brother, but don't put it off. I'll tell you what I've already told Dall. This demon is nothing new in the history of man. You and I have talked about them before. You're aware of their power and their limitations. This demon has no power over true believers."

Abel rubbed the back of his neck and said, "Well, I'm a believer, Bishop, and he certainly had power over me. That girl used my head to dig a post-hole."

Bishop Clevenger smiled. "Yes, I know, but it's like I told Dall. You and he took on Gaal believing that simply because you were believers, you could defeat a demon. The disciples were stronger believers than any of us because they'd walked and talked with Jesus daily. They tried the same thing once in the book of Matthew and failed just as you did. When they asked Jesus why they had failed to cast a demon out of a possessed child, He told them it was because of their unbelief. They, like you and Dall, believed, but they had doubts that they could actually cast out demons. You and Dall tackled Sandy with doubt in your minds."

Abel nodded his head. "Yes, well, there's nothing like a good lashing to put doubt in your mind. If I had doubts before, I'm really scared now. If that demon shows up again, he'll kill everyone who gets in his way. Dall has to leave."

Dall said, "I don't want anyone to get hurt because of me, Abel, but I have to find a way to help Sandy."

Abel was confused "She's lost, Dall. She's indwelled by one of the most powerful beings ever created. You saw what she did to us. There's nothing we can do for her. There's no one in the district powerful enough to stop her. And to top it off, Bishop Gordan has disappeared."

Bishop Clevenger nodded sadly. "Yes, Dall just told me. And he hasn't just disappeared. He was murdered by Sandy. He confronted Gaal last night and Sandy killed him. The rangers that were with her shot Hans Bowlin. Their bodies are at the coroner's office."

Abel lowered his head in grief. Bishop Clevenger stood angrily. Realizing that he was now senior bishop, he said with authority, "Their widows must know what has happened, and we must meet with the brethren and elders to decide what to do. Abel, please leave now. I want you to swing by Sampson's place on your way to Lilly's house and ask him to spread the word that we'll have a district meeting here tonight. Dall, will you help me to my buggy? Mrs. Gordan and Mrs. Bowlin will need comforting."

Abel struggled to his feet while Dall helped Bishop Clevenger toward the door.

Gaal, Smith, and Dr. Sveade studied Bishop Clevenger's house though binoculars. The rangers screwed the magnification ring on their scopes to maximum power. Dr Sveade asked, "Gaal, do you want to go down there. We've got them all contained in one house."

Gaal was surprisingly alarmed. He blurted out, "**No! No, I can't!**"

Smith shifted his eyes suspiciously at Sandy. "Why, Gaal, you went through that big Amish farmer and Dall like they were putty. You can dismember them both with one hand. I've seen your power with my own eyes."

Gaal glared angrily at Smith through Sandy's soft green eyes. "**It's not the farmer or Dall that concern me!**" Gaal's tone convinced Smith that he should not press on. He mentally ran down the list of people in the house. There was Dall, Abel Straus, Bishop Clevenger and his wife. If Gaal wasn't afraid of Straus and Dall, it had to be the bishop.

All three men stepped out onto Bishop Clevenger's porch. Abel and the bishop moved slowly, so they were fairly easy targets to acquire in the rangers' scopes. With a hopeful tone in his voice, Smith said, "Fire at will."

With deliberate but gentle strokes of the triggers, the rangers began a rhythmic sequence of fire. As the recoil of the shots rocked the rangers backward and caused the muzzles to jump off target, they allowed the weight of the rifles to quickly bring them back down on target. They had already taken the creep out of the triggers, and as the crosshairs settled down on their targets they squeezed off another shot. A full-auto burst would have been impractical. The first shot would have been on target, but the recoil of the rapid fire would not have allowed time for the rifle to settle back down on target before the following shot would make the muzzle rise even more. The string of fire would be a vertical line ending up somewhere over the roof of the bishop's house.

From two-hundred yards, confirmed kills were not as assured as they would have been had they crept closer to the farm house without being seen. The first round penetrated the 4" x 4" support post that ran from the deck to the roof rafter. It blew the post in half and continued through the house, but missed the men. The subsequent barrage was so fast and furious that all the men could do was dive for cover as pieces of wood and siding flew from the house and porch railing.

Dall bear-hugged Bishop Clevenger and jumped through the front door, landing on the floor. He then pulled the bishop behind the sofa. Abel was not so lucky. After a round ricocheted off the cast iron planter beside the bishop's rocking chair, it passed through his left thigh, barely missing his femur and femoral artery. He pulled himself behind a hand-painted milk can at the edge of the porch in which Mrs. Clevenger had filled with dirt and planted flower.

Mrs. Clevenger heard the commotion and hurried into the living room in time to see the whole front wall of the house disintegrating before her eyes. Frozen in shock, she trembled as bullets and debris zipped around her. She would have been killed, but was immediately tackled and dragged behind the sofa by Dall.

When the rangers had emptied their magazines, Abel sensed a pause in the chaos. He put his pain out of his mind and made his body move. He ran to his buggy and whipped the mare till she had leapt into a full sprint. He turned her around, causing the buggy to fishtail, and headed her toward home. As he looked at his leg, there was a large stream of blood pumping out the wound with every heartbeat. He knew he'd never make it to his house, so at the end of the bishop's drive he pressed his hand hard over the wound and turned the mare toward Sampson's place. It was much closer.

The rangers quickly reloaded fresh magazines as Gaal yelled, "THE HORSE! KILL THE HORSE! HE CAN'T GET AWAY!"

Abel continued to whip the mare as she turned toward Sampson's house, fishtailing the buggy again. The rangers quickly shouldered their reloaded rifles and set up the appropriate lead for a target moving at that speed and distance. Again they began their controlled fire, hoping to see the horse tumble end over end.

Abel ducked and released the compression of his bullet wound to cover his head with one arm as rounds zipped through the canopy, floor and seats of his buggy. The mare flinched as rounds thumped her shoulder, hips and rib cage, but ran even harder as she panicked from the unfamiliar pain. When the rangers' magazines again released their last rounds and locked the bolts open, Abel realized that the assault was over and took quick assessment of his condition. Miraculously he'd suffered no further injury, but the streams of blood from his mare's side confirmed that she had not been so lucky. He reapplied pressure to his wound and slapped the reins hard against her back.

Sandy's eyes raged as she turned. Gaal yelled, "You missed him, you fools! Now he'll warn the entire district!"

Dr. Sveade said as he motioned toward the gathering of dark spirits that encircled the district, "They may hide Dall, Gaal, but your followers are with him. They'll tell you where he is. We can still find him."

Sandy sighed in frustration and rubbed her eyes. Gaal said, "Yes, Dr. Sveade, I can find him. Finding him is not the issue. I had hoped to find him alone and kill him without having to kill everyone in the district. That kind of publicity is not conducive to a working relationship with your President and military that is based on mutual trust."

Deep inside, Sandy was glad that Dall had someone to help him. When the time was right, she would stand up to Gaal and take back control of her body, even if it meant being killed.

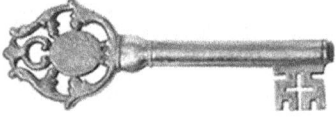

"I am he that liveth, and was dead; and behold, I am alive for evermore, Amen; and have the keys of hell and of death." **Revelation 1:18**

Sampson was still shaken from his brush with death the night before. He knew he should warn the neighbors, but he was too frightened to leave the house. He'd spent the morning moving from window to window with his deer rifle in hand, searching for rangers.

He'd heard the distant rifle shots that had riddled Abel's buggy, and thought they were intended for him. When he looked out the front window and saw Abel's mare and buggy charging toward him out of control, he ran to the road, hoping to stop the mare before someone got hurt. He knew something was seriously wrong when he recognized Abel's giant frame in the seat. Abel would never abuse his equipment or animals like that unless it was a matter of life and death. He now knew who the gunfire was directed at.

The mare was panting heavily with her tongue hanging out as she raced recklessly toward Sampson. She slowed and staggered several steps as Abel pulled back on the reins, then collapsed with her nose plowing into the gravel road. When she rolled over, Sampson saw the bullet-holes in her side and streams of blood oozing from the hole.

Abel fell out of the buggy as the weight of the mare turned the buggy over when she rolled over onto her side and died. The blood pumping out of Abel's leg answered Sampson's curiosity about the rifle-fire that he had heard a few minutes earlier.

Sampson ran to Abel and helped him to his feet. Abel clutched his leg and yelled, "Sampson! I've got to get home to Dory and the kids! The English shot at me and Bishop Clevenger! Lend me your buggy, then saddle up another horse and ride through the district! Warn everyone to be careful and meet at Bishop Clevenger's house tonight! Tell them to arm themselves! Bishop Gordan is dead and Bishop Clevenger is in charge!"

Sampson said, "I know, brother, I was there. And you'd be dead instead of Hans if you'd been with us."

Sampson felt like he was moving in slow-motion as he tied a compress around Abel's leg and helped him to the barn. Still in shock, he said, "The English did this, Abel. They're to blame."

Abel shook his head. "No, Sampson, we're to blame. All men are to blame for the misfortunes that befall us. It was our non-belief and lack of faith in the Father that led us to seek our own pleasures and solutions to our problems. If we were all living our lives according to God's will, there'd be no room for demons to dwell in our midst. It is our own pride and vanity that invites them in. Without God, they're free to whisper in our ears and lead us into sin."

After a moment of reflection about his long friendship with Hans, Abel's voice cracked as he almost wept. "Poor Hans. It's my fault. He took my place last night because I was in no shape to go. It should have been me that was killed."

Sampson had earlier hitched his gilding to the buggy in case he had to make a fast getaway. He helped Abel in and nervously watched him barely clear the gate posts as he raced out of the barn-lot. Abel yelled, "I'll pay you for the horse if he gets hurt, Sampson." He only slowed down briefly to skirt around his dead mare and overturned buggy in the middle of the road. Sampson then saddled his paint and rode hard to warn the neighbors.

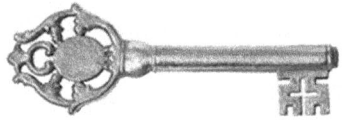

"I am he that liveth, and was dead; and behold, I am alive for evermore, Amen; and have the keys of hell and of death." **Revelation 1:18**

Once Dall had made sure the Clevengers were safe, he ran to the back door. He saw no one, so he yelled, "Bishop, we can't stay here! We've got to leave!"

Bishop Clevenger struggled to his feet with his wife's help. "No, Dall, you go. Run on and save yourself. We'd only slow you down, and we'd have no chance of outrunning the soldiers."

"I can't leave you, Bishop. They'll come here to make sure they've killed us. When the find you alive, they'll kill you for helping me."

"Run on, Dall! We'll be fine! We'll see you here tonight, if you can! If not, make your way back here as soon as you can! I'll get you out of the district where you'll be safe!"

Dall reluctantly ran and jumped off the back porch. He headed for the tree line that ran across the back of the small pasture. Once there, he would decide where to go.

As Dall was leaping off the back porch, a team of rangers jerked open the front screen door and barged in. Bishop Clevenger stood bravely in front of Mrs. Clevenger and pointed his shaky finger at the rangers. "Leave this house, sons of Satan, and abandon your cause or you'll account to an angry God for your evil!"

The rangers had no time for banter. One yelled, "Where is Roberts, old man?" He leveled his M-14 at the couple and turned the selector switch to full-auto. If he didn't get the answer he wanted, he would slaughter them on the spot.

Bishop Clevenger shook his head defiantly. "Don't waste your time trying to scare us, young Englisher. Without God's consent, no harm can come to His elect."

The ranger paused briefly as his partner looked out the back door and yelled, "Roberts is running across the pasture at the rear of the house! Come on, let's end this!"

The ranger gritted his teeth and ran to the back porch. As he ran past the bishop and Mrs. Clevenger, he raised his rifle stock up under his arm and pulled the trigger. He would cut them both in half as he ran by.

Bishop Clevenger held up his frail hand as if the arthritic old appendage would somehow stop the torrent of devastation that was coming his way. As the ranger pulled the trigger, he continued to run toward the back porch. To his great surprise, nothing happened. The trigger would not pull, as if the safety had somehow been pushed to the SAFE position without his knowledge. As he exited the house onto the porch, he looked at the safety to see why the rifle had failed to fire. The safety was in the FIRE position. The hair on the back of his neck stood on end as he searched for the reason the rifle had failed to fire.

Shifting his attention to Dall, the ranger saw him as he reached the trees. He leveled the rifle at Dall and pulled down hard on the forearm as he pulled the trigger to keep the muzzle from climbing in the full-auto firing mode. As twenty rounds cycled through the weapon, he held it firm and tried to keep the front sight on Dall's silhouette. The ranger's partner did the same.

Dall heard the fire as he reached the trees. When tree-bark, branches and leaves began flying all around him, he breathed a sigh of relief. Since the rangers were firing at him, the Clevengers were safe for now.

Dall assessed his condition as he dove face-first into the dirt. Again he had survived a sustained burst from one of America's finest battle implements. He now knew the rangers were not seasoned battle veterans. Even he knew that that particular rifle was totally uncontrollable in the full-auto mode. No experienced sniper would ever operate that weapon in any mode other than semi-auto.

When the bolts locked open, the rangers pulled the empty magazines from the rifles and dropped them to the ground. They hurriedly removed loaded magazines from their mag. vests and inserted them in the rifles as they jumped off the porch and chased after Dall. The ranger who had tried to kill the Clevengers ran slower than the other. His mouth was like cotton and his legs felt stiff and heavy with fear as he tried to figure out why his rifle had worked flawlessly when firing at Dall, but had seized up when he'd tried to fire on the Clevengers. The old bishop was right. The ranger had never believed in God, but now knew there was a God and he would soon suffer God's wrath for what he had done.

THIRTEEN

THE REST OF that evening was spent in a cat and mouse chase in which Dall had expertly used his military survival skills to barely avoid the wrath of the embarrassed rangers. He was panting hard and soaked with sweat as he collapsed at the base of the cistern at the rear of the Litchfield barn where he and Sandy had washed each night during their stay there. With a legion of dark spirits reporting his every move to Gaal, it was only a matter of time before he would be caught and killed.

As he struggled to raise himself to his knees, he clung to the concrete rim of the cistern and tried to slow his breathing so he could hear the approach of the rangers. To his great relief, he had either lost them or they were temporarily distracted by more pressing matters.

He lowered the bucket into the well and hoped the squeaky pulley did not wake Mrs. Litchfield or her deranged son. Once he had the bucket of cold water resting on the edge, he looked toward the house. When he saw no lights on inside, he tipped the bucket up and drank his fill, then poured the rest of the water over his face and head.

Dall sat back down and leaned against the well casing as he pondered his options. He would try to make it back to Bishop Clevenger tomorrow, but he had to find a safe place to hide tonight. The dark, swirling cloud of dark spirits in the distance was back-lit by the moon. He stared at them and wondered how safe he would be from the massive gathering who would report his every move to Gaal.

As the coolness of the evening refreshed him, Dall stood and wondered into the barn where he and Sandy used to sleep. To his surprise, the mattresses that he and Sandy had slept on were still in the stalls. The wash basin and bar of soap were still on the rickety table where Preacher Litchfield had placed them a few weeks earlier.

Dall went back to the cistern and drew another bucket of water. He shed his clothes, then poured the water over himself. After soaping and lathering himself up, he drew another bucked of water and rinsed. As cold as the water was, it was refreshing to be clean again. After a long petting session with Lady and Tramp, he collapsed on a mattress and slept soundly, in spite of the tiny pieces of hay debris that fell on him during the night.

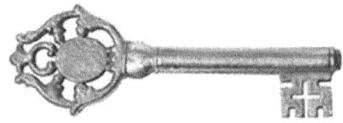

"I am he that liveth, and was dead; and behold, I am alive for evermore, Amen; and have the keys of hell and of death." **Revelation 1:18**

The next morning, Dall awoke to Mrs. Litchfield yelling instructions to Devin as he walked to the barn. Dall jumped from the mattress and raced to the door in time to see Devin lumbering toward the barn in a state of ignorant bliss, kicking small rocks.

He ducked around the corner of the grain bin as Mrs. Litchfield yell, "And be gentle with those horses! You don't have to beat them so much!"

Devin grunted an obligatory, unintelligible response to his mother and dismissed her with a lazy wave of his hand. As he entered the barn, both Lady and Tramp became frightened and
tried to back out of their stalls. The barn shook as they backed hard against the doors and walls.

Dall's worst fear was realized when Devin pick up a metal fence post that had been leaning against the wall. He panicked as Devin took a few practice swings, knowing that he intended to beat the horses. Dall couldn't allow that to happen, so he stepped out of the grain bin and said, "Devin, you heard your mother. Don't beat the horses."

Devin jumped as though he'd seen a snake. He dropped the post and stared at Dall in disbelief. As he regained his composure, his courage swelled. "You! English man! You don't live here no more!"

"No, Devin, but I still don't like to see animals abused. I know that's how your father treated them, but he's gone now. You can be a better person than that."

Devin was slow to engage, but after careful consideration, he said, "They're my horses now. Preacher said they have to be kept in submission for them to work right."

Dall stepped toward Devin as non-threateningly as possible. He shook his head and pointed to Lady. "Look at them, Devin. They're not going anywhere. They're not capable of plotting against you. They know they have to work. They actually like it. They're bred for it. You don't have to beat it into them. You're a better man than your father was. You can break that cycle of abuse. You dad beat you and your mother just like he did those horses. Did you like that?"

Devin looked at the ground and shook his head like a small child. Dall said, "The horses don't like it either. You can see that they're afraid of you. Wouldn't you like to be able to get close to them and pet them without them trying to get away from you?"

Devin looked at the horses and mumbled, "Yeah, I guess." He then looked back at the metal post lying at his feet. He raised his head slightly and looked at Dall from under the brim of his hat. Being a simple soul made him easy to read. Dall stepped into him to discourage him from picking up the post. "You don't want to try that, Devin. I'm trying to be your friend, but I warned you at the barn raising. I meant what I said."

Devin had no chance of taking Dall. He slowly turned and went back to the house. Dall anguished over Lady and Tramp as he made his way back to the Clevenger farm. He knew Devin would wait until he had left, then beat them mercilessly.

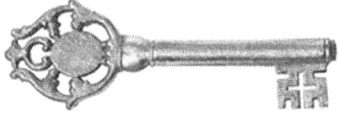

"I am he that liveth, and was dead; and behold, I am alive for evermore, Amen; and have the keys of hell and of death." **Revelation 1:18**

Dexter Waters hadn't touched his breakfast of coffee, a hard biscuit and a Styrofoam plate containing cold scrambled egg substitute and a greasy freezer-sausage patty. He waited impatiently for the jailer to open the door. To his surprise, Chief Deputy Casey Thurman stepped through the metal fire-door that divided the jail from the rest of the Sheriff's Office. He said, "Morning, Agent Waters. What a beautiful morning for an arraignment."

Waters glared bitterly at Thurman and extended his hands to be handcuffed. "You're enjoying this, Thurman. I hope I'm around to see your face when you take a fall for this."

Thurman handcuffed Waters and said sarcastically, "Maybe you will be, Waters. If I ever screw up as badly as you have, maybe we'll be cell-mates at the state prison."

"I didn't screw up, Thurman! I was sold out! There's a difference!"

Casey shrugged his shoulders. "I'm sure there is, but either way, you've got some significant hurdles to overcome in front of the judge this morning. And since we're talking about your shortcomings, how in the hell did you ever get so stupid as to let the worst policemen in the history of American law enforcement catch you? That's the biggest embarrassment of all."

"Thurman, you know that once I tell the court that I'm an F.B.I. agent, the judge will release me after a phone call to my supervisor. Once he hears that I was working a federal case, he'll view this whole thing as it really is, a violation of bureau policy, and let the bureau handle it administratively."

Casey said, "He may, but in this case your violation of bureau policy resulted in a violation of Missouri State Statute. And I think I know old Judge Pettigrew pretty well. You may hope he'll be satisfied with the good judgment of the bureau, but he hates you feds almost as much as I do. He'll wait to see if the U.S. Attorney steps in and declares jurisdiction before he drops the charges. Better be prepared for the worst."

Waters sat nervously through the arraignment of three other felony prisoners before it was his turn to face the judge. He became more frightened with each arraignment.

Judge Pettigrew was a frail little man who looked as physically capable as a concentration camp survivor, but he wielded the power of his bench with the passion and vigor of a Greek Spartan swinging his sword in defense of the Thermopylae Pass. Not only were the accused scared stiff, but onlookers, attorneys and law enforcement officials alike walked on eggshells while in his court.

Judge Pettigrew was diabetic, and his demeanor on any given day was largely determined by how bad he felt. He'd already lost a foot to diabetes, and his kidneys had failed to the point that he had to undergo dialysis three times a week. He looked as though he could slip into eternity at any time.

Waters stood when his name was called and started toward the bench. He casually looked around the courtroom and caught the determined stare of two men he didn't know. Years in the bureau had conditioned him to spot federal agents from a mile away by their dress, sunglasses and hair style. They were obviously here to see if he would betray the secrecy of the investigation.

He stood erect at the bench and stared confidently into the sunken, hollowed eyes of the fowl-tempered magistrate. With a scowl on his face, the judge read the charges through gritted teeth. Waters noticed that the agents had quietly moved to each side of him. He glared suspiciously at one, then the other, but they only stared despondently at the judge.

The judge continued reading the charges, and Waters was surprised that the judge would allow the agents to flank him so closely. The judge hadn't inquired about their identity, and seemed completely unfazed that a prisoner before him on a felony arraignment was in such close proximity to people who weren't his attorney, had no obvious standing in the case, and could possibly be armed. The judge read on and the agents sandwiched Waters so tightly that he was wedged between them shoulder to shoulder, an obvious attempt at intimidation.

When the judge had finished reading the charges, his eyes burned with hatred as he looked at Waters over the top of his reading glasses. Waters looked expectantly at the judge, hoping he would ask the two agents the nature of their business and determine their standing in this case. To his shock, Judge Pettigrew glared only at him.

Waters looked angrily at the agent to his left. Something seemed wrong. He couldn't put his finger on it at first, but then he realized why the agent didn't look normal. The agent was impeccably groomed and his suit was immaculate. His hair was perfectly combed and his face was flawless. There wasn't any beard stubble or a wrinkle or blemish anywhere. He appeared to be a mature man, but his skin was like that of a newborn baby. It looked as though he had just been created. Closer examination made Waters gasp. The agent was also not breathing.

Waters quickly looked at the agent to his right. Again, the agent appeared as a fine China doll, perfectly formed. Waters studied him hard and found that his chest was also not swelling as his lungs inflated. Neither agent was human.

Judge Pettigrew became impatient with the prisoner in front of him. He yelled, "Mr. Waters! I've read the charges! Are you so apathetic that you can't pay attention to the reading of the charges against you, or are you displaying your blatant contempt for the integrity of this court?"

Waters snapped to attention and stared at the judge in complete shock. By the angry glare of the magistrate, it was obvious that the judge couldn't see the two agents. They were only visible to Waters. The judge yelled, "Mr. Waters! I will not have the propriety of this court tampered with by your charades! Is your preoccupation with other things around you a display of contempt for this court? Yes or No!"

Stark fear consumed Waters. His voice trembled as he asked, "No, your honor, but can't you see these two men beside me? They're crowding me so tightly that I can't move! Look at them! Look hard at their faces! Can't you see anything strange about them?"

Unfazed by Waters' complaint, the two agents continued to stare at the judge. They leaned harder against Waters, compressing his shoulders and chest, making it hard for him to breathe and completely unnerving him.

Judge Pettigrew appeared as a child playing in his father's office chair. The chair was large, and his small, emaciated frame didn't come close to filling it. He leaned back in a full spread of righteous indignation and looked on both sides of Waters. Seeing nothing, he leaned over the bench and growled impatiently through his gritted, gapped and crooked teeth, "Mr. Waters, you will not disturb these proceedings with your feeble attempts to fabricate an insanity defense! I would strongly suggest that you speak with counsel before you attempt to spar with me! I'll return you to your cell and have the public defender speak with you! When you approach this bench again, you'd better have your act together and display an appropriate sense of humility and reverence for this court if you harbor any expectation of ever being released on bond! If you intend to test the resolve of this court, you'll find yourself remanded to the county jail under the worst possible circumstances! Am I perfectly clear?"

Waters broke down and cried at the realization that these two agents were not men at all. He wondered why they had bothered with the charade since he was apparently the only person who could see them.

Throughout the preparation phase of this investigation, he had been made aware that the bureau was looking for a demon inside the Amish district, but he'd never really believed in demons or angels. He had always figured the bureau would chase their tails until they finally accepted the fact that there were no such things as supernatural beings. He only accepted the assignment because it would look good on his resume at promotion time.

Waters believed the Amish deaths were results of a vicious, masochistic mortal, that's all. Even the encounter with Sandy after she had been indwelled by Gaal had not fully convinced him. He somehow believed that Sandy was embellishing the role to gain a favorable outcome for her and Dall. Nothing he had seen so far had frightened him as much as these two.

The appearance of the two fallen angels, however, had destroyed any and all preconceived notions that he'd ever held about eternity and spiritual beings. If these spirits were real, then so must be Satan, the angels and God. As frightened as these two fallen ones were, how much greater power did Satan and the angels have? And he couldn't even get his mind around the power of God.

He nodded his head as tears of terror rolled down his face. When the court deputy stepped up to Waters and took his arm, the two agents stepped aside and followed closely behind as the deputy led Waters back to his cell.

Judge Pettigrew adjusted the nose-clip of his oxygen tube as he scanned the courtroom through bloodshot, angry eyes. When he spotted the public defender, he raised an arthritic index finger and motioned for her to approach the bench. As she approached, the judge said, "Ms. Brown, I'm assigning you to Mr. Waters. Ask the prosecutor to let you look at the case file. If he refuses, bring me a motion for discovery. Go counsel him on the requisite evidence and documentation necessary to support an insanity plea. Then determine if he has the resources to retain his own counsel. If he does not, please represent him at his arraignment. I won't allow any person charged with a felony to represent themselves."

Ms. Brown walked by the prosecutor's table and he held the case file up in the air. She took it and sat in the pew directly behind him and familiarized herself with the evidence. Fifteen minutes later, she placed the file back on the prosecutor's desk and whispered, "Thanks", then hurried off to consult with Waters, hoping to escape before the ogre on the bench found an excuse to eat her for lunch.

The English Man   Mike Smitley

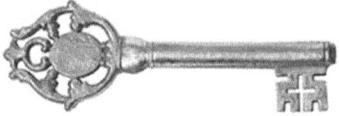

"I am he that liveth, and was dead; and behold, I am alive for evermore, Amen; and have the keys of hell and of death." **Revelation 1:18**

A resounding boom echoed throughout the building as the steal cell-door slammed shut behind Waters. He looked around and sighed with relief when he saw that the two demons were not with him. He trembled as he staggered to the washbasin and turned on the cold water. He splashed several handfuls of cold water in his face, then wiped his hands on the legs of his jail coveralls.

He leaned in close to the polished metal mirror that was bolted to the wall over the basin. He assessed his situation and longed for the good-ole days back in the Kansas City field office. He then walked on weak legs to his bunk and collapsed on it.

Waters decided that focusing on the shock of his situation would not get him out of it. He would be facing the dying judge from Hell soon and he needed to plan a strategy. He thought about the old judge and believed the judge looked more demonic than the demon that he'd been sent here to find.

When he opened his eyes, Waters sat up quickly and scooted to the corner of the bunk with his knees up in front of his chest. His porcelain-faced keepers had suddenly reappeared. He looked at the cell door, but it had not been opened since the jailer had locked it.

Both demons moved to the bunk and sat unnervingly close to Waters. They were still dressed and groomed as if they had just stepped out of the pages of an upscale society magazine. When they spoke, it was as if one mind drove both beings. Their mouths and eyes moved in perfect synchronization. They said, "DEXTER, WE ARE OF THE LEGION OF GAAL THAT GATHERS IN THE DISTANT SKY. WE ARE MANY, AND HE HAS SENT US TO YOU."

Waters relaxed slightly as he realized that these two may be his ticket out of this mess. His voice cracked with fear as he asked, "How can you help? Can you make these charges go away and get me out of here?"

Both demons spoke simultaneously. "YES, DEXTER. WE ARE ABLE TO PERFORM MANY GOOD WORKS."

He said, "You'll have to excuse me. I've never talked to fallen angels before."

Both understood Dexter's ignorance and nodded in perfect sync. "WE KNOW YOUR HEART, DEXTER. YOU HAVE NEVER BEEN A BELIEVER, BUT WE WILL REVEAL THINGS TO YOU. WE ARE NOT NEPHILIM. WE ARE AMONG THE FALLEN. THERE IS A DIFFERENCE. WE ONCE DWELLED IN HEAVEN WITH THE PRINCE OF THE POWER OF THE AIR, BUT HE AND WE WERE CAST DOWN TO EARTH BY THE MOST HIGH."

Waters said, "You said you were Gaal's followers. Does that mean you're some of those who want to overthrow Satan and approach God for salvation?"

Again, both spoke in perfect synchronization and with identical voices. "YES. WE ARE OF THOSE WHO WILL FIGHT THE GREAT BATTLE WITH THE PRINCE OF THE AIR. IF WE WIN, WE WILL LAY OUR VICTORY AT THE FEET OF JESUS AND ASK HIM TO MAKE INTERCESSION ON OUR BEHALF TO THE FATHER."

Waters asked, "Why go to Jesus? He's just the son. Why not go straight to the top and ask God Himself in the first place?"

Both said, "WE WILL ULTIMATELY PROSTRATE OURSELVES BEFORE GOD. YOU WOULDN'T KNOW THIS, BUT IN JOHN 14: 6 WHEN JESUS WAS ENCOURAGING HIS DISCIPLES, HE TOLD THOMAS, *'I am the way, the truth, and the life: no man cometh unto the Father, but by Me.'* WE ARE NOT MORTALS, BUT THE SAME NARROW GATE APPLIES TO US, THE FALLEN. SINCE JESUS IS THE ONLY ACCESS TO GOD, WE WILL MAKE OUR PETITION TO HIM. AND IT IS WRITTEN IN REVELATION 1:18 THAT JESUS HOLDS THE KEYS TO HELL AND DEATH."

Waters shook his head in disbelief. He'd never read the Bible and couldn't discuss the matter intelligently or discern the truthfulness of what the fallen ones were telling him. He asked, "What if Jesus doesn't like you? What if he refuses to allow you access to His Father?"

Both fallen ones waved their hands in the exact same motion and spoke in perfect stereo. "WE ARE NOT CONCERNED. JESUS AND THE FATHER ARE ONE. IF JESUS HEARS OUR PLEA, THE FATHER HEARS ALSO."

Dexter said, "Yeah, I've heard about the trinity; The Father, Son and Holy Ghost, but that doesn't seem possible to me. How can all three be one being?"

In unison both said, "IN JOHN 10: 30, WHEN THE ANGRY JEWS SURROUNDED JESUS IN THE TEMPLE OF SOLOMON, HE SAID, *'I and my father are one'.* WHEN OUR

KNEES TOUCH THE HALLOWED GROUND IN FRONT OF CHRIST'S THRONE, WE WILL BE BEFORE THE FATHER. YOU'VE NEVER SEEN THE TRINITY, BUT WE DWELLED WITH THE FATHER BEFORE OUR FALL. WE SAW THE FATHER, SON AND HOLY SPIRIT WITH OUR OWN EYES. WE ENJOYED CLOSE FELLOWSHIP WITH THEM DAILY. ONCE YOU'VE SEE THEM, YOU WILL BELIEVE."

Waters relaxed a little as the conversation continued. He then turned the discussion to his plight. He looked at the two with smug arrogance and asked, "So, what are you and Gaal going to do for me?"

Both said, "WE ARE NOT FOR YOU. WE SERVE A GREATER CAUSE, AND OUR LOYALTY IS FIRST TO THE FATHER, THEN TO THE ONE WHO WILL APPROACH THE SAVIOR ON OUR BEHALF. AS WE SAID, WE KNOW YOUR HEART. YOU WANT TO SAVE YOURSELF. YOU HAVE NO CONCERN FOR ETERNAL MATTERS. YOU HAVE NO REGARD FOR THE DAMNATION THAT WE FALLEN WILL SUFFER IF WE FAIL. WE CANNOT FAIL. YOU WILL TRY TO SAVE YOURSELF. THAT WILL DESTROY OUR PLANS, SO GAAL HAS SENT US TO SILENCE YOU. YOU WILL NOT BETRAY OUR CAUSE TO ANYONE. WE CANNOT LAY HANDS ON ONE OF THE ELECT BECAUSE THEY ARE COVERED BY THE LAMB'S BLOOD OF CHRIST AND WE ARE SUBJECT TO HIS AUTHORITY, BUT YOU ARE NOT WASHED IN HIS BLOOD. YOU DO NOT WEAR THE SPIRITUAL ARMOR OF SALVATION. WE WILL TAKE AWAY YOUR ABILITY TO BETRAY US. YOU WILL NOT HEAR, SPEAK, OR WRITE."

Waters instantly panicked when the reality of the fallen's mission sank in. He began to cower and tremble in fear as he screamed hysterically for the jailers to save him.

The jailers were presenting the visitor log to Ms. Brown at the booking desk when they heard Waters scream over the intercom. After the second scream, his next scream was instantly cut off as if someone had cupped their hand over his mouth. Since she was there to represent him at his arraignment, Ms. Brown hurried after the jailers as they raced to Waters' cell. They stopped suddenly at the bars and backed away in fear.

Ms. Brown screamed and fainted when she looked through the bars at Waters. He was on his knees in the middle of his cell with his head bowed, quivering in fear and excruciating pain. He raised his head and arms, hoping someone could help him, but both jailers slid down the wall and collapsed to a seated position as they began screaming.

Dexter's ear canals, mouth and eye sockets were gone. They were filled in with bone, and there was skin over them as if they had never existed. His arms were gone above the elbows and there was old-growth skin over the stumps as though he'd been born without them. The fallen had done their job well. Waters would never hear, speak or write again. His life would be spent as a prisoner in a dark shell, cut off from the outside world. Not only could he never communicate with anyone, but the fallen ones had taken away any possibility of him being able to end his suffering. He could not even kill himself. He was doomed to a lifetime of sustenance through a feeding tube in his stomach and imprisonment in his dark solitude.

"I am he that liveth, and was dead; and behold, I am alive for evermore, Amen; and have the keys of hell and of death." **Revelation 1:18**

Mrs. Clevenger was still unnerved by her close call with death at the hands of the rangers. She had swept up the debris inside the house, but the porch and exterior wall were riddled with bullet-holes. She fought through her fear and maintained her composure as she delivered drinks to the angry, indignant men gathered in her living room.

Bishop Clevenger began the meeting. "Dear brothers in Christ. I've asked you here tonight to lay out a plan of action to deal with these English who have invaded our district. I believe you've all heard about the deaths of Bishop Gordan and Hans Bowlin."

Elder Dunlevy said, "Bishop Clevenger, now that Bishop Gordan is dead, you're the leader of this district. Speaking on behalf of the other elders, we support you. Can you tell of the details of our brothers' deaths?"

Sampson Bettendorf was eager to tell his story. He stood and said, "I was there! As you all know, Bishop Gordan had ordered that we all take turns as three-man teams to patrol our district and confront the English. Last night we found the English soldiers and confronted them. Bishop Gordan insisted they explain themselves, and he was killed. The person who killed him was that English girl, Sandy."

Elder Dunlevy said, "Bishop, we're not equipped or trained to deal with these godless English. Who can help us?"

Dall stood and said, "Gentlemen, first of all, let me explain something. The Bible tells us that we do not struggle against men. We war against principalities, meaning Satan. The person who killed our brothers was a demon named Gaal. He is now indwelling the body of Sandy Parsons. Now, you all know Sandy. There isn't a gentler person on earth. She wouldn't hurt anyone, but this demon that is in her is a monster. Abel Straus and I tangled with him when he had just taken her over. He almost killed us."

The men in the room looked around. Sampson knew they were looking for Abel, and said, "He's at home recuperating. He suffered severe spinal cord injuries in the fight with the demon. Today he was shot during the attack on Bishop Clevenger. He's got a bullet-hole in his leg. He'll be down for a while."

Dall was passionate in his defense of Sandy, but it fell on deaf ears. Mr. Carter said, "We don't care about your sister, Dall. You both entered this district under false pretenses. You lied to us all and brought the wrath of this demon upon us. We want you out of here, and soon."

As the men grew angrier, Bishop Clevenger intervened. "Brothers! Brothers, listen to me! This demon was in our midst long before Dall and Sandy arrived. They just came here to help rid us of the demon. You all remember the disappearance of Wilhelm Dresselhaus and the death of Levi Croft. This demon killed them. And we still haven't found the body of Preacher Litchfield. I spent last evening with Ruth Bowlin and Sarah Gordan. They're devastated by the loss of their husbands. Rather than pointing fingers at others, let's remember our Christian duty and minister to the need of these Godly widows. And now that I am bishop, I want to bring something else to your attention. While Bishop Gordan was in charge, this district had treated Wilhelm's widow, Lilly, with great contempt. That ends here and now. Lilly is Amish. She may be outspoken about the behavior of some of our members, but maybe someone needs to speak out. She's a dear soul, so let's open our hearts to her and minister to her needs also."

Most of the men lowered their head in shame. Elder Dunlevy said, "Thank you, Bishop Clevenger, for reminding us of our Christian duty. And let us not forget the lashing that we gave Dall. That was uncalled for, and we must not only repent and never lash another man like that again, but we must approach Dall as a group and ask his forgiveness. Speaking for everyone here, Dall, will you forgive us?"

Dall said, "You weren't even there, Elder, but yes, I forgive everyone who lashed me. But for now can we focus on a plan to bring this demon out into the open and cast him out of Sandy?"

Everyone looked at each other. It was apparent that they all had the same doubts about their ability to cast out demons that Dall and Abel had when Sandy almost killed them. Sampson said, "I'm sorry, Dall, but I think I speak for everyone here. We know what he did to Abel, and no one here is a better man than Abel Straus in a brawl. If the two of you couldn't whip him, we're not willing to try."

Dall looked at Bishop Clevenger. The bishop nodded his head and said, "He's right, Dall. No man should ever take on a demon if he has doubts about his ability to draw on the name of our Lord for strength. I know it's a sour testament to our lack of faith, but it's better to admit that shortcoming than to forge ahead in arrogance and false hope and get ourselves killed. You and I will talk about this demon after the meeting. I am bishop now. This unclean spirit is my responsibility, and he will not prevail."

After several more minutes of discussion, it was decided that even though it was the Amish way to handle their own problems and not associate with the English, this was a special circumstance. Someone would go to the county sheriff for help. Since it was federal agents who were working with Gaal, approaching the F.B.I. was out of the question.

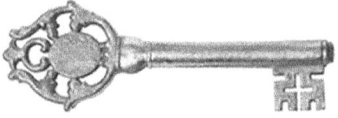

"I am he that liveth, and was dead; and behold, I am alive for evermore, Amen; and have the keys of hell and of death." **Revelation 1:18**

Dall waited patiently in the lobby while Sheriff Holden and Chief Deputy Thurman conferred. When the secretary said he could go in, he walked into the sheriff's office. To his surprise, he found Curly seated in the chair beside the one that he was to take. Curly was visibly shaken and had just finished a hard cry. Dall knew he had gotten Curly in trouble.

Casey said, "Have a seat, Dall. We were just explaining the need for proper protocol to Curly. He told us that you called him the night he arrested Agent Waters. Now, although we deeply appreciate your tip, we would appreciate it if you would go through us next time. Curly is eager to please, but we care about his safety. As proud of him as we are, we want him to have proper back-up next time he goes to make a felony arrest."

Dall leaned over and patted Curly on the back. "I'm sorry, Curly. The chief deputy is right. It was careless of me to pull you into this without going through them." Dall turned toward Casey and said, "I apologize for that chief deputy. You're right. But this was my fault. Please don't be too hard on Curly. I have a lot more experience than him and should have known better."

Sheriff Holden said, "Don't worry, Dall. We're not going to cook him and eat him. We just want everyone to work together. And we especially don't want Curly to get hurt. And if he runs up against that little arm-breaker, he'll be killed for sure. This is a federal investigation, and we're just a local sheriff's office. The feds have ordered us to stay out of this matter, so we're hard-pressed to stick our noses in it. We really went out on a limb by arresting Waters."

Dall asked, "Oh, yes, Waters. How did his arraignment go?"

It was at this point that Dall realized that Curly hadn't been crying over the chief deputy's chastising. He broke into tears again and said, "Oh Dall! It's horrible! I've never seen anything like it! You've got to see his body!"

Dall stood in shock. "He's dead? What happened?"

The sheriff stood and took his hat of the hat-rack. He said, "No, Dall, he's not dead. But since you're the undercover for the F.B.I. in this case, I guess it's okay to show you. You're technically a federal agent. Come on." The sheriff, chief deputy and Curly all got in the sheriff's car and drove Dall to the hospital.

Curly raved all the way to the hospital about the horrible condition of Waters. Dall tried not to hurt his feelings, but he didn't believe a word that Curly had said. As they arrived at the hospital, Sheriff Holden told Curly to be quiet so they could talk. The sheriff said, "Dall, for all intents and purposes, Agent Waters is dead. We've secured the cooperation of the hospital administrator, and we're keeping Waters in seclusion. The staff has got some big-shot pathologists flying in from the east to examine him."

They were met by the doctor in the hall as they approached Waters' private room. After Dall had been introduced, the doctor explained his findings. "As soon as we received Mr. Waters, we immediately ran a

C.A.T. scan to find out what had happened to him. The scan showed that there is solid bone where his ear canals, mouth and eye socket had been. There are no ears, teeth, tongue, eyes, nothing. The only feature in the solid mass of bone that is his face is a small protrusion that used to be his nose, with a single nasal passage leading to his lungs. His face is a solid mass of bone. And he has no hands or arms below the elbows."

Dall looked at the door of Waters' room in disbelief and walked in. The doctor and sheriff followed. He walked up to Waters' bed and put his hand on Waters' leg to gauge his response. Waters turned his head toward Dall, but had no idea who he was. The doctor said. "He can't hear or see anything. He has no idea how to communicate. Without his eyes, ears or hands, he's essentially incapable of receiving or sending any communication of any kind. And his arms are just short stumps. Everything at the elbows and below is gone as though they never existed. As soon as he arrived here, we installed a stomach tube so we could keep him alive by pouring nutrition drinks directly into his stomach, but it's going to take a therapist with lots of time on their hands to get him to where he can communicate, if it can be done at all."

Dall turned away in shock. The sheriff took him by the arm and said, "Come on, Dall, let's go talk."

He led Dall to a conference room, and Curly and the chief deputy followed. When all were seated, the sheriff said. "Dall, we all know what happened to Waters. The chief deputy and I didn't like him much, but no one could predict that this would happen. He had been in front of Judge Pettigrew only a few minutes before he screamed, so there are plenty of witnesses who know he was normal only a few minutes earlier. Alterations to the human body like these could not have healed in a few minutes. Can you help us here?"

Dall looked at Sheriff Holden, then nodded. "Has the F.B.I. been by to see him?"

Sheriff Holden said, "No. Smith visited him the night before his arraignment. The jailers couldn't hear everything that was said over the monitor, but it was apparent that they were arguing. I suspect that Waters was going to blow the whistle on the investigation. I'm sure the feds will deny any knowledge of him now."

Dall sighed heavily. "I didn't like the guy, but I wouldn't wish this on anyone. I can't imagine the torture that he's going through." After a long pause, Dall said, "I guess there's nothing to be gained by withholding information at this point. The investigation has collapsed and I'm on the run." Chief Deputy Thurman asked, "On the run? You?"

"Yes. You remember the girl that I was with? Well, she and I were put in the Amish district to locate a killer. There had been two murders in the district, and the F.B.I. was playing up the hate-crime and serial murder angles to justify going in and taking the investigation away from you. There was another reason they wanted inside that district; a much bigger reason."

Sheriff Holden held up his arm with the cast on it. "Yeah, we know. It has something to do with that little girl that broke my arm."

Dall nodded. "Yes, it does. That little girl was a manifestation of a demon. This demon has played an important role in world history, and has in the past tried to manipulate powerful men."

Casey asked, "Why?"

Dall shrugged his shoulders. "I don't expect any of you to believe this, but this demon is the leader of a large faction of the fallen angels here on earth. They fell from grace and were cast out of Heaven with Satan when he tried to elevate himself to an equal status with God. Many of those fallen angels realized that they'd made a mistake and they want to somehow redeem themselves and avoid the lake of fire spoken of in the book of Revelations."

Casey said, "I don't find it hard to believe. I'm a believer anyway and have known for years that there are demons here on earth carrying out Satan's mission. After that little girl broke the sheriff's arm I'll believe about anything."

Sheriff Holden said, "You won't get any debate from me, Dall; my arm won't be the same for months. How can we help?"

Dall said, "Well, this brings me to the reason that I've contacted you. I'm here on behalf of the leaders in the Amish district. There have been three more of them killed. And it appears that the F.B.I. is behind it."

Casey and the sheriff perked up. Casey asked, "How?"

Dall said, "The girl that I went undercover with was Sandy Parsons. She was a field agent out of the Phoenix office. The F.B.I. has employed the services of a man named Milton Sveade. He's an expert on world religions and had worked with the allies during World War II. The allies had discovered that the Germans had established contact with a demon that was going to help them win the war. When that failed, the allies wanted to talk to this demon and see if there was some way to use him and his followers to bring future conflicts to an outcome favorable to the

United States. This demon's name is Gaal. He has taken over Sandy's body and is using her to kill everyone who stands in his way. He wants to form an alliance with the U.S. military and the President to combat the Antichrist that will come to power at the beginning of the Tribulation. He and his followers think that if they can defeat the Antichrist and Satan, maybe God will provide a means of redemption for them."

Sheriff Holden shook his head. "Man, that's complex. A guy could go crazy trying to figure out all the possibilities with that scenario. Isn't the future set in stone? Isn't that all outlined in books like Daniel and Revelations?"

"I'm no expert, Sheriff, but I think so. It's in Revelations and a few other books. For all we know, Gaal could be Satan himself. I've secured the help of the district bishop, and he's pretty smart about these things. He agrees with me that mortal men are not capable of matching wits with a demon. A demon can take any form he wants, and there's no way to confirm what he says. All we have is scripture to verify what they say. And the bishop and I believe that God recorded the events in Revelation through the pen of John the Epistle because He had already set the future in stone. That includes the fate of the fallen angels and non-believing mortals. I guess it's possible for God to change His mind, but He obviously has known about Gaal and his followers wanting redemption for centuries. If He had any plans of redeeming them, surely He would have said so in the Bible. I don't know, but I don't trust this demon. He's killed people and indwelled Sandy. I've got to find a way to help her."

Curly was completely lost. When Dall looked at him, Curly corrected his dumfounded stare and closed his wide-opened mouth. Thurman asked, "How can we help? You know if the feds find out that we're tampering with their investigation, we'll be up on charges in federal court."

Dall thought for a few seconds, then said, "Sandy is too strong. She almost killed me and Abel Straus. The bishop and elders met last night and asked me to come to you for help. The F.B.I. has snipers who are taking out anyone that Gaal sees as a threat, so you can't come in there without being shot. Can you contact the St. Louis office and ask them to look at the two bodies that you have in the morgue? If they see Mr. Bowlin and Bishop Gordan, then look at Waters, maybe they'll realize that the secrecy of the investigation is compromised. If they relay that information to the director, maybe they'll pull the plug on the investigation to avoid unfavorable publicity and a congressional hearing. Then Gaal will have no one to do his bidding in Washington."

Casey said, "You know that won't work. They'll hustle Gaal out of the district and bury the whole thing. I'm sure the project is deep black."

Dall said, "Not if you threaten to go to the press. They won't want the national exposure. They certainly won't want to explain themselves to congress."

Casey perked up. "Yeah, they'll have to back off. We've got an ace up our sleeve. We have Waters, and they have no idea where he is. The press would have a field day with him."

Dall said, "True, even if Gaal kills him, you'll still have the body. That'll shut the F.B.I. down, but how can I get Sandy back?"

No one had an answer. Sheriff Holden finally said, "I'm sorry, Dall. Exorcism is out of my league. She may just be one of the casualties that we can't do anything about, like Waters."

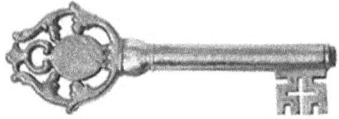

"I am he that liveth, and was dead; and behold, I am alive for evermore, Amen; and have the keys of hell and of death." **Revelation 1:18**

Abel groaned as he shifted his weight to his other side. Every movement was agonizing. Dory and Lilly Dresselhaus were tending to his injuries, but without the benefit of prescription pain-killers, he was forced to suffer with whatever over-the-counter meds and home-spun concoctions that Lilly could come up with.

Dory was trying to keep house, take care of the family and relay Abel's instructions for the farm work to Isaac. She greatly appreciated Lilly's help.

Evening was approaching and Abel wanted to talk to Isaac. It was only when Dory called for him that she discovered that he was missing.

Dall had made his way through the open country to Abel's farm. As he eased up to the back porch he heard the commotion from inside the house. Abel was struggling to get his boots on, and Lilly and Dory were pleading with him to stay in bed.

Dall knocked on the back screen door and waited to be invited in. Dory ran to the door and pushed it open when she saw him. "Dall! Come in here! Please talk some sense into this stubborn man! He's not in any shape to be out of bed!"

Dall hurried to Abel. He knew Abel was hurting and searched for a place that he could put his hand that would not cause him excruciating pain. He gently put his hand on Abel's arm and said, "Abel, what's so important that you have to go out? You should be in bed."

Abel had been hounded by the women and was in no mood to explain himself. He growled, "Isaac has gone out! It's getting dark and he'll surely run into those soldiers! If he meets Gaal, he'll be killed for sure!"

Dall looked at Dory. "Why? Why would he go out, Dory? Doesn't he know how dangerous it is to be out at night?"

Dory began to cry and said, "Yes, he does, but he's not been thinking straight lately. He's been angry with Dad and does just the opposite of what Dad says, just to annoy him."

Dall said, "I'll go look for him, Abel. You get back in bed."

Abel stood and towered over Dall. "No! I know where he's gone. I'm going after him. He won't listen to you. He'll do what I say."

Since Dall couldn't talk sense to Abel, he went along to help if he could. As they walked, Abel said, "I think he's gone to Massey's pond. That's where he goes to meet up with Sampson Betendorf's daughter, Katie."

Abel limped noticeably from the bullet-hole in his leg and the pain in his neck and back. Dall put his arm around Abel's waist to help him. They heard the kids talking as they approached Massey's pond.

Abel hurt too much to be tactful. He was prepared for anything as he barged through the brush into the opening, even if he found them undressed. He didn't care. The stakes were too high to worry about hurt feelings.

Both were dressed, but Katie screamed before she could recognize Abel. He was so angry that he charged Isaac with clinched fists, ready to lash him for his disobedience.

Isaac stood his ground, although he was visibly shaken. Before Abel could reach him, Dall grabbed Abel's tensed arm and said, "Abel, let's think about this. Bishop Gordan is dead, so lashing may not be the right thing to do. You've been trying to lash him less; this may not be the time to start again."

Abel looked into the fearful eyes of his son. He swallowed his anger and said, "Isaac, this is the worst possible time to be out at night! You know what happened to me! We've talked about the power of this demon that haunts our farms, and you've dared to risk Katie's life by bringing her here!"

Isaac had no defense. Katie spoke up and said, "It's my fault, Brother Straus. I came by your farm while Isaac was cleaning stalls and asked him to bring me here. I should have stayed in the barn to talk to him."

Abel fought back the pain, but he could not hide the tears rolling down his face. He said, "That's right, young lady! You've put both of your lives at risk! I should be in bed and Isaac should be at the house protecting his family! Come on. I'm taking both of you home!"

Just as Katie was gathering up her cloak, Sampson Betendorf stormed into the clearing. Anger shot from his eyes, and Abel knew how uncontrollable Sampson could be when he was angry. Sampson started toward Isaac, and this time Isaac had the good sense to back away. As painful as it was, Abel hurried to get between them so Sampson wouldn't hurt Isaac. He got in front of Sampson and put both hands in Sampson's chest. He pleaded, "Please! Brother Sampson, please! I'm not in any condition to stop you tonight, but please, if our friendship has ever meant anything to you, please spare Isaac. He loves Katie very much. He has not taken her virtues."

Dall also stepped in front of Sampson. He said, "Sampson, we've got a much bigger problem here tonight. We're all in danger. Please, help us get the kids home before we're all discovered by the rangers. None of us are equipped to handle them and Gaal."

Sampson finally took his angry glare off Isaac and looked into the Abel's watery eyes. He slowly nodded his head and said, "Kids, let's get home. Isaac, you and I will talk about this. When your father is not in so much pain, we will talk, then meet with the elders and discuss your punishment. You may try your father's patience, but you've tested mine for the last time."

With that, all turned to leave. As they reached the edge of the clearing, all stopped in shock as they were confronted by Sandy. Gaal said, "LET'S NOT LEAVE SO SOON. WERE YOU SO FOOLISH AS TO THINK THAT YOU COULD LEAVE YOUR HOMES WITHOUT MY LEGION KNOWING OF YOUR TRAVELS? WE HAVE MORE TO DISCUSS."

All were stunned to find themselves facing Sandy, Smith and two rangers with fully loaded M-14s. Dall, Abel and Samson pushed the kids behind them and stood between them and Sandy. Abel said, "Take me and let the others go."

Sandy smiled and shook her head as a gentle night breeze blew her long blond hair off her shoulders. In the glow of the moonlight Dall thought she had never looked more beautiful. It was so hard to believe that she was capable of ripping all three men to pieces. Gaal said, "IT IS NOT YOU THAT I WANT. I SHOULD KILL YOU ALL, BUT IT HAS BEEN POINTED OUT TO ME THAT I MAY HAVE KILLED TOO MANY PEOPLE ALREADY, AND THAT ANY MORE KILLING MAY JEOPARDIZE OUR CHANCES OF SECURING A REDEMPTIVE PROVISION FROM OUR LORD."

She pointed to the rangers and said, "YOU TWO TAKE THE CHILDREN AND ESCORT THEM HOME. SEE THAT THEY ARRIVE SAFELY. NO HARM IS TO COME TO THEM."

As the rangers moved toward Isaac and Katie, Abel stepped into them and grabbed one by his jacket. The ranger quickly gave Abel a sharp butt-stroke with the rifle across the face. The pain of the blow sent spasms down Abel's spine, landing him flat on his back in the dirt.

Seeing that the ranger intended to empty a magazine into Abel if he resisted again, Dall stepped forward and said, "No, Gaal. It's me you want. Let the others go."

Sandy circled Dall slowly and smiled as she sized him up. Gaal said, "YES, DALL, IT IS YOU THAT I WANT. I'LL SPARE THE OTHERS IF YOU COME. YOU KNOW ME. MY WORDS CAN BE TRUSTED."

Dall turned to Sampson. He could see that Sampson was completely enraged at the rough treatment that the ranger had dealt Abel. His fists were clinched and he was leaning forward on the balls of his feet, ready to lunge. He was a man of incredible strength and entirely capable of killing either of the rangers with his bare hands, but Dall knew he would be chopped to pieces before he could lay a hand on one of them. Even if he managed to disarm and incapacitate the rangers, Gaal could pull Sampson's massive body apart in seconds and not break a sweat.

Dall hurried to Sampson and said, "No, Sampson! This is not your fight. This is between me and Gaal. Go to Abel. Help him home to Dory and Lilly."

Sampson glared angrily at Sandy, but quickly lost his nerve when she glared back into his eyes and slowly started toward him.
He bent over and helped Abel to his feet, then put his arm around Abel's waist for additional support.

Dall looked at Smith and said, "I guess you're not running things anymore, Smith. What's your role now?"

Smith shrugged his shoulders and said, "I serve Gaal now. We've contacted some key members of the joint chiefs and they're ready to meet Gaal. There's really nothing that anyone can do to stop it now. Our mission is complete. We're finally going to get our alliance with a large portion of the angelic realm and the protection that Gaal and all of his fallen can give us against the Antichrist, and he and his followers are going to get their good works to lay at God's feet when they ask Him for redemption."

Dall said, "There's a lot of ifs in this whole thing, Smith. If they can convince the joint chiefs to go along with the alliance. If they can convince the President to accept it. If they can defeat Satan and his loyal followers. If they can get God to accept their good works. If God hasn't already determined their fate as written in Revelations. Lots of ifs Smith."

Sandy circled Dall and said, "Yes, Dall, lots of ifs. The joint chiefs and the President are not a worry. They'll be so enamored with the fact that demons are real and that they can use us against future enemies that they'll fall all over themselves to welcome us. But God is the unpredictable element here. Yes, it is true, He has preordained our fate, but your finite minds can only comprehend what you read in scripture. There is much that you cannot know. For example, Satan goes back and forth to Heaven and talks to God, as stated in the first chapter of Job. Although most of their conversations consist of Satan bringing accusations against the saints, and Jesus interceding on their behalf, there are other things that are discussed. If God would consider our redemption, it would not necessarily be written in scripture if it did not pertain to man. I also have spoken with the Father on many occasions. I believe He will grant us our wish."

Dall pivoted and kept Sandy in sight. He didn't want her to have his back. He asked, "Then if your mission is a success, what do you need with me and Sandy? Let us go."

Gaal laughed with an evil grunt. "No, Dall, I need a vessel like Sandy. She'll present me in the best possible light. And you! You cannot be allowed to betray me. You will not go away quietly. You can't. You are a dedicated believer, and you will never let me exist in peace. You will devote your life to

DESTROYING MY ALLIANCE WITH AMERICA. I HAVE PROMISED MY FOLLOWERS THAT WE WILL KEEP OUR SINS TO A MINIMUM TO KEEP FROM ANGERING THE FATHER, BUT YOU ARE A NECESSARY SIN. YOU MUST DIE."

Gaal started toward Dall, and Sandy began her assault on Gaal from within. She rose up and screamed loud as she could for him to stop. She struggled with Gaal with all her strength to take control of her body.

Dall pulled the automatic pistol from the back of his waistband and leveled it at Sandy. If it had been anyone else, he would have emptied the magazine into them and spoiled Gaal's plans.

He leveled the pistol at Sandy, but couldn't pull the trigger. If he killed Sandy, Gaal would simply inhabit someone else and pursue his alliance with the government. He had to find another way to save her.

Sandy smiled as she gently took the pistol from Dall's hand. She threw it in the brush and back-handed Dall hard across the face. The blow knocked him backward, landing him on his back unconscious. She picked him up in a fireman's carry and carried him to the well where he'd found the bodies of Preacher Litchfield and the missing young people. Deep inside her, there raged a war of wills between Sandy and Gaal.

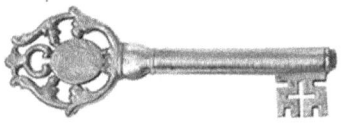

"I am he that liveth, and was dead; and behold, I am alive for evermore, Amen; and have the keys of hell and of death." **Revelation 1:18**

Sampson was getting tired from carrying Abel and was glad when Abel regained his senses enough to support his own weight. Both sensed the other's concern for Isaac and Katie as they walked. They both slowed the pace so the kids could put some distance between them and the rangers.

Abel and Sampson listened intently to the conversation between the rangers. It was apparent that they did not intend to let them live, in spite of Gaal's directions. Abel whispered to Sampson, "We've got to take these English men, Brother Sampson. It'll mean our deaths, but Isaac and Katie deserve to live their lives."

Sampson agreed. "Yes, Brother. We're both recipients of the grace and righteousness of God through the sacrifice of His son, Jesus Christ.

We've lived our lives, and our reward awaits us in our Father's Kingdom. I look forward to living close to you in Paradise, brother."

Both men had been struggling along with their arms around each other to support Abel's broken frame. The rangers had grown tired of the slow pace and prodded the men with the flash suppressors on the ends of their muzzles. That was the break that Abel and Sampson needed. They bid each other farewell with a pat on the back, then turned together and charged the rangers. They normally wouldn't have had a chance, but the rangers had become complacent and had gotten too close. They were confident that neither farmer posed a threat.

Abel was the one who was injured, and the rangers showed him no respect. As far as they were concerned, he was incapable of hurting anyone. To their surprise he fought through his pain and charged with the ferocity of a lion. He ran over the ranger, wrapping his arms around him in a bear hug. As he drove him backward, the ranger squeezed the trigger, but Abel was already past the muzzle. The burst went into the air as Abel picked him up and body slammed him to the ground with Abel's entire weight crashing down on him. Abel felt the ranger's ribcage break. To put some finality to the matter, Abel placed his forehead against the ranger's nose and crushed his face with his head. The ranger let out a loud grunt as all the air was forced from his lungs, then never moved a muscle.

The second ranger was too preoccupied with Samson to help the first. Samson was slightly slower than Abel, and did not get past the ranger's muzzle before the ranger pulled the trigger. The split second before the rifle discharged Samson pushed the muzzle aside and the five-round burst went past his ear as he charged the ranger.

With the force of a runaway buggy-mare, Samson hit the ranger with his broad chest, knocking the rifle from his hands. He encircled the ranger with his arms and ran him into a tree. He then interlaced his fingers and bear-hugged the smaller man with all the force that he could muster. The ranger spit up blood all over Sampson's shoulder as his ribs and back broke. When Sampson felt the man go limp and heard no more bones breaking, he let the man collapse to the ground.

Sampson stood over the ranger, panting hard from the exhilaration of the fight. He looked Heavenward and yelled, "Yes! Gracious Lord and Savior! Your mercy abounds!"

When he looked around to see how Abel had fared, he saw Abel rolling off the ranger and groaning in pain. He hurried to him and knelt beside him. "Abel, my brother, can you walk?"

Abel didn't try to get up. He said, "Let me lay here, Sampson. Go on and make sure the kids get home okay."

Sampson didn't have a chance to leave. Both kids had heard the commotion and ran back to them. They helped Abel to his feet and dusted off his shirt and trousers. Abel said, "I'm okay, kids. Go on to the house. Isaac, load your gun and protect everyone. We'll be along later."

The kids hurried toward the house, but Sampson looked at Abel and asked, "Why are we not going home?"

Abel hung his head and rubbed the back of his neck. "Sampson, do you remember the lashing that we gave Dall?"

Sampson lowered his head and said ashamedly, "Yes. I regret that."

Abel nodded his head and said, "As do I. Dall is being led to his death as we speak. I can't in good conscience go to the comfort of my soft bed knowing that Dall is being killed. I tried to whip that demon once, but I was weak in my faith. He hurt me bad, but that doesn't hurt as much as knowing that I owe Dall a debt for wrongly lashing him, and that I'm letting him down when he needs me most. He's an Englisher, but he's a believer in the same God that I worship. That makes him a brother. I want another shot at that demon. This time I'm going to whip that little girl like a low-down, no-good, yellow-bellied, egg-sucking dog."

Sampson smiled and said, "It's a little humbling for a man our size to take a lashing from a woman, isn't it?"

Abel nodded. "Yes, brother, but that woman has the strength of ten men. I now realize that Gaal is not alone inside her. There are many in there with him. But many or one, Dall befriended me, and I can't let a friend go to his death alone. That is not the Amish way. We're men of God, and we don't let a brother go to his destruction alone if possible. God tells us that when two or more believers assemble and pray in His name, He will be there and answer our prayers. Bishop Gordan is gone and Bishop Clevenger is in charge now. He would tell me to go to Dall. You can go if you want, but Dall is our brother and I'm going to help him."

Sampson looked indignantly at Abel and asked, "And what am I? I'm as much a brother to Dall as you are! I'll come with you and we'll both pray to God to help us defeat this fallen devil! We two combined will surely receive the grace of the Father! And besides, you're not in any condition to help anyone!"

Abel looked over at the ranger that he had just crushed. Sampson looked also, then said, "Well, okay, maybe you are, but that demon will be a lot tougher than those little girly-men. Come on; let's go see who's got the stronger God, that demon or us."

Both men picked up the rangers' rifles. Abel was able to find the magazine release lever and removed the half-empty magazine. He pitched it aside, then bent over and opened the ranger's magazine pack. He removed a loaded magazine and inserted it in the rifle.

Sampson had never handled an M-14 before, and fumbled with it, searching for the magazine release. When he couldn't get the magazine out, he searched for the safety. As he pushed and prodded each lever and button, he had finally put his finger inside the trigger guard to see if the safety was on. He pulled the trigger by mistake and lit up the night as the rifle emptied the remaining rounds in the magazine. He didn't have a good grip on the rifle and it trampled all over him before he could regain his grip and throw it to the ground.

Abel covered his head as the rifle danced around in Sampson's arms. Every fired round caused the rifle to jump violently, and Sampson could never get it under control. When it hit the ground with the bolt locked open, Abel uncovered his head and said in a frightened tone, "Brother Sampson! Your father certainly failed you in the lessons of firearms safety! I've already been shot once! Do you mind not doing that?"

The spanking that Sampson had just taken from the rifle had scared him and he heaved as he tried to catch his breath. He glared wide-eyed at Abel and panted, "Damnation, Abel! That cursed English contraption almost ate me alive! How do you work that confounded thing?"

Abel picked up the rifle and put in a loaded magazine. He showed Sampson how to operate it, then both headed off after Dall.

"I am he that liveth, and was dead; and behold, I am alive for evermore, Amen; and have the keys of hell and of death." **Revelation 1:18**

Dall awoke and found himself lying on the ground by the well casing. The stench from the rotting bodies that used to occupy the well still emanated from its depths. He knew he would soon be its only occupant. He shook the stars out of his head and looked into Sandy's dark eyes. He then looked around, but Smith was not there. Sandy bent over him and Gaal said, "GLAD YOU COULD JOIN US AGAIN, DALL. SANDY AND I WERE HAVING QUITE A HEATED DISCUSSION ABOUT YOU."

Dall struggled to a seated position and rubbed his neck. "I hope she's winning. I don't relish the idea of going back in the well."

Sandy stood erect and put her hands on her hips. Gaal said, "WELL, DALL, I'D LIKE TO SAY THAT DEPENDS ON YOU. SANDY HAS GRACIOUSLY CONSENTED TO GO ALONG WITH ME IF I WILL SPARE YOUR LIFE. SHE SEEMS TO THINK IF YOU PROMISED TO KEEP YOUR MOUTH SHUT, THAT I COULD TRUST YOU AND LET YOU LIVE. BUT YOU'RE A BELIEVER. YOU CAN'T ALLOW ME TO LEAVE THIS DISTRICT WITH HER, CAN YOU?"

Dall sighed deeply. "No. No, Gaal, I can't. As believable as your story seems, you're a dark spirit. It's contrary to your nature to tell the truth. And long before God ever laid the foundations of the earth or created the universe, He predetermined the course of mankind and angels. The events written in the Bible were set in stone by Him, and nothing you do will ever change one letter of Revelations. You and the rest of the demonic world will spend eternity in the lake of fire. This whole redemption and alliance scenario is nothing but a scam to trick mankind and further Satan's plans. As a matter of fact, I suspect that you're really Satan himself."

Gaal exploded in anger. Sandy grabbed a mature pine tree and ripped it up by its roots. She threw it at Dall and broke a chunk out of the concrete casing of the well when Dall rolled out of the way.
Sandy stormed up to Dall and grabbed his shirt. She jerked him to his feet and pulled him close. Gaal yelled, "THE PRINCE OF THE AIR WOULD HAVE KILLED YOU A LONG TIME AGO! I'VE BEEN PATIENT WITH BOTH OF YOU LONG ENOUGH! I WANT SANDY, BUT THIS COVENANT IS GOING TO TAKE PLACE WITH OR WITHOUT HER HELP! I REGRET HAVING TO ADD ONE MORE SIN TO MY ACCOUNT, BUT GOD WILL FORGIVE ALL OUR SINS IF HE'LL FORGIVE THE ORIGINAL ONE!"

Dall cried out in pain as Sandy grabbed his shoulder and began to pull him apart. She stopped suddenly when Abel yelled from behind her, "Release my brother!"

Dall collapsed to the ground in pain. Sandy turned and glared at Abel, then pointed her finger at him. "I SPARED YOU LAST TIME, YOU IGNORANT PEASANT! YOU'LL BE IN THE ARMS OF YOUR GOD TONIGHT!"

Abel yelled through gritted teeth, "Demon, you inhabit a body that is not yours! It is not my desire to kill that child, but I won't let you hurt anyone else!"

Gaal snarled, "THIS CHILD WILL LIVE! TURN YOUR WEAPONS ON YOURSELVES AND BE SPARED GREAT PAIN!"

Abel pulled the bolt-handle of his rifle to the rear, then let it go, picking up a round out of the magazine and ramming it into the chamber. He leveled the M-14 at Sandy as she charged. Dall yelled at Sampson and Abel to not shoot, but they were gripped with fear and heard only their heavy breathing and thumping hearts.

Abel gripped the rifle and held it tight under his arm, then used his left hand to push down on the forearm. He pulled the trigger and pushed the barrel down so it wouldn't rise while being fired in the full-auto mode.

Sampson copied Abel's technique and fired his rifle as well. In four seconds, both rifles had spit out forty rounds that would have shredded any other creature on earth.

Sandy stopped her advance and staggered backward as the hollow-points ripped large pieces of flesh from her body. Dall saw leaves and pieces of bark fly from the trees behind her, and knew she could never survive such carnage.

A small column of smoke rose from muzzles as the bolts locked open, signaling empty magazines. Abel and Sampson stared in total shock at Sandy. Dall struggled to his feet and gasped as Sandy levitated to her feet and looked down at the massive injuries to her body. To everyone's shock, she looked up at the stars and held her palms upward. The streams of blood stopped flowing, the massive holes in her front and back closed and the bloodstains on her clothes vanished. Sampson's voice trembled as he asked, "Abel, is now a good time to pray?"

Abel now resolved himself to the fact that he was about to meet his Savior. He said solemnly, "Yes, brother, if we have time."

Both men threw the rifles aside and sprinted in a full charge at Sandy as they uttered a brief prayer for God's grace and mercy.

Seeing that the men were calling on the name of Jesus, Gaal panicked and charged them at full-speed. He sensed their faith and knew they now had the power to expel him. In the blink of an eye, Sandy closed the twenty feet and collided full-force with seven-hundred pounds of Amish muscle.

Her one hundred and thirty pounds was no match for the two farmers. They hit her with their chests and wrapped their arms around her as they drove her backward to the ground and crushed her under their collective weight. Dall strained to see through the cloud of dust to determine how badly Sandy was hurt.

To his surprise, Sandy mustered the strength to throw Abel and Sampson off her. They flew six feet in the air and landed ten feet away. Both were shaking the stars out of their heads as they struggled to their feet to meet her attack.

Sandy again levitated to her feet and charged the stunned farmers. She punched Abel in the chest, knocking him backward ten more feet against a tree. He grunted hard as the wind was knocked from his lungs and blood again oozed from his wounded leg.

Samson saw the blow that Abel had taken and exploded in anger. Abel was in agony and could not take any more punishment. Sampson sprang to his feet and rushed to defend his brother. He grabbed Sandy by her neck and lifted her off the ground. He punched her hard as he could in the face, knocking her backward and landing her on her back only a foot away from Dall.

Seeing that this was the opportunity that he had been waiting for, Dall jumped on Sandy and grabbed her arms. Sampson charged in and threw his full weight on top of her. When Abel saw that the two men had managed to get Sandy on her back, he fought through his pain and charged her also. He jumped on her using his forehead to head-butt her hard in the face.

Sandy went limp for a second. Dall yelled. "We've got him!"

Sampson yelled, "Now, Abel, cast him out of the girl!"

Abel was now spitting up blood from the collapsed lung that his fractured rib had punctured. He spewed blood as he prayed. But before he could utter the Lords name, Sandy's eyes popped open and she sprang to life. Gaal screamed something in an ancient dialect, then gave Dall a murderous glare.

Like a kick from a mule, she punched Dall in the face, knocking him off her. She then used her free arm to grab Abel by the throat so he could not complete his command for Gaal to leave her. Abel choked as she raised her foot and put it in the middle of his chest. With a hard kick she threw him ten feet backward, turning him upside down and landing him hard on his head and neck. This was the exact same fall that he had taken the first time he'd fought Sandy. His already-injured spinal cord could not take the strain. His neck broke, killing him instantly.

When Sampson saw Abel collapse in an unnatural heap after landing on his head, he realized that Abel was dead. Sampson's rage drove him to insanity. Seeing that he was all alone in the fight, Samson began punching Sandy in the face as hard as he could with his massive fists. She showed no ill effects and slowly stood while hanging on to Sampson's shirt so he could not escape.

He continued to batter her face with every ounce of strength he could muster, but each blow merely turned her head briefly. She immediately recovered and looked lazily into his eyes. She felt nothing from his crushing blows.

Sampson was heaving from exhaustion and fear. This strategy wasn't working. He threw one last desperate punch, but Sandy seized his fist and grabbed his arm, then broke it as if it were a small twig. With his arm dangling at an unnatural right-angle, Sampson collapsed to his knees and cradled his arm as he rocked back and forth in pain and tried to stop the profuse bleeding from the jagged bone that had protruded through the skin.

Gaal cleared his throat and brushed the dirt from Sandy's clothes. Dall was regaining consciousness as he said, "It is over, Dall. I offer you this victory as evidence that God has blessed our cause. You three believers did your best to defeat me and I have prevailed. The God who created everything that is and set the universe in motion has not honored your request. I still am and I still have Sandy. This was preordained by our Lord before the foundations of the earth were set. I and all of my fallen now know that we will defeat Satan and be spared the lake of fire. If it were not to be so, you would have defeated me."

Sampson quivered in pain and looked at Dall. Dall had no answers and shook his head in defeat as he dropped his stare to the ground. Both men and Gaal were completely shocked when another man stepped into the clearing. The man was familiar to all, but none could believe the transformation that he had undergone. Once they'd looked through the gentle glow of his youthful face, they could see that it was Bishop Clevenger.

The bishop no longer bent over and shuffled his feet in arthritic stiffness. He walked gracefully with a youthful limberness, and stood upright in complete righteous indignation at the beating that the three believers had taken. In a strong voice, he said, "Dall and Sampson, your faith was strong tonight. Don't listen to this deceiver. Your defeat was not an indictment of your cause. God was with you, but you were just a little slow in calling His name. Rather than taking this demon to God in the first place, you tried to overcome him with your own strength. You tried to kill him with your weapons rather than rely on the power of God Himself."

Dall said, "I don't believe anything Gaal says, Bishop! It's his nature to lie!"

Bishop Clevenger moved to keep Sandy in front of him as she circled him, searching for the most opportune time to jump. He said, "You're right, Dall. He is a liar. I've dealt with this devil before. He and I are old acquaintances. Once he defeats Satan, he'll be just like Satan and continue to deceive mankind. He'll not approach God for forgiveness, but be corrupted with Satan's power and continue to try to overthrow God, just as Satan has. But this demon will not prevail, and the evidence of that is God's intercession now through an unworthy vessel such as me."

Gaal raged in anger. He screamed as Sandy charged the bishop. Bishop Clevenger smiled with a calm, confident bearing and charged Sandy with the speed and agility of an NFL linebacker. If Sandy had the strength of a legion of demons, elderly and crippled old Bishop Clevenger had the strength of the one true God. Sandy grabbed the bishop by his chest, but Bishop Clevenger grabbed her by the throat and bent her backward till she was on her knees. Gaal gurgled and, for the first time, Dall saw stark fear in his eyes. Bishop Clevenger said, "Beast, I would pull you from limb to limb, but it is my desire to preserve the body of this child. In the name of our Lord, Jesus Christ, I command you to leave this child. Be gone from this district and take your gathering with you!"

The entire countryside echoed as Gaal screamed in pain. He and his legion immediately left Sandy and she wilted in the death-grip of Bishop Clevenger. In the distance, Dall could see the moonlit gathering dissipate in the night air.

The bishop sensed Sandy's weakness and released her. Dall crawled to her and held her head as she regained consciousness.

Sandy slowly awoke and the effects of all the punishment that she had sustained as a result of Gaal's indwelling began to reappear. Every place where she had been punched by Dall, Abel and Sampson swelled and turned color. She began to gasp for air as the forty bullet-holes slowly opened and began to bleed. She then lost consciousness.

Dall panicked. He yelled for her to hang on as he tried to compress the wounds, but he could not compress them all. She was bleeding to death in his arms.

Bishop Clevenger gently knelt beside Dall and said, "Release the child, Dall."

As tears streamed down his face, he yelled, "She'll die!"

The bishop smiled and said in a calm voice. "Oh ye of little faith." He then placed his hand on Sandy's chest. As suddenly as her wounds had appeared, they faded away and she slowly awoke. When she saw Dall, she wrapped her arms around his neck and wept as he held her close.

Bishop Clevenger stood and smiled at them. He then turned his attention to Sampson. He knelt beside Sampson who was still rocking back and forth in pain. His face was pale from loss of blood and he was slipping into hemorrhagic shock.

With an angelic glow, Bishop Clevenger said, "Be of strong faith, brother." He gently took Sampson's broken arm in one hand and used the other to grip the dangling wrist. He pulled it out straight and placed the two broken ends together. As the ends of the bone came together, they made a muffled grinding noise. To Sampson's surprise, there was no pain. Bishop Clevenger then gripped the broken arm and said, "It is healed, brother."

Sampson stood and shook his arm to test its strength. It was as though it had never been broken. Dall helped Sandy to her feet as Sampson walked over and knelt beside Abel. He swelled with tears and touched Abel's chest. He looked into Abel's blank face and cried. He gently closed Abel's eyes, pushed his mouth shut and cradled his head close to his chest.

Abel had landed on his head, and his neck was displaced as the broken spinal cord pressed against the skin on the side of his neck in a hideous deformation. Bishop Clevenger knelt beside Sampson and said, "Don't grieve, Sampson; he only sleeps." He took Abel's head with both hands and pulled it out. He realigned the spinal cord and pushed Abel's head into its natural position. He then pressed his hand against Abel's face and said, "Awake."

Abel slowly opened his eyes and looked around. Samson wiped the tears from his eyes, smiled and said, "Welcome back, brother."

With Sampson's help, Abel struggled to his feet and stretched. He moved his head around in a circle to stretch the stiffness out of his neck. With disbelief in his voice, he said, "I can't believe it. I don't hurt anywhere. My neck, my back, my ribs, nothing hurts. He looked down and felt for the bullet wound in his leg, then said in total amazement, "My leg. It's healed."

Sampson said, "That's a miracle. You were dead."

Abel searched his memory and said, "Yes, I had to be. No man could see the things that I've seen while alive. I didn't have time to go inside, but I can tell you that from the outside looking in, the gates of Heaven are indescribable. I saw just a glimpse of Heaven through the gates. There aren't words to describe the beauty."

Sampson patted him on the back and said. "We'll both get a better look someday. Come on, let's go home. He turned to Dall and said, "Come, brother. You're no longer an English man. You became Amish tonight. Your home is with us."

As they turned to leave, Bishop Clevenger shuffled up to them. He'd lost his angelic glow and was again arthritic and crippled. He grabbed Sampson's arm for stability and said," Lend me your arm, brother. I'm afraid God has returned me to my former self."

Abel and Sampson picked up the M-14 rifles. Abel slung one over his shoulder, then he and Sampson held on to the ends of the other and placed it under Bishop Clevenger. He sat on the rifle and both men carried him out in a seated position.

FOURTEEN

SANDY HAD GREAT reservations about trusting the bureau. She called the S.A.C. at the St. Louis office and filed a complaint against Smith. After a short investigation, she was told that there was no one at the bureau by that name and title. She now knew that Smith was Army, which explained why he had such free access to Army rangers and had no allegiance to Waters, leaving him to rot in the silent darkness of his shell.

She became particularly suspicious when she asked about Dr. Sveade. The S.A.C. refused to discuss him. When she called Headquarters, the receptionist refused to let her talk to the director. She was always routed to an agent who kept insisting that she reveal her location and come in for debriefing.

After several failed attempts to get some answers, she mailed her resignation to the director along with her reasons for not trusting the bureau and a strong warning not to trust Smith, Sveade or any supernatural being that they tried to introduce. She said she had lost control of the C.I., Dall Roberts, and he had fled the district to parts unknown.

She and Dall hid out in the district for several weeks and moved from farm to farm. The F.B.I. sent several teams of agents into the district, searching for them under the pretense that Dall was a fugitive and was facing criminal charges in Houston. They were propagating the notion that he was dangerous and was keeping Agent Parsons against her will. The Amish knew better and refused to talk. The F.B.I. also found that as uncooperative as the Amish were, Sheriff Holden and Casey Thurman were even more uncooperative.

Bishop Clevenger had called a meeting of the entire district and declared that Dall and Sandy had completed their indoctrination into the Amish faith, then baptized them officially as Amish. With that, all the men had gathered at a site on the back corner of Abel's farm and erected a small cabin for Dall and Sandy. Two days before they moved in, the entire district showed up at Abel's house and watched Bishop Clevenger join them in marriage.

The F.B.I. may have known before the investigation that the Amish was a closed faith, but they had no idea how secretive they could be until they started asking for information about Dall and Sandy. They finally gave up and moved their search to other parts of the country.

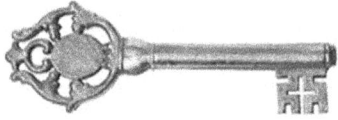

"I am he that liveth, and was dead; and behold, I am alive for evermore, Amen; and have the keys of hell and of death." **Revelation 1:18**

Dall washed up after a long day of building cross-fences with some of the other men for Bishop Gordan's widow. Much of their time was spent helping the widows, including Lilly Dresselhaus.

The sun had set below the horizon and a dim golden glow hovered over the distant trees. Dall sat in the old cane chair on the front porch of his new cabin and put his feet up on the railing. He was wearing only his boxers, and the evening breeze felt wonderful. He was so relieved to see that the gathering had gone, whoever they belonged to.

The screen door opened with a loud creak, and Sandy eased up behind him. She leaned over and handed him a glass of iced tea, then encircled his neck with her arms. She kissed his shoulders and said. "You need a shave, baby. You're starting to look Amish."

Dall patted her hand and said, "I like it here, Sandy. I know it's hard work and the pay isn't good, but we could have a good life here."

She sighed. "It's too close to the St. Louis office, Dall. Someone will spot us when we go to town. We can't hide out here forever. We'll have to move on to Oregon someday. We'll find work and start over."

"I know, honey, but not yet. Let's give the F.B.I. time to grow tired of looking for me. I'm really enjoying this life. I especially like the men here."

Sandy bent over him farther and slid her hand to his lap. She moaned and said, "Yeah, well, you won't like them so much if they find out how much we make love. We're not even trying to have children. They'll impose church discipline on us, then what will you do?"

"Not a chance. Things have lightened up since Bishop Clevenger took over. The men don't lash their kids as much, and I've heard the other men talk. They're all loving their wives more. I don't think anyone will judge us. And besides, that's between us. No one has any business knowing what we do in our own bed."

Sandy then stepped around in front of Dall. She was wearing a shear gown with nothing on under it. The glow of the sunset illuminated her anatomy as she said, "Then come on to bed, Brother Roberts, and let's see how many old Amish laws we can break."

Dall gulped the last of his tea and sat the glass in the railing. He stood and swept Sandy up in his arms, then carried her inside. Oregon beckoned, but for now there was no place that Dall would rather be than right here. He and Sandy had never loved anyone like they loved each other now.

Several hours later, Sandy awoke from a sound sleep as Dall gently eased out of bed and got dressed. He put on his boots and quietly left the house, making sure he did not let the screen door slam.

Having retained her old suspicious nature from her years with the bureau, Sandy could not resist the urge to follow him. She waited till he'd stepped off the porch, then quickly dressed.

By the time she had eased out of the house, Dall had disappeared into the darkness. She could only guess where he had gone. Since he had become such good friends with Tramp and Lady, it was a pretty good bet that he had gone to the Litchfield farm for a visit.

Sandy gave up trying to find Dall, and was resting by a corner-post in the shadows of the timber when she saw a large mass moving in the moonlight toward her. She knelt down and watched as Dall walked by within thirty feet of her leading Tramp and Lady by their reins. They were both sporting saddles and bridals from the Litchfield barn.

She wanted to confront him and remind him that horse stealing was still a crime, and knowing how vital horses were to the Amish farming operation, may even be a hanging offence in this district, but she decided to follow and see where he was taking them.

When Dall reached the gate that led to the road bordering the north side of the Straus farm, she saw a pickup truck with a horse trailer attached to it. As Dall led the mounts through the gate, the shrill voices of excited children echoed across the fields as the kids were introduced to their new pets. Sandy didn't know who the man and kids were, but aside from the horses, one silhouette was unmistakable. It was obvious that Curly had assisted Dall in the rescue of the horses.

Sandy hurried home and made sure she was undressed and in bed when Dall slipped quietly into the house. As he eased into bed, she wrapped her arms around him and asked, "Where have you been, Mister Roberts?"

Dall sighed and said, "Oh, I went for a walk and did some thinking."

Sandy sighed and mumbled, "Funny, you smell like horses."

Dall thought for a few seconds, then said, "Well, I did go visit Tramp and Lady."

Sandy patted his back side as she turned over to go to sleep. She said, "Yeah, I know. I hope they enjoy their new home." Dall sighed heavily and shook his head. He fluffed his pillow and realized it would take a long time to get the cop out of Sandy.

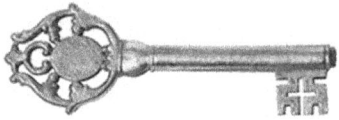

"I am he that liveth, and was dead; and behold, I am alive for evermore, Amen; and have the keys of hell and of death." **Revelation 1:18**

Shock and grief swept through the district as the information about the bodies from Massey's well was released by the sheriff's office. When the members realized that their disobedient teenagers had been killed rather than banished from the district, there was a general mistrust and hatred for Preachers Litchfield and Croft. The murders were laid at their feet since everyone had too much affection for Bishop Clevenger and the other elders and preachers.

After Isaac's testimony at the inquisition that he'd been attacked by Preacher Croft, Bishop Clevenger preached a two-hour sermon on balancing strict obedience to Scripture with love for others, then assured the members that that kind of lashing would no longer be tolerated.

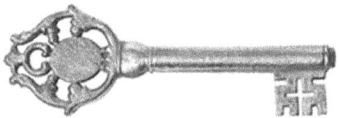

"I am he that liveth, and was dead; and behold, I am alive for evermore, Amen; and have the keys of hell and of death." **Revelation 1:18**

Weeks passed. Isaac could no longer accept the doctrine and constraints of the Amish faith. He moved a few miles north of the district and took work with an English man who owned a construction company, and was teaching Isaac the trade. Isaac was bunking in the English man's barn until he could afford his own apartment.

He had just washed up one evening when he looked down the road and saw a familiar horse and buggy coming his way. His anxiety rose, but there were some things that needed said and he was now a man. He would face his father with courage.

Abel pulled the young gilding to a stop in front of the barn-lot gate. He stepped out and waited for an invitation to come into Isaac's quarters, but Isaac came to the gate. Abel extended his hand to his son to show him that he was now a man in Abel's eyes.

Isaac refused to shake Abel's hand, which broke Abel's heart. He cleared his throat and said, "Son, I hope you'll listen to me for a few minutes. I've got some things to get off my chest."

Isaac braced for the worst. His father had been very vocal about Isaac's decision to leave the faith, and he feared that Abel's anger had not dissipated. He asked angrily, "Did you being your whip with you?"

Abel lowered his head and nodded. "Yes, if that's what it's going to take to resolve this, I've got it."

Isaac swelled with anger. He gritted his teeth and said, "Then you'd better use it, because I'm not coming back!"

Abel stared into the angry eyes of his son. He slowly turned to the buggy and retrieved the harness strap that had the buckle on the end; the one that he'd lashed Isaac with over a year ago. Isaac's heart sank when he saw the strap and recalled the pain that it had inflicted.

Abel stepped through the gate and stared at Isaac through lazy eyes with the strap hanging at his side. Isaac refused to back down and glared back at Abel. To his great shock, Abel slowly extended his hand and gave the strap to Isaac. He then removed his shirt, turned and put his hands on the gate. He bowed his head and waited for the lashing to begin.

Isaac choked with emotion. He gritted his teeth and clinched the strap hard as he shifted his weight back and forth on shaky legs. This was the moment that he had been waiting for.

Abel waited, but the lashing did not come. He slowly turned and found tears streaming down Isaac's face. After all these months, he couldn't bring himself to hurt his father.

Abel put his shirt back on and said, "Isaac, I came here today to balance the scales in our relationship. If a lashing will square things with us, then I want you to give it to me. I deserve it. I'm here to tell you that all those times I lashed you, I was wrong. We were laboring under some unbiblical laws of Bishop Gordan. Everything had to be done a certain way, and we couldn't deviate from that, no matter what. All that mattered was that we all complied with his laws. Bishop Clevenger has showed us that that is pure legalism. God does not condemn us for each and every little transgression. His grace covers us, and He doesn't sit up there in Heaven looking for every little opportunity to hammer us. He forgives believers for every sin, and expects us to treat each other with the same grace and love. As Amish, we should keep ourselves separate from the world, and strictly adhere to God's word, but we shouldn't become so obsessed with obedience to Scripture that we lose our compassion for others."

Isaac stared at the ground and now felt ashamed for even wanting to hurt his father. He dropped the strap and wept openly. Abel said, "I know why you left the faith, son, but I want you to know that even though the faith demands that we disown you, your mother and I will no longer allow that to bind us. You'll always be my son and I'll never abandon you. As long as I'm alive, I'll proclaim my love for you and my other children, no matter how far out of God's will they may stray. If anyone wants to challenge my priorities, I'll tell them. God forgives you and will accept you into Heaven, even if you're not Amish. And I will accept you as my son, even though you're not Amish. You are more important to me than being Amish. And if it gets me excommunicated, then so be it. I'll no longer be Amish."

Isaac choked back his tears. He finally said, "I can't come back, Dad."

Abel held his hand up and said, "That's okay, son. Every man has to live his life in his own way. I'm just telling you that I'm sorry for all the pain I caused and I want you in my life. Will you please come over and see us from time to time? Your mother misses you terribly. Judith and baby Jack cry for you every night when we pray. Abel looked over Isaac's head at the horizon and choked back his emotions as he wrestled with the awkwardness of his words. "And I guess I miss you more than anyone."

Isaac broke down and collapsed into Abel's arms as he cried. Abel wept with him and rocked him from side to side as he had when Isaac was a small child.

When both had regained their composure, Abel said, "I've brought your things to you." He reached in the back of the buggy and started unloading bags of clothes and Isaac's personal belongings. He continued, "And listen, son, you're going to need transportation. There's a used, red pickup at the Chevy dealership in Shelbyville. I've looked it over and I think it'll suit your needs just fine. I'll stop by and pay for it on my way home. If your boss will give you a ride, you can pick it up any time you're ready."

Isaac shook his head in disbelief. He swallowed hard and said, "Dad, this wasn't all your fault. You don't have to buy me a truck. Part of my problem is that I've been living with a lot of guilt. I've never told you, but I felt so responsible for Preacher Croft's death. I had sneaked out of the house and was meeting some of the other boys at Massey's pond. He cornered me and was beating me. That's how I got the marks on my face that time Mom go so upset. I got scared and pushed him down. He hit his head on a rock and I thought I had killed him. After talking to Dall and Bishop Clevenger, I realized that I hadn't. I knew who did, but I couldn't tell anyone."

Abel looked at Isaac in disbelief as he leaned in closer and asked, "Who did it, Isaac?"

Isaac looked skyward and sighed. "It was Katie's dad, Sampson. He hated me so much. He'd followed me out there to catch me with Katie. I thought I had killed the preacher, but Dall and Bishop Clevenger said I hadn't. Sampson killed Preacher Croft because he thought he would hurt Katie if he caught her out there. It was all my fault. I should never have led her astray. I should never have started meeting her out there in the dark. It was too risky."

Isaac lowered his head and thought for a few seconds. He then mumbled sadly, "Anyway, she's not going to see me anymore, and there's no way that Sampson can be charged now, so I guess it's okay to tell you. You won't tell the sheriff anyway."

Abel stared at Isaac for a long minute. Isaac looked up at him, wondering why he was so quiet. Abel said, "It wasn't Sampson who killed Preacher Croft, Isaac. It was me. At that time in my life I was struggling with my faith. I realize now that I really wasn't saved. I had become influenced by dark spirits. I was so confused and spiritually conflicted. I wanted so much to protect you, yet I was being pulled to obey Bishop Gordan's laws. When I saw Preacher Croft raise that hammer over his head to strike you, I lost my sanity. When you pushed him down and ran, I waited till you'd gotten out of sight, then seized him. The evil in me had given me so much strength that I almost tore him to pieces. I'm sorry that you've lived with that guilt, son, but you did nothing wrong. I'm the guilty one."

Isaac stared at his father in total disbelief. He thought back to the night that the sheriff and Chief Deputy Thurman had confronted him and Katie at Massey's pond. He remembered the pictures of Preacher Croft and how shocked he was at the carnage that the preacher had suffered. He'd never known that his father was capable of such violence. He said, "I'm shocked, Dad. I didn't know you could do that."

"I shouldn't have. I should have been stronger and cast that demon out of my heart long before he got such a strong grip on me. I should have had the courage to raise you according to God's word, not Bishop Gordan's. I should have let them kick me out of the faith rather than alienate my son. If you have to turn me in to the English authorities, I'll understand."

Isaac again swelled with tears. "I could never do that. I didn't think you cared that much for me. I judged you too harshly, Dad." Abel stepped into Isaac and wrapped his big arms around his son. He rocked him gently and patted him hard on the back.

Abel stepped back and said, "And you've judged young Katie too harshly. I saw her on my way here. She said to tell you that her father has softened up a little since his encounter with Gaal, and you can start courting her again. But you'll have to re-think leaving the Amish faith, and this time she wants everything done in front of Sampson; no sneaking around. And if you return to the Amish faith, Bishop Clevenger said he'd baptize you. And we've built a small cabin on the backside of the farm. Dall and Sandy are living in it now, but they'll be moving on soon. You and Katie can live in it as long as you want after you're married. And she said to tell you that if old Sampson doesn't come around, that ladder is still on the ground under her window when you're ready to use it."

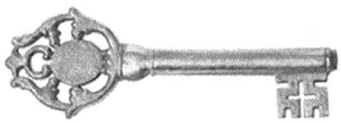

"I am he that liveth, and was dead; and behold, I am alive for evermore, Amen; and have the keys of hell and of death." **Revelation 1:18**

    Dall's beard had grown long enough that he felt confident he could go into town without being recognized. He met his friend, Curly, at the diner and bought him lunch to repay him for all his help. Dall was shocked at the bill. When he told Curly that lunch was on him, Curly took advantage and ordered up. Dall had a chicken sandwich, and Curly had three double-cheeseburgers, a large order of fries, three refills of root beer and pie. He couldn't make up his mind between the apple and blueberry, so he ordered two slices of each.

    Dall paid the tab and loitered for a few minutes as he watched Curly strut proudly back to the sheriff's office. He couldn't help but laugh at Curly's arrogance.

    When Dall glanced at the paper stand, the front page grabbed his attention. He hurriedly deposited some quarters and opened the door. He ripped a paper out and let the door slam as he read the front page article in total shock. The headline read: ***U.S. STRIKES MOST SIGNIFICANT ALLIANCE SINCE WORLD WAR II.*** The subtitle read: ***FOREIGN RELATIONS EXPERT FROM PRIVATE CONSULTING FIRM HELPS AMERICA DEVELOP STRATEGIC POLICIES TO DEAL WITH FUTURE THREATS TO NATIONAL SECURITY.***

    It wasn't the headline that had caught his attention so Dramatically; it was the accompanying photograph that made his heart sink. Directly under the caption was a photo of the U.S. President shaking hands with the private firm's representative. They were surrounded by the joint chiefs and S.A. Smith wearing a U.S. Army uniform. The rep for the firm was none other than Sandy Parsons.

Dall knew that Sandy was with him, so Gaal must have been so pleased with her persona and image that he manifested himself as her to carry out his plan.

The covenant had been forged. There was nothing he could do now to stop it except hope that God would work His perfect will and use it to further His perfect plan. His main concern was for Sandy. With the alliance in place and Gaal using her body, he would not let her live to expose him for what he was, and Dall knew Sandy well enough to know that she would never stand still for Gaal impersonating her.

With Gaal's legions pumping information to him, Dall had been foolish to believe that they were safely hidden in the district. Gaal knew exactly where they were. And if he knew where they were, so did the F.B.I. and any other hit squad that Gaal could covertly assemble. He quickly searched the sky and stared in disbelief at the gathering of strangely familiar storm clouds over the horizon, then ran to the pickup that he had borrowed from Lilly, and sped home.

Thank you for reading THE ENGLISH MAN. For other novels by Mike Smitley, please read:

IMPLIED CONTRACT
GHOST HUNT: The Sequel (sequel to IMPLIED CONTRACT)
PREY
DEAD FILES and
OUR MISSING

All available through Father's Press and all E-Book distributors.

Mike Smitley

Milton Keynes UK
Ingram Content Group UK Ltd.
UKHW032142170324
439604UK00012B/1807